# After Everything

# After Everything

A NOVEL

## Suellen Dainty

**ATRIA** BOOKS

NEW YORK    LONDON    TORONTO    SYDNEY    NEW DELHI

**ATRIA** BOOKS

A Division of Simon & Schuster, Inc.
1230 Avenue of the Americas
New York, NY 10020

First Atria Books hardcover edition July 2014

**ATRIA** BOOKS and colophon are trademarks of Simon & Schuster, Inc.

For information about special discounts for bulk purchases, please contact Simon & Schuster Special Sales at 1-866-506-1949 or business@simonandschuster.com.

The Simon & Schuster Speakers Bureau can bring authors to your live event. For more information or to book an event, contact the Simon & Schuster Speakers Bureau at 1-866-248-3049 or visit our website at www.simonspeakers.com.

Interior design by Kyoko Watanabe
Jacket design by Yoori Kim
Jacket photograph by PHB.CZ (Richard Semik)/Shutterstock

Manufactured in the United States of America

10   9   8   7   6   5   4   3   2   1

Library of Congress Cataloging-in-Publication Data

Dainty, Suellen.
  After everything : a novel / Suellen Dainty. — First Atria Books hardcover edition.
      pages cm
1.  Middle-aged persons—Fiction.  2.  Family life—Fiction.  3.  Friendship—Fiction.
4.  Man-woman relationships—Fiction.  I.  Title.
  PR9619.4.D33A38 2014
  823'.92—dc23                                    2014016986

ISBN 978-1-4767-7137-3
ISBN 978-1-4767-7139-7 (ebook)

*For my family*

# After Everything

# Chapter 1

HE HAD LOOKED forward to this all weekend. He had looked forward to it throughout his solitary walk across the river, a chill spring wind snapping at his legs. Now, as he saw Jeremy at their usual table in the corner, he looked forward to the next two hours. After so much of his own company, a good lunch was just what he needed. Already Sandy was wondering how he might extend proceedings into the late afternoon.

Time spent with Jeremy was the only constant in his life, sanctuary against an ominous pile of debt, a divorce he never wanted, and children he found increasingly difficult to understand.

"So, what will it be?" asked Jeremy, waving a dog-eared menu. "I'm for the usual sausage and mash. What about you?"

"Same," said Sandy, stretching his legs under the table.

Eating at Arthur's was like enjoying a family meal cooked by a beaming grandmother, except you paid at the end. Arthur had cooked in the same cramped space in Royal Hospital Road for thirty years. Apart from the fraying edges of the napkins, nothing had changed. The walls were the same tobacco color. There were never any substitutions on the menu of grilled brown food. The concept of rainbow cuisine and cantilevered vegetables would never reach this room. No diner would ever wear a black T-shirt or fiddle with an iPad between mouthfuls.

It was safe, comfortable, and predictable. Like the friendship between Sandy and Jeremy, it was based on the solidity of shared time. Arthur didn't rate his clients by postcode or job description. He just liked to look out from his kitchen and watch people enjoying themselves.

Manuela, Arthur's daughter who had begun serving them as a blushing teenager and was now a stout mother of three, appeared at the table with a bottle of Rioja. She knew them well enough to anticipate their order.

"To us," said Sandy, filling their glasses. He had been drinking too much lately, but Jeremy wouldn't say anything, at least not until Sandy fell off his chair. Even then, perhaps not.

Jeremy made his usual salute and conversation resumed. Chelsea's chances at the weekend? Which was the better long-term investment, heavy metals or wind farms? The two of them didn't go in for revelations about feelings and motives. The well-worn chat about football scores and stock prices gave them all the support they needed. It was an arrangement that had suited them since school.

"How are the kids?" asked Jeremy, after he had analyzed the weekend game.

"Emily's off to India next week," Sandy replied. "A self-discovery thing. On a one-way ticket."

"Always something to worry about, these children," said Jeremy. "Rosie is so involved in her property deals that she got her assistant to text me last week saying she was sorry not to have been in touch." There was a pause. "And my godson?"

Sandy knew from Penny that Matthew was struggling to stay out of trouble. He wondered if somehow Jeremy had heard about it. No, that was impossible. Sandy was being paranoid. And he didn't want to confide in Jeremy about his son, or himself. "Matt's doing great."

Their food arrived, shiny fat sausages curved beside a mound of mashed potato flecked with brown mustard seeds. A bowl of steaming peas came separately. The restaurant was now full, warmed by a comforting fug of food and people sitting close to each other. Sandy rubbed his feet against the leg of the table, feeling the last of the chill seep away. He should get out more.

Jeremy was holding forth on his latest theory of economic opportunities offered by recession. "McDonald's and Microsoft started during hard times," he said. "Chances to create new businesses are everywhere."

Jeremy had always been one for positive thinking, even after what happened at university. Nothing, it seemed, could shake the knife creases from his trousers, his perennial air of prosperity. Jeremy was his very own rock. Perhaps that was why Sandy had come to depend on him so much, particularly in the last year.

There was a couple sitting on the other side of the room, the woman about Penny's age, early fifties. There was something of Penny about her neck and jawline, the way she fiddled with her earring. She was gazing into her companion's eyes, hanging on to his every word. Penny used to look at Sandy like that.

He put down his fork, already speared with the end of the sausage, the chewy part he liked best. He was no longer hungry. He drank some water and then more wine, before remembering to offer the bottle to Jeremy. But Jeremy glanced at his watch and signaled Manuela for the bill. "No more for me. It's a frantic afternoon. There's a load of conference calls to get through."

Sandy couldn't remember the last time he'd had a frantic afternoon. He arranged his face into a smile and slapped a credit card from his wallet on the table before heading downstairs for a quick pee. Back at the table, an embarrassed Manuela was holding his card between her thumb and forefinger.

"I'm sorry, Sandy, it's been declined."

Jeremy handed Manuela a fifty-pound note. "Bloody banks. Always getting it wrong. Couldn't organize a piss-up in a brewery. We'll sort it out later."

Before Sandy could say anything, Jeremy slapped him on the back and was gone. Sandy found himself alone on the pavement. It began to rain, first a light spatter, then a heavy downfall. Water began to creep through the soles of his shoes and he wished he'd remembered an umbrella. There was the usual jangling chorus of sirens and straining bus engines. He rocked back and forth on the edge of the pavement, rain dripping down the back of his neck. Should he go back into the restaurant and wait it out? Have a coffee or perhaps another drink? But the idea of sitting alone in a room full of people, especially near a woman who reminded him of Penny, wasn't appealing. He shook his head like a dog and walked towards Battersea Bridge.

By the time he reached the river, the rain had stopped as suddenly as it had begun. There was some slight warmth at the back of his neck from the afternoon sun, but his feet rubbed against his damp shoes and his big toe, the gouty one, began to throb. He headed towards the cluster of shiny apartment buildings sprouting on the other side of the bridge, the sun glittering on their balconies. None of them had existed when he and Penny moved to London nearly thirty years ago, when they held hands in the street and she was always smiling. There was the Battersea Power Station and the redbrick mansion flats along Prince of Wales Drive. That was it.

Two joggers pounded by, neon Lycra flaring against an insipid sky, a sharp tang of sweat in the air. Their energy exhausted him. A year after the divorce, the pain of Penny's wanting to end their marriage just as he was finally ready to commit to it was acute. He buttoned his coat, dug his hands into the pockets, and felt the frayed lining come apart.

He thought back to the autumn evening when he had come home early. He'd had this idea of eating supper in the basement kitchen with Penny and the children, the four of them, the way they used to when everything was fish fingers and ketchup, with the old upright piano in a corner behind the table. Walking back from the bus stop, he saw them through the window. Penny had her arm draped over Emily's shoulder. They were smiling and listening to Matthew. Sandy hurried downstairs to join them, the warmth of the flat flushing the cold from his cheeks. The three of them had looked up from their Thai takeaway, surprised. He might have been a burglar.

It was as if a family trinity had formed during his surreptitious affairs, his trips away, and his boozy nights out with Jeremy and the others. Now that he had tired of all that, he couldn't manage to rejoin his own family. Penny and the children weren't interested in his clumsy overtures: invitations to films they had already seen, exhibitions in which they had no interest. He was the outsider trawling the perimeter.

Sandy was halfway up the hill now and his calf muscles were straining. He kept on along the uneven pavement, his gouty toe jarring with each step. Threads from his torn coat pockets clung to his fingers and he couldn't rub them off.

The problem was that he had been away too long. It appeared Penny thought the same thing, but she had a different solution to his dogged efforts. "I don't want to be in this marriage anymore," she'd said, looking straight at him, not busying herself with kitchen tasks as she usually did when she wanted to talk about something.

She might have rehearsed a speech in front of the bathroom mirror. "There is no one else. I just want to be on my own. It would be better for all of us." He had protested of course, told her it would hurt the children. Penny sighed. She spoke slowly and clearly in a low voice that was foreign to him. "They've grown up now, in case you haven't noticed. Emily is about to graduate and Matt is working. They're ready to move out. We all need to get on with our own lives."

In an uncharacteristically efficient way, she'd hired a lawyer to divide their assets, diminished by the huge mortgage on the flat in Onslow Gardens. Within months, Sandy found himself living in 545 dilapidated square feet in the outer reaches of Battersea, his collection of framed gold records gathering dust on top of the cupboard.

At the top of the hill, he paused for breath. On the common opposite, two men were pushing those newfangled buggies, high off the ground with three large wheels, like luxury wheelbarrows for babies.

He knew the divorce was more his fault than hers. He could have tried harder. But still. He kept saying that to himself. But still. It hurt. He tried writing a song about it, the way he used to write songs about his feelings when every stray note that came into his head turned into an international hit. Nothing happened. All his best songs, the ones that had topped the charts, had been written with Penny beside him.

The men with the buggies were saying good-bye to each other. They peered down at each other's babies and embraced in that modern male A-frame way before turning in opposite directions. One of them carried a rucksack with a large teddy bear sticking out of the back pocket.

Then Penny had moved to France, on her own, away from the familiar streets of West London. "Surely it's not that bad, that you have to move to another country," he'd asked after the final round of documents were signed.

"You have all your friends here," replied Penny. "Jeremy and Peter and Tim. I want a new start."

Sandy wanted a new start as well, but with his wife of twenty-eight years beside him, not on his own. Faced with that new steely gaze of hers, he didn't have the nerve to tell her.

He thought about walking around the common, but his feet hurt and he'd done that yesterday. He might stop at the pub across the road. Just for the one, to delay going back to his flat.

# Chapter 2

IT WAS DONE. The paint on the walls was the most idyllic shade of duck-egg blue she'd ever seen, the swag of each brocade curtain so geometrically perfect and the placement of the armchairs and sofas around the fireplace so pleasing that she lost track of time gazing at it.

Her meticulous efforts had been worth it. Penny had spent hours calculating figures in her notebook, ensuring the distance from the fireplace to the walls was equal on both sides and that the porcelain lamps were placed precisely in the middle of the French oak side tables. She'd painted each rose-colored vein of the marbled cornice with a feather, dusted everything, and plumped the sofa cushions. She'd even combed the fringe of the embroidered rug so each strand lay parallel to its neighbor.

Tall ceilings and gracious windows; every aspect in excellent proportion. Her drawing room was a place of great beauty and nothing was going to dent the pleasure of her creation. She would clean up the last mess of brushes, paint tins, and cans of polish, then walk down to Sarlat for a celebratory coffee. Just one last look before she pushed the door closed.

That was the only disappointment. The doors, even though they were polished mahogany, were too small and thin to take proper handles. She'd had to improvise by gluing brass buttons on them. Everything else in the Georgian doll's house project had been perfect. The box containing the kit had arrived on time with none of its hundreds of plywood pieces broken. The myriad packets of screws and hinges had been clearly labeled. She'd managed to understand the instructions, and she'd discovered through dawn sessions on eBay that she had a cool head for successful last-minute bids. As the east coast of America slept, she'd snaffled a miniature brass chandelier, four pairs of wall sconces, and best of all, a hand-carved rose marble bath with its original taps, so small that it fitted in the palm of her hand. It was very satisfying.

She straightened her legs and tugged at her bra strap. A side section of her breast escaped under the wire and she pushed it back into captivity. These days new parts of her were constantly jiggling their way to freedom. Bun-sized pads of flesh popped out above each side of her trousers every time she lifted her arms. A wedge of belly sprang up over her jeans when she sat down, and bits of her backside refused to remain inside the elastic cocoon of her underpants. The surprise was that she didn't mind.

Penny had always imagined she'd care about losing her perfect male-catnip body with its sharp hip bones and flat stomach, her perky embonpoint, her jaunty backside. Why else had she crunched and lunged and jumped for all those years, pushing herself until she grunted like a pig? And in between the sweating and pounding, those interminable hours taming her hair into perfect bobs, flips, tumbled curls, or ethnic frizzes, depending on the year and the fashion. All that time lost each day primping and painting, then inevitably frowning at the mirror.

Her stunning face and body had been her only sources of self-reference for so long and she had tended to both with meticulous care. But it turned out she didn't mourn the loss of either. At night after bathing, she tenderly patted herself dry and brushed her graying hair, relieved that Sandy was not around to peruse any new bulges. There was no one to view her except herself.

It was a good feeling, she told herself as she stored the last of the paint tins in the spare cupboard and looked around for her basket. On the kitchen step, a lizard bathed in the weak morning sun. It raised its head and stared at her with unblinking eyes as she passed. There was a moment when she realized that her trousers were speckled with paint and that she should go back and change. No, she thought. No one will be looking at me. Another advantage of invisibility.

Since puberty, her inner and outer selves had been refugees from warring tribes forced to inhabit the same house. The interior Penny was like her Yorkshire mother, a person who ironed tea cloths and saved jam jars, someone with quiet values of loyalty and duty. "Good looks are all very well," her mother said as she caught the ten-year-old Penny gazing in the hall mirror instead of polishing the cupboard beneath it. "But a good character lasts much longer."

Penny learned to be suspicious of her glamorous exterior. But no one except her mother was interested in her good character. When her absentee father took her to a belated lunch for her fifteenth birthday and told her she was turning into a knockout, she decided it was much easier to make do with the happy accident of natural aesthetics and ignore the guilt about its unearned rewards.

She became accustomed to people staring as she walked into restaurants, even expected it. But the other part of her, drip-fed by her mother's homilies, kept whispering that beauty didn't make you clever or good, that it was a temporary delusion. The whispers had stopped some years ago. Time and gravity had produced their own silent harmony.

Here in the Dordogne, she snipped away at her own hair and bought plants with the money she saved not buying expensive face creams. She wore sensible shoes and shapeless clothes. When she caught sight of herself in a mirror, she barely recognized her own round and ruddy face, so different from the lean anxious blonde staring out of old photographs. These days she was content with her doll's house project, her garden, and her home, surprised by how much she enjoyed the company of this newly integrated self of hers.

She loved her house too, the way it nestled into the lee of the hill and looked out over the valley; the way only an outline of rough-cut stone was visible from the road, as if whoever built it four hundred years ago wasn't interested in looking out at passersby, or having them look down on him or her. She liked that the house was long and low, only one room wide, with windows on each side. Every morning she could walk from the kitchen through the hall and into the sitting room, never once losing sight of the silver dew bathing each blade of grass. She didn't mind that every wall and floor sent the yellow bubble in her spirit level veering off center. She cherished its imperfections and never tired of the way the sun seemed to rise in the center of her narrow bedroom window.

The gentle half-hour ambles to and from Sarlat were her only exercise these days. She didn't crave the endorphin rush, her joints didn't seize up with arthritis as the trainer at the gym once threatened they would, and she couldn't care if she never worked up a sweat again.

The path was empty and silent, except for the rhythmic slap of her shoes on the dirt and sporadic birdsong. The air was crisp, even though the first of the spring wildflowers were peeking up between the boulders on the hill behind her. Ahead, the steeply pitched roofs and church spires of Sarlat floated above the mist. It was Wednesday, market day. Soon the cobbled streets would heave with contingents of English retirees braying to each other over the heads of local farmers with their cages of chickens and baskets of vegetables.

Everything was a tourist website cliché, but she didn't care; she never tired of the broad, lazy river, the blond stone buildings clinging to the hillside, and the tiny dim cafés with their impolitic haze of unfiltered tobacco. There was nothing to do here except watch and be. Even Jean-Pierre, the one whom all the villagers shook their heads at when he passed, couldn't destroy her sense of calm. One morning she had woken to Jean-Pierre leering through her bedroom window, trousers at half-mast and swinging an enormous penis from side to side. In London, she would jump when the doorbell rang. Here, she sat in bed and giggled as she watched him jump down the ladder and run off, clutching his trousers around his knees. She'd got up feeling invincible and gone outside to dig her vegetable garden all morning, planting neat rows of courgettes, aubergines, and tomatoes, ignoring the bleating telephone, always from England, always someone wanting something. She'd never imagined being alone could be so pleasurable.

A kite cruised above her, its shrill whistle echoing from the hill behind, and she stopped on a bend to admire its effortless flight in a pale sky of torn clouds. There was a faint scent of cypress on the breeze, replaced as she entered the town by the smell of warm yeast and pungent garlic *saucisson*. From the stalls in the market square, she bought a bag of field mushrooms, half a dozen eggs with manure and tiny feathers still on their shells and then, an unusual extravagance, one small white spring truffle. The stallholder raised an eyebrow.

"You have guests, madame?"

"No," said Penny, already salivating from the scent. "It is all for me. *Je suis une gloutonne. Merci.*" She stowed them in her basket. Scrambled eggs with truffle shavings and a glass of wine. Supper for a queen.

The entrance to the café was blocked by a warring English family. A dark-haired man struggled to control a complicated multiwheeled stroller containing a screaming toddler.

"How in the hell does this contraption work?" he hissed.

"Let me do it. It's a bit tricky, I'm sorry," said his flustered wife.

A prepubescent girl, all affronted attitude in a denim miniskirt and a tight T-shirt, rolled her eyes.

"I'm starving," she whined. "And I don't see why we had to walk all this way."

Penny skirted them and walked into the café. She wanted to tell the woman not to bother with her squabbling family, to leave them and go off on her own. Instead she smiled, the polite curved mouth of a stranger. Once Penny was like this wife, trying and failing to unite her family during tedious weeks each summer spent arguing in towns and villages throughout Europe. Sandy always complained about the accommodation she'd booked, Matthew refused to eat anything except cheese sandwiches, and Emily never once looked up from her book.

Coffee ordered, she picked up a two-day-old copy of the *Guardian*. She stretched out her legs and began the crossword, almost giddy with her good fortune to be beyond the annual nightmare of family holidays in particular and much of family life in general. Those interminable hours spent encouraging or commiserating with Sandy as he lurched from hit to miss, while hugging Emily and Matthew until they wriggled free, always trying and always failing to make everything all right.

She loved her children without measure and looked forward to their video chats, emails, and texts. But the weight of that love, how its responsibility had nearly suffocated her for so long that she barely remembered a day when she didn't feel breathless from it—all that had disappeared. Although it was frightening in the beginning after the divorce, she liked her freedom now. She liked it a lot, and some time ago had concluded it was arrogance that had made her assume responsibility for the success and failure of others.

There were still two unsolved clues in the crossword. *See post go out in March* (5, 4). She twirled her pen. It couldn't have anything to do with ides or mail because it didn't fit the other clues. Nothing came to her. *Breaking up may be wonderful* (8). Again, nothing. She couldn't be bothered to try any longer. She was still pleased with herself about finishing the doll's house. She'd browse the recipes in the back section of the newspaper and see what tasty bits and pieces she might cook for herself.

After her first winter in the Dordogne, when she'd discovered where the various shops were, how to chop wood and to operate the temperamental woodstove, after she'd scraped and sanded, tiled and grouted, even installed a lintel by herself, she decided the main disadvantage of living alone was the disappearance of her table manners. Most of the time she ate like an animal, gnawing bones or standing over the sink with bits of fruit and raw vegetables dripping down her chin. It was a minor drawback. She could still remember to use a knife and fork when she had to.

A couple at the bar were eyeing her table. It was time to go anyway. On her way home, she stopped at the English estate agency just off the Place du Marché des Oies. Nigel, the manager, let her use his office computer in exchange for vegetables and scurrilous gossip about models and pop stars she used to know in London. It was more powerful than her old laptop at home, and he never minded that the gossip was often a decade out of date.

Nigel was out pursuing a sale, but the surly Francine, his secretary, nodded and pointed to the empty desk at the back of the office. Penny maneuvered her basket between the filing cabinets and the water cooler and sat down. Already her mouth was watering from the smell of the truffle.

# Chapter 3

JEREMY BOOKED FOR lunch at Albert Hoffmann's new place. The restaurant fulfilled all his criteria. It was comfortingly expensive, he would inevitably see someone he knew, and it was less than a hundred meters from his offices in Piccadilly.

The tiny section of London between World's End and the Ritz Hotel was his tribal habitat. It didn't matter that he was one of the very few British people living there anymore. Nor did it matter that he chose a houseboat moored on the river in Chelsea as his home instead of one of the white stucco houses favored by the swill of international wealth always washing into London. He continued to see the King's Road and its tangle of side streets as he always had: a slightly bohemian village full of workers' cottages and pubs on most corners where he could always find a man to talk to, or a woman to chat up.

He glanced at his watch. There was just enough time to read through this last email before leaving the office. It had taken an inexplicably long time to write. Every word was the wrong one and yet there seemed no correct alternative. Every phrase was a mangle. The more he tried to be clear and concise, the more obtuse and abstracted each paragraph became, until the whole thing was such a mess that he had to start again. His final version was not much better, but it would have to do. He closed his laptop and wiped the aluminum cover. Sometimes it was hard to stop looking at the screen.

Apart from a sleek and impractical phone with the buttons too close together, the computer was the only object on his desk, a large slab of marble that the interior designer had placed in the feng shui commanding position: against the wall, with the widest view of the room, and out of line with the main doorway. He'd have preferred looking at the wall but was happy to go along with her suggestion if there was the faintest whiff of profit at the end.

Jeremy's personal taste ran to the clubby and comfortable with some good pictures. But that was too dated, he'd been told, hence the French gray walls, the thick mud-colored rugs woven in what looked like crop circles, and the anorexic gilded sculpture on the sideboard. Conservative, but still on point, was the message. By comparison, the floor above, where his small team of quants and brokers worked, was cramped and strictly an auction job lot. Not that they noticed. All of them, with their firsts in mathematics and physics, were barking mad as far as he could make out. The kid called Theo ended every sentence with a brisk shoulder rotation. The man sitting next to him, whose name Jeremy never could remember, blinked and stuttered at the same time, and Sam, the leader of his team, the one who devised that nifty automated algorithm, preferred not to speak at all unless it was completely necessary. But they did their job and they did it well.

Jeremy put his phone in his coat pocket and walked to the lift, emerging onto the pavement near Fortnum & Mason. A group of Chinese tourists was ogling installations of upmarket groceries. Twenty years ago he would have felt a boyish surge of superiority, a smug sense of belonging in this place of architectural grandeur. These days he knew better. The era of empire was over. These descendants of diligent rice farmers and merchants were about to inherit the earth. It was their turn and they deserved it. They worked harder and longer. So did their obedient children. If he did what he told his clients to do, he'd genuflect in front of the tourists, kiss the hems of their coats, and thank them and their country for making his comfortable life possible. Instead he smiled in a mine-host kind of way and skirted their little group.

As he approached the restaurant, he thought of Sandy. The night before, he'd pondered the matter on the deck of the *Jezebel*, swathed in a blanket while exhaling imperfect rings of cigar smoke. A five-year-old San Cristóbal La Fuerza, earthy with a slight floral taste. It was okay, but he wouldn't order them again. You really couldn't go past a Montecristo No. 2.

With the death of Jeremy's mother three years ago, Sandy was the person who had known him longest. Unlike his mother, Sandy had never disagreed with him. Jeremy remembered him in the common room at the beginning of the first term, sitting silent and bolt upright on the sofa as the others sprawled everywhere in their languid way, talking of shooting and stalking as they waited for Sandy, the new boy, to say something so they could dissect him in that casual, cruel way of theirs.

The black river slapped against the sides of the *Jezebel* as the mooring rope sawed against the stanchion, making a rasping noise. The ashtray slid along the deck before slowing as the keel settled in the water. Jeremy carefully stubbed out his cigar. The crisp tobacco aroma had changed to a stale sour smell. He put the ashtray to one side and wrapped his blanket tighter.

Sandy had been clever enough to get the only bursary but also naïve enough to believe that if he liked people and was pleasant to them, the favor would be returned. Sandy didn't understand that at this particular school it was acceptable to be poor, because that meant you were clever enough for a scholarship; or rich, because that meant your brains or lack of them weren't important. It was okay to spring from a gene pool swarming with lunacy and its variants. But it was unacceptable to be suburban and ordinary. Sandy's background was suburban and ordinary.

None of this concerned Jeremy, even at the age of thirteen. His own provenance provided a passport to travel with impunity. Depending on whom he spoke to, he could say with complete honesty that his grandfather began his working life at the age of fourteen in a Midlands grocer shop, or that his grandfather ate his last potted shrimp at White's, before dying of a heart attack on the pavement of St. James's Street.

He could map the aristocratic genome from his mother, with a discernible route back to Mary, Queen of Scots. There was no money, however, which made it easy for her to accept a marriage proposal from the son of a grocer. It helped that he had done something ingenious with refrigeration seals and cottoned on to the concept of globalization earlier than most. Updated versions of the seals extended the shelf life of foodstuffs and liquids in every corner of the planet, including Jeremy's most recent indulgence, a triple-zone wine cooler.

Jeremy had never regretted making Sandy his friend, which was why the present matter—Jeremy couldn't bring himself to call it anything else—was unsettling. The loss of control, things falling apart. He knew it hadn't been easy for Sandy. Jeremy had helped out for years, loaning money he knew would never be repaid, taking Sandy's pitiful five-figure pension pot into his fund when the normal entry was half a million minimum, organizing the sale of his back catalogue when things went bad, always paying for lunch and dinner.

He would have helped more, had he known how difficult things were. It was part of the contract of friendship, and in his own way, Sandy had already paid his fair share. More than his fair share. Jeremy had to admit that. But he chose not to think about that particular time in their past. Some memories were best excised if friendship was to survive.

Now, outside the restaurant, he was buoyed by the thought of the lunch ahead. As usual, he was the first to arrive. Tim, who was wedded to his car, had whinged about the congestion charge, but Peter hadn't said anything, probably because he knew Jeremy would pick up the tab. It would be odd without Sandy at the table. The four of them had been meeting three or four times a year ever since university, and he couldn't remember a lunch without him.

From his corner table, where he could see everyone come and go, Jeremy surveyed the room. Tables not too close together, a good weight to the linen, and a fine array of Riedel glasses in front of each chair. The lighting was flattering but not too dim. He could still make out the Freud lithographs of whippets and nudes. All very satisfactory.

Eating in restaurants was foreplay for the three things Jeremy liked best: sex, money, and chat. He loved the theater of a good front of house, the flourish and swirl of waiters and sommeliers, the delicious decisions of sea bass or *poulet de Bresse*, an unctuous daube or delicate spring lamb, each so seductive in its own way. There were only so many good meals left in one's lifetime and Jeremy had decided long ago to waste as few as possible.

He would have the boned pig's trotter. Hoffmann always did that so well. Then a bottle of the 2006 Château Talbot. It wasn't a decision of extravagance. As Jeremy only drank half a glass at a time these days, he preferred it to be memorable.

# Chapter 4

IN THE FRONT of the office, Francine was telling a couple with Lancashire accents how easy it was to find skilled craftsmen eager to renovate the derelict barn they'd been looking at. She was fibbing, of course, but the couple would find that out for themselves. Penny logged on to her email account, curious to see a message sent only minutes ago from Jeremy, who usually made do with a Christmas e-card, if he remembered at all.

She moved the mouse in circles around the desk, then opened the email. It had a picture of a golden eagle flying over a blue sky banded across the top of the page and came from Jeremy's business address. He called her his darling woman, said that she should have chosen him and that she still could.

Sandy, he wrote, had reached some kind of crisis point, not only because he didn't change the world but also because he couldn't control it or anything else in his life. It might have been harder for Sandy because he had been successful so much earlier than many others. It was difficult to say.

Penny had the unkind thought that Jeremy Henderson took far too long to get to the point. Perhaps that was part of his business strategy: bore his wealthy clients into stupefaction so they would sign over their investments to him just to end the conversation.

What was Jeremy talking about? A breakdown? An accident of some kind? Sandy seemed perfectly fine when they spoke before Emily left for India. Perhaps not completely fine. But functioning, in his characteristically dysfunctional way.

Penny read on. Now Jeremy was quoting "Anthem" by Leonard Cohen.

She didn't need to be reminded about Leonard Cohen. She was the one who'd dragged Jeremy and Sandy to hear Cohen at the Isle of Wight festival, whenever it was. She knew all the words of every song, from "Suzanne" to "Sisters of Mercy." They'd never heard of him. Jeremy had gone on about razor blades and Sandy had passed out. She'd worn her new black-and-white bell-bottoms.

She scrolled down. Jeremy said Sandy was making a good recovery and that she was not to worry. Recovery from what?

"It could have been an accident, but apparently passersby said he almost threw himself into the path of an oncoming car near the common. He's not seriously injured but it could have been much worse. The hospital wanted to put him on the risk register. I talked them out of that, but it would mean so much if you could come back."

She sat for a minute, understanding for the first time. Jeremy thought Sandy had tried to kill himself and he assumed she already knew about it. Her immediate reaction was to say that of course she'd return as soon as possible, that she'd telephone Sandy and contact Emily and Matthew. The mental list began: flight times, asking the farmer down the lane to check on the house, arranging somewhere to stay in London. All the while a sharp prick of nervous perspiration on her back.

Suddenly she was furious, with no clear idea why. She picked up her basket, reeking with the rich scent of truffle, and stomped out of the office, ignoring Francine, who asked if she'd turned off the computer. All the way along the street she fumed, the beauty of the town invisible to her. A gritty wind picked up and stung her face as she passed the ancient town walls and climbed the track, forgetting to pick some wildflowers for the kitchen table. She walked faster and faster until her knees shook and she heaved for breath.

Typical of Sandy to fall apart and let someone else pick up the pieces. And typical of Jeremy to assume she'd drop everything and rush to help. Jeremy wouldn't have bothered to contact her if Sandy had married again, or if he had pulled off a big deal. Damn Jeremy with his psychobabble and his fashionable quotations. Jeremy hadn't bothered to notice her unhappiness during Sandy's stream of affairs with eager-eyed young things from the music industry. He'd never said a word when Sandy dashed off to Los Angeles or New York, forgetting birthdays and school concerts and prize days.

No, she would not call anybody. Sandy was alive. Jeremy had said his injuries weren't serious, just bruises and concussion. He would recover in his own time. He could solve his own problems.

She rushed into her house, locking the door behind her with shaking hands. Why should the messy past return to slice through this new, carefully constructed life of hers? That was the real reason she'd come here. Not because of cheaper house prices and reliable summer warmth, not in the hope of building a new network of acquaintances or friends. The only person she wanted to get to know better was herself. The only thing she wanted was peace.

emily.ellison@gmail.com

To: mattman5@hotmail.com

Hi little brother. Miss you, also worry about you too. All alone in the big city, no big sister to boss you about, nag you about keeping clear and clean. I had a thought. Why don't you come over here, chill for a bit, bathe in the wonderful light? I'm in this hill town place, sort of like Varanasi but not. Couldn't hack Delhi, too many people. Dharamsala was too stupid for words, full of pizza shops, sushi bars, and hamburger stands. Everyone selling something, enlightenment on special, 24/7. Goddamn place full of goddamn phonies, as our mate Holden Caulfield used to say. One guy I thought was a monk—he was in the full robes with the shaved head and beads—said he'd take me to a cheap hotel and then tried to jump me in a lane. No problemo for me. He was half my size. LOL. I kneed him and that was that.

Here is so much better. Cheap, clean—well not too dirty—and I've enrolled in these amazing classes at the local ashram under a holy guy called Rosheme. No one has seen him for three years, but he has a crowd of followers, all sorts. It's so good, the best. There's this sacred cave I go to, up in the hills, and I meditate there. There's peace there that I've never felt before. I can't really describe it properly. You have to be there.

Why don't you come, now the job is no more? And you can tell me about it in your own time. Don't worry about Mum. She's okay now and I bet she'd give you a ticket. Don't worry about anything or anybody, least of all Dad. And please, stay away from that load of losers.

Remember I love you. xxe

# Chapter 5

PETER AND TIM were only minutes late. They looked approvingly around the room before picking up their menus. Peter chose the braised beef cheek while Tim took far too long to decide on roast turbot.

"So weird, just the three of us," said Tim. "Do you think we ought to pull up a chair for Sandy, just in case?"

Jeremy glared.

"Just a little joke," said Tim. "My pathetic attempt to say I miss him not being here. Is he okay?"

"He was very lucky," said Jeremy. "No broken bones, just bruises and concussion from where he hit his head. The car was only going twenty miles an hour. The driver was in complete shock, said Sandy threw himself in front of his car. Sandy told me he'd tripped. It's impossible to know what really happened. But why would he do something like that?"

"Why does anyone do anything?" Tim hunched his shoulders, a kind of inverted shrug. "Because their life isn't working and they can't stand it any longer?"

Jeremy thought about how Sandy had looked as he'd helped him out of the taxi that morning. Some kind of chalky paste coated his stubble and his hair was pasted to his skull in greasy strands. There was a fine crosshatch of lines on his face that Jeremy had never noticed before. Sandy stumbled and nearly fell on the pavement and Jeremy grabbed his elbow to steady him, his fingers pressing through the soft skin until they reached bone. He threw his other arm around Sandy's shoulder as he wrestled with the stiff lock on the front door and together, arm in arm, they made their way up the narrow stair-case to Sandy's flat.

Jeremy had never been there before. Somehow they'd always met on his side of the river. He was shocked by the collapsing sofa covered in old newspapers, the empty bottles on the floor. He could tell Sandy was embarrassed, almost pushing him out of the door before he collapsed on the sofa, saying there was no need to stay, that the hospital had organized someone to come by later that day.

"Do you think he needs to go to some kind of rehab, like the Priory?" Jeremy asked Peter and Tim, immediately regretting his question. He fiddled with the stem of his wineglass as an image arose of Sandy sitting in a semicircle of strangers sharing their secrets. Sandy didn't carefully measure the facts and calculate the consequences of every pause in every statement the way Jeremy did. With one exception, Sandy just blurted out whatever had happened.

Jeremy swallowed some wine. It wasn't as good as he remembered and there was a burning sensation at the back of his throat. Maybe he had acid reflux or worse, an incipient ulcer. He checked the drift in his thoughts and was about to steer the conversation away from rehab when Tim interrupted him.

"The last place Sandy needs to be is in Roehampton surrounded by models and addled rock stars," Tim said, looking affronted. "He'd think it was Friends Reunited. Sandy needs something more connected with reality." Tim had that blaze in his eyes, the one Jeremy associated with religious zealots, the one he always saw when Tim talked about psychology. Maybe that's the way all therapists were. However, he was relieved that Tim had rubbished the notion of rehab. Money saved as well, because Jeremy would have been the one to pay for it.

"I'd imagine that Emily going away probably didn't help," continued Tim. "Fathers and daughters, all that sort of thing."

Peter began dissecting his beef cheek. "I didn't know they were so close." He dolloped pureed potato on top of the meat and chewed slowly. "God, I could eat this forever," he said. "Sandy wouldn't have let on that anything was wrong. Not showing signs of any emotion and that Peter directed television commercials. What mattered was that all four had known and liked each other longer than almost anyone else in their lives.

Tim and Peter had stopped talking about wine and returned to the subject of Sandy. "How things have changed," said Tim. "Remember him at Oxford? Quite the golden boy."

Jeremy sniffed the remaining dregs. Sometimes the bouquet was almost as good as the taste, but not this time. He should have checked that there was food in Sandy's flat and got his secretary to make an online order. He'd call Sandy when he got back to the office.

He checked his watch. "Got to go. There's a kid coming by at three o'clock with a lazy ten million and I need to put it to work, for him and for me."

The waiter was already hovering by his side. Service was included but Jeremy added another ten percent to the bill and punched in his PIN.

"Lunch soon?"

Tim and Peter nodded, still drinking their coffee. Jeremy stood up and patted both their shoulders. "Okay, until then, *mis amigos.*"

He returned to his office feeling gaseous and bloated. He worried about his meaty breath. He fretted about worrying and tried to conjure up a lovely confident feeling but failed. Just before the kid arrived, he belched loudly and loosened his tie.

is one of the few things the English are still good at. Of course Sandy always appeared just fine."

"Fine," said Tim. "*Fine* is just an acronym for *fucked-up, insecure, neurotic,* and *emotional.* Sandy and I talked about it once. He laughed."

Jeremy was put out. No one was acknowledging that he was the one who'd helped Sandy for so many years, or that he'd been the one to collect him from the hospital. He changed the subject.

"Albert used to cook those beef cheeks in his old restaurant off Grosvenor Square. The whole thing takes three days. You have to skin the cheek of sinew, marinate it, and then cook it incredibly slowly. Albert told me himself . . ."

Peter and Tim weren't listening. They'd begun a separate conversation about wealthy Chinese businessmen favoring top Bordeaux vintages. Jeremy surveyed the room again. A woman two tables away, with wild brunette hair, was appraising his little group, a smile hovering. Behind her was a large gold-framed mirror. Reflected in it was a trolley laden with cheese, and an incongruous trio made up of himself, a balding man with a tendency to freckles and bulkiness but with an undoubted air of affluent authority; Tim, a slight figure with an old-fashioned mop of salt-and-pepper curls wearing an ill-fitting jacket; and Peter, the good-looking one. No one ever noticed what Peter wore. What would the woman have made of Sandy, his quick gestures and crooked smile giving a false impression of youthfulness until closer inspection revealed the drinker's belly under the shirt and the bloated flush along his cheeks?

Jeremy's eye traveled on. Although the restaurant had opened only a month ago, it looked as though it had been here for decades, something he approved of. Jeremy dealt with constant fluctuations throughout his working day, so he didn't like change in his private life. Sally and Isobel would disagree, but ex-wives were like that. Isobel once snarled that he showed more loyalty to his friends than to his family. Maybe she had a point.

Sandy was his closest friend. It didn't matter that Sandy was a songwriter and Jeremy worked in finance, just as it didn't matter that Tim had given up property development to become a psychologist

# Chapter 6

SHE WASHED THE eggs and put them in a bowl by the sink, and brushed the dirt off the mushrooms and the small truffle with an old toothbrush. The kitchen smelled of musty earth, garlic, and something richer, like postcoital sweat. But she wasn't salivating. Her mouth was dry. She could feel her lips pursing, that telltale vein jumping in her neck.

She left the pile of cleaned mushrooms and walked into the sitting room. There it was, her beautiful doll's house silhouetted in front of the window. She had done a good job. The reddish brown of each hand-painted brick, the dove gray of the tiled roof, the cream of the porch columns. Carefully she opened the door. How sweet its interior was, how precise, exactly as she had left it.

Here was the sofa that fitted into the palm of her hand, with cushions she'd stitched herself from one of Emily's Liberty print smocked dresses torn too badly to repair. And the matchbox sized mirror hanging on the wall, its frame encrusted with fake diamonds from Emily's fairy wand, discarded when she was seven.

The beds upstairs were covered in striped quilts made from the beloved baby rag Matthew had taken everywhere until he was five, when he threw it into the garbage bin with a brave flourish. She had retrieved it, carefully washed it, and put it in her box of special things. Snuggling under the quilts were the survivors from his first collection of Lego men. Inside the pillows, sewn from her mother's collection of doilies and linen handkerchiefs, she had secreted a milk tooth and a lock of hair from each of her children.

On the sofa was a new catalogue from the doll's house company. She flicked through the pages, stopping when she reached something called the Grosvenor House. It was enormous, shoulder height, with a Palladian façade, white like a wedding cake. She counted the rooms. Fifteen, including a parlor, two kitchens, a servants' sitting room, bedrooms, and nurseries. A grand family house.

That would be her next project, taking a satisfyingly long time to complete. Lovely dawn raids online from her sitting room, hours spent contemplating paint charts, entire days spent varnishing and marbling. There were still so many things stored in the special box. Matthew's tattered teddy bear, a Playmobil farmer and his wife, lace handkerchiefs from her mother, and Emily's taffeta fairy wings.

To mark her decision, she went to her desk and pulled out bits and pieces from the drawer to make a vase of flowers. It would look just the thing in the bow window of the Grosvenor House.

She traced the circle of a euro coin on some cardboard, then cut it out with a pair of manicure scissors. She glued a thumb-sized candlestick onto the cardboard circle and covered its base with sticky wax, making sure it was smooth all the way around. Now the flowers. She took a spray of miniature artificial roses and prized each one from the bunch, then measured, cut, and pressed them into the wax. She unfurled each tiny artificial leaf and blew the dust off each yellow bud.

The telephone rang and she jumped. The long shadows of trees played in the courtyard. Making the vase had taken longer than she thought. Perhaps the telephone would stop. It did, but then began its raucous sound again.

"Hello," she said.

"Pen, it's Angie." The breathless, husky voice hadn't changed. "Have you read your email?"

"Yes, actually I have." Penny knew what was coming and she was already annoyed. "Although what I'm meant to do about it over here, I'm not quite sure."

There was a well-meaning pause and the sound of inhaling breath. "Tim just called me from the car on his way home. I thought you might want someone to talk to. It must have come as a shock. I mean, I know you and Sandy aren't together, but somehow you've always seemed so connected. Tim says Sandy always talks about you so much."

"Really?" replied Penny. "I knew from the children that Sandy wasn't in good shape and that money is tight. But he's in the same boat as a load of other people. I don't recall him having suicidal tendencies."

Over the faint static there was another pause. Penny pictured Angie sitting near the whispering Aga in her cozy kitchen in the perfect farmhouse outside Ludlow, only miles from the cottage Penny and Sandy had once owned. Angie would be drinking something herbal from a thick mug and wearing one of her floaty-sleeved vintage numbers.

Penny imagined Angie was preparing one of her long speeches, delivered from a platform of smug satisfaction that she and Tim had survived where others had fallen. Penny dusted the desk with the sleeve of her jumper.

She heard Angie inhaling, as if she was smoking a cigarette. "Things were bad. Jeremy took Sandy back to his flat from the hospital. They'd found one of Jeremy's cards in Sandy's wallet. Apparently the flat was horrendous—buckets in the bathroom catching drips, dirty clothes everywhere, a month's dishes growing mold in the sink, bills piled up, not even opened, and empties everywhere you turned."

Penny stopped dusting and began fiddling with the miniature flowers. One of the buds was stained rusty brown. Perhaps she could wash it. "I still don't understand," she said. "If it wasn't an accident, why would he have done something like that? I mean, he has the support of his friends. That must count for a lot. They've been lunching and drinking and droning on about football for decades."

"None of them saw anything wrong with Sandy," said Angie. "The only one who noticed anything was Carolyn de Farge . . ."

There was a pang of obsolete jealousy, still familiar. Had Sandy had an affair with her as well? "What has Carolyn de Farge got to do with anything? I haven't seen her since we were picking up the children at the school gates."

"You know how bad news travels. Carolyn told Jeremy she'd run into Sandy on the King's Road one morning, that he stank of alcohol and looked like he'd been sleeping rough. He told her he'd had enough of everything. She feels dreadful that she didn't contact anybody. Things might have been very different."

"I'm sorry to hear all this, truly I am," said Penny. "But Sandy always put on the brave face, tried as hard as he could never to let me know what he was feeling. I used to imagine he confided in Jeremy and the others, that I was the odd one out." She remembered resenting them, wanting Sandy to have lunch with her occasionally instead of his friends, longing for him to seek her undivided company for an hour or so in the afternoon. "Sometimes I thought he cared more about them than he did about me."

There was a puzzled silence. "What on earth do you mean? Are you trying to say Sandy was gay in some way?"

"No," said Penny. "Well, perhaps yes. I mean, I used to think they were emotional homosexuals. Everyone talks about bromances these days. Brad Pitt and George Clooney, David Beckham and whatshisname."

"What absolute rubbish." Angie snorted. "Tim and I have always been each other's best friends and Sandy was devoted to you and the children."

"For a bit."

"We're digressing. The point is we think you ought to try to come over, if only for Matthew and Emily."

Penny put down the flower and began pushing back her cuticles with some savagery. "Em is in India and Matthew is away. I haven't even contacted them yet, so I'm not sure how I'd be helping. And I'm quite busy here. Can't someone else help, one of his old girlfriends? Heaven knows there're enough of them. Why don't you contact one of them."

"Penny, you and the children are his only family. He's going to need you. I know this comes as a shock. It must be hard for you."

Penny wanted to say that the only hard part was this tortuous conversation, that there was a difference between Sandy needing her and it being convenient for everyone else if she ran to his side. She wanted to hang up but couldn't seem to manage it.

"I'll think about it," she said finally. "But Sandy and I have been divorced for more than a year now. Our lives are completely separate. We're friendly, but we're not friends. There's a difference."

There was another silence. Penny knew Angie would hang on until she got the answer she wanted.

"All right," Penny said. "I'll try."

She said good-bye, just as angry as she'd been when she'd read Jeremy's email. There was no right decision. If she stayed in Sarlat, there would be the inexplicable guilt that she couldn't erase; if she rushed back to London, she couldn't play the role of the good wife healing the fractured former husband. Still, there were the children to consider. If—and it was a monumental if—Sandy became more aware after this episode, perhaps he would be kinder to Emily and Matthew. But they were adults now. What need, or wish, might they have for a retrospective parent–child relationship? She had no idea how they'd react.

The hills outside had turned umber with the low sun. It would be dark soon. She went to the shed for the axe and spent the last half hour of the day splitting knotted pine logs from the great pile behind the shed. She kept chopping until the wheelbarrow was full and the blade of the axe was speckled with tiny globules of sticky resin. In the weak evening light, they might have been drops of blood.

She would light a fire tonight, early. She would fry the mushrooms gently in a little unsalted butter and scramble the eggs, taking care they didn't overcook and become rubbery. Then she'd shave fragments of the precious truffle over them. She'd eat the lot with a glass of Montravel, then go into her sitting room and read as the logs crackled and spat before collapsing into a fine powder ash. After that, she would go upstairs to bed.

# Chapter 7

WHERE WAS HE? Not in his own bed. He was lying on something different, narrower and shorter. There was a chill draft playing on his uncovered feet. Through the open window came the hum of traffic and the cawing of seagulls. The last thing he remembered was seeing the men with their buggies on the common. Everything went dark after that. A gripping headache, then the nauseated, gagging feeling. The vomiting. A nurse, her figure dark above him. Deep dreamless sleep under a thin blanket, knees tucked up to his stomach as he shook and stared at the air-conditioning vents in the ceiling.

He opened his eyes. Looming in front of him was the familiar green wall of his own flat. He was lying on his sofa, dressed in unfamiliar tracksuit bottoms and a long-sleeved checked top. Where had these clothes come from? How did he get from the hospital to his flat? Who had put a pillow under his head? He had no idea. He felt only one thing: terrible shame.

There was something scuttling outside the door, then a loud knock. Sandy dragged himself upright and, steadying himself against the wall, stumbled to the door. A figure with his back to Sandy crouched in the dim light of the hall, foraging inside a bag. Thick gray hair, a black jacket and jeans. The figure swung around and Sandy saw a man in his sixties with a long face and a beaky nose.

"Hi. I'm Rupert. I've come from the hospital to see how you're going, check you over. Your friend Jeremy arranged it. No needles, no blood. Promise." He smiled, showing a row of neat white teeth. Berserk little black wires began dancing at the edges of Sandy's vision. He was going to pass out.

"Do you need a hand?" asked Rupert.

"Thank you, but no," grunted Sandy. "I'm feeling much better." The ignominy of meeting a stranger while wearing tracksuit bottoms was too much. He wanted this Rupert to know he had once been a star of the music world, that managers and agents had spoken the name of Sandy Ellison with respect, sometimes reverence. He'd shared Peking duck at Mr Chow with Mick and Jerry. He'd walked in Richmond Park with Ronnie and Jo, flirted with Stevie Nicks, and swapped guitar notes with Mark Knopfler.

He wanted to name all his hits—singles as well as albums. Rupert would have recognized some of them, surely. He might even have rushed to buy a copy when the song was released, taken the vinyl out of the sleeve, played the haunting melody Sandy had created, and been transported to another place.

This Rupert would be listening to the radio on his way to work or unloading the dishwasher. He would hear Sandy's song and remember when he'd kissed the one that got away, the scent of them, the feel of secret skin. He might forget the title of the book he read last night and the film he saw last week, but not Sandy's song. It would still echo somewhere inside him.

"May I come in?" Rupert's question cut across his reverie. Sandy nodded and crept back to the sofa. The pillow was damp and stained with brown spittle. He turned it over. There was a pile of dirty clothes in the corner and a full ashtray on the mantelpiece, but there was nothing he could do about it now.

Rupert brandished a blood pressure kit and gestured for Sandy to roll up his sleeve. He strapped on the gray cuff and began pumping air into it.

"Your friend insisted that you'd get proper care here. The hospital had its concerns, whether it was an accident or not, but your friend said he'd take all responsibility."

Now Sandy remembered. It was Jeremy who had picked him up and brought him home. How had Jeremy known where he was? Through the fog of a dull headache, he tried to concentrate on what Rupert was saying.

"Your blood pressure isn't too bad. High, but not hysterical. Do you do any exercise at all?"

Sandy was too exhausted to dissemble about walking whenever he could or playing the occasional game of geriatric tennis. He opted instead for pathological honesty.

"None at all," he said. His throat hurt.

Rupert smiled and pulled off the cuff. "You must have given yourself quite a shock. Had you been drinking?"

Sandy was confused. What was Rupert talking about?

Rupert continued. "When you stepped onto the road, when the car hit you?"

So that's what had happened. A car accident. Sandy had a sudden memory of a loud bang and the smell of rubber. Someone shouting.

"Your blood alcohol level was high. Alcohol can be a powerful depressant," said Rupert. "How much do you drink, would you say? How many units a night?"

Sandy rolled down his sleeve. "I don't count. Too many."

"And smoke?" he asked.

"Loads," said Sandy. "That's the thing about smoking. It goes with everything. Good times, bad times, and anything in between."

Rupert didn't reply. He plugged the ends of a stethoscope into his ears and placed the other end on Sandy's heart. He smelled of soap and something sharp and clean, like eucalyptus. For a second, Sandy felt that if he could lean his head on the doctor's shoulder, then everything would be all right, that Rupert could lay his freckled hands on Sandy's shoulders and make him whole again. But that was a ridiculous notion and Sandy pulled away.

"You've had a nasty knock and you've got mild concussion. You need to take it easy." He put the stethoscope back into his bag and turned an unblinking gaze on Sandy. "Was it an accident, or did you do it deliberately?"

"I don't know," mumbled Sandy. "I don't remember. I think it was an accident."

Rupert cocked his head and lifted an eyebrow. "So your friend said."

"Things weren't working out," Sandy whispered. His mouth seemed invaded by fine grit. "Everything became very difficult." He wanted to tell him in some detail how incredibly difficult everything had been, but Rupert was already heading for the door.

"I'll arrange some follow-up appointments. Take it easy. Get some rest. Try not to drink, if you can. You'll be surprised how much better you'll feel."

"I don't remember much," Sandy whispered again. His head hurt. "Perhaps I tripped."

Rupert lifted both eyebrows. "From the pavement to the middle of the road? If you say so. You might consider talking to someone. Therapy, combined with the right drugs, can be very effective. But you have to take it seriously. Recovery won't be like having a drink and getting a quick buzz. Here's my card. Call me at any time, day or night. I'll let myself out."

Sandy staggered into the kitchen. The weak afternoon sun played on pots of dead geraniums left behind by a previous tenant. He leaned against the windowsill. Chimney pots, television aerials, and satellite dishes rose from neighboring roofs to meet a clear afternoon sky. He made his own clouds, blowing little puffs of condensation on the window.

What had happened to him? To Sandy, the hit maker? He'd never quite worked it out. It can't just have been the arrival of punk, Brit-hop, garage, or grime, because ballads were perennial. People still fell in and out of love. Someone's heart always hurt and a ballad hit the spot the way a bass beat never did.

Was it that he kept writing the same sentimental songs while everything around him changed? Maybe. But for whatever reason, by the time Sandy had realized his idea of a perfect note was out of fashion, he was also out of step. He tried not to mind. But he did. His moments of riding on a wimpling wing with his hero Gerard Manley Hopkins as his muse ended soon after Fred, his faithful assistant, mentioned something called Auto-Tune.

Sandy had always imagined that his gift of combining the right note with the right word to create a hit was a kind of divine intervention. He always knew immediately if a voice or instrument was off-key. He had a special ear for music.

Yet another illusion. Sandy's ear for music was no more than a computer program devised by an American oil engineer called Andy Hildebrand. Auto-Tune made every note pitch-perfect. An unlikely career segue from drilling sites to pop music, but apparently all in a day's work for Andy.

Sandy couldn't blame his decline on Auto-Tune and Andy Hildebrand, because the mining engineer didn't even write songs. But it was something visible, a name he could google, a smiling gray-bearded image he could sneer at for replacing his beloved fuzzed compositions with squeaky-clean digitization at the same time his own life began to lose its clarity.

mattman5@hotmail.com

To: emily.ellison@gmail.com

You're not going all religious, are you? Can't see you with a shaved head and a begging bowl, so don't get too carried away. That town sounds good. I'd join you, but no job anymore means no money. Mum called the other night. Dad is okay now. Hard to know what happened. Mum says he needs help and understanding but she's got the red voice back.

Remember that? Dad always got it more than us, probably because she was mad at him more. When the red voice stopped, I thought it was because she and Dad were finally getting along. But it turned out to be the opposite. She was there in her body, but she was gone in her head, and then she really was gone. Anyhow, I haven't heard the red voice for years, so I guess she's pretty angry about it, although she won't say so. Same same. I went to see him and he said it was a blip, that he got confused. Hey, don't we all.

Don't fret about me. I'm good. Although, had a little slip last week, and spent two days in bed feeling pretty shitty. Then they told me not to bother coming into work again. Surplus to requirements. Sam moved out of the flat. He's gone to Sydney and this complete dickhead, Arthur, moved into his room. He does something in the City and never looks up from his iPad, completely straight. He'd never heard of GHB, for starters.

That was my little slip, a good one though. I had this dream thing about flying, just above the ground, like the little yellow man on Google maps except speeded up. Really speeded up. Then I fell asleep at the kitchen table and Arthur told the others he thought I had a problem. I don't. I just like it every now and then. So, no nagging. I'm cool, everything under control.

# Chapter 8

TIM DIDN'T LIKE lentils but somehow had never managed to tell Angie their floury texture stuck in his teeth and lay like a dead weight in his stomach. Angie always served them with sausages oozing red oil and stinking of garlic. It was a minor deceit, but after twenty-five years of marriage, he could scarcely confess now. Considering Angie's multiple sensitivities, the way she could extrapolate a minor nuance into a giant issue-laden dialogue, it wasn't worth it.

If he said, "The thing is, I've never said it before this, but I'm not that keen on lentils. Not many men are. And those sausages make my breath stink," then she would say, "But you've never said anything before. Why didn't you tell me? I thought you liked them. You always said you liked lentils and sausages."

He might reply, "I don't think I ever said I liked lentils and sausages. I just ate them because you cooked them." After a silence during which he could imagine her mind whirring and clicking, she would say that he should have told her. She'd ask if he was trying to tell her she had stinking breath. She'd say, "Aren't we meant to be honest with each other? Isn't that what our marriage is about? What else haven't you told me? How many more secrets have you got?"

Occasional indigestion was so much easier.

They were in the kitchen. Angie had lit the wood burner. The Aga was on its highest setting and Tim was hot. But Angie felt the cold and preferred to heat any room she was in rather than wear an unflattering bulky sweater. Angie liked to change for dinner and apply makeup, even though dinner was always in the kitchen and only the two of them. It was part of her ethos of making a childless marriage work. Without children to twine them together, Angie had made herself indispensable as both siren and secretary. To Tim, it remained one of her most attractive qualities: her implacable belief in them as a never-ending couple and her unwavering confidence in their love for each other.

In the early London days, she would drive him around Battersea and Brixton, taking notes of run-down houses for sale that he might be able to buy and sell. When he fell into negative equity in the 1990 recession, she juggled the accounts for months in a futile effort to stave off bankruptcy, and she stayed awake with him night after night discussing what they might do. Never the singular, always the plural.

Tim played with the lentils. He was tired after the long journey from London and wanted to slump in front of the television for an hour or two, have a beer, and go to bed. But he couldn't. Angie had to tell him every word of her conversation with Penny and about her trip into the Ludlow antique rooms. The matter of Sandy had to be discussed again, in case any aspect of it had been overlooked.

"Penny's become hard. I think bitterness has set in," said Angie. "Can you believe she was hemming and hawing over coming back to see Sandy? She actually said she was busy. But what does she do over there all day? There is only so much time you can spend weeding and growing vegetables."

Sandy's accident—the distinct possibility that it had been a failed suicide bid—had created great excitement for Angie. She needed examples of the frailty of others to remind herself and Tim how lucky they were. It was a bonding exercise, one at which she excelled. So they went through the whole thing again. Angie sipped her supermarket sauvignon blanc, rather quickly, he noticed. Sauvignon blanc was another thing he didn't like. He preferred red wine but wasn't prepared to have a three-hour discussion about it.

The meal was finished. The bottle was two-thirds empty. He had drunk half a glass at most. How much had she put away while he was driving home? Since Sandy's abortive suicide attempt, he'd become acutely conscious of his own alcohol consumption and that of others. He sipped instead of gulping, and alternated each mouthful of wine with water. He noticed the yeasty smell of it on the breath of strangers in the street, the telltale red blotches on their cheeks and under their eyes.

No. Angie wasn't one of them. The smooth bob of her youth had made way for a tangled auburn mess that hung below her shoulders and hovered above her brown eyes, giving her the appearance of a bedraggled loyal spaniel. But her eyes were still clear, her face bony and drawn back over her cheekbones.

She sat across from him, his friend and his wife. Angie was his unassailable ally. She was the one who had kept him going through the bouts of uncontrollable weeping and the black depressions after he lost his nerve for white-knuckle property development. It was her idea for him to retrain as a psychotherapist dealing mainly with retrenched men of a certain age.

He was reluctant at first, but Angie persuaded him that he was so empathetic, so good with people. "Why not get paid for something you do for nothing anyway?" she argued. "You're always listening to other people's problems. And it's a growing market. You have to see that." After some weeks of cajoling and flattery he agreed, gratified to hear that he was, at least, good at something.

He loved Angie, he depended on her, and he couldn't imagine life without her. But sometimes, like tonight, he would have given anything to be on his own.

"Penny should have involved herself more in Sandy's work," Angie said. "She always looked sniffy about it, like it was just a bit beneath her. If she wanted that sort of conventional life, she should have married a banker. If she'd been more supportive, things might have been different."

An image of Penny standing on her own at the side of the Soho recording studio flashed into his mind. It was past midnight and he could see the dark shadows under her eyes even in the dim light. Sandy was greasing up to that girl singer, Kate someone or other. Tim had forgotten her surname. He remembered looking away as a girl's head bobbed up and down in the sound engineer's lap behind the mixer console. There was the usual white powder on the table and a case of Puligny-Montrachet, all the bottles opened and sweating condensation. There was a case of Cheval Blanc as well, again every bottle opened. Kate whoever-she-was had ordered them as part of her contract, along with foie gras and caviar. But everyone was gobbling crisps and drinking beer from the can, except Penny, who was clutching a Diet Coke.

"Come and join us," Tim had said.

"But Sandy says I always talk about the wrong thing," Penny replied, her eyes darting around the room and settling on Sandy edging closer to Kate. "He says I don't know how to relate to people in his industry. And I'm so clumsy. I might trip and fall over a plug or something. I have nightmares about it."

Tim laughed, but he knew she meant it. People saw Penny as the jaw-dropping babe, but behind the glamour, he always thought of her as tentative and afraid of upsetting everyone.

"She had the children to look after," Tim said, swallowing the last of the sausage. "She couldn't go traipsing off after him all the time."

"That's what nannies are for," Angie replied. "And what good did it do her anyway? They're not exactly the best-adjusted kids. Emily is wandering around India, and Matthew can't even hold down a job."

The implication was clear. If Angie and Tim had had children, they would have been different, happier and more accomplished. They would have chosen between medicine or law. That's it, kids. Take your pick. Under the pastel vintage clothes and artfully messy hair, Angie could be a brutal member of the bourgeoisie.

"That's a bit cruel, don't you think? Emily is a wonderful girl. And Matthew just hasn't found his way yet."

Angie raised her eyebrows and began to clear the table, one of the few things she liked to do alone. Tim felt the lentils subside into a lump in his stomach. He told her he was going to telephone Peter and went into the sitting room. A fire blazed there as well. He chose the least lumpy sofa and pushed a paisley shawl to one side, then punched in Peter's number. While it rang, he thought up an excuse for the call. That media stock Peter and Jeremy had taken a punt on, up something like thirty-seven percent in eighteen months, despite the recession. He would ask Peter the name of the company. Better not to mention Sandy immediately. He suspected Peter and Jeremy thought of him these days as the kind of guy who had learned to multitask and was no longer able to read a map: in short, as having turned into an anxious girl.

Peter sounded rushed. "I'll email you the details tomorrow. It's doing well. Even old Frieda has put something in it." Frieda was Peter's live-out lover. "Talking of which, I have to meet her in fifteen minutes. Some new art thing she just has to see."

"Great. Thanks," said Tim. "Angie spoke to Penny today, asked her to come over to see Sandy. Penny didn't sound too keen on the idea, said she was busy."

"It's her decision," said Peter.

Tim could hear the jangle of car keys. "Penny said she'd speak to Matthew and email Emily in India, see what they thought."

"A bit late for family therapy, don't you think?" asked Peter. "They're grown up now. Leave them be. Benign neglect and all that sort of thing. Let's just concentrate on helping Sandy. But it's good that Angie spoke to Penny."

"I'll call tomorrow, tell you about it," said Tim. But Peter had already hung up.

# Chapter 9

PETER PERCHED ON a windowsill, watching Frieda walk between the groups of earnest nodding heads clustered around the paintings. She had her back to him but he could guess what she was thinking by her movements.

A tilt of her head to one side indicated interest in what the person opposite her was saying. A tilt combined with a simultaneous swivel of her neck was a sign that she had spotted a potential client, and a sweep of her right hand through her crop of thick black hair meant that she was bored and any minute would make her excuses and turn away.

Before he met Frieda, Peter would never have imagined that he would be happy to sit on a drafty windowsill deducing a woman's thoughts by the angle of the back of her head. But he was happy, sitting alone, watching her move among strangers as he thought about kissing the whorls of hair on her temples or tracing the curve of her spine with his forefinger.

From her side of the room, Frieda turned to him and smiled, a flash of white teeth. The smile said that she would be with him as soon as possible, but at the moment there was work to be done and could he possibly wait just a little longer?

Yes, Peter thought, smiling back at her and crossing his legs to disguise an unexpected erection. He had all the time in the world for Frieda, although he didn't fully understand why.

They were in Hoxton, at the private showing of a dealer who specialized in native Australian art. A lonely-looking Aboriginal sat in the corner producing low groaning noises from a didgeridoo, as waiters dressed in long black aprons served prawns and Foster's.

Frieda liked to keep abreast of current trends. She owned a gallery on Theobald's Road, dealing in what she called twentieth-century modern: minor surrealists, Lichtenstein and Warhol lithographs, and bits and pieces in between. She was good at it, trilling down the telephone to potential clients, alert to any hint of a sale.

Peter followed Frieda's progress around the gallery. He watched her talking to the dealer, a tall thin man with a walrus mustache who kept stroking her arm. Peter watched more closely until Frieda swept her right hand through her hair and moved away of her own accord. She was wearing one of her habitual black asymmetrical dresses, a slash of red lipstick her only makeup. Peter saw that she was getting plump, but he didn't mind. Neither did Frieda. She just went off to her favorite Japanese designers and bought bigger clothes.

A waiter offered him a beer. He was unexpectedly thirsty and drank half the can in two swallows. As Frieda chatted to an elderly couple, a young girl with tossed blond hair sat beside Peter and smiled. She had that lustrous confidence produced only by an expensive education followed by a history of art degree from the Courtauld or Cambridge.

"Don't I know you?" she asked, sipping her Foster's and smoothing her hair. Peter smiled but kept watching Frieda.

"I'm Hannah," the girl continued. "I work in the gallery here." Peter was sure he didn't know her because he had the best visual memory of anyone he knew. But he was accustomed to the question because he resembled a lot of other people, brooding French film stars in particular.

His own kind of good looks (Christopher Lambert crossed with early Gérard Depardieu, but with floppy dark hair that kinked over his ears) had had its apogee thirty years earlier and he'd been very grateful for the steady stream of girls it had brought him. Even silverback Jeremy had envied his easy success. Now he didn't care that much about being handsome. At least he thought he didn't. Frieda didn't agree.

"Dear Peter," she'd said near the beginning of their relationship. "There is a reason you like cities, not the country. Cities have shop windows and mirrors and you can look at yourself in them. And you do. You never miss. No harm, no shame. I still like you."

The blond girl next to him crossed and uncrossed her legs. They might have been unfurling flags. Peter turned to her. Hannah. That was her name.

"Wonderful exhibition," he said, "but you'll need to excuse me. I have to drag my girlfriend away, otherwise she'll never leave." Hannah smiled graciously, but he could see she wasn't used to any man, particularly an older man, walking away from her.

Later, lying in bed waiting for Frieda to join him, Peter called out to her. "I didn't think much of that exhibition. Everything looked like acrylic pixels." She was still in the bathroom doing something complicated with the tiny wire toothbrushes she carried everywhere with her.

"I'm not so sure," said Frieda, joining him in the bedroom. "I think those painted stories of the dreaming are so beautiful. And there is a market for them. Some artists can sell for half a million."

She took off her clothes, folding each garment and placing it in her leather overnight bag with her toothbrush and jars of face cream. Peter was used to women leaving bits and pieces behind, as if laying down a trail on territory about to be colonized. Empire builders, he called them. The Cecilia Rhodeses and Roberta Clives of our times.

Frieda never left anything. There was enough mess in his flat already, she said. On the occasional nights when he stayed in her minimal monochrome house off Marylebone High Street, she packed everything of his into a plastic bag and handed it to him at the front door in the morning. Somehow these rigid boundaries made both feel more secure, more able to enjoy each other.

Frieda stood at the end of the bed. She wore the most glorious underwear. Silk bras with cunning embroidered lace inserts around her dark brown nipples, cleverly draped sheer camisoles and satin French knickers in beige and cream with hand-stitched hems. He had drunk too much and eaten too little at the gallery opening, but the swell of her breasts and the sight of a stray tendril of lush pubic hair excited him and she knew it.

"So, a good night just now and a good day just been," she said, unclasping her bra. Her breasts jiggled. "Some uppity puppy walked in off the street. Apparently he'd liked comic books when he was a kid and so his mother went out and bought him a set of Lichtenstein lithographs—you know, the whaam, splat fighter ones—for his thirteenth birthday. Can you believe it? Now the precious darling wants a new kitchen for his Notting Hill flat and so he's selling them. And I've got just the buyer."

Peter nodded approval, waiting for her to take off her pants, something she did with erotic elegance, like a sepia-tinted Degas. "Can't match that," he said. "I spent today filming bog rolls in a bathroom and trying to get a stroppy toddler to sit on the loo. I kept asking myself would Danny Boyle be doing this. The child was hideous. The mother was quite sexy though."

"Really." Frieda smiled. She got into bed and lay beside him, smelling of the amber soap she always used. "How sexy?"

Her hand played with the hairs on his stomach and he turned to her without answering. They kissed gently and he moved towards her, grateful for the familiarity of her body and the way they made love with uncomplicated passion. He never tired of her slow easy thrusts and the way she knew exactly when to reach between his legs and gently stroke his balls until they tightened and he came so sweetly.

Just before sleep, she asked about Sandy. "How is he doing? Has he recovered?" Frieda was intrigued by Sandy. Sometimes Peter was jealous of her interest in him, particularly as she never pretended to be anything other than bored by Tim and Jeremy.

"He's getting better," said Peter. "It's going to be hard for him." He stroked her neck. "There were times when I thought you found him attractive. There was a bit of the green-eyed monster going on."

Frieda snorted. "You, mister matinee idol. Well, well, I'm flattered. But no need to be jealous. I don't fancy men like Sandy—too fair-skinned. I'm sure he wasn't the world's most attentive husband, but he seems kind and self-deprecating in his own funny way. When I asked him about his songs, he just shrugged and said he'd been lucky."

"Perhaps he was," said Peter.

"We all need some luck," said Frieda. "And the four of you intrigue me, not just Sandy. I mean the four of you together. You never talk properly to each other. You're all too busy drinking and eating and having your little boy chat-chats about football and silly games."

Peter slid his hands under the duvet and warmed them between her thighs. "Thank the Lord you don't do that Brazilian thing. I love your bush. And anyway, we're men, not boys, and we talk about other things apart from sport."

"Like what?"

"Movies, plays, the markets, news. The whole world really."

"That's lipstick and nail varnish gossip for boys," Frieda replied. "That's not talking. That's not saying what you think, telling someone else how you feel. Be honest, it's not. I've watched you. You speak in an entirely different way when you're with them. You're so abrupt and hard. Jeremy is the arrogant head boy, Sandy is his grateful little fag, and you and Tim are the underlings. Have any of you ever actually confided in each other? About something that really matters?"

Peter played with her hair. "We're not lady-boys, you know. And may I remind you that's how you and I first came across each other—during one of our little boy chat-chats, as you call them."

Frieda smiled and kissed his cheek. "I haven't forgotten. Why would I want to forget something so good?"

They had met three summers ago, one of those rare warm London evenings when the city glowed, a gentle breeze meandered through the streets, and harassed commuters looked up from the pavement and thought, Yes, this is why I live here.

He and the other three were at La Famiglia in Langton Street after watching Andy Murray win against Jo-Wilfried Tsonga at Queen's. Jeremy was a member and he had organized the tickets and a car to pick them up from Baron's Court. The four of them had a table in the garden at the back. Sandy always made fun of the plastic canopies, but they all liked the fried courgette flowers too much to take him seriously. Peter couldn't finish his second course of squid risotto, and a dark-haired woman at the next table leaned towards him.

She had deep-set brown eyes, an aquiline nose, and the air of a louche and elegant smoker. There was something about the way she tapped her thumb and forefinger on the table, like stubbing out a cigarette on an invisible ashtray. Not at all his usual lean blond shiksa.

"If you're not going to finish it, may I?" She took the plate and began eating his meal without waiting for an answer. Her companion, a young man who he later found out was her nephew, blushed. Peter was taken aback by her boldness and impressed by her greed as she finished his risotto without speaking, scraping up the last grains of rice with a spoon.

"Very good," she said in a low pleasant voice with no discernible accent. "Although the rice might have been a trifle more al dente." She handed the plate back to him and continued her conversation with the young man. On the plate, speckled with squid ink and olive oil, was her card. Peter took it and rang her the next day.

mattman5@hotmail.com

To: emily.ellison@gmail.com

Hey Em,

Forgot to say. That Jump place you wanted me to go to before you left . . . It was okay, but I could think of better ways to spend a weekend. Not a total waste of money, but too full on really. We had to trust our intuition and jump into the future, leaving the past behind. They kept telling us to write letters to all the people who had disappointed us in our lives. I started writing one to Dad but didn't finish it. They told me I wasn't being serious enough and then they tried to get me to sign up my friends. A lot of people there kept bursting into tears. The leader didn't do anything to help them. He was too busy texting.

Mum said we should try to feel some compassion for Dad. I don't see why. He's such a fucking tosser and she's forgotten all the times they couldn't even be in the same room together without hissing at each other. I can't keep up with her. One minute it's the red voice. The next she's calling for peace and understanding. She's different now from how she used to be in London. What's got into her?

I'd like to join you over there. Maybe if I get this new job as a courier and I can save some money. We'll see. Keep in touch. Watch out for the men in orange. Small is powerful. I should know.

# Chapter 10

IT WAS A mistake to return Amy's call. Experience had taught him never to go back. But Jeremy was out of sorts. Sandy was part of it. He couldn't dispel the memory of Sandy at the hospital. He looked so old and defeated, his eyes fogged by drugs as he tried to get out of bed, the flimsy gown gaping around his bare buttocks. It was as if Sandy's failings and failures might somehow prove to be a viral contagion and Jeremy couldn't risk any chance of infection.

Then, after three meetings and far too many telephone calls, Ronald Hudson Junior, the owner of the lazy ten million pounds, had decided to play elsewhere. Jeremy was annoyed, not so much by the money but by his own failure to read the situation. He'd been so sure the deal was all but done. He only suggested the second and third meetings as a favor, thinking it would bolster the American's confidence if the investment strategy was outlined in the painstaking detail so beloved by his backroom team.

Jeremy had liked Ronald Hudson Junior, although part of that, of course, was due to his family's trust fund, which he'd estimated as being worth at least half a billion, with the first tranche of ten million slipping Ronald's way on his twenty-seventh birthday. Jeremy had checked with a pal in New York. A second tranche of twenty million was due when Ronald turned thirty-three.

What had made his white-shoe family decide on those specific ages? Was anyone wiser, more able to make sound financial decisions, at twenty-seven than a year earlier? Or a year later? Jeremy knew his reputation was that of a manipulative and devious old Turk. This was unfair. He could still be kind every now and then, just to convince himself that he was able to summon something approaching compassion.

Random acts of kindness, that phrase coined by that American writer whose name he couldn't remember. He'd employed a sixty-year-old secretary because he knew she needed the job more than a perky twenty-five-year-old. He'd taken time with a shy young man and promoted him ahead of a more confident, bullying colleague.

He'd decided to be kind again and show young Hudson the subtle maneuvers of the City that Jeremy knew so well. In return, Hudson could push some younger business his way. New media, tweeting, streaming, all that. But he wasn't interested and Jeremy hadn't realized. It was a slip and he didn't like it.

He fretted he might be losing some of the finesse and confidence that had contributed so much to his success. The entire point of Jambhala Investments was to imbue the person sitting opposite with Jeremy's own gold standard of bravura, to make them inhale it down to the last penny in their bank account. Even the name of his company had been carefully calculated. He didn't want any of the predictable references to Greek mythology or the movement of planets. He'd decided on the Buddhist god of prosperity not because he was a follower of the Dalai Lama, but because it was different and it might attract Asian investors.

It was his particular gift to demystify global economics into domestic common sense, and that was the reason he'd decided on his own boutique operation instead of joining one of the big dick swingers. He was better with people. Jeremy liked being good at whatever he did.

Bananas, coffee, cocoa, wheat: he could make dietary staples sing with the prospect of profit, even in the middle of a double-dip recession. Collapsing Eurozones, hurricanes, floods, and earthquakes were not just economic or ecological disasters but new opportunities for growth. Aristotle had the right idea. Nature does abhor a vacuum.

Brand-name toothpastes and washing powders? Perfect for emerging Asian markets; whole towns and villages, millions, even billions of people wanting to convince themselves of their new middle-class status, to brush off third world poverty by stacking Persil or Palmolive in their cupboards and brushing their teeth with Colgate.

The ten million pounds that got away was a blip. It was a reminder to keep alert, not an omen of impending failure. The important thing was to make a decision, even if it turned out to be
wrong. You could always make another decision. To be tentative, or
even to appear to be tentative, was the beginning of the end. He'd
seen it happen too many times. What began as a reflective moment
became an occasional pause and then a permanent faltering, eventually picked up by the person sitting opposite. No one wanted that. It
sniffed of doubt, and doubt stank of failure.

What he needed was a quick injection of confidence. So he returned Amy's call and asked her to dinner at the new restaurant off
Sloane Square. Even if the dinner went badly, at least he could say
he'd been there.

The restaurant was in a street behind the Royal Court, with fiery
red walls and banks of orchids everywhere. The maître d' showed him
to a table next to a giant aquarium stretching across the whole of one
wall. A scarlet-colored fish with a hideous protuberance on its head
gaped against the glass as they inspected their menus. Their waitress
told them the fish was a man-made hybrid called a flowerhorn cichlid.

. "Who'd pay five thousand pounds for one fish that you can't even
eat?" she said in a broad Australian accent. "No worries for some
people, hey. Ready to order?"

Jeremy had already decided on the grain-fed beef, but Amy shook
her head.

"I'll come back in five minutes."

The waitress smiled, displaying perfect dentistry, and turned
away. Jeremy admired her bottom. As Amy dithered between fish
and steak, he wondered where all the waitress's countrymen and
-women had gone. Only a minute ago, London restaurants had been
teeming with strong-backed Amazonian Australians full of delightful
insouciance. Suddenly, lemminglike, they had disappeared. He and
Sandy once speculated where they'd gone. Surfing in Morocco? Trek-
king in Bhutan? Or back to their motherland? They'd been replaced
by nervous Eastern Europeans with sallow complexions who rarely
smiled. When they did, their dental work was not as impressive, but

he and Sandy had agreed their waiting skills were marginally better. Amy finally decided on halibut. Jeremy caught the waitress's eye. She took their order and disappeared again.

"You're not much fun tonight." Amy pouted. "I like you better after a few drinks."

"Ah, but who's the one who really is better after a few drinks? You or me?" he asked, annoyed by her slouching across the table because she was young and could get away with it.

Amy ignored him. "Anyhow, what happened?"

"What do you mean?"

"You just stopped calling." She flicked her hair from one side to the other and stroked the stem of her glass with her thumb and forefinger. He knew she wanted the gesture to be an erotic reminder, especially when she licked the corners of her mouth at the same time. But it wasn't working. The only thing he felt was boredom. He'd call Sandy after dinner. He'd seemed almost chipper when they last spoke. Perhaps they could meet back at the houseboat for a quick nightcap.

"We go out for a couple of months and then I don't hear from you."

He reached for his knife. "Nothing happened. I got busy. Deals, business, you know."

"If I did know, I wouldn't be asking."

"I'm not one for the long term, if that's what you mean."

"Two marriages, one kid. Okay. Not doing that again. Got it."

She fell silent and Jeremy asked about her new job in corporate events. Amy asked about his work. The halibut arrived, with a crop of miniature vegetables strewn around and a gyroscope of fried onion on top. Amy gushed about its appearance. Jeremy thought for a second that she was going to take a photograph of her plate, but her mobile remained in her handbag. His steak was thankfully unadorned and beautifully marbled, but he wouldn't come here again. The place was too fashionable. They discussed polo, skiing, and another new restaurant in an old Mayfair hotel. Jeremy hoped that Amy was on one of her diets and that he wouldn't have to endure a further half hour's conversation during cheese or pudding.

"I couldn't eat another thing," she announced brightly. Jeremy smiled and called for the bill, not bothering to ask if she wanted tea or coffee. Outside, a taxi disgorged a noisy group of late diners. He hailed it and opened the door for her.

"I'll call you. We'll have lunch," he said, kissing her on one firm plump cheek while paying the driver and waving the taxi away, relieved to be on his own. He walked home along the King's Road and then down Edith Grove. At some time in the last twenty years it had stopped being a dismal row of shabby terraces and become a desirable place to live with carefully tended window boxes and freshly painted front doors. He hadn't noticed.

The lights of Battersea Bridge glittered over the river and a cold wind blew papers and plastic bags against his legs. As he walked down the jetty towards the *Jezebel*, he remembered Sandy making fun of Amy, roaring with unapologetic laughter when she thought Led Zeppelin was an actual person. Sandy was right. She was stupid. He wouldn't call her again.

He looked at his watch. Too late to call Sandy now. He went to sleep much earlier these days. Jeremy would telephone in the morning and arrange something. Sandy was always ready for lunch or dinner at a moment's notice. He always picked up the telephone and had time to talk. Sandy understood. He was there, the way a wife or a girlfriend rarely was.

When he got back to the *Jezebel*, last night's ashes from the fireplace had drifted over the books and furniture, leaving a fine silt and giving the room a ghostly hue. Domestic disorder unsettled him, so he rummaged in the kitchen cupboard for a cloth and began wiping everything clean: tables, picture frames, bookcases, and books. When he finished, he began restacking the books into neat piles, the paperbacks all together, then the larger hardbacks and finally the heavy photograph albums.

There were twelve of them, all leather bound and engraved with gold Roman numerals on the spine. A decade ago, Sally had taken one look at his shoeboxes of random photographs and swept them off to be chronologically organized into albums as a birthday present. Second wives took things like that seriously. Perhaps they wanted to edit a past that didn't feature them.

There were holiday albums of the two of them, diving off boats and grinning happily in Turkish restaurants, strolling around Capri, and lounging back on a gondola in Venice. Because Sally was a generous and kind woman, there were complete albums of his childhood and his first marriage, featuring the doughty Isobel and Rosie.

He ran his fingers over the armchair nearest the fireplace, checking for dust before he sat down. Some of the pictures in the early albums were yellowing and curled up at the corners. Others had become unstuck and floated from the pages as he turned them. There was Rosie playing tennis with Isobel, dashing to return her serve, then blowing out the candles on her birthday cake. He traced the outline of her pudgy cheek with his finger. How old was she then? He couldn't remember and half the cake was out of frame, so he couldn't count the candles.

He used to creep into her bedroom at night and listen to the steady rhythm of her breathing as she lay with her arms flung out in an attitude of flight; he would almost weep with love for her. For a time she had made him good. She had almost, but not quite, saved him from himself.

It was different now. Rosie was wild and single, living in Dubai and selling exorbitantly expensive apartments off plan. Despite the recession, she was doing just fine. Although she sighed at his procession of young women and urban slang, she understood about the houseboat, how it suited him in a way a Notting Hill or Kensington stucco mansion never would. He missed her. Perhaps he would fly to Dubai this summer. He'd tried last year, and the year before, but she'd postponed both times. Isobel, however, was always welcome.

A tug passed under the bridge. Its wake slapped against the side of the houseboat. The wind had picked up. Too cold now to sit outside wrapped in a blanket and smoke his Montecristo. He opened the earliest album. Here he was in his short trousers with a brutal haircut, running free in the regimented garden in Cumbria, his stern mother glowering in the background. There he was clutching that obese black rabbit, playing cricket for the local under-elevens side, and then in the ridiculous school uniform of boater and tailcoat; Sandy beside him, tall and skinny with a thatch of blond hair, clutching his music prize on speech day.

Sandy was eligible for bullying in so many ways. Transported to Wiltshire from the center of Ewell, he would never have survived without Jeremy's patronage. He was credulous right from the start, clambering out of the family Humber, gawping at the statues and pictures in the main hall. His parents didn't help, with the mother dressed in some Ascot race day ensemble and that drunken father of his bringing up the rear. On that first night in the common room, Sandy had been so pleased to be included, to be considered worthy of conversation.

"Where do you live?" one of them asked. His name was Jamie Robinson. He used to trap mice in the school kitchens and dissect them alive. He was also prone to pulling down his trousers and igniting his farts with a cigarette lighter. But he was popular and the others followed him.

Jeremy saw Sandy's Adam's apple jiggle in his neck and knew, even at thirteen years old, that this was one of the scissor points of public school life in which Sandy's reply indicated he was going to belong or be excluded for the next five years.

"Six Newlands Road," Sandy replied, just that bit too eagerly. Jeremy watched and waited.

"Ah, a number not a name," said Robinson. "Now where might that be?"

"Just near the station, in Ewell," replied Sandy in that same eager way.

"Of course," said Robinson. "Of course it is. Tell me," he went on, after a pause and a glance around at his circle of smirking friends, "I come from up north myself. How's the shooting down there, in Newlands Road?"

Jeremy saw the Adam's apple working double time as Sandy tried to think of a suitable reply. He knew that any minute Sandy would blush scarlet and would then start to blub.

"I tell you what," continued Robinson. "A few of us are going down to the range in a bit, let off a few rounds. Why don't you join us?"

"Actually," said Jeremy, walking across to Sandy, "he can't. Ibstock needs to see us now in his study, something about the house tennis."

Jeremy turned to Robinson. "Watch out for his serve. It's lethal."

Sandy got up and followed Jeremy out of the room.

"But I'm not very good at tennis," he said, as they clattered down the wooden staircase.

"It doesn't matter," said Jeremy. "Ibstock doesn't need to see us either."

Jeremy stopped on the landing. Under the dim, fly-speckled wall light, Sandy appeared bewildered and grateful in equal parts. "Stay away from Robinson and mind your own business for a bit until you get the hang of things. Okay?"

Sandy nodded, a pathetically grateful nod. More than forty years later, Jeremy knew it wasn't pure kindness that had made him save Sandy. It was also an innate sense of the balance of power. Robinson, whom he'd known at prep school, was gathering his troops, and Jeremy needed to increase his own ranks of supporters. You could control people through kindness as well as cruelty.

He kept flicking through the dusty album pages of stiff smiles on sports days, half-terms, and holidays, until finally the two of them were on the pavement of Broad Street, arms outstretched to embrace the golden life of Balliol. He had never doubted his right to that life and the luminous one he knew would inevitably follow. This was what he'd been bred for, the best club in the world. Sandy may not have been so sure, but by then he knew better than to voice any doubts as he carefully wired his new Marantz speakers to the turntable in his room across the corridor from Jeremy.

Jeremy turned the page, adjusting his spectacles to look at the blurred Polaroid. He and Sandy were standing outside that pub near the Folly Bridge. Tim was between them. Jeremy and Sandy's hair was long and about to get longer, but still kempt, unlike Tim's wild shoulder-length curls. Peter wasn't there. He must have taken the

picture. All three of them were drunk and staring across the road. He moved the light closer to the photograph.

It was more than thirty years ago, but he recognized clearly the stunned dazed state that comes to young men at the first sight of beauty, the physical shock of it that dilates the pupils and makes them giddy. That was why the three of them were staring. They'd just caught sight of the most beautiful girl in Oxford. Tumbling dark hair, porcelain skin, brown eyes, and a wide red mouth with an unusually full lower lip. A worn paperback of Ovid clutched against the jiggling breasts, tiny waist above the lean hips, long legs striding down the road. Polly Beresford, intellectual siren of the early seventies.

She was almost abreast of them when she slowed and smiled, not at him, or the other two, but at Sandy. "Hello," she said, strands of hair blowing across her face. Bedazzled by lust, Jeremy wanted to reach across and smooth the strands of hair off her face, anything to make her notice him. But she kept smiling at Sandy.

"Liked your point about Donne yesterday," she said in a voice like running water. "I'd never thought about it like that."

Sandy blushed and shrugged. "Thanks," he muttered.

Her eyes roamed across the group and settled again on Sandy. "See you next week then." With that she was gone. Tim and Peter made the usual elbows-in-the-ribs type of jokes, but Jeremy remained silent, jealous that she had spoken to Sandy and ignored him, the main man, the better bet.

He shut the album. He wouldn't think about what had happened to her, to him and Sandy. Not tonight. Not after the failure of the day's deal, and fobbing off petulant Amy. He had worked hard to forget that time in his life, harder than he'd studied to remember tracts of prose and lists of dates for exams, harder than he'd worked to build his career. Afterwards, he and Sandy never spoke about it. They had chosen to excise it from their minds and they had succeeded.

But sometimes when it was late, or when he was weak and drank more than one glass of wine, he knew the memory could not metamorphose into anything else. The facts remained, like DNA, carbon dating, the hard drive of an obsolete computer.

# Chapter 11

THE ZOLOFT THAT Rupert had prescribed had to be kicking in. Sandy spent his days in a benign fuzz, the kind of mood that usually came over him when he was extremely anxious, when he nodded and answered by rote but didn't properly listen to what people said. He emptied a savings account to pay next month's rent and some of the more pressing bills. He cleaned the flat and the next day lugged his collection of bin ends and cut-price Rioja to the corner bottle bank, listening as the glass smashed against the metal. An oddly pleasing sound, he thought as he walked home.

He replied to the get-well card sent to him by Carolyn de Farge. He remembered seeing her in the street some time ago. He'd been drinking hard the night before and it had taken some minutes before he remembered who she was: a friendly and unassuming woman from the children's school days. She must have got his address from Jeremy. He emailed Emily in India to say his accident was just that— an accident. He said the same to Matthew and Penny. He knew they didn't believe him, but that would have to do.

Two mornings a week, usually on Monday and Friday, he walked across Battersea Bridge to have coffee with Jeremy. Jeremy made a fantastic cup of coffee with a perfect caramel *crema*. Sandy sat in the saloon watching the sun play on the colors of the Ziegler carpet while Jeremy fussed in the galley, measuring and grinding his specially roasted single-estate organic fair-trade beans in his daily pursuit of the perfect espresso. No quick and convenient coffee pods for Jeremy.

"Emily thinks I should get some counseling," he called out.

Jeremy's voice was muffled by the noise of the coffee machine. "About what?" he asked.

"You know," said Sandy. "About the thing, the accident. She keeps nagging me about it."

Jeremy appeared at the door. Although his sleeves were rolled up and his collar was unbuttoned, he looked alert and formal as if about to address a board meeting.

"Do you think that would help you?" he asked, handing Sandy a small porcelain cup. "See what you think of this blend. Could be my best yet." Jeremy sniffed his own cup and swallowed the coffee in one gulp. "Did you know coffee starts to lose flavor fifteen seconds after extraction? I know Tim can't wait for you to be in therapy," Jeremy continued, "I think he's spoken to Peter about it. But is it for you?"

Sandy tried to ignore the lick of paranoia, then succumbed to it. Clearly the three of them had been discussing the mess of his life and what should be done. They'd probably consulted Penny as well, Skyping each other in four-way conversations about his drinking, debts, and general incompetence.

He didn't want to think about any of that. His actions that afternoon had taken on the quality of a dream. Sitting in Jeremy's capacious armchair, watching the sun on the water, it seemed that someone else had walked into the path of an oncoming car and that nothing had actually happened to him, Sandy Ellison. He had his life back. Granted, it was not a life many others would covet. But it was all he knew.

Jeremy had disappeared into the bedroom. There was a clatter of coat hangers and a whooshing noise of a jacket being shaken.

"I don't know," Sandy called out. "Emily is very insistent though, and thorough. I told her I've stopped drinking, that I'm feeling good, but she won't give up. She's told me where to go and when, although how she worked all that out from a small town in northern India is a mystery."

"Why don't you think on it for a while," said Jeremy, emerging from the bedroom, jacket buttoned, ready for another busy and productive day. "Got to go, late already." They left the boat together. Jeremy had a car waiting for him. The driver scurried around to open the door and gestured to the bottle of water and the stack of newspapers waiting on the seat. Sandy waved Jeremy away and turned for home.

Later that day, mostly out of boredom, he rang the number Emily had given him and found himself agreeing to join a self-help group of people who had attempted suicide. The meetings were held on Wednesday evenings, in a church hall near Clapham Junction. On the way to his first meeting, sitting on the bus, Sandy imagined an ominous half-moon of plastic chairs and a therapist ringleader urging everyone on to messy public confessions. He was dreading it, but part of him wanted to please his daughter. He thought of the men on the common, with their buggies and their babies tucked up inside. They would know their children so much better than he knew Emily and Matthew.

The hall was hard to find, as it was badly lit and surrounded by a tall beech hedge. Sandy pushed through the squeaky gate. In front of him was an unkempt garden with the last snowdrops drooping from the day's rain. He lit a cigarette and smoked it in the shadow of the hedge. When he could delay no longer, he walked into the hall. A man about his own age, with a full grizzled beard, was ambling up and down, elbows crossed. Three teenage girls and one boy, about Matthew's age, were stacking yoga mats to one side. They looked so young, like children.

"Hey, I'm Imogen," said a girl with spiky hair. "You timed your entry well. We've just finished setting up. Although I don't get why those yoga women can't stack their own mats." She sprawled on a couple of long sofas surrounded by a group of armchairs and began scratching horizontal red weals on the inside of her wrist. Sandy winced and looked away. The boy and the other two girls flung the last of the mats to one side and flopped down. The man with the beard took up a position near the window, with his back to the group. Sandy smiled in what he hoped was a friendly way and approached the sofa. They were talking about music.

"Have you listened to *After the Gold Rush*?" asked the boy. "It's just ridiculous it's so good. The first time I heard it, I realized how many people had straight-out copied him."

"I feel that way about Janis Joplin," said Imogen. "Same same but different."

Sandy couldn't help himself. "Hey guys." He laughed. "That's my music, old people's tunes. Neil Young is even more ancient than me. Don't you want your own music?"

"Sometimes," said the boy. "But sometimes your music is better. Oh, I'm Duncan."

Sandy nodded. "I'm Sandy."

The two girls mumbled something. A man of about forty rushed through a side entrance and joined them. With a cheery Australian accent, redolent of sun and a commendable self-esteem, he introduced himself as Justin.

"It's Sandy, isn't it? We spoke on the phone," he said, shaking hands with a firm, almost painful grip. "We only need first names here."

The week before, Emily had emailed him that traveling through India was like watching a Michael Palin documentary, except that she could smell toilets and dirt and spices all at once. He now knew what she meant. Group therapy was like everything he'd ever read about or seen on television. It was both familiar and unreal. He wouldn't have been surprised if there were tripod marks on the floor and some overeducated git with his underpants hanging out of his trousers waltzed in and shouted "Cut!" or "Action!"

There was an element of performance in the room. He imagined Imogen and the others preparing their lines before they spoke, the stage fright before the public confession. What would he say when it was his turn? That he drank too much but didn't consider himself an alcoholic, although his friends and family probably did. That he had no memory of what happened that afternoon other than a desire for oblivion. That his life was a fog of unpaid bills and occasional bailiffs and that he subsisted on meager royalties from a string of largely forgotten pop songs. That he didn't bother listening to music anymore or trying to compose it, and he missed Penny and his children more than he thought was possible, that more than a year after the divorce he could not bring himself to refer to Penny as his ex-wife.

"Sandy?" Justin called him to attention. "I'd like to start this evening with an exercise that I hope will allow everyone to trust each other. It's very simple. Just stand up, in a circle, and hold hands. Lean into each other, feel the support you can give each other. Let yourself go."

What a load of horseshit, thought Sandy as he got to his feet. What was the point? If you let yourself go, you might never find yourself again—the part of yourself that you chose to recognize, anyway. The rest of you, whatever and wherever that was, might pack its bags and leave home for good. He had a bizarre image of bits of himself fleeing down an unnamed road, desperate to escape the flawed housing of his psyche for a cheery refurbished new residence.

No one else seemed to think it odd for a group of people not known to each other to stand inside a church hall on a chilly late spring evening and hold hands. "What the hell," Sandy muttered to himself. He shut his eyes and leaned forward. There was an alarming sense of vertigo in the split second between leaning and someone supporting him. But Duncan beside him was surprisingly strong and held him steady. It was all about trust, Justin told them; trust in yourself and others.

"I'm not here to tell you everything is going to be fine," said Justin. "I'm not that big on the word *fine*. A lot of people say they're fine and it means something very different."

Sandy wanted to hold up his hand as if he were back in the classroom. Yes sir, he knew the meaning of *fine*. Only recently one of his oldest friends had told him. *Fine* means fucked-up! Insecure! Neurotic! And emotional! Somehow this new interpretation of a previously anodyne word had entered the universal vocabulary, like *twittersphere, mani-pedi,* or *bestie.* As usual, he hadn't noticed. But now he was in the loop at last.

After coffee, Imogen sat next to Sandy and began talking about cutting herself. Sometimes, she said, she sliced her skin just above a vein and played with it. She'd imagine the blood oozing from the safety of its blue casing. It made her feel powerful and alive. It felt so good she wasn't able to stop.

"Why did you start?" he asked, repelled and intrigued all at once. "What made you think of such a thing?"

"Don't know," she replied, with a funny small shrug. "Lots of my friends do it. Not together, though. I always do it on my own. Sometimes I feel like I'm floating through the sky, looking down. It feels good to be so high above myself and everything. Get away from all the shit. And then I couldn't stop."

He thought of Emily. How brave and confident his daughter always appeared, how sensible and sober. Emily might have been beset by grim fears too. But he wouldn't have known, because he never asked.

Parenthood was another thing that had changed without his being aware of it. He had no recollection of ever spending any time alone with Matthew or Emily, of going to their schools or reading them stories. If he'd thought about it at all, which he rarely did, he would have told himself that his job was to provide money and Penny's job was to look after the children. Most men would have said the same. Work sucked up time and energy. Families mattered when you were older, when you had time to think properly, when it was too late.

Smoking was banned inside the hall, so he and Imogen went outside for a cigarette. Yellow light played on the lawn between the hall and the church. Through the light mist he saw the faint indentations of animal tracks in the grass: cats or foxes following a familiar route to food or shelter in the hedge. The nights were still cold and he shivered in his coat, wondering why Imogen was wearing a T-shirt.

He finished the cigarette quickly and lit another. Imogen's confidences, given so freely, made him anxious. Every social group had its unwritten commandments. Disclosure was high on the list here. Sandy dreaded the evening that he couldn't put off, the one when he would have to talk about himself.

He leaned forward to light Imogen's cigarette. She smelled of musk and cloves. In the sulfur flare, he saw her little pointed breasts, bare under her T-shirt, and knew immediately she'd seen him looking at her. She smiled, this child coquette with a taste for razors, and cocked her head to one side. He stepped back, embarrassed. He hadn't meant to look at her breasts. He wasn't like Jeremy, always up for the press of young flesh.

"What do you do?" Imogen drew on her cigarette and exhaled in a rush.

"Not a lot," said Sandy, nonplussed.

"No, not now. I mean what did you do when you did something. You know, your job." There was that upward inflection at the end of her sentences. Why did every sentence uttered by anyone under twenty-nine have to end up being a question?

"I used to write songs," he said. "I wasn't John Lennon, but sometimes I did okay." He shrugged. "I had an ear for music and I was good at the piano at school. I didn't set out to work in music, but I went to work in a recording studio as a summer job and it started from there. I was all set to become a lawyer."

Imogen studied him. "You talk like a lawyer. Kind of posh."

Sandy smiled. "Far from it." He recalled the three-piece mock-brocade suite in Newlands Road, the anxious vowels of his mother and the gruff façade of his father as they tried to mix with more assured parents on sports days.

"I'm a long way from being posh and my parents were incredibly ambitious for me. So I can understand my father being livid when I went off the track he'd set up. But I couldn't be a lawyer, I loved music too much."

He didn't tell Imogen how much he was mocked in his early days as a studio runner for his Received Pronunciation and his habit of carrying handkerchiefs. Not that it mattered that much. Apart from his friendship with Jeremy, he'd never fitted in at school either, and home was always a place best viewed from the rear-vision mirror.

Music was the only place where he felt entirely at ease. No class, no cliques; just pure notes hanging in the air. Although he did like the irony that eventually his old-fashioned musical education gave him a jump start ahead of his more fashionably spoken peers.

"I suppose I knew when I heard a sound if it would work as a song or not . . . if it would be a hit. But it didn't last, so I guess it was luck more than anything else."

He stubbed out his cigarette against the brick wall and threw the butt into the garden. Imogen made him pick it up. "It takes ten years for a butt to decompose and birds can mistake them for food," she scolded.

"I've never met an ecological smoker before," Sandy said.

"I'm stopping soon." They walked back inside. In the hall, she turned to him. "You're okay," she said. "Not as bad as you looked when you first walked in. I thought you'd be a complete tosser."

"I don't know how to take that," he said. Imogen smiled. She handed him her butt and walked towards the sofa. Sandy went to the kitchen and found a bin for the ecologically unsound cigarettes. His hands had soil on them and smelled of smoke. He washed them at the sink and gazed at his reflection in the window. The harsh fluorescent light accentuated his jowls and the pouches under his eyes. He needed a haircut. Apart from that, he looked the same as he did before.

But he didn't feel the same. He'd lost purchase with the path of his familiar cynical self. He didn't know how others saw him anymore, so he had no idea how to see himself. He'd always imagined that Jeremy, Tim, and Peter considered him a good friend, affable and sometimes witty. Now they undoubtedly thought of him as a psychological weakling, an opinion probably shared by Matthew and Emily, and definitely by Penny.

He dried his hands and went into the hall to collect his coat. It was later than he thought and everything was empty and silent. Imogen was sitting on the sofa, her knees tucked under her chin.

"I thought everyone had gone," he said, wanting her not to be there.

She smiled. "Well, not me," she said.

Surely she wouldn't want to flirt with him. He was an impotent gray-haired old man and she was only a few years older than Emily.

She patted the sofa and he sat down, making sure there was significant airspace between them.

"So who did you write songs for?" she asked.

"You're far too young, you wouldn't have heard of any of them."

"Don't know about that." Imogen smiled. She had little pointed teeth, shiny pink gums. "I'm pretty good at my music. Try me."

He was almost too tired to talk. "They were just people."

"You shouldn't be so hard on yourself," she said. "That's what my shrink says anyway." The radiators along the walls hissed, then sighed. "Where do you live?" she asked.

"In Battersea. The cheapest bit." Sandy picked up his coat. "I'd better get going. I'll miss the bus otherwise."

Imogen raked her hair with her hand. "I live just up the road. You should come by sometime."

She tapped the coffee table, as if it were a drum, and stood up. "I'm off then. See you later."

Sandy sat for a while listening to the radiators hiccup and fall silent. He heard the distant rush of water through pipes, then nothing at all. His neck was stiff and his buttocks ached. He stood up and began walking towards the bus stop.

emily.ellison@gmail.com

To: mattman5@hotmail.com

Sometimes you're such a fuckwit it makes me furious. You told me, you swore to me you were not going to do drugs again. Why do you have to keep flirting with this? You will end up like Dad if you don't watch out. Is that what you want?

I'm so tired of all this family fuckwittery and how I've somehow been promoted to counselor and fixer. Dad just mopes around that fetid little shithole in Battersea. And all Mum seems to do is glue bits of wood together and make toy houses out there in France on her own. They're hardly embracing reality. You email me about GHB ecstasy, or whatever you call it. You know what I think? I think you should stop that, get a job, get an existence of your own.

We had it okay. Not as good as some, but way better than so many others. Were we beaten, sold off as child slaves, or something like that? It's just a divorce, it's just what happened. Yes, Mum drank too much and there were those times when she threw up and pretended she had a virus. And yes, we knew that girl who kept ringing all night asking to speak to Dad wasn't his secretary. I'm not saying it didn't hurt or leave a mark, I'm saying stop using it. Move along.

Okay, end of lecture. Everything is wonderful here. It's not the same old thing of dancing at Gaz's on Thursday nights and getting hammered afterwards with the usual bunch of people you've known since you were a kid. I just feel anything is possible now. Does that sound stupid? I'm so happy here. Everyone I meet is happy. Even the babies don't cry, and God knows if you look at what is probably their future, there isn't a lot to laugh about. But they don't seem to care about money and stuff the way we do. Even all the palefaces, people like me, we're learning stuff, we're thinking and growing. Sometimes when I read texts and stuff from the lamas at the ashram, and listen to talks there, I get so excited I can't sleep at night.

I'm living in this tiny little flat about a quarter of a mile away, just off the main square. There's a woman, Annie, living above me who works for an NGO helping to build schools. She's been here for thirty years and says she's never going back to England. Apparently she was at Oxford about the same time as Dad. She knew who he was and used to see him and Jeremy around, but she didn't really know them. She left without finishing her degree after something happened in her family, said she couldn't see any point in going on. I like her a lot.

There's a big prayer festival soon, a puja. Loads of people come into town for it. Then there's a big celebration when it ends. Can't wait. You should come. I looked up the flights yesterday and they're cheap. You fly into Delhi and get a bus up here.

Think about it. Dear Matt, crazy poodle, I'm not pissed off with you anymore. Just take it easy.

# Chapter 12

IT HAD BEEN a delicious silent morning digging between the crevices in the stone courtyard, teasing out the bindweed that threatened to smother the more fragile erigeron and nigella. Bullies, Penny thought, as she left the weeds in the sun to wilt and die. You won't have everything your own way. Other plants have a right to space too. The work had given her a stillness of mind in which calm had begun to grow again. There was no sound except for birdsong and the occasional whisper from the pine trees as the breeze played along their branches. She lay on the uneven lawn in the last of the morning sun. The grass tickled her neck and bare arms. She imagined millions of root fibers slowly unfurling underneath her, tiny shoots forming, waiting for the earth to warm so it would be safe to push up to the light and air. She hoped it would be a kind summer.

Over a lunch of bread and slightly moldy cheese, she decided to prune the small row of olive trees along the side of the house. She looked up the procedure in her out-of-date Royal Horticultural Society encyclopedia before hunting out the secateurs, the long-handled loppers, and a jar of tree paint. Another satisfying aspect of living alone: she could do whatever she wanted, in whatever order she decided.

The renegade suckers at the base of the trees were easy to snip away, and she cut them into small lengths for a bonfire. The dead wood was next, and she switched to the loppers, squinting against the afternoon sun as she inspected each branch before deciding which ones to chop, being careful to leave a stub of wood on the main trunk. She thinned the live stems, making sure she could see the sun between the branches and the trunk, before daubing tree paint onto the fresh cuts.

The debris was almost completely raked away when she heard a car on the lane and then, annoyingly, turning down the rough track leading to her house. It was Nigel, corseted into his salesman navy sports jacket and trailing an attractive young couple behind him. He rolled his eyes at her when he was sure the couple couldn't see, as if to say he knew he was interrupting her and he was sorry, but here he was and here were these strangers, and let's make the best of it.

"Penny, darling," he said in exaggerated vowels. He kissed her on both dirty cheeks. "Just passing with Liz and Greg, who're looking for a house around here. They spotted yours from the car and said how lovely it looked."

She gave a strangled smile in their direction, knowing it would have been Nigel's idea all along. Closer, the couple was not as young as she'd thought and they had about them that unmistakable London luster of self-satisfied prosperity. She wiped her hand on her trousers and offered it to them. They pumped her arm up and down and bared rows of expensive teeth.

"And so I thought," continued Nigel in the same unnatural tone, "I thought I might just pop in and ask if you wouldn't mind them having just a little look around, to see what can be done with a bit of imagination and, of course, so much taste."

There was no excuse she could offer without appearing churlish, so she invited them into the house, glaring at Nigel when their backs were turned before remembering his generosity with the computer and how she enjoyed their gossip sessions in his office.

"Tea or coffee?" she asked in a high polite voice, a waitress in her own home.

"Tea would be fantastic," said Liz, inspecting the kitchen and peering into the hall. "Would you mind? A quick nose around, everything looks so divine. Greg, darling, just look in here."

They disappeared into the sitting room. Penny heard them exclaiming over flagstones, beams, and fireplaces in a way that suggested they'd never seen such things before that moment, and then the clatter of their feet as they returned to the kitchen.

"That doll's house is just adorable," cooed Liz. "Your grandchildren must be in heaven when they visit."

"Actually, I don't have any grandchildren," Penny replied. "Just a little hobby of mine, I'm afraid."

"Amazing," said Liz. Penny always thought people said things were amazing when they believed the opposite.

"It's so rude, I know," continued Liz, "but do you think we could just have a little peep upstairs? I love what you've done here. Perfect. Did you use a local designer?"

Penny was about to say she'd done it herself, but Liz was already cantering up the stairs, pulling Greg behind her. The thump of their footsteps shook the kitchen beams as they passed through her bedroom into the bathroom. She heard windows opening and shutting and then the toilet flush.

"Really," she said to Nigel.

He shrugged, helpless in the face of an impending sale.

"I owe you," he muttered. He took mugs off the shelf and placed them on the table. Greg and Liz bounded down the stairs and strode into the kitchen.

"Don't you love this place?" enthused Nigel. "The perfect bolt-hole from London. An hour and forty in the air, a quick drive from Bergerac, and you're here. You'd pay twice as much in Somerset or Dorset for the same space. And you'd be crawling along the A303 for most of the summer. On Saturdays, you don't even make it from the M25 to Stonehenge in under two hours."

For someone who had lived in Sarlat for nearly twenty years and rarely visited the motherland, Nigel had an encyclopedic knowledge of English motorways. Penny sometimes thought he studied Google maps at night.

"So much less hassle to fly, and you know how cheap flights are these days," he said.

The couple nodded. No one appeared to have calculated the time spent getting to any London airport, queuing, waiting to board and take off, and then collecting their luggage at the other end. Penny knew Nigel would be furious if she mentioned such trivialities. She poured tea as the couple interviewed her about builders, tiles, bathroom fittings, waste systems, and heating costs, as if they were about to move in. Patiently she answered their queries. Yes, she was lucky. The house was in good order when she bought it a year ago. Wood burners were very efficient, especially this one, which heated water and some upstairs radiators as well. She'd done most of the decorating herself and local tradespeople put in a new bathroom and refurbished the kitchen. No, she didn't intend to sell and had no idea of her profit if she did.

Nigel galloped to the rescue here. "Penny would double her money, even in this financial climate," he said. "People just love this area. It's full of writers and artists, a fantastic community. And the food and wine is out of this world. It's heaven here, isn't it, Pen?"

"Absolutely," she said. "No moldy pensioners in our town. Everyone here is just riveting. The collective IQ is off the chart."

Nigel glared at her. It turned out Greg had recently sold his plumbing company and was taking a sabbatical while considering his next venture.

"It's been all go for the past few years," he said. "Making so much money we haven't even had time to make some kids." He grinned at his own joke.

Liz looked out to the hills. "Are you going to put a pool in?" she asked. "The courtyard is the perfect place."

Penny could imagine nothing worse than spending her summers inhaling the stench of chlorine.

"I hadn't thought of it," she replied.

There was a silence. If they left soon, she'd have time to sow a couple of rows of carrots. But Nigel was determined.

"Penny used to live in London," he said. "In South Kensington, Onslow Gardens. Her husband is a famous songwriter. Famous in the industry of course, the public might not be so aware—but that's his job, isn't it, Pen? To make other people famous, not himself."

Nigel turned to Greg and Liz, who were clearly impressed. Penny

raddled fool who now lived on a White City council estate. One of the many reasons for his present low-cost postcode dated back to 1984 when he hired a twenty-four-hour limousine service to be available outside his Mayfair flat, in case he wanted to shop or cruise. The next week he went away on a world tour for a year and his assistant forgot to cancel the booking. Joe also forgot about the million-acre sheep farm he'd bought in northern Australia and the cruiser in the South of France. While she was on the subject of Joe Fleetfield, she'd like to point out the irony that Joe's monster hit, "Never Give Up," had been written by a man who had done just the opposite.

She also wanted to tell Liz that the performance or recording was the death of the song as she knew it; that what she had loved about Sandy and his music was the sight of him at the piano, the way the afternoon sun gilded his head as he played his songs for her. She would stop whatever she was doing and watch his long fingers stretch along the keys while his foot kept a steady rhythm on the piano pedal. His voice was thin and sometimes cracked on the higher notes, but there was an honesty to it that made her heart leap as each note echoed around the basement kitchen.

"Do you think it's good enough?" he would ask shyly. "Is it all right?" She would ruffle his hair and kiss the back of his neck, telling him he was wonderful, that the song was wonderful. She had felt herself a seamless part of him then, before he gave the song away to someone else and made it into something she no longer recognized. She never stopped being jealous of that.

Instead she offered Liz and Greg a fresh pot of tea and some Elizabeth David flourless chocolate cake she'd baked some days ago.

"Are you sure?" cheeped Liz, holding out her mug.

"I say," said Greg, "I won't say no."

Outside, pigeons squabbled in the pine trees.

"So. What was he like? Joe Fleetfield, I mean. You must have known him really well? Was Joe a normal guy?" Greg spoke the name with reverence.

"I met him once or twice," replied Penny. "He was more my husband's friend." She didn't add that Joe and Sandy were inseparable when Sandy's contagious choruses had pubescent girls weeping and screaming at Wembley. Nor that Joe had less time for Sandy as sales fell, and no time at all to tell Sandy he'd been replaced by some hipper, younger duo. That had been left to Joe's rat-faced lawyer.

"But," she said, "he seemed, as you say, a perfectly normal man."

Liz and Greg nodded, as if this was something they'd guessed all along. Penny never understood why people like Greg and Liz thought that prancing around a stage and flicking your groin at thousands of screaming girls, some so excited that they wet themselves, might be a normal thing to do. And not just once, but week after week, month after month, sometimes even year after year.

Nor did she understand why people considered glamorous, even desirable, a world that regarded the saying "No blow job, no backstage pass" as perfectly acceptable conversation. But these were thoughts she kept to herself. She poured fresh tea into their mugs and passed slices of cake. Nigel smiled approvingly.

"Don't you miss London, though?" Liz said. "Do you ever get back there?"

"Actually," said Penny, annoyed by the pitying look she saw on Liz's face, "I'm flying there next week. My ex-husband hasn't been well and I'm going to see him. I'm going to try that new travel agent in town, Nigel. So let's have lunch tomorrow."

# Chapter 13

THERE WAS ANOTHER handwritten envelope, large and stiff, in his mailbox. He recognized the looped handwriting. Carolyn de Farge again.

"It would be so good to catch up, hear your news," she wrote on one of those Keep Calm cards. "I walk in Kensington Gardens every day and we could meet at the Serpentine Gallery, have a stroll and some coffee somewhere."

She had added her mobile number and email address underneath her name. Odd, thought Sandy. He placed the lolly-pink card on the kitchen table. Or perhaps not so odd, now that he recalled Penny's fondness towards lost causes and emotional down-and-outs: the childhood friends who occupied the spare room for far too long after some domestic drama, the hours she spent on the telephone listening to other people's problems. One evening he'd been so jealous that he had pulled the telephone socket out of the wall. Carolyn must have decided to put him on her list of charitable projects. Sandy was simultaneously flattered and insulted by the cards, but he was also very bored and, after three days, he sent an email saying he could meet at the Serpentine at four o'clock, which meant he would be back in time to watch the evening news.

There was a new female presenter called Catherine to whom he had become irrationally attached, noting if she looked tired, nodding in appreciation if she wore a flattering blouse, and returning her smile before the commercial break.

He particularly liked to see her bare arms when she was interviewing people. How elegantly she waved them about as she remonstrated with politicians about their failures and subsequent economies with facts. How neatly she pointed to moving graphs and charts before she turned to address the camera, and therefore Sandy. He knew his infatuation with the presenter was pathetic, but it got him through the hour when he usually started drinking, and somehow after that he was happy to remain sober for the remainder of the evening.

On the day of his meeting with Carolyn, he woke sweating with a fierce headache. A mystery ailment, the perfect excuse for a cancellation. He was painstakingly jabbing a text message to her when he heard a ping and there, at the top of his inbox, was an email saying how much she was looking forward to their meeting that afternoon. Sandy deleted his text and looked up bus timetables instead.

During the last hours of sunlight, Kensington Gardens was full of dog owners clutching small plastic bags of turds while their charges ran wild before the long hours of enforced continence began, relieved only, if they were lucky, by a late night whip around the block. Sandy leaned against the railing and watched a three-legged dog bounding about. It was cold and his toe hurt. He should have worn a scarf. He was about to go into the gallery to get warm when a horn tooted and a tiny car, shiny and pillar-box red, braked almost at his feet. The door swung open and a beige cashmere arm waved in his direction.

"Here I am," Carolyn called out. "Hop in before you freeze."

Sandy folded himself into the seat and she pulled out onto the road.

"Too cold for a walk," Carolyn said. "Let's go for coffee instead."

As she zipped through the gates and headed west, Sandy shifted his legs. The seats were uncomfortably close together. Each time Carolyn moved her arm or leg, she brushed against some part of him. There was an instantly recognizable female scent, sweet and close.

"You don't mind," she said, "about the walk?"

"Do I have a choice?" he asked, and then, as she pulled anxiously at her neck with her free hand, said, "Of course not. It might still be spring, but it's cold out there."

She flicked on her headlights and turned into Ladbroke Grove. "Could we have coffee at my place?" she asked. "I've left the handyman there and I need to pay him." A younger, more virile Sandy might have considered this a possible proposition, but he knew that lame ducks and lust were not compatible. She was merely being kind. And Carolyn was as he remembered her: pleasantly unremarkable and plump. Not his type at all. Something of a relief, he thought, not to have to worry about unbidden erections and where they might lead.

Inside the house, Sandy tried not to look around as Carolyn retrieved a thick wad of cash from her bag and counted the notes out for the handyman, then gave him an extra forty pounds as he packed up his equipment.

"For your good work," she said. The man, about Sandy's own age and gray with fatigue, spoke no English. He looked perplexed and tried to give the money back. Carolyn shook her head and, after some minutes of mime and elaborate gesticulation, they made themselves understood and the man left the two of them on their own.

They sat with their mugs of coffee in a kind of conservatory off the kitchen. French doors led onto a terrace and then a garden where severe pyramids of immaculate topiary were outlined against the dimming light. Everything in every direction was clipped and polished, reeking of a purchasing power far superior to Sandy's own. Yet Carolyn didn't seem to belong in her own house. Sandy couldn't imagine her choosing the enormous curved sofas and the bleak modern pictures. He couldn't see her turning over lamb chops on the hob, which was bigger than his kitchen table.

"I wanted to say how sorry I was to hear about what happened," said Carolyn. "I didn't realize when I saw you in the street that day how terribly bad you must have felt then. I mean, I thought you looked so down, but I didn't do anything, didn't ask how you were, I just kept on shopping. And then I heard, in a roundabout way through Jeremy, that you . . . that you had that dreadful accident."

Sandy laughed. No one, including himself, could bring themselves to say the three little syllables: *suicide.*

"I have problems explaining that myself," he said. "And I was there, or at least they tell me I was. In the beginning, I couldn't remember much and I pretended it was an accident. But now, let me give it my best shot. Suicide. There it is, out in the open at last. And not at all difficult."

He meant his words to be lighthearted, but Carolyn's face crumpled and she began to weep.

"Please, I didn't mean to upset you," he said. "What is it?"

She scrubbed her face with her hands and didn't answer.

"Whatever it is, it can't be that bad," he said, shifting away from her on the sofa. As an afterthought, he patted her arm. She collapsed against him. Her head leaned on his shoulder. He regretted responding to her cards. He wanted to disentangle himself from this woman he hardly knew and slope off back home to admire his evening news presenter.

"I know how you felt," she whispered. "I feel the same way too. And still I walked away from you."

"But I haven't given it a second thought," said Sandy, still trying to extricate himself. "And the whole thing has its advantages. I've given up drinking and I don't even miss it. Really. Well, sometimes I do and then I think of the money saved."

"Please, no more jokes."

Somewhere upstairs a clock struck six times. If he left now, he might make it back in time for the news.

"Can you stay and talk for a bit?" she asked. "Just for a little while."

"But your husband must be due home," said Sandy. Had he met her husband? What did he do? He couldn't remember.

"He's in Salisbury. Some medical malpractice case." She stood up and paced around the room, rearranging pots of orchids and piles of books as she went. She raised her shoulders almost to her ears, then let them flop.

"I know I have everything, just everything. House here, holidays four times a year, children doing well. But I can't stop crying. I tried antidepressants but they made me feel so anxious. And I still cried." Her voice rose. She tittered and scraped her hair back.

"Then last year my husband sent me away for a fortnight to this kind of rehab place, where you try to reconfigure everything, help yourself to feel better. Someone in his chambers went and everything completely changed for him. But nothing happened for me. I still see a therapist each week, but I don't know if I can go on. I'm terrified."

"Come on," he said, edging away from her. Suddenly he craved a drink. He wanted the insulation of alcohol to wrap around him like a woolen coat. "You'll be okay."

"I'm not so sure anymore." Her voice broke. "I think what I miss is being busy all the time, now the children are so much older. Before, I didn't have a moment to think about anything except looking after them and my husband—the shopping, the cooking, organizing the cleaner and the gardener and the nanny. But that isn't a life. It's directing traffic. I keep thinking if we're going to live that much longer now, we've got to make it count for something."

She started to weep again, large tears dripping down and collecting at the end of her nose. Sandy wanted a cigarette, the sensation of breathing down sharp smoke so he could think for a minute about how to reply.

"I'm sorry, but you're talking to the wrong person. My life management skills are minimal at best. I wasn't a good husband and I regret that, very much. I've only just realized I never spent any time with my kids. I'd never thought about it before. I'm a late-onset loser. I peaked early and never got used to it."

Carolyn smiled timidly. "It's not a competition. There are no prizes for who's lived the most fatuous life." She wiped her eyes. "Besides, you're not such a loser. I think you're much nicer now than you used to be."

"You mean failure becomes me," he said. "Perhaps you're right." He considered the notion. It was fully dark now. The topiary pyramids cast long shadows in the lights from neighboring houses. He had missed the news. He wanted to get up and leave. He wasn't used to talking without drinking. Without drinking there wasn't much to say.

She came across and sat down next to him, turning her face to his and kissing him first on the cheek, then on the mouth. She smelled of fresh coffee. He hadn't been physically close to a woman since the divorce and the feeling was alarming.

It was uncomfortable perched on the oversized sofa, feeling the weight of her sitting next to him, seeing her small fingers clasped together. He shifted and crossed his legs. He tried to move away, but Carolyn moved closer and placed her hand on his knee. She kissed him again, with her mouth closed, pure like a first kiss. Her eyelids fluttered against the stubble on his cheek.

He worried about flaking lip skin, cigarette breath, bits of lunch between his teeth. Her hand was still on his knee, moving up to his groin. He felt himself shrivel and then begin to sweat. Her hand stopped moving upwards and began rubbing his thigh in slow circles. His penis jumped like a minnow in a stream, then retracted. It wasn't used to this. He wasn't used to this.

For a moment he was outside himself, peering in through the French doors. He saw his belly straining against the serviceable worn Marks and Spencer shirt; his bony shins bare and pale above his socks. He saw his bunched-up trousers, his body contorted into a half-sitting, half-slouching position with his knees pointing one way and his shoulders turned in the opposite direction, lank gray tufts of hair curling over his collar. An impotent old man kissing a sad rich housewife. It was ridiculous. He would remove her hand from his knee and extract himself from this situation.

But he didn't move and then she kissed him again, the same pure, dry-lipped kiss. There was something so trusting in the way her body turned to his, something so alien to seduction, that he softened and bent towards her. Her mouth was warm and tender and he returned her kiss. She withdrew and licked his lips, starting from one side and moving to the other. Still he didn't move except to open his mouth just a little, an involuntary movement. Her tongue probed the delicate skin inside his lip. She reached for a switch on the wall behind the sofa and the room fell dark.

Sandy was scared. He heard the sweep of clothes being taken off and landing on the floor, her small, sweet voice saying his name. Deft fingers unbuttoned his shirt and slipped it off his shoulders. They unbuckled his belt and undid his flies. Somehow his clothes were on the floor and he was lying naked and sober next to Carolyn from the school run.

It was the first time in many years he had been anywhere near a female without a full bar rolling inside his gut: beer to make him jovial before dinner, wine to produce some sort of conversation during the meal, and then something stronger afterwards. Without that armor, he had no idea how to stroke a breast or caress a nipple. All the small activities that came before intercourse had vanished from his consciousness. His entire body felt unnaturally sensitive, as if layers of skin had somehow sloughed off. He imagined pale nerve endings jerking in alarm, and he lay stiff and still.

She was the one who touched his chest, teased his nipples, and circled his stomach with her forefinger. She was the one to move closer so her breath played on his neck and her hand could trace the grizzle on his thighs and make its way to the dead weight of his penis hanging between his legs.

She'll give up now, he thought. She won't go on. There would be a rueful smile, a quiet apology, and he would burrow into his clothes and scuttle away. If they ran into each other again, they could pretend this thing, this embarrassing incident, had not happened.

But she did go on. Her fingers kept moving in slow, steady circles, displaying a confidence not seen in her teary confessions. His poor, tired organ began to flutter before subsiding. It stirred again and he felt something like hope and then nothing except shame, until suddenly it went up and stayed up. He was hard for the first time in years and, in spite of everything, he smiled in the darkness.

He relaxed and grew warm, the way he used to feel after the first drink of the day. She leaned over him and he felt himself slide into her, secret and warm. She began to move.

He'd always assumed the masterful position, had tolerated foreplay as the means to the end. He'd been keen on the grunt, the deep penetration, the energetic thrusts, the slap of flesh on flesh. He'd been used to women, Penny included, who writhed with precision and moaned stridently, who efficiently fingered their clitorises as they drove themselves towards orgasm.

This was different. So sweet and slow. So kind, measured, and comfortable, an act of tenderness between friends. He could feel the slippery folds of her, how she lengthened and thickened as she circled her hips and caressed his face in the dark until they came together in a dreamlike moment of pleasure that continued far longer than anything he could remember. Afterwards they lay entwined on the sofa, the flush of her face hot on his shoulder.

He felt her cheeks curve into a smile. "I didn't have that in mind when I suggested a walk. Really. You must believe me. Or do you think I'm a terrible old tart?"

"Well, just a bit, not that much. No need to sing the Carole King song," he said. "It was something of a surprise, though. A nice surprise. What's the word I'm looking for? Languorous? Lovely? I'll go for lovely."

She kissed his shoulder, the soft part just under the bone. "I'll go for that one too," she said. They were silent for a while. He thought she might have fallen asleep, but there was a voice in the dark. "Talk to me. Tell me something about yourself."

Sandy felt an internal shuddering, as if his ribs were about to collapse. Whatever postcoital ease he had felt vanished. He didn't know what to say.

All his conversations, sober, middling, and drunk, were predictable. They traveled familiar circuits. There was the Morse code of the male clan, where he felt safe. There was the other stuff women liked to hear, the linguistic foreplay of anecdotes about school and childhood, dogs and parents, old girlfriends and childish crushes. His marital dialogue had been predictable, consisting of children, domestic trivia, possible household renovations, bills, and holiday plans.

Even now he might be able to bluff his way through a conversation with former colleagues about the music business—deals and studios and the big old days. But the idea of an untethered conversation bobbing in the air like a helium balloon was terrifying.

"You know who I am," he began, after clearing his throat. "You know my ex-wife and my children, where I used to live. You know I used to write songs. Now, I'm in the arse end of Battersea in a rented flat on my own. I don't do much of anything. I can't think what to do anymore."

"Come on," she said, her arm resting on his chest. "You can do better than that."

"What?"

"When I was little," she said, "I wanted to be an archaeologist. I thought it would be fantastic to find out how people lived thousands of years ago. But then someone told me you had to spend months brushing dirt off stones with paintbrushes, so I changed my mind."

He told her his childhood ambition was to become a doctor. "My father worked in an insurance office. I didn't want to do that and I liked the idea of making people feel better, of driving around the country with a black bag beside me. But then I realized I hated the sight of blood. It made me want to vomit. I still vomit sometimes, but not at the sight of blood."

They shifted closer together. There was a shawl on the arm of the sofa and Carolyn drew it around them.

"My father drank a lot," said Sandy. "He used to stagger up the staircase to bed every night. My mother explained it away by the war, all the horrors he'd seen. But she didn't explain why she joined him by the drinks trolley night after night. He died about a year ago, soon after my divorce. My mother's still alive, in a nursing home outside Woking. I'm a shitty kind of son. I haven't seen her for months.

"Anyhow, I hated the smell of alcohol when I was a kid. I remember the whole house reeking of stale whisky and Dunhill cigarettes in the morning. I started drinking at Oxford with Jeremy. Then I wondered what had taken me so long. Everything was so much easier. Talking, sex, life. The funny thing is that when I started drinking, Jeremy almost stopped. He's a committed one-glass-a-day guy now."

Now he was almost gabbling. He'd start on about his dead puppy soon and how his father despised him for not being able to catch twenty tennis balls in a row. Having dreaded a conversation without an agenda, he was beginning to understand how people might want to lie in the dark and talk about anything that entered their heads, how liberating that notion might be. Just to open your mouth and speak of hopes and fears. But how could he speak to someone else about these things when he refused to acknowledge them to himself?

He shut his eyes and saw Polly, sitting cross-legged in dappled shade by Jericho Wharf. She was wearing overalls with daisies printed on them, and her hair was pulled back into a ponytail.

It was late afternoon, a golden haze hovering above the canal. The intention was to grill each other on pronunciation in Chaucer, but the heat had made them too lethargic to study and they were idly discussing Donne and beauty. Polly told him that she disliked the way she looked, the way men slavered over her like hounds after prey. "Two hundred years ago, I wouldn't have rated a second glance. Two hundred years from now, I might be considered a freak. It's just that I fit the mold now, and I can't stand the way most men look at me. But you're not like them," she said, with the faint hint of a question in her voice. He shook his head, almost truthfully. If she hadn't told him that she'd been in love with the local vet in her Cumbrian town, and they planned to marry after she graduated, he might have fallen hopelessly for her. As it was, he was content enough with their friendship, and if he was being honest, he enjoyed the status of being her companion and confidant. It was the first time he had considered female beauty as a kind of tyranny, and it made him protective of her and their easy conversations.

"You're certainly not like that friend of yours, Jeremy," Polly continued.

Jeremy had recently discarded a first-year student, making fun of her flat chest in public, and the girl's mournful face with red-rimmed eyes had become an uncomfortable fixture wherever they went. "He didn't have to be so cruel," Polly said. "It's almost as if he enjoyed hurting her."

Sandy defended Jeremy. "He's not like that. He's not a bad person, just a bit thoughtless."

Polly would not be persuaded. "You wouldn't humiliate someone like that, I know you wouldn't." She was right. He wouldn't because he was always so grateful to any girl who paid him attention. Jeremy regarded it as his due, nothing less.

Carolyn nestled closer and gently massaged his forehead. The push of her fingers on his temples was soothing, almost soporific. The words were already gathering in his mind, mushrooming into the narrative he had never disclosed to anyone. He had carried the story for so long that its weight was now an accustomed part of him. He and Jeremy had sworn to each other. They would never speak of it again. It had never happened. Tempting as it was to think of whispering these things to this warm stranger, he wouldn't do it. He couldn't tell her. Not now, not yet.

His hand was on her stomach and he recognized the small, hard ridge of a cesarean scar. Penny had one in the same place. He compared his life to Carolyn's, the squalor of his flat against her dust-free surfaces. He saw her diary bristling with appointments for lunches, hairdressers' appointments, and elegant dinners with lawyers discussing recent court triumphs. He had nothing except a pile of bills and dirty laundry.

It was stupid and fanciful, but he allowed himself to imagine them far away from London, in the country somewhere, Wales perhaps, in a small cottage with a kitchen fire, a piano in the corner, and hens clucking in the yard. He knew it was a dangerous, sentimental fantasy, but he indulged himself anyway, lying there in the dark.

He saw her by the stove. He saw himself bringing in wood and them both in bed, making love under a quilt. They would bring nothing of the past with them. They would talk of nothing but the present and the future. He would tinker on the piano and wait for another perfect note.

"What are you thinking?" she asked.

"About an old song, by Crosby, Stills, Nash and Young," he said. "I knew Graham Nash a bit. We were going to do something together once, but it never happened."

He thought he might fall asleep, but she began to talk of her own youth. She'd gone to secretarial college in Cambridge. "So now my husband tells people I studied at Cambridge. He thinks people are impressed by that sort of thing. I suppose I must be too, because I don't contradict him."

She told him how she'd been in love with the same boy all through her teenage years. That was the real reason she'd gone to Cambridge. He was reading economics and she'd followed him. She became pregnant and he dumped her.

"I had an abortion," she said. "No one knew. I got the train down to London from secretarial college one afternoon. I've never told anyone this before. For years afterwards, I couldn't even remember where I went to have it. And then earlier this year I was driving across Putney Bridge with a friend and she pointed out this redbrick building on the corner, just near the river. She said it used to be an abortion clinic. Then I remembered. I'd been driving past it for years and completely wiped it from my mind."

"I'm sorry," he said, envying the ease of her confession. Women were different like that. Penny had relished sharing her secrets. So had the others, confiding physical peculiarities of past lovers and childhood traumas. How trusting they were, offering them up like gifts. Then he must have fallen asleep because his head jerked up from his chest with a painful crack and he knew he should leave.

As he stood up, his knees creaked and there was a painful twinge in his lower back. Carolyn was fully asleep and he arranged the shawl over her shoulders. Pulling on his clothes, he stepped over to the window and trailed his fingers through beads of condensation. He drew a circle on the glass, surrounded by wriggly lines. It might have been a spider or the sun. He couldn't decide.

mattman5@hotmail.com

To: emily.ellison@gmail.com

Forgot how fierce you can be and have been trying to work out who you inherited it from. Not from Mum—she's too soft and sensitive. And Dad—you never know where he stands on anything. Remember how everyone at school envied us the cool life and the glamorous parents. That was a joke. Mum was always lemon lips and Dad just slept all the time, when he managed to find his way back home.

No more memory lane for me. Got that courier job. I get to ride this scooter all around London. I nearly kill myself once a day, or someone nearly kills me, but it's good money and I'm like this living street directory. I might just get to bathe in Buddha's light after all. In case you're wondering, I've been as clean as the proverbial.

# Chapter 14

ONE DAY TIM would be able to afford his own cleaner and a plush Harley Street address. But not yet, so each week, in the back seat of his Jeep, he carried a small basket carefully packed by Angie with dishcloths, ecologically friendly toilet cleaner, and some kind of whiz-bang handheld vacuum cleaner. He arrived early, well before the clients. He was meant to be dusting their neuroses, not his office.

This week, there was a new one, again from the City and no doubt again enraged by the unexpected removal of what he'd thought was a lifetime tenure to guzzle from a trough of never-ending cash. Tim had had a lot of these lately, referrals from a colleague he'd met at Goldsmiths. The last client, barely twenty-eight and pushed off his desk with three hours' notice, complained about his redundancy payment. "I mean, my boss, when he was moved on three years ago, got enough to pay off his mortgage and buy a vineyard in Galicia. I got basically nothing."

Tim stowed his cleaning basket in a cupboard and quickly read the new client's file: Dan Warburton, thirty-one, single, and very angry, according to the colleague. The colleague was not wrong. Punctual to the minute, Dan arrived and flung his motorcycle helmet on the floor.

"C-c-c-unt," he stuttered by way of introduction. "F-f-fucking cunt. I did nothing wrong. Nothing."

Tim arranged his face in what he knew, because he'd practiced many times in his bathroom mirror, was an expression of calm acceptance that any amount of bile this angry young man disgorged would be absorbed and, in time, removed. He positioned himself in neutral stance, upright behind his desk, hands on his knees, and waited in silence.

He wanted to tell Dan that this time of shame and fury and fear would pass, that in six months' time, or two years at most, it would metamorphose into a dinner party quip. He could refer Dan, by now stamping up and down the small office, leaving dirty imprints of bike boots on the beige carpet, to the Cambridge study indicating insecure employed people were just as anxious and depressed as recently unemployed people. Or he could mention the baseline of happiness theory, which argued that after extreme events, people tended to return to their own level of happiness, whatever that might be.

Instead he made a mental note to buy a bottle of carpet shampoo. Dan flung himself into the chair and began to cry, fat tears coursing down his cheeks.

"Why not tell me what happened?" asked Tim, inching the box of tissues towards him.

Tim knew he was a wounded healer. Each time he heard what was essentially the same story—that of a man stripped bare of his job and therefore his self-esteem—his own fear returned, freshly bitter, appeased not one jot over the last decade. The impotence, the shame, the not being good enough, the past-midnight feeling that he'd never be good again. And yes, he admitted to himself, he was jealous of the people who managed to keep it going—Jeremy most of all and then Peter. He even used to envy Sandy, who at least had done something that kept paying him a pittance.

He'd tried so hard, worked his balls off. What did he end up with? Nothing except a bloody mountain range of debt, accusatory glances from bank managers and accountants, as if to say, "Who's been a silly chap then?" And no sympathy from his father, who looked up from *Match of the Day* and muttered he should have gone into the civil service instead. He'd survived because of Angie, but there was still a part of him that wanted to be strong and successful, to be an alpha male like Jeremy, and that part of him festered beneath the guise of the loving husband and the benign, enabling psychologist.

Dan's tirade cut through his meandering thoughts. "I know I st-st-stutter," he said. "I know I'm not good with clients. But I didn't need to be. I'm a good quant."

For the first time he looked directly at Tim. Under his freckles his face was mottled, his eyes puffed and bleary. "You know what I mean, don't you? By a quant? Arbitrage? Game theory?"

Tim recognized the terms from occasional forays online, but his actual understanding was minimal. "Go on," he said, nodding and hoping he could remember the basic lingua franca.

"I was writing a s-s-stock movement prediction program and I was testing it at work. I was going to refine it and s-s-start my own business." Dan looked sheepish. "I know I s-s-shouldn't be testing my own program at work, but how else was I going to do it? I would have got s-s-sacked for that alone."

Tim kept quiet. Silence was always best. Dan gulped air like a goldfish and Tim passed him a glass of water.

"And one evening, after the markets closed, I was running s-s-some tests from the accounts and I got into the boss's files by accident. I opened one of his folders and there was all this s-s-stuff." His face turned puce. "I'd never s-s-seen anything like it. I mean, I've never got into porn myself, but I know loads of men are meant to get off on it. But this was s-s-something else. It was little girls, ten, eleven years old, doing these things. It was hideous. I didn't want to know anything about it. I wanted to forget I'd ever s-s-seen it.

"And then, I heard him come back into the office and the next thing he was right behind me. I'm pretty sure I'd closed everything down before he saw my s-s-screen, but s-s-somehow he knew I knew. I could just tell. He kept leaning over me, stinking like an old cigar and asking me what I was working on. I told him I was doing some predictive s-s-stuff, but he didn't believe me. The next thing I was s-s-sacked. He said he couldn't keep me on because of the recession, that I was uncooperative and not up to the mark. What an arsehole, with his private clubs and fancy lunches. Fat fucker with his posh accent. And the worst thing is my girlfriend tells me not to worry."

Dan looked at Tim as if he wanted to strike up some kind of male camaraderie. "Don't you hate it when they do that? She's a doctor, so no one is going to sack her. How do they know what it's like?"

Tim wanted to agree with him. He'd never been able to understand Angie's implacable confidence that everything would be all right. She was like some twenty-first-century Julian of Norwich, intoning that all shall be well and all manner of thing shall be well. He was jealous of her strength, her common sense and ability to adapt. If she was disappointed or upset, she attacked the garden for a morning or went to bed for an afternoon. That appeared to solve everything from infertility to bankruptcy. It was harder for him, with his black depressions, his secret anger, his shriveling impotence.

Sometimes he hated needing Angie so much. It seemed unnatural for a grown man to want to cling to a woman and never let go, even though he made jokes about it, how old men were the new girls, with their moobs, their propensity to cry in public, and their newfound dependency on the partners they'd kept at arm's length for so long. Was that why the four of them had clung together since university, although their careers, or lack of them in Sandy's case, had diverged so sharply?

It wasn't as if they talked about anything new or different or even acknowledged the consequences of what they said to each other. When Peter said he was bored of football and giving up his box at Stamford Bridge, the others knew immediately that he wasn't going to Hollywood after all. Everyone said it was a great idea when Sandy moved across the river. "I envy you, mate," said Jeremy without a pause. "You'll be fit as a trout, running around that park every day." They must have known Sandy's money was running out, that his days as a hit songwriter were over, just as they must have known that Jeremy was making great gobs of money from the stock market and that he, Tim, was making nothing at all.

Although Tim had called Sandy after he came out of hospital and asked if he wanted the name of a good therapist, he was secretly relieved that a psychologist's protocol prevented him from taking on clients he knew as friends. He didn't want to talk openly to Sandy. Within their little group, he wanted nothing to change.

almost laughed out loud. She knew what she looked like, plump and getting plumper with a frizz of mad gray hair and her face covered in dirt. She could see the couple trying to accustom themselves to the notion that the odd woman sitting opposite—albeit an odd woman whose house they coveted—once led a glamorous and fashionable life.

"It was a long time ago," she said. "And I'm not married anymore."

Nigel would not be deterred. Penny knew what he was doing. If he could persuade the cashed-up Greg and Liz that this area was sophisticated and possessed a Saint-Paul-de-Vence or Saint-Tropez allure at half the price, then a sale was pretty much assured. Greg and Liz wanted more than a pretty house and a quiet life. They wanted glamorous neighbors, acquaintances with a provenance of sophistication.

"Sandy, Penny's husband, wrote songs for Joe Fleetfield. His records sold loads. And he produced every album by that Kate . . . what's her name, Pen?"

"Can't recall right now," she replied.

"Really?" breathed Liz, slamming her mug on the table. "You don't mean Kate Mostyn? And Joe Fleetfield was my favorite of all time. I fell in love with Greg listening to those songs. 'Never Give Up' was my favorite."

"How splendid," said Penny.

"And that Kate," offered Greg, "what a babe, fantastic voice. What was the name of that album?"

Penny shrugged, pretending not to remember.

"Oh, she knows everyone," said Nigel proudly. "Eric, Paul, Keith. The stories she could tell. But she's terribly discreet, of course. Until you get to know her."

Penny went to the sink. If they didn't leave in a minute, she'd scream. Was she mad to care more about carrots than concerts, to prefer solitude to this inane chat about things that didn't matter anymore?

She wanted to tell Liz that Kate Mostyn, under her mournful fringe, was a bitch and a pathological liar; that Joe Fleetfield was a

Scraggy clouds scudded across the sky. What were they? Cirrus, cumulus, altostratus? Did it mean it was going to rain? He'd completely forgotten about Dan and his mottled face, his anger and rage. He had to concentrate, try harder.

Dan was screwing up his eyes and trying not to weep. "I'd report him, but I know he'd have deleted everything by now, probably s-s-smashed his computer and replaced it. Or maybe no one would care. One of the guys got drunk a month or so ago and took a dump in a wastepaper bin. Everyone thought it was hysterically funny.

"The thing that really pisses me off is that my life has been ruined and his goes on uninterrupted. I bet that he's f-f-forgotten my name already. Lording it up in Knightsbridge or wherever he lives. I'll never get out of Peckham."

Tim nodded, but he wasn't listening. He was letting Dan's rage wash through him. Other people's anger always made him calmer. His Goldsmiths colleague said it was a normal response. Everyone walked away from the sight of a traffic accident relieved that they had survived. Psychologists were only human. They couldn't contain all the mental angst heaped on them every day in fifty-minute increments. They had to have their coping mechanisms.

Dan's time was nearly over. Tim made all the right noises and said all the right things with the appropriate body language. He smoothly concluded the session and made an appointment for another at the same time next week. He saw three more clients. The first was summoning courage to ask a woman to dinner for the first time since his wife left him a year ago. The other two were trying to salvage marriages that were sinking along with their bank balances. He'd have to refer both to couples therapy, but he wanted to wait until they felt more secure. That might take some time as both wives had entered the jugular zone.

"I told her," said the last client of the day, sweaty and pale, "that we couldn't afford to move to Notting Hill. We'd have to wait until I'd got a better job. She just told me to work harder. I don't think I can do all this much longer."

At that moment, as the still-unidentified clouds disappeared and the afternoon sun skittered across the balding head of the man sitting opposite him, Tim felt a rush of gratitude for Angie and his own good fortune to be married to her. He forgot his darker moments, his occasional jealousy and resentment of her competence. He decided to cancel his regular booking at the B & B in Wandsworth and drive home in time for dinner with his wife, to tell her about his day, about Dan and his rage against the cruelty of the workplace, how he had to pretend to know about game theory, and what the harridan wife had said to her beleaguered husband. Therapists weren't meant to discuss things, except with other therapists, but Angie was different.

# Chapter 15

IT WAS THREE a.m. A fierce headache lurking at the back of his head. A tight scalp, as if the brain beneath it was about to explode. That might be the best thing: for room service or the maid to walk into suite 547 of the Nonamia Hotel in Tverskaya Street, brush past the potted orchids and see Jeremy on the floor with his tortured brain spattered all over the red-flocked sofas.

How ironic that he'd survived the subprime crisis, steered clear of the collateralized debt obligations, always been suspicious of Madoff for reasons he could never quite decide, only to be gouged senseless by his shareholding in a Russian coal mine that turned out to exist only in computer-generated images emblazoned over the glossy pages of the prospectus.

He'd known it was a risk, but wasn't everything? He thought he was safe. Now he was just like the rest of the failures he despised, a fool who tried to take a quick, ill-considered profit. He hadn't hedged his own bets, and that was the whole point of a hedge fund. You covered yourself either way.

The client accounts had been swept to cover the prospecting fees and the extra payments necessary in a town like Moscow. The money, plus a healthy increase, would be back in their accounts before the next quarterly statements were due. All he had to do was find a way to airbrush the figures until he traded his way clear. It was supposed to be a win-win. It had turned into a fucking bloodbath. Pretty much everything had gone and it would be a long time before he got it back. If ever.

The family trusts and the big clients' accounts were all but empty. London's wealthiest divorcée, the former budget airline stewardess who'd been awarded thirty million from that gay German prince, was cleaned out. So was the couple from Inverness who'd sold their leaky lodge and twenty thousand acres of prime stalking for twenty million to some dry-cleaning magnate. And, of course, Sandy. How was he going to tell his closest friend that all his money, every last pitiful penny, was gone?

There had to be a solution, but where? How? What had made him do something so stupid? He didn't need to. He wasn't strung on the wire like others he knew. His reputation, up to now at least, was solid. A steady pair of hands. Not the biggest, but all the more reliable for it.

Then it came to him, sitting on the ridiculous flocked velvet sofa, the reason why. He'd wanted to prove to himself he hadn't lost his nerve, that he was still a silverback to be reckoned with. All because that young American had taken his business elsewhere.

He crossed the room to the window. Six lanes of traffic droned underneath. A neon sign advertising Ferrari cars flickered uncertainly. Under the sulfurous streetlights, stick figures in voluminous down coats made their way between slag heaps of leftover snow. In seven hours lines of tourists would form an orderly queue to file through Lenin's tomb in Red Square. The stallholders outside the Metro would be preparing for the day's trading; the rich would continue to spend.

He'd always taken the long view, unlike most of his peers, whose memory lasted only as long as the average CEO tenure—about five and a half years. No wonder they kept making the same mistakes. They were too young to remember and too arrogant to learn that interest-only mortgages were popular before the 1929 Great Depression too.

He used to distribute tidbits of economic history to clients and fund managers, most of whom could barely remember Nick Leeson's name and had forgotten all about Jeffrey Skilling. He'd explain the Gaussian probability distribution and Keynesian theses to recent widows, newly minted divorcées, and eager young market traders. It felt good to see them nodding attentively, imbibing his experience and wisdom. If only he'd taken his own advice.

Not that he'd suffer. There was enough to see him through. The *Jezebel* was safe, the pictures, the cash in Zurich. Reinvention was also a possibility. Others had done it. He'd thought he'd never have to.

It was his injured pride, the inevitable destruction of his reputation that stung. Hubris. Nemesis. Bloody Greeks. Id. Ego. Alter ego. Bloody Freud. Schadenfreude was all that was left. Jeremy knew that far too much of his natural self was tethered to plush material things that shouldn't matter: the respectful glance of maître d's, the impeccable tailoring from Huntsman, the knowledge that if he wanted something, he could have it. That was the reason his wives had left him, because under the luxury enfolding them like cashmere, there was not much there.

"I can't be with you any longer," Isobel had said. "It's like living with a mirage." Sally had just removed herself with a series of eloquent shrugs. At the time, he didn't understand. He thought he was real enough. He thought he knew himself well enough. Most of himself anyway. Other parts were less clear, deliberately so.

If he managed to get out of this, he'd be so clean and neat that he would be held up as a model of probity and financial caution. He would stop cigars for a year and give the money to school-building projects in third world countries. He would call it a day with the young girls. He would find some respectable divorced woman about his own age. He would try to like her children, if there were any.

A nerve in his shoulder went into spasm and he winced. Suddenly he wanted to speak to Rosie. He wanted to bask in the reflection of her adoring childhood gaze, the one that said he was the daddy who would do no wrong, who could fix everything. He wanted to hug her and inhale her fresh-skinned confidence in him. But Dubai was in the same time zone as Moscow. She'd still be asleep.

He thought of Amy, forgetting how bored he had been when he'd last seen her. What time was it in London? He might catch her before she went to sleep. He scrolled down for her number and rang it. There was a message, spoken in breathy, urgent tones as if she was about to either have an orgasm or rush off to some life-changing event. He couldn't call Sandy. He couldn't tell Sandy what had happened.

He picked at the embroidery on the sofa. Bits of it came away in his hand. The whole country was like this hotel suite: a sumptuous stage set that, when you touched it, began to disintegrate. The taps didn't work in the bathroom, so what good was the Philippe Starck bath? The toilet took an age to flush, and last night, tossing in the emperor-size bed with its mountain of pillows and cushions, he'd discovered toenail clippings in the sheets.

Jeremy knew what he wanted. He knew it was wrong, that it would solve nothing, but at that moment, he needed oblivion. Not the bleary fog provided by more than one glass of alcohol, but something sharper, more savage.

On the road below him, a car skidded into a telegraph pole and crumpled as the car behind it smashed into it. He watched the pileup grow until it was almost the length of the block. He could go down to the bar, have a drink, sit for a while. Something was always happening in a bar in a big hotel. But he would have to talk and make some kind of effort. And he would have to get dressed. He retied the belt on his bathrobe. He didn't want to get dressed. He didn't want to make an effort. He walked over to the desk, picked up the telephone, and rang down to the concierge.

This was one of the few efficient things about Moscow, Jeremy thought as he heard the tentative knock on the door. He paused before opening it. He could just sit there, not get up. The knocking would stop after a while. He could muster what his mother used to call self-control and let the moment pass. But he knew it wasn't a moment. It was a sick addiction that lay sleeping for months until he thought it had gone away, before returning to seduce him again.

Sandy was the only person who suspected it might be something more than a preference for young women. He'd come to the *Jezebel* for coffee one morning, earlier than arranged, and seen one of them leaving. "Jesus Christ," he'd said. "A bit young, even for you. How old is she? She looks just a kid." Jeremy had said she was twenty, but Sandy didn't believe him. The girl had told Jeremy she was sixteen, but he knew she was lying. He'd picked her up at the usual place the night before.

There was that other time, when he and Sandy were both prof-ligately single. In an unguarded moment, he'd sent Sandy an email with a picture of a naked prepubescent girl, legs splayed. He'd ex-plained it away by saying someone had sent it to him and he'd for-warded it by mistake instead of deleting it. "You need to get things in check," said Sandy.

"You're a fine one to talk," snapped Jeremy. He knew Sandy wouldn't mention it again, to him or the others. Sandy was like that: loyal, always thinking the best of people. Little Mr. Sunshine with his perfect note moments bubbling up under the wry chat. Where had that got him?

There was another knock on the door. Jeremy ushered the girl into the room. She said her name was Natasha, but he didn't care. She stank of cheap scent. Her dark hair was scraped into a ponytail and she wore a fake leather jacket over a cropped T-shirt. In the dim light, he saw her bad skin under the thick makeup, her crooked teeth, her slightly bandy legs under the black miniskirt, and the scuffed stilettos. If he was a cliché of a jaundiced Western businessman exploiting an underage girl, she was the cliché of a postmillennium Moscow child hooker. He would have preferred someone prettier, but she would do.

Just before he motioned for her to take her clothes off, he felt faint. He might just pay her and tell her to go. But by then she had turned around. He saw her budlike breasts, the faint outline of her ribs, the thin whorls of pubic hair, and her shy, brave smile that asked, "Do you like me? Am I pretty enough?" He led her to the bed, lay her down, and turned her over.

# Chapter 16

THE MATRON HAD been firm. Visiting hours were from four to five p.m. There was a pause before she hung up. Standing in the public telephone box at Waterloo, cursing his dead mobile and straining to hear above the loudspeakers, Sandy understood what the pause signified. If he had visited his mother regularly, he would be aware of the visiting hours.

At Woking station, waiting for the bus to Mayfield House, he knew there was no excuse for not visiting his mother for five months. He didn't have a job. He wasn't ill or infirm. He didn't have a car, but there was an intricate network of buses and trains to take him anywhere on the British mainland. He could scarcely tell his mother that his failed attempt to kill himself had reminded him he owed her a visit. All he knew was this: from the moment he shut the door of Carolyn's house and heard the locks snap behind him, he ached to see his mother.

The bus was late and full of schoolchildren shouting to each other. He sat behind the driver and peered over the tops of hedges until he saw a row of Edwardian brick chimneys looming above a line of laurels. He got out at the next stop and walked back along the lane, through the tall wrought-iron gates and down the tarmac drive bordered with fluorescent rhododendrons.

He hated rhododendrons and he hated Surrey, its smug respectability, its neat copses and enclaves of ostentatious houses dotted among the rows of modest semis like the one he grew up in. But his mother had always aspired to the architectural pastiche of Esher and Woking's private estates, admired the little boutiques and teashops. So here she was, eking out her last days shuffling from her bedroom down to the dining room and back again, absurdly grateful for the beige slop they called meals and any help she might need in the bathroom.

He stood by the desk in the empty hall for some minutes. A vase of chrysanthemums, the flower of choice for the budget-conscious, was on the hall table next to a pile of pamphlets extolling the virtues of spending the "time remaining" in Mayfield House. Under the smell of floor polish and disinfectant was a whiff of boiled vegetables.

No one appeared, so he made his own way up to his mother's room, remembering how upset she had been on her first day to see her name on the door as Margot Ellison. "That's not right," she said, gripping Sandy's arm. "It should be Mrs. James Ellison. Can you let them know?" But he was running late and told himself he didn't have the time to quibble with staff about arcane etiquette.

The carpet on the stairs was frayed and dust balls gathered in the corners. The castellated towers of the old wing cast Gothic shadows on the landing where new fire doors had replaced the original mahogany ones and the old bedrooms had been demolished and rebuilt into a modern, cost-efficient brick block. The effect was schizophrenic.

He pushed through the door. It sounded like a refrigerator opening. The door to his mother's room was open, and a cleaner was stripping the bed of sodden linen, wiping down the plastic sheet covering the mattress. Everything stank of disinfectant. The walls were bare, the curtains gone from the window.

Where were her pictures of him and of his father, the drunken James? The watercolors on the wall, the Yardley English Rose talcum powder on the shelf? Where was the little Turkish rug by the bed, the one she'd asked for, so her feet wouldn't get cold on the linoleum when she got out of bed at night? It tore at his heart, this sad, small box, emptied of all belongings.

Had she died and no one told him? Had there been messages on the answering machine in Battersea? Messages he'd erased without listening to them, thinking only of avoiding impatient debt collectors. "Mr. Ellison, your mother is unwell, please call when you receive this message. . . . Mr. Ellison, your mother is very ill, please call as soon as possible. . . . Mr. Ellison, we're very sorry to have to tell you this, but your mother has passed away."

"Excuse me," he stammered. "My mother, Mrs. Ellison . . . ?" Every word a plea that she still be alive, even though he felt sure she must be dead. The cleaner looked up, a tired gray-faced woman in her late fifties. She smoothed a clean sheet over the bed. Her hands were red and swollen.

"Who?" she asked. Her accent was thick Eastern European.

"Mrs. Ellison," said Sandy, very slowly. "She used to be in this room." Heart hammering, a boy again, small and helpless.

The woman glared at him. "Miss Margot, you mean?"

"Yes."

"Who you?"

"I'm her son," said Sandy, and then in case the woman didn't understand, "Miss Margot is my mother."

"Hmph," replied the cleaner, stuffing a pillow into its case. She took forever to speak. He would go mad waiting for her reply. She flung the pillow on the bed.

"She move. Different room. Down hall. You no come."

He could have hugged her. His mother was alive, just down the hall. He still had a chance to make it all good again.

"Thank you," he said, and repeated it again just in case. "Thank you."

But she had already turned her back on him.

Sandy hurried down the hall, glancing into each room until he found his mother at the end of the corridor. She was sitting upright in a floral patterned armchair, still in her nightdress and dressing gown. He was about to bowl in and surprise her with a hug and kiss when he saw she was asleep, her head skewed on the pillow stuffed behind her neck. Her thin silver hair had been cut in a jaunty schoolgirl bob, secured at each side of her head with bright pink hairgrips. She'd always had long hair, meticulously arranged in what she called a French pleat, but clearly no one in Mayfield House knew how to do that for her, and someone had chopped the lot off.

He tiptoed inside. The photographs, the watercolors, the rug by the bed: everything was the same, except for her. In her chair, she appeared shrunken, half the size she used to be. Large, wrinkled dewlaps hung below her jaw, and her skin was pale and thin like crinkled tissue paper. There was a small line of drool on her chin, and he wiped it away with the handkerchief that lay on her lap. She sighed and turned her head. Sandy thought she might wake up, but she didn't.

He sat on the floor at her feet. Her slippers had fallen off; he put them back on, carefully easing each one over her cracked and horned toenails, pulling them over the yellow callused skin of her heels. Little flakes of skin came away in his hands.

He leaned his head against her knees and hugged her, feeling at first the ribbed pattern of her chenille dressing gown, then the faint stubble of her legs, and under that, the frail bones of her shins. There was that familiar sweet close smell about her. He shut his eyes and held on tight.

"I'm sorry they cut your hair, Mum," he whispered into a fold of her dressing gown. "I'm sorry for everything and I love you. I've messed it up again and I don't know what to do."

He sat for some time. Shadows from trees and sunlight played with each other on the wall opposite the bed. He couldn't see out the window because it was placed above his head, just below the ceiling. He knew about clerestory windows, how Egyptians first used them to illuminate temple columns, how medieval artisans built them into cathedral walls so people could still see but not be distracted from their prayers.

But who would design such a room now with so little consideration of its inhabitants? Who would deprive an elderly man or woman of a pleasure as simple as looking out a window or feeling a breeze, however slight, against their face? A third question came, unbidden and unwanted, requiring an answer: Who would neglect their only surviving parent for months on end?

He listened to the clang of trolleys in the hall. He heard people laughing and walking quickly, the sad hiss of wheelchairs' rubber tires pushing along the linoleum; the drip of the bathroom tap, each rasping breath his mother took, and the rub of her legs against the rough fabric of the armchair. He was not quite awake, not quite asleep, and it seemed that his mother reached down to his head and stroked it with her blue-veined and splotched hand.

"Don't fret, darling boy, it won't be so bad when you grow up," she whispered. "It won't hurt so much."

It was like being tucked into bed after a story, her cool kiss on his forehead, the bedside lamp being switched off and the hall light safely shining into his room; like being allowed to lie in her bed during the day when colds and fevers kept him out of school. So calm and peaceful, just the two of them, the way it had been when his father was out or sleeping it off. He could stay here forever.

Then there was a loud crash outside the door, the sound of something breaking, and someone swearing. Sandy jerked his head, immediately alert, with a fierce crick in his neck and stiff from sitting on the floor for so long.

"But I am grown up," he whispered into her knee. "I'm fifty-eight, Mum." He realized he must have been dreaming, because when he struggled to his feet, he saw his mother still asleep and he knew he had to hurry to catch the last bus back to Woking.

emily.ellison@gmail.com

To: mattman5@hotmail.com

Do you mean it? Really. You might come here? Oh Matt, that would be a very fine thing. Get away from the madness of our parents. One of the many great things about being here in India is all that stuff doesn't seem to matter that much. Don't get sucked in. Mum and Dad can fix themselves up if they want to. I think we should live our way now.

There is this teacher here who says we'd all be so much more content if we stopped trying for happiness and love, all that stuff in Dad's pop songs. He says all that trivial stuff passes and we should look for truth instead, and then we would be truly happy. Oh, and that woman I told you about, Annie. Apparently her sister died when she was young, in her twenties—the sister, I mean. Poor her. I'd be lost without my brother. Anyhow, I'm thinking of moving into her place. She has a spare room and it might be good. We're going walking in the mountains next week. No cars, no noise. Fresh air. Yes, yes. And yes again. Miss you. Stay clean and clear.

Xxe

Forgot to say one of Dad's worst efforts is high on the ringtone pop charts here. One by that greaser Joe Fleetfield. He came to dinner once and rubbed up against me in the hall when he thought no one was looking. I was all of fifteen. Funny how you and I don't like music that much. Can't imagine why.

# Chapter 17

PETER DECIDED TO take up Frieda's offer to cook dinner for everyone at her flat. She'd been characteristically practical since Sandy had disappeared just before Penny had left Sarlat. No one had any idea where he was. Frieda was the only one who thought to offer Penny a place to stay, knowing she didn't have a flat in London and guessing she wouldn't want to bunk down in Hoxton with Matthew and his flatmates.

"Are you sure?" asked Peter. "You've never even met Penny."

"It's fine," said Frieda. "Besides, I'm curious."

"And kind," he said. "Thank you." He went to kiss her, but she waved him away with hands greasy from butter and herbs. Cooking was another of their shared pastimes, but with carefully delineated responsibilities. Peter chopped with Frieda's range of surgically sharp knives while she presided over tasting, adjusting, and seasoning. They'd decided on tarte tatin and Richard Olney's spatchcocked chicken stuffed under the skin. Under her precise instructions, Peter chopped garlic, oregano, and parsley, and grated parmesan cheese before prizing the chicken skin away from the meat.

"Careful," said Frieda, looking over his shoulder as she mixed ricotta and the herbs in a bowl. "Do it slowly, otherwise the skin will tear. Shall we add some mushrooms? Or courgettes? I think courgettes, don't you?"

Peter nodded.

"So," said Frieda, "why do you think Sandy has gone missing?"

"Avoiding confrontation, looking for attention. It's hard to say," said Peter. "Tim and Angie will have their own ideas, no doubt all very touchy-feely. He's been gone less than a couple of days. Maybe he went to a spa or a retreat. I've tried Jeremy, but he hasn't called back. I even tried Jeremy's secretary. She says he's away, didn't say where. So who knows?"

Frieda wiped down the bench and began scrubbing bowls and knives. She was methodical like that, cleaning as she went along.

"All this fuss about one well-fed, relatively prosperous man who lacks willpower to organize his life. So what if he isn't as successful as he used to be? There are millions of people all over the world who aspire to his kind of failure—running water, shelter, freedom of speech. Need I go on?"

"We're selfish and self-obsessed compared to our parents." Peter began wiping everything dry. "Ah, the mantra of my Finchley youth—Dad telling me every day he came to this country with one pair of bloody underpants. 'I tell you, my boy, work, work.'"

"You still do, and very hard," said Frieda. She didn't mind that he hadn't made it as a movie director, that he earned his living from television commercials. Frieda said she liked herself well enough to like him for himself.

He looked up, across to Frieda's sitting room with its wide oak-planked floors, the Saarinen dining table, the Eames chair in the tall bay window, the Craigie Aitchison pictures of sheep and Bedlington terriers on the walls. Everything so beautiful, so perfectly positioned. He was the only untidy thing in her precise, poised life, but Frieda didn't appear to mind.

Peter thought he might be falling in love for the first time and wondered what it would be like to be married. He'd always considered his parents' coziness as claustrophobic. Now, with Frieda by his side, he was not so sure. Watching her stir the apples in a pan, seeing her breasts rise as she paused to brush back her hair, he was overcome by lust and tenderness in equal parts. But he knew better than to interrupt her while she was cooking.

"Dad never took anything, even a cup of tea, for granted," Peter continued. "It's the curse of our generation, don't you think? Always wanting more, bigger, better."

"Watch it," said Frieda. "You're in danger of entering old git territory and I'm not going there. Tell me, what was Sandy like when you met him?"

"Oh, Tim and I were pure grammar school—polyester shirts and nylon sheets. Jeremy and Sandy weren't at Eton but one of the famous ones. Winchester or Harrow. It mattered then. To us they were like something out of *Brideshead Revisited*. All that was missing was bloody Aloysius the teddy bear. Jeremy was very driven, always got everyone to do what he wanted."

"Nothing's changed there," said Frieda. "But I was asking about Sandy."

"Sandy always looked up to Jeremy, always agreed with him and did what Jeremy wanted to do. It was as if they had some secret bond. Maybe they buggered each other back in the dormitory. Tim and I could never work it out. Sandy was charming and sensitive. It's an old-fashioned thing, I know, but he had lovely manners. One of his teachers had told him politeness could disguise shyness. He was reading history, but he was mad about music even then, all that early San Francisco psychedelic stuff. The Electric Prunes, Iron Butterfly, Vanilla Fudge. And country too. Emmylou Harris and Gram Parsons."

Peter grabbed a wooden spoon and held it up as a microphone. He was well on his way through a rendition of "Boulder to Birmingham" when Frieda flicked him on the backside with a tea cloth and laughed. "Move on, my baby, to the new century, the new music—Adele, Kings of Leon."

"Or best of all," said Peter, putting down the spoon and reaching for a glass of water, "the new silence."

Frieda's upper lip was beaded with perspiration. He gently wiped it dry with his forefinger and embraced her. He loved the feel of her, her ampleness and softness and her smell: slightly salty with that smell of amber soap blended with it. She never wore scent, yet another thing he found tantalizing.

All his women before Frieda wore scent like a suit of armor. He could identify and date his affairs by smell alone. Light floral scents during his twenties. Then fruity warm scents and after that the powerful overbearing perfumes of the eighties, which he loathed because they permeated everything and made him want to gasp for air. No one before Frieda had come to him smelling of herself.

The tarte tatin was out of the oven and the chicken almost cooked when Penny arrived. Peter hadn't seen her since she'd moved to France. He barely recognized the plump gray-haired matron at the door, dressed for the garden in shapeless trousers, sensible flat-heeled shoes, and a kind of flapping jacket in varying shades of beige.

Almost defiantly antifashion, he thought, as he picked up her tapestry holdall and walked her through to the kitchen. How incongruous she looked against the stainless steel worktops and lacquered cupboards, how different from Frieda's geometric chic.

The two women looked each other up and down, in that female manner which took less than a second to clock the shape of calves and ankles, size of girth, and manner of dress. They smiled. Despite their differences, they seemed to like each other. He was relieved.

After the business of showing Penny her room and the small bathroom off it, and pouring glasses of wine amid desultory chat, they went into the sitting room.

"Thank you for this. It's very kind and I appreciate it," said Penny. Her voice was still clear and girlish, the only thing about her that had not changed. She sighed and stretched her legs. Surprisingly hairy legs, Peter noticed.

"It's been a bit of a day." Penny sipped her wine. "God, that's good. Where on earth do you think Sandy has gone? Maybe he ran away to avoid seeing his ex-wife." She giggled in a way Peter couldn't remember.

Frieda smiled. "Don't tell Angie that when she and Tim arrive. You'll be in for an hour-long sermon on the benefits of truth and reconciliation."

Peter tried to decide what was different about Penny. Her appearance, of course, but there was something else, something invisible yet apparent. It was as if by losing her looks she had found herself. All the old shy self-consciousness had disappeared. In its place was a wry good humor. It suited her, made her sexy. Did she have a lover? he wondered.

Even the appearance of Angie and Tim, and the relentless concern shown by both towards Penny and the missing Sandy, failed to perturb her.

"It must be so hard for you, Penny," Angie kept saying. "Has he got any money? Did he take his phone? Has anyone called the police? Has he contacted the children?" Her voice rose excitedly with each unanswered question.

"I tried his mobile, but it's turned off. So who knows," replied Penny, helping herself to more chicken. "There's no point calling the police just yet. He'll show up when he's ready. I haven't contacted Emily and Matthew yet. There's no point in making them worried. I just hope he appears sooner rather than later. I can't abuse Frieda's hospitality and stay here indefinitely. Besides, I've left the vegetable garden half-planted. If it doesn't rain, my carrot seedlings will perish."

Peter saw the disbelieving look passed between Angie and Tim and then Frieda's quick wink in his direction. The wink told him that Angie and Tim, the seamless married couple, were beginning to annoy her. Frieda had already smiled politely through Angie's description of her preferred version of chicken stuffed under the skin, which involved olives. Frieda disliked olives in food and also disliked talking about recipes while eating. It was trivial, he knew, but Peter loved knowing this about Frieda, and even more, he loved the fact that no one else at the table could guess her thoughts except him. He refilled everyone's glass.

"That's a joke," said Penny. "Sort of. I have come here to try to help. But all of you need to understand Sandy isn't part of my life anymore. His problems aren't my problems. I only care enough to try to help him if he wants to be helped."

"But what if he's done something?" Tim asked. "Something harmful to himself? I've already been to the flat. It doesn't look as if he's been there. Surely we should be out looking for him. We'll never forgive ourselves if we don't try to find him."

Angie took his hand. "Tim's right. I think we need to take this much more seriously."

"He probably just forgot to tell anyone," replied Penny. "He is approaching sixty after all, and I don't think Sandy is the self-harming type, despite the accident."

She spoke in a measured way, but her foot was drumming on the floor. Frieda must have noticed as well; she offered cheese as a diversion. "Cheddar. I thought you might like it as a change from goat and all the runny stuff."

# Chapter 18

BACK AT WATERLOO station after he'd visited his mother, Sandy had stood under the timetable boards, buffeted by waves of rush hour commuters. He'd wanted to ring Jeremy, or Peter or Tim, but his mobile was dead. He missed Penny. The groups of teenagers lolling on the edges of the concourse reminded him of Matthew and Emily. He thought about going home, but he couldn't face his own squalor and the certainty that he would start drinking once he shut the door behind him. So he walked along to the departure board and bought a ticket to Axminster.

Three and a half hours later, he was standing in the foyer of a rundown hotel on the beachfront at Lyme Regis. The receptionist looked him up and down.

"No luggage?" he asked.

Sandy shook his head and paid for two nights. His room was at the back and overlooked a dank courtyard. He lay on the bed flicking through television channels and watching the cobwebs in the corner of the ceiling eddy in the draft from the window. The room was mean and uncomfortable, with a cramped bathroom smelling of mold. It suited his mood and he fell into a deep, dreamless sleep until morning. He stayed in bed until the afternoon, then walked aimlessly up and down the Cobb looking at the boats. The wind was pure and cold, laced with salt. Only the most intrepid of tourists came at this time of year.

Margot had taken him here for a fortnight each August. She rented a house on the hill and each day the two of them walked down to the seafront through the park. On the way back, he was allowed an ice cream. His mother bought one as well and they ate them as they walked. It was the only time he ever saw his mother eat in public.

"Such a shame," she would say, beaming between licks and slurps, "that your father is too busy to join us here." She would take his free hand and swing it back and forth.

He suddenly craved a double whisky, salivating at the thought of it warming the back of his throat and slipping down to his stomach. He lurked at the door of a pub for some minutes, trying to fool himself that he'd only have the one. He visualized the half-full glass, the boozy smell, the quiver as he lifted the glass to his mouth. But then he recalled what everyone at the meetings had said about alcohol and depression. He remembered Justin's acronym of HALT: hungry, angry, lonely, tired? Take care! Images of the hospital rushed back: the nausea, the vomiting, and the black headaches. He crossed the road to a café and gorged himself on a greasy kebab and chips, washed down with lemonade and a Zoloft. He found a pharmacy and bought a razor, toothbrush, and toothpaste before returning to his room, to more mindless television.

He knew he couldn't stay here, away from everything and everyone, indefinitely. Apart from anything else, he couldn't afford it. But Sandy was tired of himself and the business of relentless self-examination. In this anonymous box of a room, its bland cream walls and cheap ribbed carpet, there was some respite. He was just another person in just another room. He thought of Carolyn, what had happened. Again, it seemed a dream: that someone else had walked into her house, made love to her, and listened to her secrets. A kind and loving dream, one to cherish, but he didn't want to see her again. The feeling would be mutual. He was sure of it. Their lives were so different, an unequal and flawed equation in every way.

Sometime after midnight, he flicked onto MTV, to some dusted-off collection of clips entitled *Where Are They Now?* Whirling around in his ridiculous cape was Joe Fleetfield, miming "Never Give Up."

One of Sandy's biggest and best songs, three million singles sold, his very own take on sprung rhythm, released a week before "Let's

Dance." Not the best timing in the world: who could compete with the dual talents of David Bowie and Nile Rodgers? Nor did it have the thrill of the new, like a Jim Steinman song for Bonnie Tyler, or the mellow harmonies of the Eagles. But even to his jaundiced and critical ear, it still sounded respectable. After so many years, it still worked. A shame about selling that particular part of his catalogue, but the bank wouldn't increase his overdraft and he'd needed the money to pay an enormous tax bill.

He'd written the song in the car, on the way back from seeing a house in Richmond that Penny wanted to buy. She wanted somewhere with its own garden, not a communal one. But the house, tucked away in the Vineyard, was too expensive. By comparison, Onslow Gardens was a bargain.

The traffic had slowed to a crawl on the Hammersmith flyover and he was tapping his fingers on the steering wheel when a series of notes came into his head, like the swell of a wave. Then another came, and another. By the time he got home, it was all there. He sat at the kitchen piano and turned on the tape recorder while Penny cooked supper. He wrote the lyrics later that night, after everyone had gone to bed.

> *Jenny, are you leaving,*
> *The sadness behind you, grieving*
> *For the love that never came,*
> *Don't cry, I'll try,*
> *My love, my love, the future won't be the same*
> *As the past.*

Undoubtedly corny and it owed more than a little to old Gerard's "Spring and Fall: to a Young Child," but no one would have made the connection except him. Even that snotty Craig Pritchard at *NME* said if Sandy Ellison kept composing like that, he'd be sure of a place in the pop canon. He mentioned the album Sandy had written for Kate Mostyn, said his work was classic poetry, not just tunes with lyrics. Best of all, they said he understood the weird beauty of the human heart. How good was that from a magazine that normally poured vitriol on pop music?

Sandy read every word of the article at least a hundred times on the day of publication and had read it again countless times since. There were times when he believed every word. He knew he could turn a pretty phrase into a catchy verse, and he knew when the hook of a chorus would transform a pleasant tune into something people couldn't stop humming on the bus, when a string section would bring tears to a teenager's eyes.

At other times, later on, he was not so sure. Could he take eternal credit and feel a lifelong sense of accomplishment for something that popped into his head during a traffic jam and took all of twenty minutes to complete? What would have happened if he'd been cruising along the M4, the long bit without services between Reading and Heathrow? He'd have forgotten all about his artful little finger tapping on the wheel, the half-formed notes in his head, long before he reached London. His biggest hit would never have been written and he'd never have known.

It seemed to him that he had very little to do with the entire process. Songs came calling, uninvited but always welcome. All Sandy had to do was keep the door open. The monster he wrote for Kate Mostyn came to him in the bath. He was washing his hair when he remembered what a girl had said once, about him liking her, but not enough to make it worthwhile. He wrote at least five songs while mowing the lawn when they had that cottage near Tim and Angie. Something about walking up and down in straight lines.

He knew his songs weren't symphonies or even sinfonias. He'd never sweated, pondered, or deliberated on anything. Now, in this flea hole, his life deconstructed by group therapy, Sandy saw his success as nothing more than fantastical will-o'-the-wisp serendipity.

He heaved himself off the bed and into the bathroom. A quick pee and into bed again. It took all of three steps. On the small television screen, Joe was striding around the stage, flicking his cape like a demented matador in preparation for the big ending. Eighteen takes for that one, each time Sandy asking for a bit more, just that little bit more. About two a.m., he'd called Joe out of the isolation booth and given him a piece of paper with each verb underlined in thick black marker pen.

"I don't want you to emphasize the pronouns," said Sandy. "I want you to emphasize the verbs."

Joe looked puzzled. He lit a cigarette and watched as the line of smoke floated above their heads to merge with the thick blue fug under the studio lights.

"The doing words," said Sandy. "*Grieving. Leaving.* The words that mean you're doing something, feeling something. Okay?"

Joe stubbed out his cigarette and went back into the booth. Sandy's grammar lesson was worth it. The producer and sound engineer had been pissed off until they replayed the final mix and agreed with him about the verbs. When they also agreed that the half sob in the last line was not such a bad idea, Sandy saw the opportunity to persuade them to insert some birdsong at the beginning, as a nod to two of his heroes: Hopkins and Stevie Wonder, who'd done the same thing for Minnie Riperton some years before.

It was July, he remembered, almost dawn when recording finished. Everyone else had already left. He was in the foyer of Olympic Studios, waiting for the driver to take him back to Onslow Gardens. The usual thick summer mist lay across Church Street. Perhaps it had something to do with Barnes being on the river. He was sure that the song would be a hit, and it was.

"How do you know?" Penny had asked sleepily when he got home. "How can you be so sure?"

"Trust me," he replied, and smiled, turning towards her in the warm bed.

Someone, maybe Peter, had recently told him Fleetfield was living on a council estate, bloated and unrecognizable. Perhaps their lives hadn't diverged as much as he'd imagined. He turned off the television and fell into another deep sleep. The next morning, he caught the bus to Axminster and then the train to Waterloo.

There was a worrying moment on the bus back to Battersea when he thought he might not be back in his flat in time for the news and Catherine, but he made it with half an hour to spare. The answering machine blinked at him. Three messages. The first two were from Peter and Tim, asking him to call and let them know that he was safe. The third was from Penny.

"Just because I come to town, you don't have to leave," she said. But there was a smile in her voice. "Seriously, we're worried about where you are, how you are. Give me a call when you get in, please. I'm on my mobile."

Buoyed that they cared enough to worry, Sandy spent the remaining minutes before the news ringing everyone back and apologizing in a jovial way for going AWOL.

"I'm sorry," he said to Penny. "It was a spur-of-the-moment decision. I didn't think to let anyone know. I didn't think anyone would worry."

She laughed. "Of course we worry when you disappear. Particularly since . . . well, you know. As long as you're all right. Emily tells me you're going to meetings, group therapy. That's good to hear. You take care of yourself."

"I'm trying," he replied. "Let's have a quick coffee before you fly back?"

Was there a flicker of a pause, or did he imagine it?

"Sure," she said. "Ten o'clock, the place opposite South Kensington tube? I can go on to the airport from there."

Irrationally pleased, he turned on the television and admired Catherine's skillful dissection of a fibbing politician. Her lipstick matched her blouse. She looked well.

He ate a large bowl of pasta and let its bland taste fill him like a warm bath. The last forty-eight hours had been confusing. Now that he was back home, it was hard to work out why he'd run away. It wasn't all to do with the overdue visit to his mother. He knew he was scared, terrified even, of two words. *Hope* was a word he'd come to despise. Hope was rubbish. Hope was the refuge of fools. Whatever he considered himself to be, it wasn't a fool. The second word, *truth*, was best left unexamined. No one knew what it was anyway. Everything was subjective.

He had to get a grip, cut back on the Zoloft. He was beginning to sound like Penny. Tim had always said they were turning into a bunch of old women, crying at the cinema while women became the new men, enjoying their strength as the steel entered their hearts. Perhaps Tim was right. And yet as much as Sandy tried to slide back into his accustomed thought patterns, he couldn't.

mattman5@hotmail.com

To: emily.ellison@gmail.com

Money mounting up. Surprising how much you can save in the clean and clear mode. Almost enough for a flight to Delhi. I looked at the visa application online. They want to know every last detail about you. It'll take forever to fill in, so I may as well start now. It's good for six months. All quiet in Sarlat and Battersea, as far as I can make out.

Don't go off and live in a cave or anything until I get there. There are goddamn phonies everywhere, you know. Miss you, sis.

# Chapter 19

SHE WAITED UNTIL all the passengers had pushed through the departure gate, then followed the last straggler and gave her boarding pass to the surly stewardess. "Passport," the woman snapped, as Penny fumbled in her bag. "You'll need to hurry. The gate's shutting now."

Penny scurried down the stairs and onto the crowded bus. After half an hour during which she listened to mothers attempting to quieten their screaming babies and watched children bash each other with their backpacks, the bus finally lurched towards the plane.

She didn't care that she had to stand, hanging onto a strap like a peak-hour commuter, or that the man behind her had the breath of a dead animal. She was going home, to her house and her garden, away from the mess of Sandy and the past. They had been friendlier when they met, but they were still not friends. He looked older than she remembered. He was also funnier in his usual self-deprecating way, although he still talked about himself more than anyone else. Penny knew that he was reaching out to her and she chose not to respond. She wanted him at arm's length. For reasons of family loyalty, probably misplaced, she would always defend him because he was Emily and Matthew's father, but she didn't want to worry about him anymore.

Frieda and Peter had been kind, more than hospitable. She liked Frieda, her wit and her good humor. Another good thing about getting older. Years of faulty acquaintanceships based on husbands' careers or children's schools provided an antenna for true common ground. You knew when someone was going to be a friend. Frieda, despite her impeccably minimalist style in furniture and clothes, had turned out to be a keen gardener and, like Penny, a fan of the old-fashioned designers: Gertrude Jekyll, Lawrence Johnston, and Christopher Lloyd. She'd made Penny promise to email pictures of the garden and the doll's house.

"You don't think it's a stupid thing to do, pointless?" Penny asked. "I'm sure that's what the children think, and others as well."

Frieda snorted. "It's no more stupid to paint a doll's house than to paint a canvas. It's wonderful to have something of your own, a way to express yourself. That's what art is, isn't it?"

On the last night, Peter was running late for supper. Penny and Frieda chopped, seasoned, and tasted in a companionable rhythm. Peter looked slightly put out when he arrived to sea bass cooked in a perfect salt crust, the table laid, and Penny pouring the wine.

"I feel obsolete," he said, nuzzling Frieda's neck and kissing Penny on the cheek. Frieda brushed him off, like a buzzing fly. How ironic, thought Penny. Peter had always been so dismissive about his stream of lean blondes, with their glossed hair and pouting mouths. Now he was in thrall to a plump dark-haired woman who resembled his mother. It made her like Peter more.

The best thing about her three days in London was seeing Matt. He was so pleased about his courier job and his steady, if minuscule, income. She didn't have to ask about the drugs. His eyes were clear and his cheeks flushed healthy and pink as they walked back to Old Street after lunch at some overpriced chophouse near his base.

"I guess Sandy will sort something out eventually," he said, wiping his eyes against the grit-laden wind.

"Why are you calling him Sandy?" asked Penny. "He was always Dad before."

Matt shrugged. "It feels better."

When she hugged him good-bye, his shoulder bones felt as fragile as birds' wings. "I love you, dearest boy." She tried not to cry.

"I know, Mum," he said. "I love you too. Don't worry."

It was raining when the plane landed at Bergerac. She scurried through to the car park. Only an hour more before she turned into her rutted lane, then pulled into her own driveway, the best part of going home, leaving the other world behind and embracing her own life again. Tomorrow morning she would wake in her own bed and watch the clouds rolling over the mountains down to Sarlat. She would be happy.

The car made a rasping noise when she tried to start it, then sputtered into silence. She tried again, pumping the accelerator pedal before remembering that would only flood the engine. She would go mad if she couldn't get home tonight. Walking around her garden and sitting at her kitchen table were her magnetic north. Away from them for any length of time, she became disoriented, doubting herself. A deep breath. She turned the key again. This time she was in luck. The engine coughed, and began running smoothly.

The rain was becoming heavy now, the sky was bruised and gray. She drove alert and upright, listening to the slap of the windscreen wipers and breathing in the moisture-laden air through the window. At each bend and glimpse of the river, her sense of anticipation grew. She could feel the smile on her face. She might have been going to meet a lover.

It was nearly dark when she turned off the main road and began climbing up the hill, past the neat modern brick bungalow of her nearest neighbor, the pile of stone that used to be a barn, and then the last length of lane, where few people ever came and the overgrown hedges brushed against the side of the car. She turned into her bumpy little drive and stopped on the side of the courtyard. Home at last. She sat for a bit, watching the last light ebb away behind the mountains and listening to the rain on the pines.

The courtyard flagstones were slippery, and in the dark she took small, careful steps to the kitchen door, making a mental note to replace the bulb in the sensor light the next morning. She unlocked the kitchen door and reached for the switch. The light flooded out into the courtyard, so bright.

She didn't scream or run back into the darkness or rush for the phone. She stood in the doorway and clutched her stomach, as if someone had punched her, hard, and she was waiting for the numbness and shock to disappear. All her plates, cups, mugs, and dishes had been smashed and lay in shards on the table and on the floor. The refrigerator had been emptied, its contents flung everywhere; weeping fruit, squashed tomatoes spattered with what she thought was blood at first, but on closer inspection was jam, studded with splinters of glass. Under the sweet smell of the fruit, there was another odor: urine.

She picked her way to the dresser. They were gone. Her mother's Georgian silver teapot and milk jug. The drawers were upturned on the floor. She righted them. The silver teaspoons and coffee spoons, always kept in their velvet-lined boxes, were gone as well.

She should leave the house, get in the car, telephone the police from her mobile. But something kept her moving, past the debris in the kitchen and into the hall. They had flung her vase of spring foliage against the wall. Leaves and twigs lay in puddles of water. Wind gusted in from the open front door. The key was still in the lock. Nigel was right. She should never have left it on the outside ledge. Still she moved on, into the sitting room, dreading what she knew she would see.

They had smashed it into matchwood, every meticulously painted column, every tile, every delicate piece of furniture. All her secret memorabilia stamped on and destroyed. She stepped on something sharp, like a nail, and bent down to pick it up. It was the mangled head of Matthew's Lego man, hurled from his bed and his quilt. No sign of his body among all this mess. They had thrown her precious doll's house around the room. The ash from the grate was flung everywhere. Everything was dead, desecrated. She slid down the wall and began to weep, crumpled into a heap on the floor.

After that, there was the shivering, the feeling of being flayed, then unimaginable tiredness. She wanted to sit there and not move, to keep her eyes closed and see her house as it was before she left for England: the morning sun playing on the honey-colored fruitwood table, the sprig of mimosa on the kitchen bench, her Georgian doll's house outlined against the window.

She told herself not to be stupid. She could have surprised the intruders, been raped or murdered. It's just things, she kept saying to herself, just things. Things don't matter. I am safe now. They have gone. I am safe. I will telephone the police. After they come and inspect everything, I will lock the door, go upstairs, and go to bed. It will be better in the morning. I won't give in to the fear. I'm not twelve anymore, dreading coming home every day to the empty house, terrified to open the door and never telling Mum because she had enough to worry about with working so hard and never enough money. Nothing happened then. Nothing will happen now.

She made her way up the stairs, exhausted by each laborious step. There was a moment on the landing as she snapped on the lights when she thought they might still be in the house, waiting for her. But all was completely quiet, everything familiar and exactly as she'd left it: the neatly folded pile of linen on the window seat waiting to be stored in the cupboard, the pile of books on the hall table.

Nothing had been touched in the bathroom either. Her night-gown still hung on the hook behind the door, the potted jasmine still scented the room. But in the mirror another version of herself stared back, white and wild-eyed. I am safe, she repeated to herself like a prayer learned by rote. I am safe now. They will not come back.

After the police go through the house, I will wash my face and clean my teeth. I will sleep with the lights on. I will bathe in the morning, and then I will clean my house. I will sift through the wreckage to find what I can and make everything good again.

The bed was perfect, just as she'd left it, freshly made with the thick linen sheets she liked. The bottle of mineral water was by her bed, the copy of *Bring Up the Bodies* with the bookmark peeking out from the pages. But something was missing. Perhaps it was her fractious nerves, but she couldn't work out what it was. She moved closer to the chest of drawers. So they had found that as well: her mother's jewelry box with her modest engagement ring and her cultured pearl necklace. All the things she had planned to give to Emily.

# Chapter 20

SANDY SWADDLED HIMSELF in domestic routine. Eating. Clearing up after eating. Eating again. Not clearing up after eating. Watching Catherine on the evening news. Every afternoon he walked, mostly around Clapham Common, noticing the green fuzz of new growth on the trees under the mizzle of spring rain. Coffee with Jeremy occupied two of his weekday mornings except when Jeremy was away on business, which was often. Last month it was Brazil and India. This week it was Moscow.

He was beginning to look forward to his meetings in the church hall each Wednesday. They provided a coda to his week and he liked Duncan and Imogen. Two of the girls had left, replaced by an anxious skinny woman with bleached hair whose name Sandy never caught. Imogen's attendance was erratic, and when she did appear, her sleeves were rolled down and her eyes were bloodshot. When Sandy asked her if she wanted to go outside for a cigarette, she told him to fuck off.

"Sorry," he said, and retreated to the coffee urn. He would never get it right. Duncan appeared beside him and took three biscuits from a plate.

"It's not to do with you," he said, puffing as if he'd walked up a hill. "You needn't be offended. It's just hard for her a lot of the time." He was so painfully thin. The shanks of his thighs were visible under his jeans when he sat down. The tip of his nose was still red from the cold outside and wisps of gold-red hair peeked out from under his beanie.

"I seem to offend most people sooner or later. I'm used to it," said

Sandy. He sipped his coffee. It was brackish and undoubtedly instant. He thought of Jeremy's perfect espressos. "I guess it's our turn soon, the moment of truth." Sandy laughed. It came out as a nervous cackle. The little group may have appeared casual, but everyone was expected to speak at some time and he knew it. "I'm still working out my opening line."

Duncan wiped his nose. "It shouldn't be a circus act. Aren't we meant to just say what happened?"

"So, what did happen?" asked Sandy. "Let's practice on each other. You go first."

Duncan's face suffused with a painful blush and he flinched, as if he expected to be hit. His eyes welled up and he breathed in and out rapidly.

"I know you're in the music business. I recognized you, even though we don't give surnames." Duncan hesitated. "You came to my house once when I was little. You were going to do something with my dad."

Sandy was bewildered. There was another pause. Duncan studied a point somewhere on the hall ceiling.

"My dad is George James," said Duncan, blushing again.

"I remember—you lived in Hampstead. Fabulous house," said Sandy. "Fantastic art nouveau drawing room."

"Art deco actually," said Duncan.

"I always get the two confused."

Poor kid, Sandy thought as he gabbled on about George's talent, the way he could electrify an entire arena. Poor bloody kid. Five-times-a-night gorgeous George for a father, one of the most enthusiastic groupies of all time for a mother, and that famously open marriage. No wonder Duncan had problems.

"Your dad and I spent much more time talking about things then, instead of doing them."

Now Sandy could see that George's famous halo of golden frizz had been replicated on his son, but Duncan had nothing of his father's bravura personality, the patina of sexual confidence. Why would he? There would have been no room for anything or anyone else in that enormous house except for the parents, their egos, and their publicity-conscious libidos.

On the sofas behind them, Imogen was telling the man with a beard that she hated her life. Duncan opened and shut his mouth like a gaping tadpole.

"When I was growing up, what I remembered most was my parents having sex with all these different people," he said. "The whole house stank of it. Dad used to bring his girls in for breakfast. Some mornings I'd go into the kitchen and there'd be Mum and Dad canoodling with their lovers. Mum even had an affair with one of my friends when I was about sixteen. She said she was training him up. In the end I took my grandmother's name. It seemed easier."

"You poor little shit," said Sandy. Duncan scrubbed at his eyes with one hand and tried to disguise the trembling of his chin with the other. At least Matthew had been spared that.

Sandy's number came up a week later. He sat on the sofa, flanked by Duncan and the man with the full beard. Imogen and the newest arrival, a thirtyish mother of twins, sat chewing their nails, cross-legged on the armchairs.

Sandy tucked his hands under his buttocks and stared into the pile of yoga mats.

The ceiling lights were so bright. He couldn't bear to look at anyone's face, to see their interest, or even worse, sympathy. The room was silent and his throat felt raw. Again he thought, as he did in that sweet postcoital moment on Carolyn's sofa, how liberating and cleansing honesty might be. But the thought disappeared as quickly as it emerged.

He couldn't do it. He was the same pitiful coward he'd always been. But he had to get his time on center court over and done with as soon as possible. He'd make something up as he went along. If he despised himself for dissembling, it was at least a familiar feeling. And, he told himself, it wouldn't really be a lie. It just wouldn't be the truth. Whatever that was. He cleared his throat and began.

"I always used to say I was fine, but I wasn't. Even when I was judged a success and making a lot of money, I felt whatever I did wasn't good enough. And eventually, it was a self-fulfilling prophecy. I really wasn't good enough. I was just lucky for a while. I'd like to be able to say that something really bad came along to make my life begin to disintegrate, but nothing bad happened. It's just that the good things stopped parking themselves by my front door."

He dared to look around the room. Justin was nodding with exaggerated empathy. The black beard was picking at his cuticles. Imogen and the new woman were regarding him with interest. Polite interest, Sandy had to admit, but interest just the same. They were buying this collection of navel-gazing clichés. All he had to do was keep it up for another few minutes.

"I had a wonderful wife, two great kids, but I also had an urge to self-destruct. I fucked around. I neglected my kids. I'm not going to say I was tippling whisky before breakfast or I was beating my wife. But my life wasn't functioning."

Constructing this narrative was so much easier than he'd imagined, almost enjoyable. Like being a child again and telling a lie, then getting so carried away with the lie, and all the little details that went with it, that the lie became real and you could almost convince yourself that it was the truth. Almost, but not quite.

"My wife divorced me. I realized I'd destroyed everything we had together because of my neglect. I hated being on my own. I started drinking, not too much at first but it crept up on me. Of course I was in denial about it." Sandy smiled. He was particularly pleased he'd remembered to smile. It added a sincere touch to the proceedings. He should have been an actor.

"What drinker isn't in denial? We all pretend everything is perfectly all right. And the more it's not all right, the more we pretend. But the pretense gets to you in the end, and I ended up in hospital after I walked into the path of an oncoming car. Since then, I've thought maybe I intervened to save myself. Although I wasn't aware of it, of course. I can't remember exactly what I did, but I know why I did it. And I hope, with your help and a bit of my own strength, I won't do it again." He nodded.

Justin threw in a couple of questions about his childhood and self-esteem. Sandy paused for what he hoped was long enough to indicate the requisite level of contrition and self-awareness, then answered correctly. He'd listened to the others. He knew the score. As Jeremy always said, honesty was an overrated virtue and complete honesty was an impossibility.

# Chapter 21

THE BLEAKNESS OF the Moscow night had gone. He'd made it disappear. That was one thing Jeremy was still good at. He'd spent too many days sifting through a pile of meaningless documents and asking questions that he knew would never be answered. He had to make the best of what was left.

On the plane back to London, he began a mental draft of the email to the clients. By the time the taxi had jerked through the rush hour traffic along the A4 to the Chiswick roundabout, he'd got the wording almost right. He'd decided to write a letter. An old-fashioned letter on thick, heavy paper with his embossed letterhead, followed by an email. Action. No doubts. He wouldn't wait until the client statements went out. He'd preempt that.

Before he sent the letter, he'd gate what was left of the fund so they couldn't access it. Then he'd side-pocket the rest, perhaps into Canadian mines. There was a Toronto engineer he'd met a few times who seemed to have the right look of confidence and hunger about him. Or there was always Africa. As the taxi passed the North End Road traffic lights, then the supersized billboards advertising films he'd never see, Jeremy made his final mental revision.

"Dear . . . ," he'd write. "As you know, this has been a gloomy year for global investment."

Then he'd put in the bit about the 2008–09 returns of a remarkable 145 percent, the 2010–11 returns of ninety percent. Just as a reminder of what he'd done for them. Just as a reminder that they'd opted for the risk, that he hadn't coerced them.

He'd been invited to their houses in Notting Hill and Little Venice when they were dribbling with greed at the money gushing into their Hoare's or Coutts accounts. He'd seen how they lived. The Jeff Koons and Maggie Hambling pictures hanging on the drawing room walls, the Viking stoves in the kitchen, the marble wet rooms, the Prius cars in the garage for the nanny, everything reeking, stinking of money. He'd provided all that for them. Of course it was their money to begin with, and he'd taken his two percent and then his twenty percent. But he'd done well for them and he could have taken more. Some managers charged forty-five percent.

It seemed back then that he had an invisible divining rod for sensing market changes. Even after Lehman Brothers went down, his own client accounts merely shivered for a moment. He hadn't liked the sniff of the markets and had cashed out in June. By the end of September, he'd felt invincible. For a while anyway.

And what about Sandy? Friends and business, natural foes. He should have known better, shouldn't have taken Sandy's paltry sum as a favor. He'd done his best. Never went after Penny with any real intent or any of Sandy's women, even though he'd wanted to. Paid for everything all the time—lunches, dinners, occasional overdue bills. Years of enabling him to live in that crumbling, dissolute way of his.

The taxi turned down the last section of Edith Grove. Jeremy opened the window and smelled the dark mud of the river at low tide. From this distance, it smelled like wet earth. It was only when you got closer that it gave off the rank odor of stale urine, of something deep and rotting. People always thought of the Thames as a benign ribbon of water, but the currents were vicious. Inside the *Jezebel*, he showered and changed. He made himself a perfect macchiato with a whisper of foam and drank it in his favorite chair opposite the fireplace. Outside the tide was beginning to rise. Water lapped against the hull.

The hay-colored morning sun frolicked on the waxed oak floors and danced off the canvas of his favorite picture, the Ed Ruscha, all dappled gold and blue water, or sky, or both. Meandering across the canvas was the word *Romance*, each white letter in a different font and size.

Sandy used to say the painting reminded him of Gerard Manley Hopkins, that he might have painted something like it if he'd been born in the twentieth century and took to pictures instead of poetry. He said his heart never failed to lift each time he saw it. If he was completely drunk, he'd sway in front of the picture and give a sonorous recitation of "Pied Beauty" as Jeremy smiled indulgently.

> *Glory be to God for dappled things,*
> *For skies of couple-color as a brinded cow;*
> *For rose-moles all in stipple upon trout that swim . . .*

"You always say you don't believe in anything except what is right before your eyes," Jeremy had said once, as Sandy sunk into an armchair and raised his glass. "And here you are hero-worshipping an out-of-date, out-of-favor religious zealot."

"It's not about God," Sandy replied. "It isn't God-centric. It's life-centric. It's about a perfect note moment, when everything falls into place." Sandy thought for a bit. "Unless we're talking about the dark sonnets, in which case it's a bit different."

He had rolled his eyes and gone to bed, leaving Sandy to let himself out. Sandy was the only man in the world to relate pop art to a Jesuit priest unpublished in his own lifetime. He was a fool, but they went back such a long way.

Jeremy rubbed his stomach. There was that gaseous, bloated feeling again, a dull ache in his stomach. Something he ate on the plane. A ticket that cost five and a half thousand pounds and still you couldn't avoid indigestion. He was tired. Everything was worse when he was tired. He decided to take the rest of the day off. He couldn't face the office just yet.

## Chapter 22

THE GENDARME SAID someone would come as soon as possible, but it took an hour or longer before she saw the blue light flashing on the dark lane. She heard the car stop, then voices. They couldn't find the house. They would turn around and drive away, leaving her alone with the door still wide open. She stumbled up the drive in the dark, waving her arms like flags.

"Help me!" she screamed. "Help me!" She forgot her pidgin French, but they understood. "Everything. They have ruined everything."

There were two of them and they were kind and calm. One, portly with a mustache, found an unbroken mug and boiled water for tea. The other man stepped across the debris in the kitchen, muttering to himself. He picked his way across the debris and went into the hall, then the sitting room and upstairs.

Penny shivered. Her teeth chattered. They motioned for her to drink the tea, found a chair for her. They said it was probably a local gang. Burglaries had increased markedly since the recession hit, and there was local antagonism towards foreigners. A problem everywhere these days. They took fingerprints, swabbed, and put things in little plastic bags. They took her through each room and asked what had been taken. Penny told them about the teapot and the jewelry. Nothing else had gone. The television had been upended and her computer was still on the desk. Both were probably too outdated for anyone except her. The gendarmes said she could not stay there that night, not until a locksmith came to change the keys. They went upstairs with her and waited while she packed a bag, then watched as she drove away. In the rear-vision mirror, she saw the portly officer with the mustache wave good-bye.

It was nearly eleven p.m., far too late to land on Nigel's doorstep, but she couldn't think of anywhere else to go. She had a sudden fierce longing for Sandy, wanted his arms around her. She wanted her children. She wished she'd never moved here.

The lights at Nigel's house were still on when she climbed the cobbled lane, but she hesitated before she knocked on the door. From inside she heard the scuffle of footsteps and then Nigel asking who was there.

"It's me," she whispered through the letterbox, then louder, "it's me, Penny. I'm sorry, my house has been robbed. The police have been."

Nigel opened the door, dressed in a bathrobe, flushed and embarrassed.

On the sofa was a tousle-haired young man. There was a fire burning and a nearly empty bottle of wine on the table. "I'm sorry," she said. "I'm so sorry. I'm interrupting you. I just . . . it's just that I don't have anywhere else to go." She burst into great gasping sobs. "It's ruined, Nigel, everything is ruined. My house, the doll's house, everything in the kitchen all smashed."

Nigel put his arms around her. He shushed and cooed and rubbed her back until she stopped shaking. "You're safe now," he murmured. "Everything will be all right. You're safe."

"They took my mother's engagement ring," she cried. "Why would anyone want that?"

The young man poured her the last of the wine. "You must drink it," he said. "Slowly, sip it slowly." He made space for her on the sofa.

"I thought I was safe," she whispered, as if to herself. "I just wanted to be safe."

"You're safe now," said Nigel.

He found her a toothbrush and gave her some towels, then took her up to the tiny attic bedroom, the one reserved for visits from his mother and sister. She lay rigid in the single bed, listening to their muffled conversation, the sound of running water, and then the silence.

It was so unfair, all of it. Had she wanted too much? Everyone had told her it was stupid barricading herself in France, leaving Matthew when he was still so vulnerable. But she had to make some move after the divorce. She was drowning in London, no good to Matthew or anyone else. She was smothering him, cooking meals he didn't want to eat, slipping him cash to ease her guilt over her own incompetence. Emily, home briefly from Edinburgh, had told her to see someone, but she was tired.

The irony was that she was better off now than Sandy. There was little left after the sale of Onslow Gardens. Sandy hadn't told her that he'd increased the mortgage at a ruinous rate. But the death of her mother just before she'd moved to France had left her comfortable. A lifetime habit of margarine not butter, and shopping for bargains while pushing everything into premium bonds, had ensured Penny's economic safety. "You have been the joy of my life," her mother had written in a note with her will. Penny had studied her careful, small handwriting. "I am so proud of the person you are."

Penny was grateful but wished her mother had been able to hug her more and criticize less when she was alive, and her mother might not have been so proud of her daughter postdivorce, dull and depressed, scared to face up to Matthew's problems and intimidated by Emily's confidence.

One afternoon, walking up Hollywood Road past Brinkley's, she saw a carefully dressed woman about her age sitting at one of the outside tables, determinedly plowing through a bottle of white wine, pretending to read a book while hoping for one of those men in red trousers with a matching complexion to chat her up. That would be her one day soon, if she didn't get away.

"You can't escape who you are," Tim had told her when he dropped in one afternoon.

"Watch me," she'd snapped.

It wasn't too late to make a new life and try to discover a bit more about herself. But the problem was that she didn't have a clue who she might be. She'd been a daughter, a wife, and a mother, and none of these roles told her anything about herself except how to play the part.

Turning the pillow over now, she wept. She missed Emily and Matthew, the comfort of their small, hard bodies in her arms, how they had made her feel strong and capable. Why couldn't she make herself feel that way?

The next morning Nigel brought her a bowl of coffee and a croissant from the bakery, still warm. He told her she could stay as long as she liked. "You don't have to go anywhere. I'll go back to the house with you, make sure everything is all right."

Penny shook her head. She knew that she needed to walk into her house alone. If she couldn't do that, she would not be able to live there again.

Nigel tore off a piece of croissant and gave it to her. "Eat, my darling. Go back on your own, if you must. I'll call, make sure you're all right. We can't lose you to something like this, Pen. You're my main man, my partner in gossip. It's not so bad. You'll survive."

She had her doubts as she trundled her bag across the cobbles and began driving out of the town, leaving before the stallholders began setting up for the Wednesday market. Her shoulders ached. She craved a cigarette.

She kept swallowing as she gripped the wheel and carefully negotiated each bend of the steep road. On her lane, the farmer's wife was weeding her garden, her son toddling beside her. She waved. Penny forced a smile and drove on. No need to stop and alarm her about the break-in. They probably picked her house because she was foreign. All this time she had thought she was safe because people in Sarlat recognized her. She hadn't realized recognition meant she was an easy target.

The clouds hung low over the mountains. The courtyard flagstones were still slippery from the previous night's rain. From the outside, the house looked peaceful, undisturbed. She stood looking at its uneven roof, the different colored pointing where someone had added on a room, the windows placed haphazardly along its length. This was her home. It had given her strength and, in ways she couldn't articulate, had helped her change into an independent person. She would not be forced out by petty thieves.

Penny opened the kitchen door. The smell of urine was stronger than last night. She stood at the entrance, overwhelmed by the debris, scared and wanting to run away. Instead, she picked through the mess until she reached the cleaning cupboard. She put on a new pair of rubber gloves, locked the door behind her, and went to work. The glass in the kitchen was wrapped in newspaper and put in the rubbish bin. The hall table was polished. All the splintered wood from the doll's house went out to the bonfire.

She wiped everything clean with water and disinfectant, then emptied the bucket, refilled it, and repeated the process. She cleared and swept and scrubbed and vacuumed and mopped. She went upstairs and changed her sheets, even though she had not slept in them. She scoured the bath and the basin. She did not stop and she did not allow herself to think or cry.

In the afternoon, a locksmith came, changed all the locks and checked the bolts on the windows. After he left, she boiled a saucepan of vinegar and watched as it spat and sizzled until it finally evaporated. She put the saucepan in the sink and walked into the hall, the wooden boards still bearing damp marks from the mop. Everything smelled of vinegar and furniture polish, sharp and clean.

In the sitting room, she sat on the floor in the empty space where her doll's house had been. She traced the faint indentations of its perimeter left on the rug. Her finger slowed at one corner. Just here was the drawing room, with the equally positioned side tables and the painted cornices. Above it were the bedrooms, with Matthew's Lego men tucked under their quilts, the four-poster bed with its chintz swags. Her finger moved to the next corner. Here was the kitchen, the pine table laid for tea, the miniature pots and pans ready for the family's dinner.

Penny examined her hands, red and swollen from her work, and stared through the window at the last light fading behind the mountains. For the first time since she had come home that morning, she allowed herself to weep.

emily.ellison@gmail.com

To: mattman5@hotmail.com

Hey Matt, oh to see your sweet self again, I can't wait. You're going to love it here. At least I hope you do. A lot of people I've met have been here for years, and they seem so full of, don't know . . . is grace a crazy word? Such a relief to believe in something at last, to be away from England and the parents.

Hope I'm making sense. Don't worry, I'm still the same. I love you and only five more sleeps until I see you. Don't forget to bring some of that antibacterial hand gel stuff. And some strong mosquito repellent. I'll be at the bus stop. Xxe

# Chapter 23

PETER WANTED TO try the new steakhouse in Hoxton. It would be the first group lunch since Sandy had left hospital, and Peter thought something neutral would be best. Sandy might feel more comfortable away from their usual West London haunts. Peter particularly did not want to go to Arthur's, which he'd come to regard as a bad omen, something to do with Sandy's accident.

By silent consensus, everyone had agreed to call the incident near the common an accident. Peter thought it was something far more deliberate, and Frieda agreed with him. But he didn't discuss it with the others. It somehow seemed disloyal to Sandy. Best just to carry on with the usual lunches and conversations. A change of location, however, might be a good idea.

He suggested the steakhouse to Jeremy, who had told him it was too far away. Peter had hung up thinking Jeremy always had to be in control, deciding on the restaurant, paying the bill more often than necessary just because he was so much richer than the others. In the end, Peter rang back and suggested the wine bar in Ebury Street, familiar ground to them all.

When Peter arrived, Sandy was already sitting in the corner, studiously chewing gum. He stood up and they embraced in their usual way, making sure their torsos never touched.

"So," said Peter, after slapping him on the arm one too many times. "How is everything?" He didn't mean to sound so oblique. It was difficult to know what to say. A man couldn't ask another man what had made him do such a thing, even if they had known each other for decades.

Sandy stopped chewing. "I feel good. That'll do."

Peter was about to say how well Sandy looked, without his former bloated flush, but Tim and Jeremy arrived and they began their usual conversation of football and finance. Jeremy admitted his fund had taken a hammering, but things were looking up.

"Not like you, to take a loss. It has to be the first dip in your profits for a long time," said Peter.

Jeremy fiddled with his napkin and looked away. His face was paler than usual and there was a small arrow of gray stubble high on his cheekbone that he'd missed when shaving. Next to him, Sandy looked robust and healthy.

"You'll be back on top in a nanosecond," said Sandy, raising his glass of water to Jeremy. "Give yourself six months. You'll be bigger and better than ever."

It was typical of Sandy, thought Peter, to be so loyal, as if he'd taken a schoolboy vow to be Jeremy's cheerleader until they both stopped breathing.

"Thanks, my friend," said Jeremy. "There are some things I like the look of. Some companies in Brazil and a few other countries look promising. Now, what about our team this weekend?"

Tim thought Chelsea was on cracking form, and everyone agreed before ordering hamburgers. Jeremy chose the wine. Sandy asked for fizzy water.

The night before, Frieda had bet him one hundred pounds none of them would ask Sandy anything about what happened or why. Halfway through lunch, he knew he was in her debt. Everything was the same. There was a moment, during coffee, when Peter thought Tim was about to launch into therapy speak, but it dribbled off into an innocuous question.

"So what now?" Tim asked with a vague wave of his hands.

"You know," replied Sandy. "I thought more of the same, less of the other. I'll stay in Battersea for the time being. I only have to give three months' notice if I decide anything. Penny said I could stay with her for a while if I wanted." He shrugged.

"Penny?" asked Jeremy, signaling for the bill. "Are you two getting back together? I hear it's all the fashion. At least you know each other's habits."

Sandy shook his head. "She's just being kind." He put thirty pounds on the table and looked at his watch. "I need to get back. Thanks, guys. So, next month? Arthur's perhaps?"

They left the wine bar together. None of them, Peter knew, wanted Sandy to think they were staying behind for a postmortem. Tim said he had a client and Jeremy muttered he was late for a meeting. Peter wondered what Sandy needed to get back to. Maybe he had a doctor's appointment. Only Peter, it seemed, had nothing to do.

He decided to shop for dinner, taking more time than was necessary. He dawdled around the greengrocer's, picking up pieces of fruit and discarding them until it was made clear to him he had to either purchase or leave. He took his bags of endive, pomegranate, and apples to the fishmonger, where he peered into the eyes of dead fish, annoying the assistant when he finally chose the sea bass right at the bottom of the pile, then asked for it to be gutted and filleted.

"Lovely fillets right here already, sir," said the assistant.

"But I like to see their eyes," replied Peter. The man raised his eyebrows and took up his knife.

He chose a small piece of Stinking Bishop from the cheese shop in Judd Street, then an extravagant bottle of Meursault from the vintner near Russell Square tube and finally a box of four Waitrose chocolate truffles, dusted with the dense bitter cocoa Frieda liked so much. He was particularly pleased about the truffles.

So that was dinner organized and it was only four o'clock, hours before Frieda came home and he could start cooking. He might stop in at the bookshop on Theobald's Road.

He was procrastinating and he knew it. Peter enjoyed not working. Apart from the money, of which he had enough, having been frugal all his life and unencumbered by a series of wives and children, he'd decided some months ago he didn't care if he never worked again. Perhaps it was just as well, because no one had offered him any work for a month. He didn't care about that either.

Acknowledging this was a relief. He no longer had to maintain an exhausting upbeat persona, pretending the fulfillment of his entire lifetime lay in the invention of a new way to film dishwashing detergent, or feigning excitement over baby food. For a week after his last freelance job, he'd prowled about his flat, noting hairline cracks in the plaster of the sitting room, some bulging tiles in the bathroom. Nothing he couldn't fix in a couple of days. Frieda called his flat, one of four in an ex–council building near Great Ormond Street, the Bauhaus Box. Yet again, she was right about form following function.

He thought about Frieda as he stood at the kitchen sink, his preferred place to ponder. When he wasn't thinking about Frieda, the way she snuffled in her sleep, the delicious curve of her belly, he considered the emerging leaves on the linden tree. He noticed that some had unfurled and deepened in color. Others were still buds. He marveled at the intricacies of their shapes, that each one was unique.

He thought about Carl Linnaeus and his life's work in classifying plants and animals. All afternoon he stood in silence, looking out his kitchen window, thinking about who he was and what he wanted. He wasn't like Linnaeus, a creative obsessive able to sustain an academic passion for all his life. He wasn't like the other directors he knew, always thinking of a new way to frame a shot or film a scene, trying to reconfigure the language of cinema. Nor was he like his friends, striving for something bigger and better, despising themselves if they failed. Even Tim, swaddled in psychological enlightenment, occasionally redrew old battle plans, became expansive late at night about what might have been.

Peter was interested in doing a good job, the best he could do within the constraints of budgets and available talent. But his interests finished with the job in hand and began again with the next one. He liked doing a job. He didn't want a career.

A spring shower came and went. After noting how gracefully the leaves bowed under the weight of the rain, it came to him. He wanted to be Frieda's wife. He wanted to stay at home, as his mother had for his father. Peter liked cooking and he didn't mind cleaning.

The oven, particularly, he found curiously satisfying. After decades of working with argumentative teams, he relished daytime solitude. It made him appreciate nighttime companionship.

If Frieda was like his father and wanted a dry martini before dinner, he'd be happy to oblige, as his mother had done. He'd even buy a cocktail shaker. He'd run a bath for her, wash her back, then sit on the toilet and chat about her day while they drank her favorite prosecco.

Peter didn't want Frieda to keep him. He was no ponce. He'd thought about renting his flat and giving the money to her, keeping a small allowance for himself. Pin money, his mother used to call it. She used to change before his father came home from his accountancy office. She'd paint her mouth with a lipstick called Frozen Peaches, blurring the outline with her little finger, then she'd ruffle Peter's hair as she moved past him towards the kitchen to prepare dinner.

After so many years of elegant promiscuity, he wanted his parents' predictable measured life, and he wanted it with Frieda. Acknowledging this made him feel vulnerable and unusually sensitive. His handsomeness had always been his armor against all those doe-eyed girls that he seduced so easily and then discarded when they wanted some affirmation of his affection. He wasn't cruel to them, and he didn't lie. But he never once considered how they might feel when he stopped calling for no reason or when they saw him out with someone else.

He hadn't considered it, because he'd never felt anything for any of them apart from casual affection. He didn't understand their reproachful stares when he ran into them, or their impassioned late-night telephone calls. Only since he had met Frieda had he begun to comprehend the mad pull of the heart. He regretted the pain he had caused and felt guilty about it, while selfishly hoping that he would never have to feel it for himself.

In the kitchen, Peter checked the level of the Pernod bottle. He wanted a slurp for the fish. He laid out the ingredients for dinner. He set the table. Everything he wanted was right in front of him. Except for Frieda, and she would be home soon.

# Chapter 24

THE LETTER WAS lying on the hall mat, partly obscured by one from British Gas with the word URGENT, followed by an exclamation mark, and a mail-order catalogue. He fingered the thick paper of the envelope, studied the italic writing of his name. Alexander Ellison Esq.

He took it to the kitchen table. It might be an invitation, he thought, as he looked at the first-class stamp with a frisson of anticipation. To a party, or a dinner with people he used to know. It could be something to do with the rerecording of "Never Give Up."

He saw himself accepting some kind of award, giving a short witty speech, being clapped on the back by the industry's big swinging dicks. The *Guardian* might track him down for that section on songwriting, even though the new version of the song, by some group called Daddy's Cool, sounded nothing like his original. Too much bass.

Royalties would have been so much better than accolades. But recognition never hurt. It might be the beginning of something, an idea or an opportunity. It wasn't impossible that something could happen. He might write a song again. Imagine that. A song. Even better, imagine writing *songs*. Picking out notes on the piano, tinkering back and forth until the sounds came together; then the lyrics, bumbling in his head until, in some kind of divine miracle, they formed their own rhythm. These new songs would be sweet, like the others, but more poignant, more autumnal and full of rue, in keeping with his age and his new sobriety.

Yes.

They would be hits, recorded by divas like Beyoncé and Rihanna, downloaded from iTunes and Spotify, making it into the Billboard

Top 100: he would be back where he used to belong. On top. Money in the bank. A new postcode. A corner banquette at Scott's, smiles from the maître d'. Chummy cocktails beforehand with Jeremy and the others. No more sighs from Penny. No more rolling of the eyeballs from Matthew and Emily.

No.

He had to stop. This was the beginning of another mad moment, when illusion was so much more seductive than reality. Justin had warned against extremes of any kind. "Try to be calm," he said. "Don't start anything new, don't start having intense affairs. Remember the pussy trail often leads to Château Despair. Just be with yourself."

Justin forgot to tell him how bored he would become, being with himself, that he could get so excited about an unopened letter. He held it up to the light. It couldn't be a bill. Accounts departments specialized in cheap paper that got thinner and more like tissue with each successive demand for payment. This was a proper letter, he could tell. He would save it up, open it after he made himself a cup of rooibos. Caffeine-free. Justin had told him it would be better for him than the regular stuff. He was getting quite a taste for it.

At the kitchen bench, he put the letter from British Gas to one side and threw the unopened catalogue into the bin. He drank half the tea, then couldn't wait any longer. He slit the envelope open, took out the folded piece of paper, noticing, even before he unfolded it, the weight of it, the linen weave, the indentation made by the embossed letterhead on the other side of the page.

Odd that it was Jeremy's letterhead. Sandy didn't understand why he was writing to him in this formal manner when they'd had lunch together only the week before. A quick lunch, because Jeremy had an early afternoon meeting, but long enough to restore in Sandy that old feeling that if Jeremy still had time for him, he was still worth something.

Jeremy had commiserated about the rerelease of the song and promised to look through the sale contract of the back catalogue, to see if there was some way he could winkle out some money.

During coffee, they'd laughed about Amy, how silly and young she was. Sandy said nothing about his meetings in the church hall, his dissembling confession to the group. It seemed to belong in another world and he was content to leave it there. What was important, he thought to himself as he finished his espresso and Jeremy paid the bill, was the friendship between them.

All this went through his mind as he read the letter and then reread it because he didn't take it in properly the first time. He read the letter a third time, just to be sure. The woman in the flat above dropped something on the floor, then turned up the radio. From outside, the faint machine-gun rattle of a helicopter grew louder and louder, almost deafening. Shards of light flickered across the wall as it flew overhead.

He waited until everything was silent and still again, then looked at the letter in case he'd misread it. But he'd understood perfectly the first time. Jeremy had somehow lost every penny of his pathetically small savings and couldn't be bothered to tell him in person.

An anger without sides possessed him, and under that a hard and savage hurt. Jeremy had done it again, sacrificed Sandy to save himself. But this time Sandy wouldn't stay silent about it for decades. He'd go immediately and confront him, before he lost his nerve or went down to the off-licence on the corner. He'd tell him the truth.

On Battersea Bridge Road, the late-spring wind was eye-watering. In his rush, he had forgotten his jacket. He was cold. His heart hurt. His lungs ached as he stamped along. Rising above the trees were the roofs of the prosperous redbrick mansion blocks. He conjured up a vision of the people inside, sitting in their high-ceilinged rooms, gazing out their tall windows onto the river, secure in their measured lives and assured incomes. He was overwhelmed by a sudden need for some kind of luxury. A plate of oysters at Wilton's, a soothing silk shirt, a first-class train ticket. It didn't matter what it was. Something, anything he could eat, feel, or touch to distract him from his rage.

At the traffic lights at the end of the bridge, just as he was about to turn towards Lots Road, a car that looked like a tank, with tinted windows and huge wheels high off the ground, mounted the curb and almost ran him over. A woman driver with one hand on the wheel, the other on her mobile. She waved and pulled away, all Hollywood highlights and dark glasses. He stood on the pavement, giddy with shock, before striding down towards the pier and onto the jetty. A flock of seagulls feasting on a half-eaten hamburger screamed and flew off.

The wake from a passing tug rocked the houseboat. The deck was still slippery from morning dew. He stepped carefully to the cabin door and banged on it. He heard voices, then footsteps before the door opened and Jeremy emerged, dripping wet and wrapped in an oversized bathrobe.

"Sandy, good to see you, looking spruce." A scent of lemon filled the air between them as he grasped Sandy's elbow. Sandy removed his hand. How could Jeremy persist with this charade, as if nothing had happened? How could he stand there, all early-morning bonhomie?

Sandy felt in his pocket for the letter. "Not so good to see you. Mate." He spat out the last word. "And I'm not feeling quite so spruce." He thrust the letter at Jeremy. "You total and utter bastard. Had you already written this last week, when we had lunch, when you were pretending to be my friend, offering to help? When I was thanking you for being such a terrific friend? You fucking traitor. You shitty little coward, not even to have the guts to tell me to my face. After everything that happened, after what I did for you."

Jeremy tried to look blank.

"Don't you dare to pretend you've forgotten," snarled Sandy. "You know exactly what happened. You were there. I was there. And you were the one who used to say if you have to choose between betraying your friend and your country, have the balls to betray your country. E. M. Forster. Remember? Or are you pretending to forget that as well?"

His voice rose. A window snapped open on the boat moored opposite. Jeremy looked around.

"Come inside," he said. "We'll discuss this, but you need to calm down."

"Calm down!" Sandy shouted. "Give me a reason why I should

calm down! I trusted you with everything I had. You told me everything was safe, I would be safe. And you owed me."

Jeremy stepped out on the deck. "You need to come inside."

"Why?" Sandy shouted. "Worried that your fancy neighbors might overhear that you've managed to lose every miserable penny I had? After what I did for you. You wouldn't have your glorious rich career if I hadn't saved your miserable arse."

His rage was magnificent, purifying.

"I saved you! You fucking traitor!" he shouted again.

Jeremy paled. He grabbed Sandy, pulled him inside, and shut the door. "Stop this," he said slowly, shaking his fist in some unseen rhythm. "Stop right now. We will talk about this calmly, when you stop shouting." He might have been addressing a boisterous shareholder.

"No, we won't," said Sandy. "I won't be calm. Not now. Not ever . . ."

A high adenoidal voice interrupted him.

"John? Is everything all right? Can I have some coffee?"

She couldn't have been more than fifteen, fourteen perhaps, with a smattering of freckles under her spots, bruised shadows under her eyes, and a bath towel wrapped around her skinny body. Jeremy moved in front of her, as if to make her disappear.

"John? His name isn't John. He's called Jeremy," snapped Sandy. "And sweetie pie, aren't you a bit late for school? Don't want to get detention, do you?"

The girl looked from one man to the other, confused.

"Shut up," said Jeremy to Sandy, and then to the girl, "You need to go now."

The girl started to speak, but Jeremy took her arm and marched her out of the saloon, towards the bedroom.

"Don't you fret about a thing," Sandy called after her. "Uncle John will help you tie your shoelaces. If you're nice to him, he'll even plait your hair, give you some lunch money."

He looked around the room he had always admired, the one where he'd felt more at home than in his own flat: the Georgian chandelier, the Ruscha on the wall, the plump sofas and armchairs. He thought of his own tiny sitting room, crammed with piles of newspapers and mismatched chairs, but he no longer envied Jeremy.

All this stuff, all this upholstered luxury. It was nothing more than a façade for a seedy and immoral lowlife clothed in a Huntsman suit, all the cracks neatly obscured with clever tailoring. It had taken him more than forty years to realize it.

There was a scuffling behind him. Jeremy and the girl emerged from the bedroom. She looked even younger in her low-slung jeans and skimpy T-shirt, glancing nervously at Sandy as she scurried through onto the deck.

Jeremy shut the door behind her. "I'm sorry," he said.

"Sorry for what? Sorry that I caught you with your underage bimbo, or sorry that you lied about losing the last pathetically small amount of money I had?"

Jeremy shrugged. "It's gone. I can't get it back. It's the risk you took, everyone took. You're not the only one."

Sandy thought of the rent, the unpaid bills, the council tax. "You told me not to worry. You said everything was safe, that you were looking after everything. Why couldn't you have left my money out of it? You always said I was your poorest client. You knew I had nothing more, that was it."

Jeremy was silent, staring fixedly at a point somewhere above Sandy's head.

"And what about you? What will happen to you?" Sandy asked.

Jeremy walked over to the Ruscha and adjusted the frame. "I'm staying put."

Sandy understood. Jeremy wasn't going anywhere because he didn't need to.

"I'm going to make some coffee," said Jeremy. "Want some?"

Sandy shook his head. "You owed me."

"You can't keep calling in that old debt. I've paid up." Jeremy tightened the belt of his bathrobe.

"You can't pay up for that," said Sandy. "It's not, it never was, one of your clever little financial transactions. It—"

Jeremy cut him off with a savage swipe through the air. "Don't go there. It's over, gone. End of story. I'm late already."

Sandy persisted. "I'm not asking you to pay up, you shit. It's a pure and simple thing of friendship. You couldn't even be bothered to tell me to my face."

"Pure and simple." Jeremy snorted. "There is no such thing."

"So I see," said Sandy, and walked out, not bothering to close the door behind him. The little hardware shop was still on the corner, just before Lots Road with its collection of smart auction houses and interior design shops. As his feet hit the pavement in a clipped rhythm, he felt a sense of demarcation between him and the rest of the world, as if the air between him and it had formed an invisible force field. It wasn't what he'd had in mind when he dunked his rooibos tea bag into that lumpy mug Emily had made him as a child. He'd been all set for a day of go-with-the-flow harmony. Now every nerve was abraded, manned-up for combat.

Sandy made his purchase and strode back towards the river. No one was on the jetty. He wouldn't have cared anyway. He stepped onto the deck of the *Jezebel*. There was no sound from inside. Jeremy must have already left. Sandy ran his hand along the varnished teak decking with its solid brass nails and narrow hand-cut boards. The *Jezebel* was an object of exquisite craftsmanship, cosseted like a favorite mistress. Eight coats of varnish. Proper cotton caulking between the headboards. Hull scraped down every year. Sandy looked through the beveled glass door into the cabin, the morning sun dancing off the Ruscha. He shook the can for longer than the recommended sixty seconds and took off the lid. He rolled up his sleeves and bent down. Sandy was careful. He made sure the entire deck was covered. When he'd finished, he stood up to admire his handiwork. FUCK YOU, it said, each letter two meters high and half a meter across. He added some exclamation marks for good measure, then some swirls on the cabin windows. The scarlet fluorescent paint was even more garish than he'd imagined.

mattman5@hotmail.com

To: emily.ellison@gmail.com

I feel like Holden Caulfield, right at the beginning, when he's about to leave that school and he wants a good-bye to mean something. Remember that bit? I practically knew it off by heart. I really wanted to say good-bye to Sandy properly, and to write a proper letter to Mum, even though it wouldn't be a paper letter, just an email. But Sandy was so weird when I saw him, almost crying into his diet coke, really lame. All "Remember this" and "Remember that." He was never there anyway. So what would he remember? And Mum's cracked up because her precious doll's house is now kindling after that break-in. She keeps saying how violated she feels. Like she's Tess of the d'Urber-whoevers. See, my education wasn't a complete waste. LOL. So no proper good-bye to anyone, on the first overseas trip of my life. Goddamn phonies. Fuck the lot of them. Next week, Em. Next week, you and me, together again. Can't wait. See you at the bus stop.

# Chapter 25

TIM COULD HAVE healed the rift between Sandy and Jeremy, if only he'd had a chance. He would have sat them down, made them talk it through, shifted their viewpoints.

He'd done that with Dan the quant—worked through the rage and the tears and the fear of not finding another job. He'd asked Dan if he could imagine his boss not as a monster but as a sick and fragile person imprisoned by his own weakness.

"Think about it another way," Tim had said. It was the fourth or fifth session. Dan had stopped crying. Tim had cleaned the boot marks off the carpet. There was a kiss of sunshine in the morning air and Tim opened the windows.

"You're free now, you're out of that culture, which you say you hated. That man doesn't have any power over you anymore. It seems to me he doesn't even have any power over himself. Perhaps he's the one who should be pitied."

Dan was disgruntled. He'd become accustomed to the anger that had sustained him since he'd been fired and didn't want to let it go. Tim wanted to tell him that anger wasted time and energy, that it was depressing and corrosive. But to do that, he would have to reveal the part of himself that had smoldered for too long over deals backfiring, people he shouldn't have trusted, and more often than he liked to admit, his own lack of judgment. He couldn't do that, because therapists didn't talk about themselves. This was a protocol that suited Tim. He cared about his clients, but he didn't want to confide in them.

Dan shook his head. "I don't pity him one bit. He's the one with the money. I still don't have a job. It's so much harder now, in the recession. I still buy my suits off the peg. I always wanted to get a suit made by a proper tailor in Savile Row."

"A tailor-made suit won't make you a different person." Tim wanted to say Dan was clinging to his victim status, but that would be too aggressive.

"Your choices are wider than you think. You're a mathematician. You're clever. Up to now, you've been making mathematical models that have catered to people's greed. You could make other models that actually produced something that people needed. Or you could teach. Not so much money, but you might find it more satisfying."

Dan was doubtful, but Tim could see there was a shift. Dan would finish his course of therapy a more calm and aware person. It made Tim feel better, more useful. No, that was the wrong word. It made him feel more powerful.

He imagined renegotiating the friendship between Sandy and Jeremy. Jeremy had always been the success story, the most powerful one in the group. Now Tim could be the one to help him and Sandy. Not as a therapist of course, but as a friend. Tim could talk to them about Sandy's meltdown and Jeremy's business problems, help them to understand each other.

But the divorce between Jeremy and Sandy, it seemed, was absolute. Tim didn't like the way their little group had disintegrated. He missed the lunches and dinners together. He didn't realize how much sustenance he got from their meandering blokey conversation, how they balanced the enervating intimacy Angie demanded from him.

He loved Angie and didn't want to live without her, but she wanted his soul. It might not have been so intense if they had sex. Her intensity might channel itself into that, and then they could roll apart, content to be separate people. But he couldn't, hadn't been able to for years, hadn't wanted to. Not with her, not with anyone, even himself.

His once rock-hard erections had grown flabby and halfhearted during the years when his business imploded. He went from wanting sex all the time to faltering halfway through the act, feeling himself shrivel and slide out onto the sheet, a small, sad worm.

Viagra induced an erection so vertical it hurt, but also blinding headaches, so that was out. He read up on oral sex, tried gentle tongue flicking, finger fucking. Nothing happened. Angie remained rigidly, almost aggressively, orgasm free. He suggested a vibrator.

"A what?" came a hiss from her side of the bed, accompanied by a fierce rustle of the duvet. "I do not want to have an orgasm courtesy of a battery. How can you think of such a thing?" Tim waited for the duvet to settle. "I've told you before it doesn't really matter. I'm sorry for being cross." She reached across the pillow and patted his shoulder, which made him feel like a dopey family Labrador, and then made him think she must never have enjoyed sex with him if she was so willing, almost eager, to give the whole thing away.

All those fragrant before-bed baths, the wardrobe of Victorian nightgowns, the subsequent moans and delicate shudders of what he thought was satisfaction, might have been nothing more than a convincing act. Women like Angie, who saw marriage as an eminent profession, probably regarded sex as part of the job, like meeting targets or networking.

This made him feel even worse. Even when he was able to have sex, he probably wasn't able to satisfy his wife. Her effusive not-minding didn't help. "It doesn't matter, we have each other in all the important ways. We could have sex with anyone. What we have together is unique." His heart sank when she said this, and she said it often as they lay like spoons, insulated from each other's nakedness by sensible nightwear.

He wanted mindless and frequent copulation with his wife. He wanted to wake in the morning and slip into her half-sleeping form from behind, to fuck her forcefully at night. It would have made him feel a whole man. A primitive thing to think, but he thought it nonetheless. These days he felt like a soul sister with a flabby dick.

His thoughts were interrupted by a buzzing from his mobile. It was a text from his afternoon client, canceling his appointment, leaving an empty six hours until his evening client arrived. A warm breeze fluttered the papers on his desk. On the street below him, café owners were setting tables on the pavement, luring passersby to sit awhile in the sun.

He called Peter. "Let's have lunch. I'll come up your way."

"I'm busy," Peter said.

"Busy doing what?" asked Tim, knowing Peter didn't have any work lined up.

"Building a cupboard."

"Isn't that what Ikea is for? Come on, just for an hour. Your screwdriver won't gather rust in sixty minutes."

Peter agreed reluctantly, and half an hour later they were sitting in Carluccio's in Covent Garden, drinking house white and swapping idle comments on passing girls.

"There was a time when all these girls would be looking at us," said Peter. "Well, some of them anyway."

"Speak for yourself," replied Tim. A waiter hovered. They ordered minestrone and a salad. "So, any word from the squabbling pair?" he asked.

"Not to each other," said Peter. "Sandy's last words on the subject were, and I quote, 'I'll never speak to that double-crossing cunt again.' So I guess they're not going to kiss and make up any time soon. Jeremy said he'd saved Sandy's neck too many times, that he was going through a tough time and all Sandy cared about was himself and his pathetic investment. He said he's been bankrolling him for years and he'd had enough. It's beyond dialogue."

Tim slopped soup on his jacket and dabbed it with a napkin. "I wish I'd known. I might have been able to get them together, talk it through."

Peter raised an eyebrow. "It's not marriage counseling. It's over. Just you and me now. We can talk to them, they can talk to us, but they're not going to talk to each other. Long live the grammar school boys. How is Angie, anyway?"

"Good. She'd got some idea about opening a vintage clothes shop in Ludlow, but I doubt it will come to anything. She gets this rush of blood to the head every now and then, but then she forgets about it. I think she likes being at home, being in control of the place."

Peter took off his sunglasses. "What about you? The other half of the perfect married couple. What do you like?"

"Hard to say. Probably I like things the way they are." It was a lie. "How's Frieda?"

Peter rubbed his eyes. Tim thought it was unfair that Peter was still so good-looking, so ridiculously youthful even when he was squinting against the sun. Last weekend at the barber's shop, the owner had given Tim a pensioner discount and patted him on the back as he left.

"Frieda is Frieda," Peter said, smiling to himself. "When I think of all the others . . ."

"There were quite a few. We were envious, all those blondes weak at the knees."

Peter laughed. "Frieda has my number, as they say. I don't know why or how, because no one has ever got to me the way she has. I just love being with her. I think about her all the time. I want to . . ." He paused. Tim waited for him to finish his sentence. "Sorry," said Peter. "I've forgotten what I was going to say."

Tim had never heard Peter speak like this before. Even at school, he was flip and sardonic. "The problem with you, Peter Epstein," their history teacher once said, "is that you are quite often in error but never in doubt." Peter had smirked and got a month of detention. He didn't care. He used the time to study and top the class.

"Maybe she'll grow closer to you," said Tim. "Long-term relationships aren't always easy. Sometimes you're gagging for time on your own."

What would Peter think if he knew he and Angie hadn't slept together for over a decade, that the only fire in his belly these days was anger at his own impotence? Could he tell him? He hadn't told anybody, not even his supervising therapist. Surely he could trust his oldest friend. Angie, however, wouldn't like it. It would be a chink in the marital armor. But she needn't know. There was no rule against talking to an old friend. Maybe they could have another coffee, talk some more.

Peter glanced at his watch. "I'd better fly. I want to get the doors on and the mess cleaned up before Frieda gets back." He rolled his shoulders back. "I always hated woodwork at school, thought it was for the dimwits. I like it a lot now. Better than worrying if the crew can get through the day without messing something up. Good to see you. Let's do it again soon. Maybe I'll drag Frieda up to Ludlow one weekend."

"That would be great," said Tim. He sat alone for a bit. Actually, it wouldn't be great. Angie thought Frieda was fat and arrogant. Angie didn't like the way Peter talked to Tim and ignored her. Frieda didn't like walking or sifting through junk shops. She also suffered from hay fever that intensified with each mile away from London.

He decided to walk back to the park and get the bus back to his office. His legs were jumping and he needed to walk, as if the physical process of putting one foot in front of the other would provide a solace that his lunch hadn't given him, some escape from being himself.

emily.ellison@gmail.com

To: mattman5@hotmail.com

Time you left the old folk behind. Really. Way behind. Forgot to say.
Things you should bring. Torch, batteries for torch, one of those plug
adaptor things so you can recharge your phone, that germ-killing hand
gel stuff, a door wedge—don't laugh, it's good security if your room
doesn't have a proper lock—a money belt. Don't forget to write your
passport and debit card numbers on a piece of paper and keep it
separate from your stuff. A small padlock too. It gets cold at night, so
something warm, and proper walking shoes, not just Converse or Toms.
A waterproof jacket. I'm sure I've forgotten some things, but this is a
start. Hey, freedom days ahead.

## Chapter 26

JEREMY ONLY CALLED Penny to warn her about Sandy, to tell her he was obviously not coping, the proof of this being the damage done by the scarlet spray paint.

"I've tried everything I can think of to help him," Jeremy said. From his newly sanded and varnished deck, he gazed across the river. The reflection of clouds flushed gold from the last of the early-summer light danced on the water. On the opposite bank, the tips of the plane trees in Battersea Park were tinged pink. The sight of such rare calm beauty should have soothed him. Instead, he found it disquieting.

Messages left on Penny's answering machine had not been returned and it had taken some time to get hold of her. "It's plain Sandy is bent on self-destructing. Obviously I'm not going to press charges, but the damage done to the deck was considerable, way into the thousands."

"Why are you telling me this?" Penny's voice was pinched. "Is this an attempt to persuade me to take your side? I'm not doing that. Sandy trusted you and you let him down. As if I care about your precious deck. I'm sure it was all covered by insurance anyway, every last nail."

Jeremy had never heard Penny speak in anything other than a sweet girlish voice. Now he had to move the telephone away from his ear as she thundered without pause.

"Sandy and I may not be married anymore, but I won't stand by and see him, or anyone else for that matter, be treated so shabbily."

Jeremy turned his back on the plane trees, concentrating instead on his beloved Ruscha, attempting to stay calm. Her anger, unexpected and, in his opinion, unjustified, surely had to break soon. She would start to stutter and weep. Then he could comfort her, apologize for the upset, and ask about his godson, Matthew. But she might have been reading his mind.

"I won't be hosed down on this one. You knew his situation. You might have taken a bit more care. After everything."

The last of the sun bounced off a glass decanter, making him blink. Somewhere behind his eyes a dull thump started, then a small kick in his stomach. He regretted calling her. She knows nothing, Jeremy kept thinking to himself. Nothing. All the same, it was time for a counterattack.

"Yes, exactly. After everything I've done for him. I couldn't save him this time. I've taken a complete body blow here. I've had to get rid of most of my staff, sublet half the office to pay the rent. It'll be years before I claw my way back."

Jeremy shifted the telephone to his other ear and moved from the deck to the saloon. He paced up and down, noting with annoyance some smears on the windows. A seagull landed on the deck and began pecking at the putty on the frames. He banged the glass. The bird cawed loudly and flew away.

"It's not about you this time, Jeremy." Her voice was loud and precise. She might have been standing next to him, breathing into his face.

He coughed, something caught in his throat. He felt an unexpected swell of tiredness, but he had to continue. He needed to win this conversation.

"You sound just like him, bleating on about . . ." Jeremy stopped. He was about to say Penny was bleating on about something that had happened in another lifetime. He would not fall into the trap of acknowledgment. She didn't know anything. A fly buzzed above his head. He waved it away.

". . . bleating on about friendship and loyalty."

"You can't treat people like they're nothing," said Penny.

"Look who's talking. I'm not the one who left a kid with a drug problem on his own in London and pissed off to France to start a new life. You did that, Penny. You did that all by yourself."

"That's not true," she said.

"It looked pretty damn true from where I was standing. He's my godson, after all. He couldn't go to Sandy for money or any kind of support. He couldn't go to you, because you were too busy with your bum in the air growing muddy vegetables. Who do you think he turned to? Father fucking Christmas?"

He flung the telephone on the floor and strode back out onto the deck, slamming the door behind him. It was almost dark now, high tide. The clouds had disappeared and a greasy slick covered the water. He told himself again that Penny didn't know anything. He should never have called her. A tourist boat sputtered along the river. Passengers clustered on the deck and clicked their cameras before passing under the bridge.

Time for a drink. No. Time for something else. He checked his wallet, thick with cash, put a pack of cigarettes in his jacket pocket, and began walking towards Lots Road, past the auction houses, crossing through the streets of dinky renovated workers' cottages until he reached the small park between the New King's Road and the river. It was always quieter here, still enough for him to hear his own footsteps, hear himself breathing. He halted outside the public toilets, smelling the urine, mud, and stale beer rising from the pile of stained quilts and sleeping bags pushed against the wall.

There was a time when he might have told himself he was getting some exercise, or pondering the scope for a Chelsea Harbour–type of redevelopment, or just seeing how other people lived. There was something to be said for changing one's environment to concentrate the mind, to see things from a different angle. He didn't bother with that anymore. It was a waste of time.

The girl looked like the others, scrawny with flickering eyes and long sleeves to cover her arms. He asked if she had a light, then offered her a cigarette. It was easy after that. A bit of chat. The offer of a drink, something to eat back at Cheyne Walk. Inside the *Jezebel*, he gave her a glass of cheap wine and watched her glance around as she gulped it down.

"I think you know a friend of mine. She mentioned a guy with a boat." Her voice was flat and sly.

"It's not my boat," Jeremy said quickly. "I'm just staying here for a bit, minding it for a friend. I don't live in London anymore. I live in . . ." He paused. "I live in Hong Kong."

The girl was walking around, picking up books, putting them down in the wrong place. She ran her forefinger along the cabin wall, brushing against the mantelpiece and the bottom of the Ruscha. She stared at it, moving her head from one side to another, like an inquisitive bird.

"Funny picture," she said. "Was it very expensive?"

"I don't know." He sat down, hoping she would do the same. All his things with her fingermarks on them. It made him queasy. There was that odd full feeling in his stomach again. "As I said, it's not my boat."

"Whatever." She lit a cigarette, drew in hard. He hated anyone smoking inside the cabin, but he was loath to take her onto the deck. Someone could see them. She could change her mind and make a fuss. He was suddenly fearful of all the things that could go wrong. He'd never thought that before and even as he did so, he told himself it was a ridiculous notion. He didn't keep any cash here. Kids like her wouldn't know the value of the Ruscha or some of the first editions. They could barely manage joined-up writing. Even if someone saw him, someone he knew, he could lie, say he was telling a stranger not to trespass on the jetty.

"So?" Her question cut across his thoughts. "What now?" She stood with one hand on her hip, her head angled to one side like an old-fashioned courtesan. "Let's make it three hundred, okay?"

It irritated him that she was taking control. But he nodded anyway and motioned for her to undress. This was the part he liked best: the memory of grainy Internet images flickering through his head, feeling his balls tighten, his cock grow thick and hard as he told them to take their clothes off, and the way their breasts jiggled as they pulled off their T-shirts and he breathed in their stale mushroomy smell.

But then this one smirked as he rubbed himself. She thought she had the power over him. She was nothing. A nobody, a dirty kid with a need for quick money to feed a lowlife habit. He unbuckled his belt and snapped it at her thighs. She yelped in pain. He pushed her over and fucked her from behind. It was always better when he didn't have to look at them. He pushed harder, deeper, watching her buttocks quiver, ignoring her whimpers.

Afterwards, she didn't get up. He thought she might have passed out. Blood trickled from the corner of her mouth where he'd pushed her against the coffee table. He pulled up his trousers. He worried about stains on the rug, and then how to get her out.

"Jesus," she muttered, wiping her mouth. "You didn't have to do that, you didn't have to be so fucking brutal." She sat up slowly and gathered her clothes, began to get dressed. Angry welts had sprung up on her thighs.

"You shouldn't have done this," she repeated.

He shrugged. More than anything, he wanted her to leave. The sight of blood made him nauseous.

She stood up and walked to the door. He had the cash, plus a bit extra, ready to give her. He saw she was holding something with one hand as she took the money with the other. On the deck, with the money safely in her pocket, she opened her other hand. He saw one of his business cards, engraved in black Baskerville semibold on thick cream paper. It must have fallen out of his pocket.

emily.ellison@gmail.com

To: mattman5@hotmail.com

Sorry bro, don't forget pills for the runs. A friend (?) emailed to say she saw you looking pretty wasted last week. Hope she got it wrong. I'm not going to be your keeper over here, remember that. Let's talk when we see each other. Heard from Mum lately? She sounds pretty damn cheerful.

# Chapter 27

SANDY PICKED UP the telephone. No, he was not interested in solar panels. He didn't even own a roof. He slammed the receiver back onto its cradle and continued his online search for employment suitable for someone his age. So far he'd considered teaching music (a crowded field, he'd discovered), mediating between divorcing couples (the computer test found him judgmental and impatient), and delivering groceries (not fit enough for the inevitable stairs).

He poured his fourth cup of rooibos and drank it as he considered the dishes congealing in the sink. The odds of keeping sober, giving up smoking, and remaining solvent would increase if he found some kind of a job. The idea was to keep steady, not to explode in rage and spray-paint the deck of Jeremy's boat.

It was an invincible Sandy who strode away from the jetty, imagining that divine retribution would follow, that Jeremy would fall and Sandy would rise, that somehow Jeremy could be made accountable. But nothing happened. No one cared. After tossing the can of paint into a garbage bin, he'd called Peter, who mentioned fine print and the matter of damage to property. Sandy hung up and called Tim, who asked why Sandy had expected Jeremy to save him.

"What are you on about?" Sandy shouted into his mobile as he waited at the pedestrian crossing along Cheyne Walk. A Filipina nanny standing beside him jumped and ran off, her buggy veering from one side of the pavement to the other as the baby inside wailed.

"I didn't expect him to save me. I merely expected that Jeremy, as my oldest friend, would not throw me to the wolves."

"But that's just what I was talking about," said Tim.

"Thank you and fuck you." Sandy jabbed a button to end the call.

His hands were shaking. He tried to stay calm and think logically. All he felt was pure fear, like an animal cast out from its pack. He was overreacting. He had survived the breakdown of a marriage, the decline of a career, and growing alienation from his children. By comparison, this was nothing. But it felt like everything as he began walking back across the bridge. Swirls of brown froth slapped at the river's edge. Low rain clouds misted the horizon. It seemed to him that the sky and the earth were moving closer together. Soon he would be crushed between the two into nothing.

A female jogger pounded past. He moved to one side, clutching a metal column. The sense of betrayal and loneliness was exhausting. Why did he mind so much about Jeremy? Penny had once called it emotional homosexuality. It hurt just thinking about her.

For the first time since he'd left the hospital, he took his old route home, the one passing the Majestic store on Queenstown Road. He bought two bottles of marked-down New Zealand pinot noir and hurried back to his flat, as if he was scared someone might see him with the telltale carrier bag and hear the clink of the bottles as he walked.

Just the one glass, he promised himself, then he'd empty the rest of the bottle down the sink. The remaining bottle could stay on the shelf, in case someone dropped by. It was just a drink, and he wasn't a proper drunk. Wasn't that what Justin had said? Or suggested? Sandy couldn't remember. All he knew was that he wanted something warm in his stomach, a bit of a haze, just a tiny little bit, and it tasted so good and he felt so remarkably sober that he poured another glass, put his feet up, and considered his revenge.

He imagined Jeremy's reaction when he saw the spray paint on the yacht. He fantasized about running into him somewhere public. Jeremy would try to apologize, say he was pleased to see him. Sandy would stand very straight, because if he did that he was taller than Jeremy, and deliver the most coruscating speech without hesitation, and Jeremy would feel like dirt while everyone around them cheered for Sandy.

With delicious but unaccustomed alcohol swilling in his empty stomach, he indulged in the fantasies again and again, and then somehow the bottle was empty, then most of the second bottle, and everything in the room blurred as he passed out on the sofa. It was not a good night. He would not, could not, do it again. He told himself repeatedly. He had to find something to do, some kind of daily routine to keep at bay the occasional eruptions of anger, the sense of abandonment by Jeremy, Penny, Emily, and Matthew.

At night he dreamed of Emily running to him in the park, of Matthew's small plump body in the bath, the smell of his innocent skin. Yet he'd never bathed Matthew, never taken Emily to the park. It was false, he knew. He was inventing a family history for himself. Still he dreamed, often so clearly that he woke with their voices pealing in his ear, his arm reaching out across the empty bed.

He had to find something to do. A week later he was still looking. But even the dogs' home had a waiting list for volunteer walkers. Then he remembered when Emily was about seven, her best friend's father lost his job in the City and immediately found another driving London buses. He took Sandy's fare once on the number 90 and told him it was the best place he'd ever worked.

Sandy decided to apply. London Transport might be pleased to have a songwriter and an Oxford graduate behind the wheel, a person who, although somewhat worn, must still count as being more intelligent than most. It would be another reason to keep sober and earn some money at the same time. *Empowerment*. That was the word he was looking for.

He signed into the Transport for London site. Good. There was no age limit for applicants and there was an online test, which had to be a breeze. The first trial question required him to work out the direction of arrows in a series of diagrams. The arrows ran vertically and horizontally, but he couldn't decide on the sequence. After staring at the screen for more than a minute and noting the seconds ticking away on a clock at the bottom of the diagram, he made a guess. He was wrong.

The second question presented a series of shapes in either dots, solid black, or narrow lines, with one blank rectangle. What was the correct choice for the rectangle? Dots, solid black, or narrow lines?

He stared at the screen, put his head one way, then the other. With three seconds to spare, he opted for solid black. Wrong again.

Just what were the job requirements to become a bus driver? Would the next question be on string theory or particle physics? He clicked to continue and saw with relief a comforting multiple choice about petrol consumption. The correct statement was obvious. One out of three. It could only get better.

He was pondering an unnecessarily complicated question on American pizza consumption, and wondering why a bus driver needed to know such a thing, when the telephone rang again.

As he reached for the handset, he fumbled and it fell on the keyboard. The screen went black. Although the idea of driving a bus across London had palled increasingly as he answered each of the questions, the interruption was infuriating. Now he'd have to start again.

"Yes," he growled. Silence. The telephone was halfway back to its cradle when he heard a cough that sounded familiar in a way he couldn't immediately decipher.

"Who is this?" he asked, nervous. Another silence.

"It's me, Carolyn," said the voice.

"Ah," he said. What to say next? He wasn't up on the etiquette of greeting someone who'd shared details of a traumatic abortion after they'd had sex together on her conservatory sofa.

There was another silence before she spoke again, in a breathy voice.

"I've just walked across the bridge, through the park," she said. "Sorry about the silence. I can't work out this new mobile. How about a coffee?"

Sandy turned off his computer. His job application was over for now anyway. He offered to meet her in the café on the corner of a nearby square.

"Actually," she said with one more syllable than necessary, "I'm right outside your building."

He looked into the sitting room, the scuffed matting, the sofa with more stains than pattern. He shifted his focus to the unmade bed. A younger Sandy would have loved this, the flattery of a woman knocking uninvited on his door, the idea that sex might follow. But he wasn't so interested in sex anymore and he didn't want Carolyn to see how he lived, the tackiness of it all.

"I'll come down to let you in," he said, taking the key from the hook by the door and descending the stairs slowly. She might change her mind and walk away, he thought. She hadn't. She was standing on the pavement, wearing an expensive-looking trench coat over jeans and a crisp white shirt. Food wrappers skittered in the gutter behind her.

Her sunglasses were pushed back on her head. She looked so glossed and clean, as if the pipes in Notting Hill gushed with special quadruple-filtered water that made skin softer, hair more lustrous. He kissed her on both cheeks, regretting not shaving that morning as he told her to mind the hole in the stair carpet.

Then they were in his flat. He could see Carolyn trying not to look around, not to notice what could only be termed bachelor squalor. Her former mousy housewife aura had disappeared. There was no more anxious pulling at her neck. Standing in his kitchen, she exuded confidence and well-being.

"I just thought I'd drop by," she said. "See how you're doing."

There was an ominous prickle at the back of Sandy's neck. What did she want from him? She must know he had nothing to give her.

She had a Whole Foods canvas bag with her, which she unpacked on the kitchen table. There was a loaf of bread shaped like an exploding hedgehog, a wedge of weeping brie, three perfect plum tomatoes, some *saucisson* and Parma ham encased in thick waxed paper.

Sandy's mouth watered at the rich aroma from the large circles and rectangles of meat glistening with small jewels of translucent fat and dotted with plump green peppercorns. This was food with provenance, not mean little strips encased in supermarket plastic from mystery destinations in Eastern Europe. Her one bag of exclusive charcuterie probably cost more than his entire week's shopping.

"Do you think we should eat something?" she asked with a smile. "Everything is better after food."

# Chapter 28

JEREMY UNWOUND THE towel from around his neck and wiped his face dry. Almost immediately he felt beads of perspiration re-forming on his face. He lay back on the bench, closed his eyes, and inhaled the moisture-laden air. He imagined all the microscopic specks of urban dirt, the dead flakes of skin, the oil and sweat from his scalp leaving his body, dripping onto the floor and flushing down the marble-covered drains into the sewers of London. If he lay completely still, he could actually feel the steam opening and purifying every part of him, loosening his muscles, calming his jangled shoulder tendons.

These early mornings in the Royal Automobile Club's Turkish baths were his balm, his time spent on winning battles before they were fought. His Sun Tzu strategy. Above him taxis and buses rattled up Pall Mall, their windscreens spattered with summer rain. People scuttling to work looked up to the sky and frowned. Below the hubbub, wrapped in towels, obscured by dense fog and surrounded by giant slabs of marble, Jeremy felt safe. No one could get to him down here. Not the clients and not Sandy. Not the girl either. He shouldn't have lost control like that, but he had no real remorse. It was a transaction of sex and money, nothing more, and it had been fixed. There would be no repercussions.

He rewound the towel around his neck. This was the time he liked best, when he had the place to himself. Jeremy especially liked the last ten minutes of his half-hour sessions, where he tried very hard to think of absolutely nothing. He had planned his moves for the week (sell gold, buy rice futures) and was lying with a warm towel draped across his eyes when the door swung open. Someone cleared his throat and sat down, his feet scuffing on the floor. Jeremy rearranged his towel and tried to capture that pure safe feeling again. There was the sound of towels rustling, more scuffing, and then a voice.

"Sorry," came a broad Australian accent. "Could you tell me something? I'm a bit confused about the order of things."

Jeremy removed the towel from his eyes and slowly sat up. On the bench opposite sat a slight, balding man about his own age, skinny freckled legs protruding from underneath a huge towel. There was something childlike about him.

"I can't work out all the pools," the man said. "I mean, which ones I'm meant to go into—the hot one, the big one, the narrow one. All a mystery to me."

Jeremy explained, with what he thought was very good grace considering the interruption, that any member or guest could go into any pool, but it was recommended to shower first.

"Right. Got it. Thanks. It's more complicated here than the place at home."

The two men fell silent. Jeremy tightened the towel around his waist, gave a small wave and walked out towards the showers and the swimming pool. Halfway through his customary twenty lengths, he dropped his legs down at the shallow end for a brief rest and saw the skinny balding man emerge from behind one of the marble columns surrounding the pool. Jeremy was about to push off, but the man plopped in beside him and greeted him like an old friend. One polite question, Jeremy thought. He'd ask one polite question, wait for the answer, and start swimming again as quickly as possible.

"What brings you to London?" he asked. The man dunked down beside him, splashed water on his face.

"Bit of business. The accountants seem to think I should buy something over here, to diversify a bit. Not so sure myself."

Jeremy rinsed his goggles and put them back on his head. "Where are you looking?"

"They showed me a place in Hill Street yesterday. Do you know that area?"

Jeremy nodded. Perhaps a longer conversation was in order.

"A bit poky for seven million," the man continued, scratching his blotched forearm. "And not even a place to park the car."

"It sounds a lot, but that's probably about right for Mayfair," said Jeremy, and then, because he was on home ground and he knew how to play these things, "although you do need to be careful. I've got some pals in the property business. If you're about in the dressing room after my swim, I'll give you my card."

Jeremy slid under the water before the man could reply. All the way down the pool, he tried to ignore the tiny pulse of excitement in his stomach and concentrated instead on lengthening his stroke and breathing correctly. Exhale strongly under the water. Turn your head, don't lift it. Look for the pocket of air in your own bow wave. Inhale smoothly. At the end of each length, he made sure the man was still swimming in the lane two over, pleased to note he had an extremely crooked left overarm and a jerky leg action.

Later, walking up St. James's Street with Charlie Gibson's card in his wallet, he felt almost cheerful. Jeremy had a positive feeling about the man, and a new rich client would be a good thing. Well. More a splendid thing. No point in relying on the existing clients. No expansion there.

A two-minute Google search and his positive feeling was justified. Even with the downturn in China, Gibson owned vastly profitable mining leases in the Pilbara and, perhaps to insure himself against a slump in iron ore prices or against hefty new carbon emission taxes, was the majority shareholder in a seven-hundred-hectare algae farm in the Northern Territory. The company prospectus showed a picture of him wearing a wide-brimmed hat and a confident grin. Biofuels, he said, could well be the fossil fuels of the future.

During lunch at the Wolseley two days later, arranged by Jeremy, Gibson appeared awkward and clumsy, the kind of man who could walk down an empty street and find something to bump into. He lacked the patina of money, old or new. He couldn't decide what to eat, and when his first course, a tomato salad, arrived, he considered the cutlery for some time before picking up an implement. He was, thought Jeremy, the perfect potential client: enormously rich but just that bit gormless, needing only to be convinced that Jeremy's investment fund was a better bet than Mayfair property.

"How's the flat hunting going?" asked Jeremy.

"There's this place in South Audley Street," said Gibson, prodding his kedgeree. "A bit noisy though. You'd have to keep the windows closed. Not that the wife and I would want to spend much time here. We prefer Umbria. Got a place outside Arezzo. But the accountant says something in London would be no bad thing."

Jeremy saw his opening and launched into a smooth and plausible sales pitch, speaking of possible tax savings, his insider knowledge of integrated commodities and currency swaps versus property investments. He saved the bit about the reduced commission on large investments until last.

"That may come in handy," said Gibson. "We'll have to talk about that later. When I can concentrate. It's hard to think in London, so much noise and traffic everywhere. Every time I call home, the wife says she can hardly hear what I'm saying over the sirens. I'll have a think about it on the way back to Perth."

Jeremy was trying to tempt him with a sure tip on coffee futures when Gibson interrupted him.

"Where do you live?" he asked.

"In Chelsea," Jeremy said. "On a houseboat, on the river."

Gibson spent some time dabbing the corners of his mouth with a napkin.

"Why would you want to live somewhere like that?"

"Actually," said Jeremy, "I quite like it."

"It must stink at low tide," Gibson said, easing his shirt collar. His neck was chafed and raw. His eyes darted around the room and fixed on the upstairs balcony table. "Should we be up there?" he asked Jeremy.

"I think down here is just as good, if not better," Jeremy replied smoothly. "We can see everything or everyone who needs to be seen." He swallowed his slow-cooked lamb. It was good, but he wasn't that hungry. He seemed to feel full so quickly these days. Or maybe the meals were getting larger. He noted that his guest had barely touched the kedgeree.

"Not to your liking?" Jeremy asked.

Gibson scratched his neck. "I thought I'd try something different. Should have stuck to the tried and true. Something you can identify on the plate. No offense, of course."

"None taken." Jeremy smiled. "Let's keep in touch. I get down south every now and then."

Two weeks later, when Gibson replied to one of Jeremy's emails saying he would be in Hong Kong for ten days, Jeremy decided to go courting again. He arranged a meeting and asked his secretary to book flights and a hotel.

"Just for two nights," he said. "It's that kind of town." He was confident he didn't need any more time to hook Gibson. On the plane, he swallowed a Valium just after takeoff and slept for eight hours. For the remaining time, he stared out the window into nothing. He wanted this to work. He needed his luck to change.

# Chapter 29

PENNY LAY IN the bath until her hands and feet were wrinkled like prunes. She would be clean but nothing more. She would wear her acceptable-in-all-places linen trousers, the ones she'd bought on sale in London, and an old blue top. She would not blow-dry her hair or paint her face for him. Most definitely she would not shave her legs.

She could not let the thought of him go. The fine dusting of hair on his arms, his brown eyes, that sudden sight of him reading his book in the café, jotting something important in his notepad. His interesting mind. His body.

His body. Penny didn't want to think about his body. The slow swooping, the gasping, the shuddering, the pleasure, and the sweet sucking noise when the two bodies separated. She wouldn't think about it. It was behind her. She had put it behind her. It was worrying, though, how clear the memories were, of the wanting, then the wanting becoming the needing.

His questions. How disconcerting it was to be expected to talk about herself. Conversations with men, as she remembered them, were mostly epic monologues of unremitting boredom. She'd never minded. All that was expected of her was a sympathetic nod, an occasional question, and then the drone would start up again. It was peaceful to be left alone, to be able to think of the garden, books still to read, lists of things to do.

It had been different with Sandy, because she had loved him and their early life together. His private self, his essential sweetness, she'd found interesting. His exterior less so. Penny knew Sandy much better than he knew her because Sandy was never interested in her, only in what she thought of him.

Even during their most recent conversation, when Sandy rang on the pretext of asking how she was after the robbery, she knew it was something else he wanted. She had barely finished telling him that after the first fearful night back in the house she was perfectly all right when there was the familiar hesitant cough, the break in his voice. Then, with no preamble, out came everything: how he had trusted Jeremy and how betrayed he felt.

"I'm sorry, so sorry," she said, and meant it. As she listened, there was also a sense of detached satisfaction that he had turned to her after everything, that Sandy considered her to be his true friend: a feeling so different from the anger that had engulfed her when she read Jeremy's email about the failed suicide bid, and the subsequent anger against Jeremy for betraying Sandy.

Penny couldn't understand the change in herself at first. But that afternoon, digging in the garden in an attempt to calm herself before dinner with Robert, a three-word chorus had come into her head and would not leave. If. Only. Might. If only Sandy had been more open, everything might have been different. If only she had been more sensitive, he might have cleaved to her instead of to Jeremy and the others.

She heaved a barrowload of weeds onto the compost heap and returned to her digging. It was time to stop using those words. Penny knew that she couldn't make everything better for him. Their lives no longer belonged to each other. Prizing out weeds with savage precision, she realized, by some mysterious process, that she liked Sandy more now than she had for years, and that this mysterious process had much to do with meeting this man, this Robert, who, she had to admit, was very attractive.

Not that anything was going to happen, she told herself as she got out of the bath, satisfyingly stiff from the day's gardening. Nothing at all. Robert must have been at a loose end when he asked if he could join her at the café, when he asked all those questions, about her life, her house, why she came here, her children, the garden. How she felt when she'd been robbed. On and on.

Penny had always made her signals by sitting still, allowing the man to come closer, curving her mouth in silent acquiescence. That was what good-looking women did. Men talked, she listened. That was the semaphore of seduction.

But Robert would not be deterred by her monosyllabic answers, swiftly followed by her determined inquiries about him. Why had he come here? Did he like the Dordogne? Find it something of a tourist cliché? He didn't bother to answer, just batted back her questions with more of his own. What did she read? Where did she grow up? What did her parents do? And then, would she have dinner? Not in the café, but in the new place, just outside town. She could feel herself blush, a shy schoolgirl, as she accepted. Not for the next night, but for two nights after that. Some things were hard to change.

She dressed quickly, locked the house, and drove down to the town, the last of the day's sun turning the mountains the color of ripe plums below a rose sky. In the car, she tried to recall exactly the shades and planes of his face but couldn't. All she remembered were hazel eyes, kind and clear, and the pleasing wrinkles at their edges. Her palms were sweating. She wiped them dry on her trousers as she parked the car and walked into the restaurant. He was waiting for her at a table by the window, a bottle of rosé already open but not yet poured.

"Sorry to have kept you waiting." She was almost stammering. She might have been fifteen again, except then she would have been more confident about what was expected of her.

He smiled. Good, well-tended American teeth. "You're not late. I was early."

Robert poured water, then some wine. "What do you recommend?" he asked, handing her the menu.

"It's gizzards and livers everywhere around here, I'm afraid," she replied. "Most of the time, I feel like a Roman soothsayer, picking around at entrails."

"Nothing to be afraid of," he said. "Shall I order for us? If we don't like it, we can always ask for something else."

She nodded and tucked her hands under her thighs. Why was she so nervous? This wasn't a date, it was just dinner. And he couldn't, wouldn't, be interested in her sexual self. She didn't have one. Again, she reminded herself. That was behind her.

He chose the perfect meal: mâche and walnut salad, *confit de canard*, followed by *crottin de Chavignol*. The process of eating calmed her, and the talk between them became less a series of questions and more a conversation. He was on a sabbatical from Columbia, finishing a book on Montaigne.

"A somewhat crowded field," he said. "But perhaps there's still something left to say."

After dinner, they walked along the river, followed by a family of hopeful ducks. He told her his wife had died two years ago, of liver cancer.

"I'm sorry," she said.

"So am I," he replied. "It was hard on all of us—her, the children, the grandchildren. But time does help—although not all the time."

His wife had taught art at NYU. Piet Mondrian was the subject of her doctoral thesis. Penny felt mentally lumpen by comparison, remembering Sandy's jibe years ago that the only thing she read with any regularity was the bathroom scale.

Robert's mobile rang. She walked ahead to allow him privacy and also because she couldn't think of an appropriate and sensitive thing to say. This was difficult. It was so much easier to be alone. She was too old for dinner dates, too clumsy for the subtle gavotte of flirtation. Behind her, she heard his footsteps growing closer.

"Sorry about that," he said.

"Not at all. I really should be getting back," she heard herself saying in a high, tight voice. "There's still so much cleaning up to do, after the robbery. But thank you for dinner. It was lovely."

Robert laughed. "You clean at night? In the dark! What do you do? Wear a miner's lamp strapped to your head?"

She shrugged defensively, caught out in her lie. Her house was spotless, every trace of the robbery exorcised by her frenetic domesticity. Robert stopped and took her arm.

"I'm American and we're allowed to be direct. It makes up for our more annoying habits, like talking too loudly or asking too many questions," he said. "I'm nothing to be scared of. An occasional dinner or lunch can be just that. A chance to get to know someone a bit. That's all. I'll call you in a while, see if you're free for something."

He walked her back to the car and kissed her cheek. All the way up the hill, her face burned at the memory of his lips against her skin. Could it get any more banal?

# Chapter 30

"WHY DO I always get the impression that you're holding something back?"

Sandy kept chewing the ham and reached for another piece of bread. He wiped his mouth with his hand.

"Sorry about the lack of napkins," he said, ignoring her question.

"The thing is," Carolyn persisted, "you know so much more about me than I know about you. I've told you everything, more than I've ever told anyone."

He'd envied her honesty that night, wanted to take it for his own. Now she was acting as if there was some agreed treaty between them and he hadn't read the subclauses on the repayment schedule.

There was a peppercorn lodged between his back teeth. He tried to shift it with his tongue without Carolyn noticing, but failed.

"I miss my kids," he said. "I wish I'd spent more time with my kids."

"You could do that now if you want to," Carolyn replied. "Make a new start. That's what I'm trying to do."

"Emily is in India, and Matthew is flying out to join her for a while. It will have to wait."

He didn't remember Carolyn being so confrontational before, aggressive almost. He shifted about in his chair. How long was she planning to stay?

She brushed the crumbs on the table into a neat heap. Her hands were smooth and unlined. Her fingernails were pink, without ridges, and neatly filed.

"You could buy a ticket too," she continued. "Flights are cheap. What's stopping you? Are you frightened?"

He fiddled with the cheese for a while. If only they hadn't slept together. Being naked and vulnerable always left a trace. You never looked at each other in quite the same way again.

"I suppose I am. They may not want to see me. I'd probably be interfering in their lives."

"Are you frightened of me as well?" This new confidence of hers was intimidating. "Do you think I'm going to jump on you again? Don't worry. That's not going to happen, even if I wanted it to." She sighed, a big whoosh of air. "It's not so complicated, Sandy. My life was in a bit of a mess and now it's not. You probably don't want to admit it, but you were kind to me that night, so kind. You listened, we laughed, and it was a turning point for me. Everything started to get better after that. I like you. I've always liked you, even when you forgot to pick up the children at school."

"That was just once," interrupted Sandy.

"I know." Carolyn laughed. "And I never forgot it, because it was the only time in five years that Penny ever asked you to pick up the children. But now I'd like to know what's going on in your life. Or more to the point, what has gone on in your life. You can talk to me, you know."

He swallowed, hunched his shoulders. There was that familiar dry feeling in his mouth, the tension of shame and self-loathing. He had a violent desire for a drink and then another. He wanted a cigarette. He needed a Zoloft. Again he wanted her to go. And yet he heard himself begin to speak. He didn't want to. But it was like knowing you were going to be sick, that tight feeling at the back of your throat, the rush of sour saliva into your mouth, and realizing it didn't matter how hard you tried to swallow, nothing was going to stop you from puking your guts out.

Sandy had the dissociated thought that there were three people in the room. There was his physical self, dressed in grubby khaki trousers and a worn shirt, sitting motionless at the table, his hands tucked under his thighs. There was Carolyn, waiting for him to continue. And there was this voice that somehow suddenly developed a separate existence, then a shape he could see in his mind, tensed and crouched, like an athlete on starting blocks, breathing in and out, ready to launch itself forward. The voice came from him, but it didn't belong to him anymore. It had its own force and he couldn't stop opening his mouth and hearing all these words erupt, in sentences already formed, in a story already written.

"When I was at university, just before I left, I killed someone. In a car accident. I wasn't driving, but it was my fault."

The words hung in the room. He had said it, the thing he and Jeremy had sworn never to talk about; they had tried and almost convinced themselves that it didn't happen, that it was a random and tragic accident. But that was a lie. Polly Beresford had died and it was his fault.

"So, this is the thing I've never told anyone. You've asked me and now I'm telling you."

There was the noise of a police siren and the sound of a bus changing gears. Under everything was the dull constant hum of traffic.

"It was my fault," the voice repeated. "Everything was my fault."

He was the one who had sidled up to Polly after finals and suggested the drive to Bampton, the celebratory drink at the Morris Clown. He knew Jeremy was already drunk, barely able to stand. Still, Sandy persisted, persuading Polly that it was a lovely day, that the village was pretty, that Jeremy's new Karmann Ghia was a beauty and they deserved a break after the long nights of black coffee and cramming.

He squeezed himself into the tiny back seat and the three of them roared out of Oxford. Sandy knew that Polly got into the car because of him, because of their friendship, their casual meetings, and the trust that had grown up between them. He knew Polly disliked Jeremy and only tolerated him because of Sandy, and he knew Jeremy only wanted her because everyone else did.

Somewhere near Witney, it started to rain and Jeremy drove faster, showing off his slick gear changes as he swung through roundabouts and pushed past tractors. Polly wanted him to slow down but Jeremy laughed and put his hand on her knee. Polly shifted her legs away from him. Her hair whipped behind her, strands blowing in Sandy's face. He could smell cigarettes, shampoo, and rain, feel the engine reverberating under his feet.

Then there was a screeching sound of metal against tarmac, a flash, and the smell of burning rubber. Polly was lying on the side of the narrow road, that glorious hair matted with blood and leaves. Her eyelids fluttered like broken wings and she moaned softly for some minutes before falling unconscious. One of her long legs was skewed at an obscene angle and a shard of bone protruded from the torn denim. Her books had skittered into the ditch. Sandy hauled himself from the wreckage and knelt beside her. He cradled her head in his arms and tried to breathe life into her, the metallic tang of blood around her mouth smearing his cheeks. He kept trying long after he knew she was dead, and then he lay beside her and wept as Jeremy crouched by the ditch, vomiting again and again.

"Someone drove past us and went to call an ambulance and the police. I remember praying that maybe I was wrong, that the ambulance drivers would find that she was still alive." He couldn't bring himself to look at Carolyn. He heard her shoes scuff the floor. He heard himself continue to speak.

"By the time they arrived, Jeremy had regained control and we'd agreed on our story. I would say I was driving, because I was sober, and we'd say I'd swerved to avoid a deer and the car skidded. I told all these lies to save Jeremy from being charged with manslaughter and maybe going to jail. We swore to each other that we'd never speak about it again."

There was no blurred palimpsest on his memory. He had never poked or prodded it or rationalized it into something else because up to this moment he had tried to ignore it.

"I don't know why I did it. I think I loved him, I wanted him to be like a brother, I wanted to please him. He'd protected me at school, stopped me from being bullied. He was the only real friend I had. There are two other guys, Tim and Peter, who were at university too. They were friends as well, but not in the way Jeremy and I were.

"And now that friendship is over. He was looking after the bit of cash I had left, swore blind he would keep it safe. He knows about money, he's in that game. But he lost it all and couldn't even tell me to my face. I just got an impersonal letter. After everything. When I found out, I was so angry I trashed his precious houseboat, sprayed the whole deck with fluorescent paint. It felt good at the time, but it didn't solve anything. I could write 'Fuck You!' on his deck, but I can't rewrite what happened more than thirty years ago."

He was suddenly cold and began to shiver. He felt his nose running and he wiped it clean with the back of his hand. The light coming in through the window was uncomfortably bright.

"There is no excuse for what I did. Polly was a wonderful person. She was kind and honest and beautiful. Of all of us, she had the brightest future, the most to offer. She had parents, people who loved her, a fiancé. They had a right to know the truth."

Eventually Carolyn spoke. "That's a huge thing to keep buried inside yourself for so long. It must have been incredibly hard for you."

Sandy stared out the window. The sun glinted off something metal in the sink. His mouth was so dry. His tongue made soft sticking noises against his palate and he realized that the separate voice, the third presence in the room, had disappeared. He was still shivering.

"I just pretended it never happened," he said. "Every time it came into my mind, I thought about something else, and eventually, after a while, years actually, the whole thing became like a nightmare that you used to have as a child. It lost reality."

"Still, you never forgot it," said Carolyn. "You couldn't make it disappear."

But he'd thought he could, at first through the trusting gaze of Penny, wobbling on her bicycle to secretarial college in Summertown, then through Emily and Matthew and the cozy hub of family life. In the studio, there were the perfect note moments, as if the music would drown the screeching noise of the car crash and obliterate the sight of Polly lying dead on the side of the road. There were the random mindless affairs. The end of his marriage. Eventually nothing provided true oblivion except the steady drip-feed of alcohol.

"Everything would have continued as before, but one afternoon, I was walking home after lunch with Jeremy, and I saw these two men on the common, across the road from me. They were pushing buggies and they looked so happy, being with their babies. I don't think I ever took Matt or Emily out in their prams. I remember once going to a bar on the way home, waiting there until I was sure they'd gone to bed and Penny could give all her attention to me. I loved them, but I was so selfish. Somehow, seeing these two men made me so sad about what I'd missed and I just walked out into the road. You know the rest."

Carolyn cleared her throat. "What a dreadful thing for you to bear, to keep all that to yourself all these years." She stroked his hand. "Did you ever tell Penny?"

Sandy shook his head. He felt his chin begin to lose its bearings and wobble. His cheeks flushed and his eyes welled up.

"I was always too ashamed," he stuttered. "But that is no excuse. I just know I don't deserve sympathy or forgiveness for any of it."

"You could look at it another way," said Carolyn. "It's not a matter of deserving anything or continuing to blame yourself. You could accept what happened, understand why, and try to live more honestly from now on."

"Ah, straight from a therapy handbook, if I'm not mistaken. But what does 'understand why' really mean? Polly died and I was responsible. There's nothing more to understand."

Carolyn scooped the heap of crumbs onto a plate and cupped her face with her elbows. She looked like she was wearing a wimple. The sunlight had moved from the sink and shimmered on the wall above her head.

"I'm not a shrink. But maybe the part of you that asked Polly to get in the car was the childish part of you that hero-worshipped Jeremy and would have done anything for his approval. Maybe the part of you that lied to the police was a fear that you'd somehow lose his friendship, which had protected you. You wouldn't blame a child for his actions, not entirely, would you? But you'd hope that the child would grow up, eventually."

Sandy wanted to say he was grown up, that he couldn't begin to change now. He was too old and too scared. And then he wanted to weep and was afraid he would. He was terrified the tears would form on their own by some force he couldn't control and he would end up bawling—because under the shame, there was also an unaccustomed feeling of relief that for once he had told the truth.

# Chapter 31

THE HOTEL PORTER had just brought his bags up to his room when his mobile rang.

"Gibbo here," someone shouted.

"Who?" asked Jeremy, moving the phone away from his ear.

"Gibbo," the voice repeated, impatiently this time.

It took Jeremy some seconds to work out whom he was talking to.

"Charlie, great, good to hear from you," Jeremy said. "Looking forward to seeing you this afternoon. I think we arranged three o'clock, in the lounge downstairs. I'm at the Mandarin."

"No can do," barked Gibbo. "Have to catch up another time."

There was nothing tentative about Charlie Gibson now, no more clearing of the throat before he spoke. In his own hemisphere, he had an authoritative New World boom.

"Got a bit of a problem on one of the Pilbara sites. Need to fix it."

"I'm sorry to hear that," said Jeremy. "But perhaps you might have time for a quick meeting. It's quite some distance from London." He was almost pleading.

"No way," replied Gibbo. "I'm in the car on the way to the airport. Late already." Jeremy flung his briefcase onto the bed. The prick could have paused for a second, at least pretended to be polite.

"Give me a couple of days, she'll be apples. The sight of my face generally makes the lot of them perk up," continued Charlie. "But I'll be up here again next week, if not the week after that. Why don't you hang about? And don't give in to the jet lag. Only girls do that sort of thing."

"Of course not," Jeremy said, his voice clipped in annoyance. "I'll be in touch."

A click at the other end of the phone. Gibbo wasn't one for the old-fashioned formality of a good-bye.

There was nothing else to do except go home. To wait around for someone like Charlie Gibson to return was to exude the unmistakable smell of desperation. Jeremy thought of arranging some other meetings, a quick trawl through the expat community, but he was too tired.

He spent a sleepless night in an airless suite full of potted orchids before the hotel limousine dropped him back at the airport and he boarded the flight back to London. He'd called Rosie and asked if he could fly to Dubai for a quick visit, but she was in Doha and frantically busy, or so her assistant said. He missed her. They'd lived in two separate worlds for too long.

Another six hours before he landed at Heathrow. Jeremy jabbed at the buttons on his remote control. An air stewardess glided to his side.

"I can't bring up this film," he complained. "The screen just goes dark."

"Let me see, Mr. Henderson." A current of warm jasmine-scented air wafted towards him. She leaned over, adjusting her scarf as she fiddled with the controls. The screen was still dark. Jeremy glared and she signaled for assistance from the purser. Together they pushed and prodded, plugged and unplugged, shrugged and gesticulated. Still nothing happened.

Jeremy slowly placed his spectacle case on the table in front of him. Even more slowly he uncrossed his legs, then crossed them again. "I particularly wanted to see that film, so perhaps you might arrange another seat for me, as the controls on this one clearly do not function correctly."

He did not raise his voice. Each word was enunciated with care, with menacing effect. He didn't even want to watch the film, until he realized he couldn't. Then he wanted to watch it, very badly. He needed to watch it. He could think of nothing else except watching this particular romantic comedy about a man and a woman and their menagerie.

The stewardess and the purser glanced at each other. "I am so sorry, sir, but first class is completely full," said the man. "We are unable to move you at this time."

Jeremy closed his eyes and rubbed his forehead. "Are you quite, quite sure about this?" he asked.

"Yes, sir. The cabin is fully booked." Her accent became thicker, her voice rose. "I'm so sorry, Mr. Henderson. Perhaps another film? We have a wide selection, over eighty in total."

Jeremy stopped rubbing his forehead. "May I see the control, please?"

The stewardess smiled and handed it to him. Anything to please. He examined it, as if it were the first time he had seen such a thing, as if he didn't know how it worked or what it did. He turned it up-side down, then sideways. Jeremy did this very deliberately, almost in slow motion. Then he dropped it on the floor and stamped on it, then again and again until the back shattered. Splinters of gray plas-tic exploded on the floor. Jeremy kept stamping. Under his feet tiny colored wires pinged free of their housing. Batteries rolled under the seat. The screen in front of him silently flickered between embracing couples, soldiers shooting into the jungle, three girls drinking in a bar, and finally, just before it faded to gray, a Labrador puppy chasing a ball.

The stewardess paled under her headscarf. "I'm so sorry, Mr. Henderson," she kept repeating as she scrabbled around the floor, picking up the pieces. "I'll report the fault and make sure it doesn't happen again."

Jeremy ignored her and turned his head towards the window. The sky outside was navy under tiny stars. He wished that he was flying to Doha, to see Rosie. He imagined them eating lunch under a palm tree, making up for the years spent apart. The thought of London was depressing. He imagined himself flying away into the empty space until he disappeared. He wanted fresh air, not this stale recir-culating stuff that somehow still had a faint smell of tobacco years into the smoking ban. He hated planes. He resented being confined to his pod. He loathed the suffocating clutter of scented face towels, pillows, duvets, and fluffy socks.

The red dot above the toilet light turned to green. He undid his seat belt and walked down the aisle, seeing the stewardess duck into the galley. Locking the door behind him, he stared at himself in the mirror. His hair clung to his head in greasy strands. His face was gray and drawn and his eyes were bloodshot and puffed. He sat down on the toilet and put his head in his hands. It felt heavy and he began to cry. He hadn't cried since he was ten years old and now it seemed he couldn't make himself stop.

But after a time, he did stop. He splashed cold water on his face and scrubbed it dry, then went back to his seat. His hands shook as he pulled down his eyeshade. It rubbed against the bridge of his nose and he flung it off. If only he could sleep.

He had to get himself under control. Apologizing to the stewardess would be a start. People like that didn't take it on the chin anymore. They complained, pressed charges, demanded damages. They talked to newspapers. He pressed the button again and another stewardess glided to his side, one he'd not seen before.

"I was wondering if I might have a word with the other stewardess." He didn't know her name. "The one I spoke to before, about the film."

The woman's eyes popped in alarm. "I'm sorry, Mr. Henderson. Samira is on other duties at the moment."

"Well then, might you be able to convey to her my apologies for my bad manners? I am so sorry. I haven't slept for some time. Could you tell her that, please?"

The stewardess nodded and quickly backed away. Jeremy pressed the bridge of his nose between his thumb and forefinger. His sinuses were raw from the dry air. He tried to conjure up instances of the effortless superiority he usually took for granted: walking along Cork Street, seeing a picture, and buying it just for fun; suddenly thinking about Saint-Tropez and then to be eating langoustines and inhaling the scent of lavender on the evening air only hours later; everywhere people greeting him, acknowledging that his presence was important.

He thought of Sandy and the easy fun of their friendship. He remembered the times he'd taken a posse of stuffy brokers backstage, courtesy of Sandy, and seeing their eyes widen at the sight of that year's pop sensation, as they hopped between the snake trails of cables while ogling those tousle-haired girls. He remembered the pleasure of being with someone who liked you just as much as you liked them.

He rubbed his sinuses again. It was time to stop that kind of thinking or he would turn into a sentimental fool, just like Sandy. Survival of the fittest. Herbert Spencer had the right idea. Sandy was excess baggage. Jeremy had to look after himself first.

He shifted in his seat. It might have been designed by a genius in ergonomics, but it was impossible to get comfortable. His buttocks ached and there was a painful crick in his neck. He moved his head in circles. His shoulder tendons cracked in protest.

He was too smart to fail. Everyone made mistakes sooner or later. His mistakes happened later, so they surprised him. They wouldn't happen again.

mattman5@hotmail.com

To: emily.ellison@gmail.com

Hey Em,

Negotiated Delhi and will be on the bus in an hour. Kind of weird, but exciting. Is it really true that Sandy might be coming here? That would be so weird. I can't remember him going anywhere except America or some luxury island. Hope he's not turning into a parachute parent. After not noticing we were around for most of our lives, that would be hysterical. Annoying too. I wanted this to be my time. Let's make the most of it before he gets to us.

m

# Chapter 32

THIS WAS NOT the evening for a quick stir-fry, courtesy of Nigella or Jamie, and a casual slump on the sofa with a box set.

Peter showered, cleaned his teeth, and changed his shirt. He put on his black trousers, the new ones that Frieda liked. He called the restaurant to confirm his reservation of table eleven, the one in the corner.

He rang Frieda to ask what time she would be back. Her phone was switched off. He sat in the kitchen watching the minutes blink away on the oven clock, telling himself not to panic. Forty-five minutes late. Where was she? What had happened? A problem with a client? An accident?

Ah, there she was at last; at least there was the sound of her footsteps outside in the hall. He was so eager to see her that he almost ran to open the door. The evening would go to plan after all.

Frieda kissed his cheek, a cool, brisk peck. When he tried to maneuver her for a proper kiss, full on the mouth, she neatly sidestepped him and shrugged off her coat. She left it on the chair and sighed, a long, slow puff of air towards the ceiling, like a balloon deflating.

Suddenly he was nervous. "I've booked a table at our favorite," he said too quickly. "You look done in. Would you like me to run you a bath before we go?"

Frieda shook her head, three small sharp movements. There was a flush of color along her cheekbones, as if she'd been walking hard for some time. "I don't want a bath and I don't want to go out to supper. I want a drink and then I want eggs on toast. I've had quite a day and I'd like to sit down and not get up again."

She walked through to the kitchen, sweeping her right hand through her hair.

"Please," he said. "I've booked the corner table, the one you like. We'll be home early. Please." He felt a trickle of irritation. He was fifty-eight years old and this was the first time he had ever begged for anything.

Frieda opened the refrigerator and poured them each a glass of wine. "I'd like to stay in. I'm touched that you want to take me out. But you didn't check with me, and I'm tired."

The trickle of irritation became stronger, and under it grew a sense of bewilderment. He suppressed it and tried another tack.

"How was everything today?" he asked, thinking to jolly her along.

"Penny rang this morning," she said. "Early, before the gallery opened, so we were able to have a good chat. She told me the funniest story. Apparently Sandy's mum has given him some money. Not much, but enough to pay off his debts and a bit left over. You won't believe this. She grew up next to an orchard in Kent and so on a whim bought Apple shares at eight dollars each."

Peter tried to look interested, because he could see Frieda's mood improving as she told the story.

"Then she put the certificates in with her papers and forgot all about them until her lawyer came to update her will. This was when they were up to about six hundred dollars and she told him to sell them. That's about a nine thousand percent increase."

Peter laughed and reached for her hand. He loved her hands, square with stubby fingers and neatly trimmed nails.

"You know more about my friends than I do. Now, Frieda, come to dinner with me. Please."

There was an expression on her face that he'd never seen before: affection undoubtedly and—there was no other word for it—slight annoyance. It came to him that Frieda was looking at him in the way he used to look at women. So then Peter knew he must be looking at her the way women used to look at him: that eager, insecure look he found so cloying and off-putting. The more infatuated they became, the more he withdrew. He'd forgotten that and now wondered, not for the first time, whether this was a good idea.

He took the empty glasses to the sink. Behind him, Frieda said in a resigned way, "Okay, okay, let's go."

The evening could only improve, thought Peter as he helped Frieda put on her coat again. No more vacillating. He had committed to this trajectory. Besides, he had always been able to persuade others to his point of view and, he reminded himself, Frieda loved food. A good pinot noir, a perfect pink rack of lamb would lift her spirits.

Two hours later, Peter felt more confident. Frieda's mood had improved with each mouthful. "You know who I mean by Theo Wertheim?" she asked, mopping up the last of the meat juices with a torn-off piece of bread.

"Mr. Big himself, all the way from New York," replied Peter, remembering a softly spoken little man wearing, of all things, spats. "Didn't he come to one of your openings?"

Frieda nodded, chewing with relish. I love her, Peter thought.

"He's been after me for a bit."

He felt an unfamiliar flash of jealousy. "What do you mean, after you?"

"Not like that. I'm far too fat and old for him. It's business. We had lunch yesterday and he wants me to set up a new print gallery for him, in Brooklyn. Fair split of the profits for two years, then we'll see how we feel. I'd still keep on with the gallery here. A lot of toing and froing, but exciting, don't you think? I've got just enough energy left for something like this and I'll never get the chance again."

Her brown eyes were luminous with excitement. He felt a rush of disappointment that she hadn't bothered to tell him last night. They'd spent the night apart but she could have rung him.

"And what about us? Our life?"

He knew he sounded petulant and tried to think of some witty follow-up quip, but nothing came. Behind him a waiter hovered like a buzzing fly. Peter motioned for him to take away their plates, heavy with congealed fat and juices. In the awkward pause that followed, Frieda surveyed him with cool detachment, as if he were a picture that she hadn't quite decided on. She brushed the tablecloth with her hands, sweeping stray crumbs into a neat pile.

Peter rushed into the silence. "Frieda, I want to marry you. I love you and I want to marry you and look after you for all time." There. He had said it. The instant relief of it, just as quickly followed by the fear of how she might reply.

A puzzled look flickered across her face, replaced by one of kindness as she took his hand, kissing the back of it. There was affection but no passion. This was it then. He'd blown it, scared her off. Now Frieda would end the relationship, just as he had done with so many women before her. Still, he couldn't let go of her hand.

Another waiter passed their table and asked if they wanted coffee. Peter shook his head and gazed at Frieda, willing her to talk.

"Peter, dear man," she said, gently removing her hand from his. "I love you, but I can look after myself. You know that. And you can look after yourself too. I like the way things are between us. Nothing has to change. You can come to New York with me when it suits you. We'll still see each other. We'll still be committed to each other."

"But I've never felt like this before," he argued. He needed her to know he hadn't handed over his heart to anyone except her.

"No, Peter." She spoke firmly, the way his mother had spoken to him when he was a child. "Don't emotionally blackmail me because you've reached a stage in your life when you want to settle down. It's not me, it's timing that has prompted your proposal."

Not true, Peter thought. As if his feelings for Frieda were a matter of convenience, a commodity with a sell-by date. He tried to interrupt, but Frieda wouldn't let him. "You're at the stage in your life when you want to settle down. I don't. I've worked hard to get where I am, not just in hours, but in my heart, in my head. I am nobody's wife. I'm sorry . . . no, I'm not sorry. I won't apologize for who I am. You knew what I was like when we met. I don't want this to end, but I'm not changing my life for you," she said.

There was nothing else to do but summon the waiter, pay the bill, and try not to show his pain. All the way back to the flat, Frieda's arm through his the way she usually had it, Peter remained silent and concentrated on her words instead of the sting of rejection. She doesn't want it to end, he consoled himself. She says she loves me. It hurts that she won't marry me, but what she says will have to do.

In bed, he was still repeating her words like a mantra when she turned to him, touching his face.

"Here's the deal. If we're still together when I'm seventy-five, let's get married and wear purple clothes. Let's take up smoking again and have gin for breakfast and spliffs for supper. Let's get wasted on a daily basis." She put her arms around him, and in spite of himself Peter smiled.

That was the thing with Frieda. They were never at odds with each other for long and she always made him laugh. There was also that other thing with Frieda. She was right, pretty much all of the time. But every now and then she did change her mind.

# Chapter 33

SANDY WASN'T USED to traveling on his own. Before, someone else had always booked the ticket and the limousine to take him to Heathrow. All he had to do was pack his bag, yet even that task he found difficult at times. Ten T-shirts, no boxers. Four pairs of jeans, boxers, but no T-shirts. Not that it mattered. There was always a shop at the other end.

At Heathrow, the chauffeur would find a trolley and help check his bag through. Sandy would proceed to the first-class lounge, where he would drink steadily until some pretty young thing touched his shoulder and told him the plane was ready for boarding now, sir. There was always a "sir" at the end of the sentence. He would weave towards the plane, turn left, and be shown his seat, settle in with another drink, and that would be that until another chauffeur met him at his destination.

The executive lounges of New York, Los Angeles, and San Francisco were as familiar to him as his own house, but he'd rarely flown over anything except the Atlantic Ocean and continental America. Twice he went to AIR Studios in Montserrat, where he did nothing much except lie in the sun. He was there to help Kate Mostyn with the last album they worked on together, but there were no perfect note moments, only a girl with large brown nipples whose name he couldn't remember.

When the work dried up, there was no reason, or money, to fly anywhere. He didn't even have a suitcase on wheels. It took him an entire evening to buy his ticket. There were so many options. Did he want a bigger, more comfortable seat? A vegetarian or a low-salt menu? How many stars did he require for his hotel accommodation?

Travel insurance? Or a specially discounted trip to the Taj Mahal?

He spent so long pondering his choices that twice a small box appeared on his screen saying his session had timed out. Shortly before midnight, his dusty printer finally jerked into action and spewed out the ticket, complete with pages of terms and conditions.

At Heathrow, he'd finished his Starbucks with an extra shot and was perusing the shelves of best sellers in the newsagent when he heard his name reverberating through the airport loudspeakers.

"Will Mr. Alexander Ellison please go immediately to gate number five," the stern voice said. "Your flight is now boarding. Last call for Mr. Alexander Ellison. Please go immediately to gate number five."

No one called him Mr. Alexander Ellison except debt collectors. He tossed the coffee cup into the nearest bin and scurried down the corridor, practically running, his bag bouncing uncomfortably on his shoulder. Damn. He leaped onto a travelator, pushing past a group of schoolchildren. "Sorry, so sorry," he said, as he rushed on.

Gate two, then gate three. He was trapped between a canoodling couple and more schoolchildren, unable to break through. It was like wading through wet cement. Gate four. He was nearly there. He swallowed in relief and began to relax. But there was no gate five, only gate fifteen. Where was gate five? He glanced behind him and saw an arrow with the number five above it, pointing in the opposite direction.

Shit. He hadn't realized he'd spoken out loud until a teacher type turned around. "Language, please! Do you mind?" she tutted. Sandy ignored her, jumped off the travelator and onto one traveling in the opposite direction. He ran down it, losing his balance and nearly falling over as he leaped off onto solid ground.

By the time he lurched, sweating and disheveled, towards the desk of gate five, the departure area was empty except for a stern stewardess. "I'm sorry," he gasped. "I didn't realize . . . and then I got lost . . ." He was so out of breath he could barely manage joined-up speaking.

She snatched his boarding pass and tore it in half. "You should have kept an eye on the departure board. And the flight *was* announced. They were just about to unload your bags," she snapped. "I'll tell them you finally graced us with your presence."

The sarcasm was unnecessary. How was he to know you were meant to keep looking up at a board to find out when your flight was ready for departure? And there were so many announcements, all sounding the same. Again, no one had ever told him a plane couldn't take off unless both bag and owner were on board and that separation of the two caused delays.

Sandy scurried down the boarding bridge and turned right when he reached the plane. Everyone seemed to scowl at him as he lumbered down the aisle, but none of the passengers looked more reproving than the couple in his row. They had spread themselves everywhere and the woman was already in his window seat, snuggled in a blanket.

"Excuse me," he said, flapping his boarding pass in her face. He'd paid an extra twenty pounds to reserve that seat and nobody, not even a white-haired old lady in flight socks, was going to take it away from him. She sighed and heaved herself into the center as her husband rearranged their piles of belongings.

Sandy inflated his neck pillow and tucked his legs into the available space as the plane hurtled along the runway, then lifted sharply. The red tiled roofs, the sports fields, and the roads with cars buzzing like ants grew smaller and smaller until everything was left behind, obscured by pillows of clouds.

His new life was about to begin, his adult and responsible life. What was it Carolyn had said? That if they were all going to live for so much longer these days, they ought to make the extra time count.

He was doing his best to grow up at last. He didn't even miss Jeremy anymore. The slip the night after he ran amok with the spray can had been a mistake, but it had made him even more determined to stay sober, and now, right now, he was on his way to meet Emily and Matthew. He was going to apologize for being such a crap father, ask for their forgiveness, and try to start again.

The cabin lights dimmed and most of the passengers, like Pavlov's dogs, immediately fell asleep. The few remaining awake watched films or played computer games. Sandy was the only one to do nothing except stare at the whorls of pastel colors on the vinyl seat in front of him and drum his fingers on the armrest until the white-haired woman asked him to stop because she had a headache.

Sandy apologized and folded his arms. He was lucky to have this chance. Emily and Matthew could have said no when he suggested a visit. He wouldn't have blamed them. He was lucky too that Peter and Tim were still his friends. Even Penny was chatty these days. The pillow behind his neck was uncomfortable. He wished he could sleep. Penny always slept as if it were a vocation. "I'm going to sleep now," she would announce. Then she would shut her eyes and not open them until the next morning. He envied that about her.

Odd that both of them were still on their own, given the general headlong rush into geriatric romance. Only last week he'd read in a newspaper about an actress in her midseventies raving that her fifth husband was the best lover of them all.

He'd always thought he didn't need to marry again. It had seemed, during the solitary drinking days after the divorce, that a wife was in permanent residence already, an inner nagging spouse embedded in his frontal lobes with a sad look of promises broken, potential lost, and the unspoken question, Why did he let himself get into this state? The inner nag had been right to ask that question. But no more.

Eight hours later, he unfolded himself into a standing position and hobbled up the aisle, his bag banging against his stiff back. There was a moment, inside the airport, when Sandy thought he was lost again. He emerged from the toilet to find his fellow passengers had somehow disappeared along the miles of identical shiny corridors, dotted at equal intervals with identical glossy tropical plants. The air conditioning was arctic. He shivered. There had to be signs. Emily had told him to follow the signs.

But first he had to find them. Yes, there they were, bright yellow, right above his head. How could he have missed them? He made his way through customs to the arrivals hall, found the right carousel and picked up his backpack, again bought on Emily's advice, and pushed through the doors into the Delhi night.

The heat hit in a wave and a madmen's symphony of car horns battered his eardrums. The hairs on his arms and legs began to unfurl and his skin plumpened in the unaccustomed humidity. He could almost taste the smog under the diesel fumes.

Emily had told him to go to the taxi office and pay for his fare into the city. He was then to find the lane for prepaid taxis, give the ticket to the driver, and tell him where to go.

"That way, they won't see you coming and charge too much. It's not their fault, we have so much more than they do. Dad, are you sure about this trip? Great to see you, I mean, but you might find India a bit difficult," she'd written.

At the time, sitting in Battersea with a cigarette and a cup of rooibos, Sandy had no doubts about his ability to get himself from Delhi to the hill town. How hard could it be? Get on a plane, get off again. Stay in a hotel for two nights, get on a bus, get off again. Now he was not so sure. He was having difficulties finding his way out of Indira Gandhi International Airport.

He shouldered his backpack, picked up his other bag, and walked down the pavement looking for the right rank. Taxi drivers kept offering to drive him anywhere at a very good price. He kept walking as if he knew where he was going.

Midway along the concourse, a man slid into the back of a shiny Mercedes as a chauffeur stowed a set of matching metallic luggage in the boot. Once, that would have been him. For that second, sweating and confused, he missed his old life, but it passed.

The prepaid rank was at the end of the terminal. Sandy gave the piece of paper to the pint-sized driver and told him the name of the hotel. Emily had recommended a place near Lodhi Gardens, which meant nothing to him but was apparently an imprimatur for safe and reliable accommodation.

The driver opened the back door. Sandy made to get in. He smiled to himself. He had made it. He had bought the ticket himself, got on the plane himself, and found his way out of the airport. And he was sober. Everything important was ahead of him now.

Suddenly he was yanked back out of the taxi. He landed with a thud on his back, like a figure from a comic book, sprawled with his legs and arms waving in the air. There was a strange gust of spicy breath and a grunt coming from beneath him. Something jabbed his ribs. Something else kicked at his legs and what felt like a hand, a rough and murderous hand, pinched the back of his neck. His skin crawled in fear.

He was being mugged and he hadn't even left the airport. Any moment he would feel the sharp prick of a knife against his ribs, the hot gush of blood, the ebbing of consciousness. He had to fight back, defend himself. But in his confusion he only kicked himself in the ankle, and when he tried to land a punch on his unknown and invisible assailant, his elbow cracked against the pavement, sending his arm numb.

Still on his back and under attack, Sandy thought surely someone would come to help him. There must be police somewhere, a Good Samaritan. Or would he be left, a wounded and helpless tourist, dying on the pavement, his trip over before it had begun? What was the Indian word for "Help!" Or should that be Hindi? Or Urdu? How could this happen to him; how could he travel so far from his own country, his own home, and not even know what language they spoke?

He scrabbled for a footing and almost made it to a crouching position but lost his balance and fell again. This time he noticed there was no painful jar as he hit the ground, and it took a while to stand up because something heavy strapped around him kept pulling him down. The taxi driver was beside him, out of breath and muttering. So the taxi driver had saved him. What a brave, unselfish man, to save a stranger's life. He would reward him well. Give him a large wad of rupees.

Then it came to him. The heavy something that kept pulling him down was his backpack. He'd forgotten to take it off and it had jammed in the door as he bent to get in the car. He'd lost his balance and fallen backwards, on top of the driver, who'd been standing behind him, waiting to shut the door. Sandy couldn't help it. He started laughing at his own foolishness.

"I'm so sorry," said Sandy to the driver, who was scowling and dusting himself off. Being felled by a backpack carried by a pale, sweaty 1.8 meter man was probably not what he had in mind at three a.m. Sandy unstrapped himself and clambered into the back seat.

In the taxi, going through the tunnels and roundabouts and then into the wide motorway towards the city center, Sandy remembered something. The official language of India was English. Shouting for help would have worked perfectly well. He giggled again to himself. It was something he could tell Emily and Matt, make them laugh at their peculiar old dad, how he couldn't even get into a cab without first falling out of it, how he had flown nearly seven thousand kilometers to a country and he didn't even know what language the people spoke. He could make a joke out of it. It would be a start.

At the hotel, he gave the man one hundred rupees by way of compensation. The driver grabbed the money, muttered again, and roared off into the night, leaving Sandy in the empty hotel foyer. Its marble floors and mirrored columns promised luxury. The concierge, when he finally appeared, still half-asleep, spoke perfect English and wished Sandy a pleasant stay before ringing a bell on his desk. A porter appeared. He shouldered the offending backpack and motioned for Sandy to follow him through the carved doors along the corridor to his room.

The hotel became meaner and smaller as they went on. With each turn the carpet became more faded, the walls more dingy. His room, when they finally reached it, was small and smelled damp. The walls were papered violent orange, and thick black hairs nested in the corners of the bathroom.

He would not lose heart. He would shower, open the window for some fresh air, and go to sleep. But the water, when it emerged from the showerhead, was brown and smelled metallic, the towel had a rank odor of stale milk, and the bed was as hard as a plank.

He heaved the window open, leaving the mesh screen closed, and tried to sleep. In between the honking horns, the revving car engines, and the shouting, there was a dull thud as suicidal insects smashed against the mesh. The rough pill of the sheets scratched his back. His head sweated on the hard rubber pillow. He turned over. Something was rootling in the ceiling.

Under the cacophony of noise, he could hear his heart racing. The fog of anxiety that had enveloped him at the airport had disappeared, replaced by panic. What was he doing here? Did he imagine that he could compensate for all those absent, careless years with one budget trip paid for by his aged mother? Did he think there would be some circle of comforting light to lead him back to his children?

He couldn't even remember reading Emily and Matthew a bedtime story. What would he talk about? And did they even want to talk to him? In the known territory of Battersea, he had summoned up a cozy image of the three of them eating curry, visiting temples, wandering through markets. Now he was not so sure.

Penny had told him he was mad. "Don't you think it's a bit late for a gap year?" she'd asked. In the background, he could hear someone talking. "Never too late for anything," he'd replied.

"Well, good luck," she'd said. He was beginning to think he might need it, and he hadn't even left Delhi yet.

# Chapter 34

"YOU JUST MIGHT find yourself in trouble, big boy." She had a fake American drawl and smiled as she waved his business card up and down. Her teeth crossed over in the front.

"Jeremy? So that's your name. Well, Jeremy, this might cost you. I am, you know, not quite of age." She'd jumped onto the jetty next to the *Jezebel*. "I'll be in touch."

Of course she'd called him the next day. He thought he'd fixed it. She'd started at ten thousand but he'd whittled her down to less than half that and got her to sign a nondisclosure statement, carefully worded to ensure nothing would jump back up at him. He drafted the statement himself and kept a copy in his office safe.

Still, he couldn't rid himself of the anxiety that lodged high and tight in his stomach. He started chewing his fingernails again. He couldn't stop hearing footsteps behind him as he stepped off the jetty every morning. He was still rattled by his failure to seduce Charlie Gibson. The Russian debacle hadn't helped, although some clients, surprisingly, didn't defect. He'd given a rare interview to a columnist at the *Financial Times*, remembering to appear both contrite and alert, blaming his past success for his present malaise.

"We got too big too quickly," he told the journalist, a man so young that he still had spots. He had booked at Le Gavroche, one of the corner banquettes opposite the stairs. The man, whose column was called Speculator, appeared more interested in the cheese trolley and the dessert menu than in Jeremy's explanations. "There is often a negative balance between the size of the fund and its performance," said Jeremy, as he passed bread and biscuits. "Sometimes, small is better. We started that way; we intend to do that again."

The journalist nodded and took an enormous spoonful of Époisses. He wasn't taking notes or recording the interview, which turned out not to be an interview at all but a dismissive mention in the last paragraph of his column. He had called to apologize about the subheading of "Yesterday's Hero" but not about misleading him. Bastard. All of them bastards.

Jeremy settled into the business of making money. It was oddly easier without the weight of staff. The floor above his office was empty, waiting to be relet. There was just him and a secretary now. There was a satisfaction in returning to the basics he once knew so well without having to pretend he understood his team's talk of algorithms and probabilities. He took a nice profit on a week of stock exchange jitters and then on heavy metals. By Friday he was ahead by six figures, for himself as well as his clients.

He needed to maintain the momentum to keep the other stuff at bay: the anxiety about failure, the fear that he couldn't negotiate yet another successful deal, the suspicion that everything was random, that he controlled nothing.

Scaling down had been the best solution, he told himself in a taxi, crawling around Hyde Park Corner on the way home, caught up in the Friday evening traffic. He'd forgotten how he liked a small operation. Guerrilla tactics, not military might. It was a strategy that worked in finance as well as in war.

All along Knightsbridge, he planned his weekend with meticulous detail. He'd swing past Chelsea Green and do some shopping. He'd cook supper, crab linguine with chili and garlic, and have it with a glass of Sancerre. Then a Montecristo on the deck, still warm from the day's sun. Maybe a small snifter of brandy before bed.

It was at this time, when he could still smell sap and blossom before the leaves sighed under the August heat, that he loved the city most, felt at one with its brash mercantile heart, which beat so harmoniously next to its culture and history.

He ate his supper on the deck, finishing with a rocket salad. He thought about the gelato in the freezer but decided against it. He couldn't recall the last time he'd eaten a three- or even a two-course meal without feeling uncomfortably full. Feet up, he contemplated the horizon. His neighbors were out or away. The only sound came from the water slapping at the hull and a crackle of burning tobacco as Jeremy drew on his cigar. His BlackBerry rang. He ignored it. This was his Friday night. He'd worked hard, he'd done well, and he was behaving himself. He didn't want to be interrupted. It rang again. He reached over to turn it off, saw Rosie's name on the screen, and grabbed it, pleased that for once she had called him. He'd persuade her to meet him somewhere this year, if only for a weekend, or else he'd go to Dubai.

"Rosie." He felt a ridiculous smile on his face. He couldn't help himself. "How's my baby girl?" He couldn't remember when they'd last spoken. She hadn't replied when he'd phoned and emailed her about the financial hiccup. But she might have been away.

"Twenty-six at last birthday, Dad, so not so much of the baby anymore." She sounded tough and remote.

"Sorry." He was always so quick to apologize to her, the only person he ever wanted to appease. "I was thinking of coming out to see you, sooner rather than later, if that suits." He heard the plea in his voice. "I need to do some business in that part of the world, extend myself a bit."

"Dad, forget about the business. What is this website thing? What the hell have you done?"

He held the phone away from his ear and swung his feet down on the deck, nearly spilling the brandy. A fat circle of ash fell off his cigar and settled in the cracks between the planking.

"What are you talking about?" he said. "I just cooked myself a fantastic supper and now I'm sitting on the deck watching the sun set."

"For God's sake, get your arse into gear and google something called Psst!"

"Pissed?" He didn't understand what she was asking him to do. And he didn't like the coldness in her voice. "Why would I want to google *pissed*?"

"No, Dad, *Psst!* as in *Psst! I've got a secret.* It's a website. It's full of accusations against you."

"What things?" He stood up and immediately felt giddy.

"Go and have a look. Then call me back."

He didn't move, not until a disembodied voice told him to please hang up. Then he carefully stubbed out his cigar, took his brandy, went to his desk, and turned on his computer. Psst! was a gossip website with a frenetic screen of pop-ups and headlines surrounded by exclamation marks that appeared and disappeared with bewildering speed. He drained the last of the brandy. It burned the back of his throat.

By the time he'd clicked onto a story about a wife who'd been suing her ex-husband fund manager for twenty years and an analyst who claimed cocaine on his expenses, there was an ominous drumming at the back of his brain. He knew what he would find, and there it was on the breaking news section, a blind item. But everyone could guess whom it referred to. The houseboat was mentioned in an oblique way ("it seems this mover and shaker likes the river more than most"), the Piccadilly address, the Russian fiasco, and—by now his hands were shaking and his mouth was dry—a video link.

There was a rustling sound behind him, something falling on the floor. He wheeled around, rigid with fear. Was he about to be handcuffed, led away to a police car for everyone to see? But it was only a breeze through the open door, blowing the evening paper and the day's post off the coffee table. He slammed the door shut and picked up everything. He took a bottle of water from the refrigerator. He stood very still and looked out the window. The gold dome of the Peace Pagoda, just visible above the plane trees edging Battersea Park, glimmered in the evening sun.

When he could procrastinate no further, he returned to his desk, where there was nothing else to do except click his forefinger down on his titanium mouse, the one given to him by that divorcée client during her grateful stage.

Somehow, probably through habit or anxiety, he had shut down his computer. Starting it again took forever. It clicked and whirred and buzzed before the little colored ball appeared at the top of the screen. Stubbornly, almost willfully, it refused to transform itself into a biddable cursor. The drumming in his brain had turned into a fierce headache, threatening to explode.

Finally the cursor appeared. He double-clicked until he saw her, full screen, holding up her fringe to show the bruise on her temple. The camera lost focus, then zoomed in on her cut lip before traveling down to a close-up of the welts on her thighs. There was that flat nasal voice.

"This guy is an animal," she said. Her chin wobbled; tears coursed down her cheeks. "He duped me into going with him. I thought he was safe. I might look older, but I'm only fourteen. He looked so respectable, well dressed and all that. He took me to this houseboat, said he just wanted a chat, someone to talk to, and then he attacked me. He raped me."

Her voice was angry now, defiant. "Then he tried to pay me off. Of course I took the money. Who wouldn't? But look what he did to me. I'm lucky to be alive."

The screen went black. He turned off the computer. It felt like an illusion or dream. A hoax. Things like this did not happen to people like him. People like him were too clever, too embedded in fortunate gene pools, to be destroyed by people like her. He couldn't even remember her name.

He was so tired. It was all so exhausting and monotonous—the discipline necessary to keep everything at bay. Alcohol had to be rationed. Ditto cigars. One a day, never more. The games of squash, the swimming three mornings a week. The prompt sweating off of extra kilos in the steam room. Until the Russian debacle, he'd run a conservative and profitable business. He was well on the way to doing so again. He'd married two suitable women and had one beautiful and successful daughter. Postdivorce, the *Jezebel* was an acceptable eccentricity, and he was envied for the constant parade of pretty girls like Amy.

Except Amy was twenty-nine, and this one was fourteen. Those years made the difference between envy and disgust. Any solvent adult could get as much sex as he wanted these days, so why would you seek out a child? Why would you do that unless—unless what?

Unless you were sick and there was a part of you that was black and rotten. Jeremy knew that was what people thought. Now, terrified that people he knew would know, he began to act as his own defense counsel, outraged at the slurs against him.

He had done little wrong. He had not raped children in third world countries. He was not getting his rocks off by throttling himself with women's pantyhose. He had no idea this girl was under the age of consent. Had he known this, he would never have approached her. Never.

Jeremy's thoughts ran on. Compared to the activities of so many people, this was nothing, a sexual trifle, a bagatelle of the flesh. A weakness. And he paid, he paid well for something he wanted to do every now and then without the world knowing about it.

Now, sitting at his desk, noting the flecks of dust on his computer screen, it came to him why he picked up those girls. It wasn't the sex so much. He could get that anywhere. He did it because it made him feel powerful and feeling powerful made him feel alive. He wanted to introduce some risk to his life.

Laughter and shouts from a passing riverboat interrupted his thoughts. Music began. ABBA, "Dancing Queen." If Sandy had been here, he'd have gone on about Bjorn and Benny, why they were masters of the pop song, that there was a sad darkness under the bubbling harmonies. But Sandy wasn't here. Sandy, the one person who would excuse everything, understand anything, was no longer his friend.

His back ached and he hunched his shoulders, then let them drop. It just made the ache worse. From the Embankment, he heard a sudden screech of car brakes, the scrape of metal against metal, then a furious barrage of horns. He blinked, and in that fraction of a second before he opened his eyes, he saw it all. He saw himself staggering from his car as the rain hissed against his ears and he turned away from Polly's crumpled body, rivulets of blood seeping from the cruel gash in her head and dissolving into the mud and leaves; Sandy grabbing him and telling him everything would be all right as he wept and shouted again and again, "I've killed her. I've killed Polly."

And afterwards, the cover-up, and then the vow to expunge it from their memory, as they covered Polly's body with a coat and waited for the ambulance and the police to arrive, all the while Sandy's hand on his back, rubbing up and down as if to soothe a fractious baby, repeating that he wasn't to worry, that they would sort it out, that it was a terrible accident. All the time their eyes never met, because they knew it was a lie.

From that moment up to the present, if Jeremy had thought about it at all, late at night or in a moment of weakness, he had referred to it as Polly's death. Abstract, removed, a phrase absolving anyone of responsibility. A statement of historical fact.

In the computer screen he saw a reflection of himself: bags, jowls, beetle eyebrows, hairy nostrils. He was so tired. But he had to call Rosie, had to fix things up with her. Maybe it had been a bad dream. Maybe he'd imagined everything. He looked at the website again. There it was, with red letters flashing over the item. "Breaking News . . . Police investigation into City figure's under-age sex scandal. Man to be named soon . . . We already know."

His mobile kept ringing. He ignored it. Six new messages waited in his personal email, all from newspapers and television channels. Jeremy put his head in his hands. He decided to deny everything. People would believe him ahead of a girl like that. He dialed Rosie's number.

"It's not true," he lied. "It's a setup. A scam. I've already called my lawyer. Someone is out to get me. It's all innuendo. They'd have named me otherwise. We're going to sue, get that website down. It's outrageous that people can make these kinds of false accusations, that no one ever thinks to talk to the other side first. A load of scumbags."

There was silence. When Rosie spoke, she sounded no longer hard and remote but tired. "Look again. Your name is on the website. I've got about a dozen emails already."

"It's a setup, I told you. Don't believe it."

"One of the emails was from Sally Harvey. Remember her? From school? I always wondered why she never wanted to stay at our house. Now I know. She said you came into our bathroom when she was about thirteen. She said you wouldn't leave and when she began to scream, you told her to keep quiet, otherwise you'd cancel her bursary. I thought she must be lying, but then I remembered you were on the board of governors. You must have known they had no money."

"She's lying!" he shouted. "Why would I do anything like that?"

"You tell me, Dad." There was a pause. "Actually, don't tell me, I don't want to know." There was a click, and then nothing.

Hi Mum,

You keep asking what I'm doing over here and when I'm going to come back and start my real life. You ask about jobs, a career, all that, as if it's the only thing that matters. It's not and it shouldn't be. And yes, I see the irony that if Dad hadn't had some sort of career, then I wouldn't have had the expensive education and the nice house and all that. But perhaps while I'm grateful for having had it in my childhood, I don't want it in my adult life. You need to try to understand that. I'm looking for something I'll never find in England. I'm looking for peace and some kind of truth about how I live. I can't do what you want me to do anymore. And please don't take this the wrong way, but isn't that exactly what you're doing in France? Aren't you looking for your own peace too? So how can you criticize and question what I'm doing?

You say you're worried about "this Rosheme person." If you're so interested, you could look him up. He has a website. Everything is very transparent. I haven't met him, because he's been in a silent retreat for a year and won't finish for another two. But I study his readings and I follow his teaching, as much as I can. He makes sense to me, more than anything else in the world.

I'm not trying to lure Matt away. I just want him to get away from all that London stupidity and the drugs. He can't handle it. You must know that. He's much more sensitive than you think. Did you know when we were little, he used to creep into my room and lie on the floor next to my bed, when Dad was away all the time and you were crying into the wine bottle in the basement? It's probably not something you want to hear, but it happened for too long. He's not tough like me. He's more like you, fragile. He gets hurt too easily. But you survived and he'll survive. The shit makes you strong, as they say. You need to have more faith in me and Matt, more faith in the way you were as a mother to us. We're okay, you're okay. Wasn't there a book called that?

As for Dad, I know what he's like, I know he hurt you. But he is my father and I'd rather have some relationship with him than none at all. Can you understand that? I hope so. It'll be a bit odd having him here, but it will be good to see him. It's been too long and too strained. And everyone deserves another chance. I can't tell you when I'll be back. I don't know. I just know I'm happy. I feel good and I'm not about to let it go. But that doesn't mean I don't love you.

Xxe

# Chapter 35

SUNDAY MORNING. EVERY surface had been painted, polished, and dusted. Every stone had been swept, every weed pulled out, every seedling checked, and every potted plant watered to the brim. Penny checked the tracking information on her computer again. The Grosvenor doll's house had arrived in Calais from Yorkshire with admirable speed but appeared to be languishing there for reasons unknown.

The waste of a day stretched in front of her, a gloomy prospect. She needed something to stop her fretting about Emily. Penny had waded through Rosheme's website and watched countless video clips of a rotund and beaming middle-aged man but was not much wiser. He appeared to talk in riddles that Emily understood and she didn't. She was also worried about whether Matthew could stay drug-free. She both feared and envied the family reunion that excluded her.

She decided to drive to the secondhand market in Bergerac. There was a man there who sold old linen sheets, embroidered with elaborate monograms. He claimed they were the forgotten trousseaus of nineteenth-century spinsters, but some of the sheets were double length and of such a coarse weave that Penny always suspected they were shrouds. Most were creamy and thick, of a weight and weft more comforting than high thread counts. They smelled of dust and dried lavender and were thick and shiny with old-fashioned starch, often with small holes in them.

As Penny mended them, she would think of her mother and grandmother, the laundry basket between them, darning socks and pillowcases with their small neat stitches, companionable in the early evening. So peaceful, those mending sessions, even after her father

picked up his coat and left home forever, sometime after the incident with the scarf, which was all her fault, because at the age of seven or eight she was old enough to know she shouldn't go through people's pockets. But often at night, when he came home and hung his coat in the hall, she couldn't resist sneaking out of the kitchen every now and then and staring at his coat pockets, particularly when they were bulging with something that might be for her, an early present for her birthday, or chocolates for doing well at school.

One night after supper, as her father watched the evening news, she sidled out of the kitchen and tiptoed to the coat of Harris tweed, the same tweed her father said that George Mallory had worn climbing Mount Everest. She stood enveloped in its folds for a minute or two. The newsreader was going on about striking miners.

The coat smelled different. Mixed with the smell of damp wool, cigarette smoke, and beer, there was a scent of something sweet and strong. She reached into the pocket and pulled out a woman's silk scarf, patterned in bright yellow and blue. She had never felt anything so smooth. Wrapped inside was one pearl earring. She clipped it onto her ear and held up the scarf, its perfume rising above her head.

Penny was so sure he had left it for her, a surprise for her dressing-up basket. She rushed in to her father and her mother, waving the scarf, giggling with delight. Her mother sat up abruptly while her father rustled the paper, then walked out of the room. She knew she had done something wrong, but it took many hours of eavesdropping during the mending sessions before she knew what it was.

The adult Penny noted the irony of the loving attention these two celibate women, her grandmother widowed, her mother deserted, gave to their bed linen, the starched and pressed sheets so evocative of the sex and intimacy that was absent in their lives; and that she, also celibate, was doing exactly the same, even folding the sheets and towels the identical way her mother had done, arranging them in neat piles in the cupboard.

But it was learned behavior, not something encoded in her DNA, she thought as she scooped her car keys into her bag and locked the doors. Driving down the mountain, carefully braking at each curve,

she told herself again that she was not becoming her mother, that her mother would never have left England and begun a new life in France. Most definitely, her mother would not be interested in mending a dead person's sheets or going to a market where every item once belonged to someone else.

She joined the main road and immediately switched to the slow lane, happy to cruise behind an enormous Winnebago festooned with bicycles and a canoe as she planned the rest of her day. Also at the market was a stall with enormous piles of wooden fruit boxes that Penny used as shelves. They were cheap and strong and she liked to see her books resting against bare wood. She could have lunch in one of the restaurants in the town square and, by the time she got back, the day would have been dealt with. There would just be the evening then, reading in front of the fire. Alone and, she hoped, content again.

Before the break-in, if she had felt old anxieties and depressions rising, she had only to contemplate her garden and her house for them to disappear. Morning sun could lift her from gloomy dreams. A vase of budding willow stems placed on a table provided a center of calm.

A state of physical contentment was her earthly sense of heaven, and of late it was moving away from her. She was worried about herself, as well as her children. She was beginning to wake in the middle of the night, caressing her breasts and reaching between her legs to discover herself engorged and wet. What was happening? Was she becoming some kind of late-middle-aged sex fiend, addicted to masturbation to feed a craving for sex that she wasn't going to get?

She wanted to be free of all that. Sex had unbalanced her in the past, made her lose reason like a bitch in heat, glassy-eyed, flicking its tail to one side, gagging for penetration. When she'd first met Sandy, she'd lie in bed gazing at his sleeping form, willing him to wake and make love to her.

There had been no one since the divorce, although she could not say the same about Sandy, even in his present state. Men always moved on so quickly. Even Frieda, who refused to recognize sexual stereotypes, agreed with her on that.

Penny didn't want anyone else's company. There were other physical pleasures she had taught herself to enjoy here: hot scented water, a breeze on her skin, the sun on her head. All things she could control. She did not want to lose herself again. It had taken her so long to discover at least part of who she was, who she might be.

After the robbery, Nigel had suggested that she move into town. "It's too lonely for you up here, all by yourself," he said, when he dropped in for coffee one afternoon.

"But that's the reason I came here," she said, looking across at the mountains, hazed blue and mauve. "I want to be on my own. It suits me."

They were sitting in the courtyard, the flagstones still warm. Valerian and erigeron sprouted their blooms from between the cracks.

"It didn't suit you when the house was ransacked," said Nigel. "What happened with the police inquiry?"

Penny inspected a trail of ants and their cargo of crumbs. "They know it's some kind of local gang, kids. But they were smart enough not to leave any fingerprints. The things they took were not incredibly valuable, so the police are on to the next case. I can't blame them. I've changed the locks, added more security lights. The police said they won't come back. They never do. So I'm okay."

"And what's happening with Robert?" asked Nigel.

"He left a message. I haven't got back to him yet."

"Why not?"

Penny hadn't wanted to elaborate on what she thought of as her postmenopausal flush of lust. Keep moving, she told herself now as she negotiated the bends down to Sarlat and joined the road to Bergerac. It had worked for her mother. She could never remember her sitting down or sleeping late. Each day was to be attacked with a list of tasks to be ticked off, battles to be fought against dust and fingermarks. No time was to be wasted. Penny still felt indolent by comparison.

She wandered through the market, idly searching for bargains. But keener shoppers than her had already swept through. All that was left were pots without lids, rickety stools, and rusted headboards, as well as the occasional tarnished suit of headless armor. She walked back to the linen stall and carefully examined each sheet in the pile, before deciding on one with scrolled embroidery at the top and a large hole at the bottom. She negotiated her price and then bought two fruit boxes.

As she heaved her purchases to a carrying position, Robert emerged from behind a stall selling old shovels, nearly tripping her.

"Hello," she said, disliking her immediate worry that her hair was particularly unkempt and that she was wearing her baggiest trousers.

"Hi," he replied with a wide smile. His teeth really were wonderfully white, his skin so deliciously olive.

"You're all loaded up. Let me give you a hand."

Before she replied, the boxes were in his arms and he was walking alongside her towards the car park.

"How have you been?" he asked, and then, without waiting for her reply: "I called, thought you might like to go for a hike, but I guess you were out." He shrugged and smiled. Not a matter of great concern to him, then.

"How's life with Montaigne?" she asked.

"He was the most amazing guy," said Robert, jiggling the boxes in his enthusiasm. "If he were alive now, he'd give any Eastern mystic or Western theologian a run for his money. He was into the living-well, living-in-the-moment thing. And he didn't go in for major reflections. He let his thoughts lie where they fell. But hey, what thoughts."

"My daughter, Emily, always talks about living in the moment. She's in India right now, with her brother. And their father has joined them for a bit."

"That's good," said Robert.

"What? Living in the moment or their father joining them?"

"Both, I guess." Robert shifted the boxes from one arm to another. "Montaigne might say it'd matter more to their father than to them, because things matter more as we get older."

"I was rather hoping they'd matter less." Penny smiled.

"I don't like your chances," he said. "Montaigne says as we get older, we've got the opportunity to recognize that we're fallible. If

we understand that age doesn't make you wise, then that's kind of a
wisdom all its own."

Penny pointed out her car. Robert stowed her purchases in the
boot and stretched out his arms.

"Those boxes were heavier than they looked."

"Sorry about that. But thank you." She fumbled in her bag for
the key.

"Hey," he said, "are you busy this week?"

Her stomach contracted while she considered her reply. It would
be so easy to tell him she was going away. Easier still to make a date
and then cancel it at the last minute. Migraine or back problems were
always good excuses.

Or she could say no, she wasn't busy. She might even ask him to
dinner at her house, cook a daube or a roast chicken. Nothing too
elaborate. It was still too chilly to eat in the courtyard at night, but
the kitchen was fine. Even better perhaps, with no possibility of a
romantic evening in a candlelit restaurant. She shook her head and
waited.

"It's just that I have a friend coming to join me for a while and
I wondered if we could have lunch together," said Robert. "She'd
like to meet you. She used to live in London. You'd have lots to talk
about."

"I'd love to," said Penny very quickly. The embroidered sheet
slipped in her hand and she grabbed a fold of it. "Name your day. I'm
as free as the proverbial bird."

She got in the car and drove home. Just as well, all things considered. There were a few more meaningless phrases she could have
dredged up, but she decided not to bother. As she swung into her
lane, her old companion, self-pity, slipped into the seat beside her. So
unfair, the whisper came, to be driving home alone, to continue her
predictable expatriate existence while a man she didn't want to find
attractive, but did, waited for his partner to join him, and her children
and ex-husband explored a far more exotic country than the one she
had chosen to live in.

# Chapter 36

SANDY THOUGHT THE bus would be a bit of an adventure, a little road trip to see India. The concierge, a different one from last night, thought otherwise.

"Sir is going where?" he asked. He tugged the hairs of his bristling mustache when Sandy told him. "Usually that town is more popular with young people," he said.

The implication was clear. Sandy should be booking a luxury tour of the Taj Mahal and the Red Fort, not a bus ticket to a place reeling with gurus and mystics, with as many monasteries as hotels. Under the fulsome mustache, the concierge's lips pursed. "We will organize a car," he said.

Sandy held firm. Did he look so incompetent that he couldn't manage a bus trip on his own? He did feel off balance, but that was because of the changed time zones and temperatures, not because he was too stupid to find a bus stop.

"Bus," the concierge repeated. "From the terminal? In Old Delhi?" His brow knotted and he chewed at some wayward mustache fibers.

"Well then, we will organize a taxi to take you there." He looked disappointed.

Sandy shouldered his backpack and paid his bill. The taxi driver steered through elegant Lutyens avenues, sighing as he left them behind for the narrow teeming streets of Old Delhi and the bus terminal. The air smelled of spices, ripe fruit, fried food, and under that, a whiff of dank sewage. He wouldn't have known where to go without the driver's help, who steered him onto the right bus, then hoisted his backpack onto the overhead rack. He tipped him and bagged a window seat at the back, grateful for the driver's help but also glad to be on his own at last.

The bus was crammed full of weary-looking Indians returning to their villages and groups of raucous Western teenagers shouting to each other about dysentery and drugs. Sandy tried to ignore the pain in his back as the bus juddered across the ruts and potholes that passed for a road once the city was left behind. He recalled the advice given by his friends before leaving London.

Ignore hawkers, said Tim, who'd been to Kerala twenty years ago and never returned. So when the bus stopped to refuel, Sandy buried his head in his guidebook as children jiggled crude wood carvings against the window. Leave your bourgeois judgments at home, advised Peter, who'd traveled to Goa once or twice in the seventies. So when Sandy walked to the toilets, he ignored the men who goaded their chained monkeys to turn lethargic somersaults and peered up at the temple domes curving like plump breasts against the sky. It seemed the only safe place to look.

As the bus began to climb the hills, the driver, in between shouting into his mobile phone, slowed to a crawl along the straight sections, then accelerated around sharp bends, skidding and spinning gravel down into steep, cedar-covered valleys.

Sandy eavesdropped on the couple sitting in front of him, recognizing an American accent and a broad Australian twang. It was either that or give into the fear that the bus would almost certainly crash. The sight of smashed fenders, frayed tires, and—twice—a steering wheel strewn along the sides of the road did little to calm him.

"A direct connection with the land . . . so amazing," said the Australian male. His ponytail hung over the seat. Intermittent plaits fastened with red braid nestled between the black tangles. Sandy was tempted to yank one and tell him he was talking a load of rubbish. The girl's hair was cropped so close that Sandy could see the pink tinge of her scalp under the blond fuzz. He thought of Emily and Matthew, just born, their skulls still soft.

The male's voice drifted above the engine noise. "Too many machines in the West . . . we've lost our way . . ."

The female voice agreed. "Everything here is so spiritual. People here are hungry for enlightenment, not just material possessions."

The ponytail bobbed in agreement. "We can learn so much from them."

Was this the sort of half-baked philosophy Emily and Matthew were going to preach to him?

He winced as the bus jolted over a pothole. The creases of his shirt were silted in red dust and his mouth was dry. He wiped the face of his watch clean. Five hours to go. Perhaps the bus was not such a good idea after all. It was colder than he'd imagined and his only sweater was jammed at the bottom of his backpack on the rack above his head. He tried but failed to summon interest in the fields, the temples, and the people. The journey seemed interminable and the villages more or less identical. The same bit of scenery appeared to be on a permanent loop. The bus veered around yet another sharp bend and his head banged against the window. He blinked from the sudden pain and rubbed his forehead. It felt like sandpaper.

Below the road, dust and stones rolled down to a small clearing about five meters away, where a crowd had gathered around an upturned cart. In the few seconds before the bus accelerated, he saw a man clutching a rag to a bleeding gash in his forehead with one hand and brandishing a stick in the other. A donkey was lying on its side, still harnessed to the cart. The man was beating the animal. Half its flank had been ripped open and blood was dripping down its leg beneath the loose flap of skin. The donkey was struggling to stand, but its head kept bashing the ground, its lips curled back as it screamed in pain.

Sandy was close enough to see the yellow froth around its mouth and the stick bounce off bare muscles and tendons. He had to get out and help in some way, to stop this cruelty. But before he managed to straighten, the bus pulled away and the clearing disappeared behind a row of scrappy trees. He looked at his clenched knuckles, the bones white under his skin, and wondered if he'd imagined the whole thing. No one else seemed to have noticed.

All the passengers were dozing, their heads bobbing on their chests. The couple in front of him were fast asleep, her head skewed against the window as the male leaned on her shoulder. He wanted to poke them awake and demand to know exactly how this country and its people was so spiritual, why they would flay an innocent animal alive if they were so aware.

Two more hours. He should have listened to the hotel concierge and hired a driver. This whole bus trip was a mistake, a sentimental idea brought on by an affection for the songs of Willie Nelson and things he'd read about Ken Kesey and his Merry Pranksters. He moved his head in circles, trying to get rid of the ache in his neck.

Night fell in a rush. Lamps flickered on either side of the road. Finally the bus lurched into a brightly lit depot in the center of a town. Sandy sat for a minute, his ears still dinning with the noise of the engine. Half the seats were already empty when he pulled his rucksack down from the overhead rack and left the bus, his eyes watering against the smoke from the rows of food stalls. He was thirsty and filthy.

He was in a large square, teeming with jostling crowds: children trying to sell copies of designer handbags or trays of sweets festooned with flies, men and women humping battered suitcases, and Western tourists struggling with their backpacks. Among the excitable gap-year teenagers shrieking as if they were back in the playground, there was a sprinkling of gray heads and sedentary paunches, some consolation that he wasn't the only old fool on the road.

Emily had said she and Matthew would meet him at the hotel, but he still searched the crowds for his son's skinny frame, his daughter's tall, loping figure and her blond hair. But all the European girls had long hair and all the boys were skinny. Most were blond and none were his children.

He fished out the piece of paper with the address of the hotel and turned to face the taxi drivers shouting for his attention. The man nearest him grabbed Sandy's backpack and tipped it into the boot of his tiny dented car before opening the door with a flourish and gesturing for Sandy to get in. Sandy passed him the piece of paper.

"Hotel Mountain View," he said slowly and too loudly.

"Yes, yes," the driver replied, barging into the stream of chaotic traffic. "I know. Very good."

The road was mostly rubble and rock, with intermittent puddles of tarmac hinting at earlier, more prosperous times. The driver shouted at wobbling cyclists and blasted his horn like a Gatling gun. Buses painted in gaudy patterns roared past, with people squashed together on the roofs. On either side of the road were deep open ditches littered with bottles and garbage. Behind the ditches were footpaths and then a continuous row of open-fronted stalls. There were Internet and telephone shops next to ones selling pipes and buckets, and stalls selling scrawny chickens with their fragile necks dangling over wooden slabs, then on a corner, a tiny shrine in a stone niche adorned with sunset-colored marigolds. Emily was right. Everything appeared unreal, as if Sandy were watching a television documentary at home in Battersea.

The driver stopped his car with a flourish outside a hotel down a narrow lane. The mountains were nowhere to be seen. Sandy paid him and dragged his backpack into a filthy lobby decorated with bouquets of dusty plastic flowers. An ancient porter escorted him to a room off the central courtyard. Sandy went straight to the bathroom, looking for the toilet. There wasn't one, just a black hole in the floor with corrugated metal treads on either side. He'd never be able to crap into that, even if his life depended on it. He gingerly placed his feet on the treads and urinated with care. He looked for a button or a plug to flush, but there was only a bucket of dirty water. At the basin, he washed his hands and face in a trickle of brown water, using the antiseptic gel that Emily had told him to buy, then locked the door and lay down on the narrow single bed, just to be still and quiet after the hours of juddering motion.

He fell asleep and woke with a start almost an hour later. There was still another hour and a half before Emily and Matthew would arrive, so he left his room to wander through the lane, which was crammed full of tourists dawdling around stalls selling scarves and plastic deities.

A boy about twelve, thin like a burnt stick, followed him. He carried cages of birds that drooped on their bamboo perches until he prodded them with a cane to make them flutter their brightly colored wings. How could anyone be so cruel?

Sandy was beginning to loathe this notion of traveling. He'd never been entranced by the idea of the hippie trail that invariably ended in wearing a smelly Afghan coat on the King's Road, clutching Hermann Hesse paperbacks, and boring everyone witless with stories of acid dropped on the tops of mountains. He didn't even mind not being in Paris in '68, or never spotting Bill Graham at the Fillmore West or hanging out at the Chelsea Hotel in New York. He'd always felt that his own life was so interesting that he couldn't imagine a better one in another place and time.

Sandy ignored the boy, but he kept circling and wheedling. If he bought the birds and set them free, it would just encourage the boy to capture more. Sandy became angry and shook his fist. The boy shouted and swore, but at last he walked away. Sandy retraced his steps to the hotel and went to his room to wait.

He worried about the boy. He couldn't have been more than eight or nine, yet he was on his own at night. Did he have a family to go to, somewhere to sleep? Then he worried about the birds. Where were they? Did the boy feed them? Or give them water? But his real concern was Matthew and Emily, how the three of them would fare together on this ridiculous sentimental journey of his. Penny wasn't the only one who was skeptical. Tim had warned him not to expect too much. His stomach began growling, then cramping. He rushed into the bathroom and squatted over the black hole.

# Chapter 37

THE THING ABOUT a Harley Street surgery was not so much the expense of an appointment, which was always more than one expected, but the assurance guaranteed by such highly polished brass plaques at the entrance of the building. Jeremy found the right name, pressed a button, and announced himself. The heavy door, glistening with countless coats of black enamel paint, swung open to reveal a small marble-tiled hall leading to another set of heavy doors, this time of polished oak.

It was almost impossible to imagine that any malady could strike in a place protected by such impressively solid architecture. Once past the deferential receptionist, he settled himself in what must have been the drawing room, its high ceiling edged with egg and dart cornices, with a large marble fireplace opposite the windows.

He picked up the latest edition of *Country Life* and waited for his name to be called. The only other person in the room was an old woman who was clicking her teeth. Jeremy glared at her, rearranged one of the many tapestry cushions on the sofa, and snapped open the magazine. Every time Jeremy read *Country Life*, which was not often, he congratulated himself on his good sense never to have lived any part of his adult life outside central London. Tim couldn't wait to immerse himself in Herefordshire, extolling the virtues of home-made elderflower cordial and long rambles through dung-infested sheep fields. Sandy, egged on by Penny, had done his stint in a rented cottage. Only Peter and Jeremy remained faithful to the capital.

There were times when Rosie, in the full prepubescent horse lust stage, begged to move to the country. He might have eventually succumbed. Already the convenience of shunting family life to weekends and school holidays had occurred to him. But it must have occurred to Isobel as well, because she refused to move outside the Royal Borough of Kensington and Chelsea. "I'm not having you prowl around London on your own all week," she said, dishing up a Marks and Spencer ready meal. "The kiss of death to any marriage." Two years later, they were divorced anyway.

Jeremy changed position. He thought about Rosie, what she might be doing. His calls were not returned. His emails remained unanswered. Lately, he had taken to ringing her number two or three times a day just to hear her voice on the answering machine, then hanging up just as she finished speaking. She had a lovely voice, husky with a hint of a lisp. He should have moved to the country and taken up riding with his daughter. He and Rosie could have hacked out together, got to know each other.

Losing Rosie, irrevocably it seemed, hurt so much more than the Psst! scandal. He could justify his actions to himself and lie convincingly about them to others, but not to her. Rosie would never again see anything good or decent about him.

Jeremy had always hoped that at some time in her adult life Rosie would return to him. His most secret hope was that they might work together. Often, smoking late at night on the deck of the *Jezebel*, he had imagined an office with identical desks for him and Rosie, the two of them taking clients to lunch. A double act performed by the corporate elder statesman and his feisty daughter with her fierce green eyes and tumble of auburn hair. He imagined Rosie impressing them with her financial acumen inherited from him.

Jeremy shifted again. It was hard to get comfortable with so many cushions on the sofa. A dull pain banded his middle. When the receptionist called his name, he stood up too quickly and felt faint.

Assurance was all Jeremy wanted. A thorough checkup with all the usual tests would do the trick. It was completely understandable that he felt below par. There had been the undue stress of dealing with that girl, the website, and everything associated with it. Although once she had been told that her testimony could be demolished by any first-year barrister, she'd disappeared. It was one less case for the police to deal with. Psst! forgot about him and fastened its teeth in the next scandal.

It helped that Jeremy discovered, through a private investigator hired by his lawyer, that many stories on the website were provided by a financial PR minion whose employer would not take kindly to one of his staff moonlighting for a cyberspace gossip column.

The receptionist showed him into a room full of swagged chintz resembling a decorator's drawing room from the pages of the magazine Jeremy had just put down. His doctor, Felix Summerscale, rose from behind a huge partner's desk and greeted him like an old friend. For a moment, Jeremy almost believed him, although they only met in this office once a year. Did private doctors take courses in how to put people at ease? Were they graded for bedside manners along with human anatomy and infectious diseases?

"Stress," said Dr. Summerscale, rubbing his hands together to warm them as Jeremy lay shirtless on the narrow patient's table. "The curse of the successful businessman." He poked and prodded, listened to Jeremy's heartbeat, and took his blood pressure. "Nothing to worry about there," he said. "But, you know . . . stress." He shook his head.

Jeremy knew stress was dangerous. He had contemplated a stay in one of those ayurvedic places in Kerala. But that was in India and Sandy was in India. It didn't matter that Sandy was in the opposite end of the country, almost at the Nepalese border according to Peter and Tim. India was not an option. He also considered that Austrian spa, the one where they gave you Epsom salts and potato soup, and solids consisted mainly of spelt bread that you had to chew forty times each mouthful.

In the end he stayed at home. Every morning he walked down the jetty and caught a taxi to his office. Every evening he reversed his journey. Occasionally he met Tim and Peter for lunch, usually around Sloane Square. Once, coming back from the toilet, he saw their heads, bowed together in furtive conversation, snap apart at his approach. He recognized their false cheeriness at his return. It was how they had behaved towards Sandy. Jeremy would have bet his

Ruscha that they were talking about the girl, the website, the whole hushed-up disgrace of it all. It hadn't reached the mainstream press, but they knew. Of course they knew. A week after the Psst! story, Tim had called to ask if he needed any help. Peter wanted to know if he was going to sue. How odd that someone as urbane as Peter didn't know that it was almost impossible to sue a website. They were always several providers ahead of their pursuers. Jeremy told them that the story was completely false. By tacit agreement it was never mentioned again.

Felix Summerscale was pressing a finger around Jeremy's navel. It was ticklish and he squirmed.

"Sorry," said Jeremy. "So childish, to still be ticklish."

Summerscale smiled and gazed at the ceiling. He moved his finger up to below Jeremy's ribs.

"I sometimes feel bloated," said Jeremy. "Uncomfortable."

"Probably heartburn," said Summerscale. "But let's run some tests anyway. Just to be sure. Good thing you're not overweight. I see you've lost a bit since your last visit here."

He had dropped a few kilos lately, without even trying. At first it was good to see a gratifying roominess in his trousers, to fasten his belt at a different, less worn notch. But then it occurred to him that it wasn't normal at his age to lose weight without making an effort.

Maria, his cleaner, told him he was looking very trim as she arranged his shirts in neat rows, coathanger hooks all pointing inwards. "Maybe you in love, Mr. Henderson," she chortled. "And you missing person who not here for you. Too sad to eat."

# Chapter 38

DAMN. HE'D FALLEN asleep and it was already dark. He'd be late for Emily and Matthew. He flapped at the air around him but the buzzing continued, louder, somewhere beneath him. Bloody mosquitoes. His arms were already covered in hard red lumps. The buzzing turned into ringing and he fumbled for his phone.

"Dad." Emily's voice sounded tentative, far away. But the same sweet high timbre, lifting his heart. He sat up, flushed with pleasure and excitement.

"Are you downstairs?" he asked. "I must have fallen asleep, so stupid of me. I'll be down in a minute. Or you could come to the room?" He was already standing, running his hands through his hair, preparing for the beginning of making everything good and whole again. Everything was going to be all right. Not fine, as in Tim's psychological terminology, but all right.

"Well . . . ," Emily said, "the thing is, Matt isn't back yet. He went to meet some people, so let's leave it until the morning." She sounded so casual, as if they'd seen each other yesterday. "You must be tired. Besides, I've got some things to do, at the ashram."

"But I don't have anything to do." He was almost shouting. "I don't have anything to do except see you and Matthew. And I've spent two days getting here. Why can't I come to the ashram with you?"

"Dad," said Emily, in the patient but annoying tones Sandy was sure she'd learned at her mother's knee, "I haven't seen you for months. Ten more hours won't make such a difference. Get something to eat. There's a good place around the corner, the Nirvana Café. Get some sleep. We'll come by in the morning, see the sights."

"In the morning?" This was not what he wanted. This did not fit with his carefully tended dream of a joyful reunion with his children. He sighed and flopped on the bed, deflated but determined not to show it. "So, then, what time will I see you?"

"Oh, nine or ten. Okay?"

It wasn't okay, not one bit, even if it was his dream, not theirs. He'd traveled halfway across the world. He'd spent ten hours hugging his knees at the back of a plane, then another ten hours on a clapped-out bus. He'd listened to interminable inane conversations. He'd seen an animal flayed alive.

"Dad? Are you there?"

"Yes," he replied.

"It'll be great to see you in the morning and you'll be grateful for the night's rest." There were voices in the background. "Got to go."

A click, then silence. Sandy sat on the bed, watching flies orbit the ceiling. Something must have got in his eyes. They were watering. He scratched his mosquito bites and swallowed a Zoloft.

He had to keep calm if this was going to work. Did he imagine that the three of them would waltz around India like some third world reincarnation of the von Trapp family, singing as they tramped up and down the mountains? He should be grateful for any time Matt and Emily would give him. But he wasn't. He felt cheated.

The night stretched ahead of him. He couldn't keep counting flies until he fell asleep again, so he carefully locked his room and left the hotel. Outside, it was cooler than Delhi, but with the same incessant horn honking. Every stall had its own ghetto blaster, each playing a different track at a distorted top volume.

He stood at the corner of the lane, trying to work out where to go. Emily had said he couldn't miss the sign for the Nirvana Café, but he did and chose instead a small nameless place with a group of noisy Germans clustered around the central table. He was in no mood for culinary exploration and ordered lentils and vegetables. At least they would be cooked. As he waited, he flicked through the pages of his guidebook, just for something to do. Everyone was with someone except for him. He didn't want company anyway. A plate of glutinous gray stuff flecked with green eventually arrived at his table.

It was like chewing glue. He pushed it around his plate, then left and retraced his steps back to the hotel.

He swallowed a pill and tried to sleep. Someone was snoring in the room below him, jagged gasps for air, rising in tone until they became high-pitched strangled cries. There was an interminable pause before whoever it was exhaled in long and rattling sighs. Outside the manic horn hitters continued, backed by a cast of barking dogs and howling cats. He should have thought to pack earplugs. He would be awake all night. But just before dawn, he fell asleep.

By eight a.m., he had shaved and dressed with care and was sitting in the lobby, his phone beside him, pretending to read his travel guide, trying not to look up every time he heard the door swing open or the sound of approaching footsteps.

There were two giant-sized Toblerone bars in his pack, a childhood favorite of both Emily and Matthew. He was wishing he'd brought something more useful when suddenly there she was, standing in front of him, thinner than he remembered, and tanned, but still with that luminous triangle of golden hair.

It seemed to Sandy that many of his own features had been replicated in her, but in the transmutation had become finer, more delicate. On Emily, his own large nose had been chiseled into something more aquiline. His wide mouth had been plumped into pinker, fuller curves. The invisible genetic sculptor had also taken Sandy's fair skin and burnished it into a high-cheeked bloom.

She smelled of earth and sandalwood when he hugged her. Too enthusiastically, he knew, but he couldn't help it. Over her shoulder, he looked for Matthew. He always did dawdle behind. He wanted to savor the embrace but Emily pulled back, chewing her lip. Irrationally, he was angry with Matt.

"Trust your brother to be running late," he said, before remembering his own habit for tardiness. "He must have inherited it from me."

"Matt isn't running late. I don't know where he is." She slumped beside him, flushed, and began clawing at her hair. In the excitement of seeing her, he hadn't noticed that her eyes were red, that she'd been crying. "He didn't come back last night and I didn't see him at all yesterday. We had breakfast at the café and he said he was going to meet some guys he knew in London, hang out with them, and be back by the evening. I've checked his room. His stuff's still there, but he's gone."

"It'll be okay," said Sandy, trying to calm her. He scratched at a mosquito bite on his arm. It began to bleed. "We'll find him. We'll go back to the café and ask. Someone will know where he went. He probably drank too much, stayed with someone."

"It's not South Kensington, Dad, for Christ's sake. Not Battersea," Emily hissed. "This is India. People go missing more often than you think. They fall down mountains, they're attacked for ten quid in their pocket. You think it looks so safe because there are people like us, loads of tourists and Western cafés and people speaking English. It's like a parallel world. One path is safe and dandy. Step off that path onto the other one—you never know where it will end up."

Sandy felt paralyzed. Fathers, proper fathers, were confident, broad-shouldered protectors of their children. They knew what to do in crises. He didn't have a clue what to do. What had he told them when they were small? Something about retracing their steps? Or staying in the same place until someone found you? Obsolete advice, unlikely to work in a place like this.

"We'll find him," he said, to convince himself as much as her. "We'll go back to the place you last saw him. We'll ask. Someone must know, someone will have seen him." Emily was sobbing. Sandy went to hug her again.

"Not now, Dad, for Christ's sake." She pushed him away. "I don't need a bloody hug. I should have known. He was worried."

"About what?"

"What do you think? About seeing you, of course. It always sets him off somehow."

The guilt. Always the permanent stain of the bad parent, the absentee father. He would never be rid of it.

They hurried through the streets to the café. The sun was already tightening Sandy's scalp. His eyes itched from the dust as they strode past a queue of women and children waiting with their empty buckets at the public tap. "Hello, hello," the children cried from behind the folds of their mothers' saris. Sandy scooped out the coins from his pocket and placed them in a heap next to a statue festooned with marigolds. Emily took his arm and led him away to the square. They stopped to get their bearings. Sandy bought a bottle of water from a stall. He was out of breath and grateful for the brief rest.

"Can't you get a flask like the rest of us?" snapped Emily, as he drank the water in one long swallow. "Just look at the rubbish. There's no recycling here. You can't nip down to the bottle bank with your empties or leave them out for the bin man."

"I'm sorry, I didn't know." He crushed the empty bottle with his hand and pushed it into his pocket.

Emily ignored him. She covered her head with an orange-and-maroon-striped scarf. Tendrils of hair escaped around her temples and her neck. Her eyes were closed as if in prayer. The veins on her eyelids bloomed like violets and he had a sudden urge to reach over and caress them with his fingers, make her see something good in him again, the way she used to when she was a child.

But she rushed off down a lane without a word, leaving him to scurry behind her, out of breath, heart pounding. By the time they reached the café where Matt and Emily ate most of their meals, sweat was trickling down his back. He flapped his T-shirt to stop it sticking to his chest before wiping his forehead and following Emily inside.

At first he couldn't see anything, but when his vision adjusted, he saw Emily zigzagging between tables of tourists asking about Matthew. Some people didn't bother to look up from their laptops. Others were shoveling down pallid eggs and greasy bacon. His stomach churned.

"Excuse me," he said to the boy behind the counter. "Do you know someone called Matthew? Have you seen him? He is English." Every word a register just below panic. The boy regarded him with weary patience and shook his head. At the end of the café, Sandy caught Emily's eye. She was shaking her head as well.

In the street, shopkeepers were flicking water from buckets onto the footpath in a halfhearted attempt to settle the dust. There were so many bars and cafés, so many young Western tourists, and no one had seen Matthew. Apart from asking questions, Emily said nothing. Her face was tight, her eyes narrow.

Sandy's face was burning. He should have remembered a hat. He stumbled over the uneven cobbles as they walked through the streets. Emily seemed to glide ahead of him. He caught up with her, the rough straps of his sandals rubbing against his ankles. An image of Matthew, stoned and unconscious, came into Sandy's head and would not leave. Should they call the police, or contact the embassy? Emily shook her head and kept steady progress, her speech coming out by rote in every new bar and café.

"Sorry to disturb you. We're looking for someone called Matthew. An English boy. Brown hair. Short. Not very tall."

The lanes had narrowed into alleys by now. The tourists had floated away. So had the bars advertising half-price happy hours and all-you-can-eat noodle bars. Indians now predominated the rows of stalls selling electrical fittings and pipes.

"He wouldn't have come here," panted Sandy. One of his toes was stubbed and oozing blood. "This area is for locals, surely."

Emily shook her head. She kept chewing her lip.

"We're not on the other path just yet, Dad," she said. "Tourists come here too. Someone was talking about a place here, a bar. They said it's somewhere near a temple."

But which temple? The place was awash with them, as well as shrines and statues. Every street corner was marked by some marigold-clad deity surrounded by incense sticks.

"There," said Emily. "Down there." She turned off the alley into a dank narrow path, lit at the end by a purple fluorescent light in the shape of a smiling goddess. The smell of incense and stale cooking oil was thicker here. Halfway along, a heap of plastic bags and bottles smoldered in a reluctant bonfire. Sandy coughed and blinked against the acrid fumes. His eyes watered and all he could see for a moment were gray and flickering shadows, then Emily's scarf gleaming like a sunrise.

The sign on the carved wooden door said CLOSED, COME BACK LATER, but Emily knocked anyway. Loud, and then louder. She stepped back and Sandy heard the latch give, and the door opened, just a crack. Emily pushed past him and into the bar. He remained by the door, uncertain and afraid.

The room was no larger than a single garage, with a bar in one corner made from stacked beer kegs covered by rough planks. The wall behind the bar was covered with hundreds of tiny mirrors glinting in the dim light of one weak bulb hanging from the ceiling. Shelves stacked with beer and spirits covered the remaining walls. In the corner opposite the bar was a heap of large cushions around a low table littered with empty bottles and full ashtrays. There was the yeasty smell of stale beer and unwashed bodies, then cigarettes and the sweet pungent smell of dope.

Somewhere a puppy yapped. There was a sudden loud crack, as if someone had thrown something. The puppy began whimpering. Sandy stepped further inside and nearly tripped over a piece of curled-up linoleum, one of many mismatched shapes that made up the floor. His stubbed toe began to throb. He was almost grateful for the pain, to feel something else instead of panic and fear.

Emily was standing in the empty space looking exhausted and defeated. On one side of the bar was a narrow hall. He hadn't noticed it at first because of the distortions of the mirrors. At the entrance, he listened. Everything was silent. The puppy had stopped whimpering. He walked in and headed for the hall. At the end was a door, rimmed by daylight. Behind him, Emily's sandals clip-clopped on the floor. Her breath fluttered against his neck.

He prodded the door. It fell open into a tiny yard, stacked with crates of empty bottles and cans of cooking oil. A collapsed sofa was pushed against the back wall. Matthew lay sprawled on it with his head half-buried under a pillow. His mouth was crusted with vomit. It was down his T-shirt as well, and his jeans. Still breathing though. "Thank you," Sandy whispered to himself, stunned by relief.

"He's all right, he's breathing," he said to Emily. "I can't believe you knew where to find him. You're amazing."

"No, Dad," she replied. Now that they'd found Matthew she seemed to regain her energy. "It's just a process of deduction." She shook Matthew, at first gently, then with more force. He didn't move. She tapped his cheeks, rubbed his temples, and wet the end of her scarf with water from her flask and wiped his face. Sandy fidgeted behind her, heavy and useless.

"C'mon, Matt, wake up, time to go. Matt, we need to get going now." It seemed an age before Matthew stirred and opened his eyes. He looked up and smiled, wiped spittle from the corners of his mouth.

"Hey, Em," he slurred, "Angel Em. Thanks for finding me. Sorry." His eyes closed, then opened and focused on Sandy. "Sorry, Sandy," he mumbled. "Got held up."

"It's okay," Sandy replied. "We're here now, we'll take you back to the hotel. Everything will be good, you'll see."

The words came out so easily. Why wouldn't they? It was his own morning-after litany, muttered to himself more often than he could remember. He would pat Matt on the shoulder, tell him not to worry but not to do it again. Everyone got excessive now and then. No big deal.

He helped Matthew to sit up and was looking around for his son's shoes when he heard Emily behind him.

"Oh Matt," she said, drumming her fingers against the wall. "Look what you've done, look at the mess of everything."

Sandy helped Matt to his feet and together they limped back through the bar to the path. Emily was overreacting, he thought. Matt was safe. They'd get him back to the hotel. Everything would be all right. Matt would sleep it off and they'd have dinner together, plan some little trips outside the town. At some stage, maybe when Emily was off at one of her classes, he'd take Matt aside and they'd talk about their substance problems. Not quite how he had planned to bond with his son, but it might be a good time to apologize. Justin was big on the power of apologies. At the time, drinking his instant coffee in the church hall, Sandy doubted the ability of three words to usher in a new era of family harmony. Now he was prepared to give it a whirl.

Matt's head lolled on Sandy's shoulder. "Come on, boyo," said Sandy, half carrying, half dragging him back to the lane. "We'll find a taxi, get you back to the hotel, clean you up. You'll feel better in the morning. Everything will be better."

From behind, he heard Emily again. "You bloody fool."

He hoisted Matt higher and turned around, ready to tell her not to be so harsh, to give her brother a break. But Emily wasn't staring at Matthew. She was glaring at him. "You don't get it, you bloody idiot," she kept shouting. "You did this. It's all your fault."

# Chapter 39

PENNY HAD STARTED to look in the mirror again. She didn't
like what she saw. Lines careering from her mouth to her jaw, nests
of wrinkles around her eyes, and blotches on her nose. If she blinked,
she saw her mother's querulous bleak stare on her own face. She
wanted her former self back, the one who had been content with
her own company, who didn't care about her appearance or her body.

She was also angry with herself that one dinner with a man who
was clearly involved with another woman could demolish her so easily. For the first time since she'd moved to France, she was lonely. The
woman who only several months ago had sat so happily in the café,
congratulating herself to have traveled beyond the morass of children
and ex-husbands, was nowhere to be found. Someone else had moved
in, a resentful, vain neurotic spreading an atmosphere of gloom.

In a crude attempt to reestablish self-sufficiency, she took to ignoring the telephone, leaving the machine to pick up messages. But
one afternoon she forgot and picked it up, just after she'd come in
from watering the vegetable garden. The new carrot and bean seedlings were growing with ferocious energy. Each morning she would
walk down to her carefully weeded beds to find some of the plants
felled by their overnight spurts of growth. Perhaps life exhausted
them as well.

"Hello," she said, kicking off her shoes.

It was an annoyingly cheerful Robert, and she heard herself agreeing to have lunch with him, and his partner. It would be churlish to
refuse. And it would help her get over her childish crush, to see Robert with her, this woman called Laura. She had spent too much time
on her own. It would also stop her thinking about the other three in

India, remind herself that it was only arrogance that made her think she could control events, be the glue that stuck everyone together.

"What about the café just off the square?" Robert's question cut across her thoughts. "You told me they have the best gizzards in town. Let's see how Laura does on the entrails. Half past one or thereabouts?"

"Perfect," replied Penny, remembering to smile into the telephone, so she would sound pleased. She scrubbed her nails free of dirt and changed her clothes.

The path to town was already cracked and dry. A line of industrious ants crawled across the dirt, and bees droned through the last of the spring flowers. A breeze stirred through the pine trees. Above, in the cloudless sky, a buzzard circled. The morning mist had burned away, leaving the blond stone buildings of the town sharply outlined against the darker mountains.

As she reached the last bend before joining the road, she saw a fallen bird's nest on the side of the path. It was empty and broken in two. Nestled among the fine twigs and stalks was a clump of tawny fledgling feathers. She carefully picked them out and put them in the zippered part of her bag. Something for the new doll's house. A fan perhaps, to set on a table in the drawing room.

Sarlat was filling with tourists. It was early enough in the season for café and shop owners to smile and welcome the milling groups of ample-buttocked women in shorts and their skinny male companions. By the end of September, proprietors would turn surly, worn down by constant demands for instant coffee and Twinings tea bags. For now, they were happy.

Just before she entered the café, Penny raked her hands through her hair and stood straighter. She was suddenly conscious of the swell of her stomach, her breasts straining against her ill-fitting bra. Robert and Laura were sitting at a window table in the back. Penny gave what she hoped was a cheery wave and joined them. Robert jumped up and kissed her on both cheeks. Laura looked at her quizzically and shook hands with a firm grip.

"Ah, a real native," said Laura. "How do you do? Robert said he was so pleased to have met you. The first proper conversation he'd had since he got here."

Penny smiled. "That can't be true. He has Montaigne as a companion, after all."

Robert ordered a carafe of wine and they perused the menu before settling on *salade périgourdine*.

"We'll be mainlining cholesterol," Penny said to Laura. "It's got the lot—gizzards, duck breast, and foie gras."

"Good," said Laura. "We can diet when we're dead. I can't tell you how many friends of mine who've jogged and counted calories for decades and have ended up with heart attacks and ruined knees. Or worse, in a coffin."

Penny surreptitiously observed the other woman. She was rail thin, elegant in a weathered, tanned way with dark eyes and sleek brown hair cut close to her head. Despite her American accent, her jeans, and faded top, she had a *parisienne* air about her. Penny could imagine her cycling with brio about the Left Bank. Laura gesticulated and waved her arms about in a European way. Penny noticed a crop of thick dark hair under her arms.

"What in God's name is this?" asked Laura, as their food arrived. She speared a wrinkled brown ball on her fork. "It looks like a fossilized turd."

"That," said Penny, "is one of the famous gizzards. Taste it. They're good."

Laura obediently chewed and swallowed. "I agree and I retract my earlier statement. More like a fossilized testicle. Or what I imagine a fossilized testicle might look and taste like."

Penny had to admit that she liked Laura. She was interesting and funny. Robert clearly shared her opinion, patting Laura's arm as they spoke and ruffling her hair as he went to the bar for more wine.

What a fool she'd been, indulging in romantic adolescent fantasies. She was past all that anyway. So much more peaceful to have them both as casual friends. Laura looked the type to enjoy a walk. She would invite them home, for a bit of a hike through the hills, then supper. The company would do her good.

"So how did you two come across each other?"

Penny jumped out of her reverie. "In the café, another one nearby, and then we had supper together. I think he was lonely, missing you."

Laura arched an eyebrow. "He might have been lonely, but he wasn't missing me, as in 'missing,' as in 'romance.' I've known Robert a long time. I knew his wife. We worked together. Robert and I are good friends, but that's it. He suggested I visit him because I've just come out of a long relationship."

She leaned towards Penny. "You've been tucked away in the country for too long. I like Robert, but I don't sleep with men. I mean, I've tried it, but I didn't like it. It seems to me that you and Robert should get to know each other better." Laura lifted her shoulders in a Gallic fashion and tilted her head to one side. Penny blushed. What was she to make of such a comment? Did she have an invisible tattoo on her forehead? Lonely woman in search of a romantic encounter? She was saved from having to reply as Robert sat down, brandishing a full carafe. He refilled Laura's glass, but Penny shook her head.

"I have to make it back up the path." She knew her cheeks were still red. "And I have to get to the post office." She reached down for her bag before offering a tentative invitation. "Would you both like to come for supper? We could walk for a bit beforehand. There's a kind of cave and a good view from the hill above me. Friday? Around six?"

"Terrific," said Robert. His eyes crinkled against the afternoon sun. "I'll call you, get the directions."

She thanked him for lunch, kissed them both on the cheek, and scurried out of the café. She would go to the post office on her way home, check if anything had arrived for the new doll's house. She would concentrate on that.

All the way back home, striding up the path until she was hot and breathless, she felt the two small parcels in her bag knocking against her side in a steady rhythm. When she reached the courtyard, she stood gazing at the solid wall of mountains across the valley, their peaks flaming in the afternoon light, until she regained her breath.

She unlocked the kitchen door and carefully unwrapped the parcels. The first was a miniature cream Aga with controls you could actually turn, from Kent, Connecticut. She held it in her hand, carefully opening and shutting the oven doors. So intricate and exact, worth waiting for. The second parcel, from a Somerset address, was even more satisfying: a palm-sized copy of a mid-eighteenth-century console table with tapered legs and a bronzed base. Another eBay find, another early-morning pounce.

Penny dusted them and placed them next to the special box in the hall. The Aga would go in the basement kitchen, and the positions of cook and kitchen maids would be filled by a family of apron-wearing Labradors, salvaged at the end of Emily's Sylvanian Families phase. Matthew's Mickey Mouse pajamas would be cut into a pantry tablecloth and fragments of his favorite mini mirror ball, brought home by Sandy after some trip, would tile the master bathroom. The mirror ball had broken almost immediately, but she had kept the pieces for all these years. Everything would come to life once it had found its home in the new doll's house.

The house was silent apart from the ticking of her mother's old grandfather clock. This was the time of day she liked best, walking from room to empty room, feeling the last of the sun warm her face, thinking what she would cook for supper, what she would read that evening, planning the next day.

But the usual calming routine wasn't working. She was still jangling from her lunch and Laura's suggestion that she seduce Robert, or at least make some kind of play for him. Also, she couldn't stop comparing her oh-so-bourgeois and solitary life in France to the one that Emily, Matthew, and Sandy were no doubt enjoying in India.

She had become obsessed with domestic hygiene. She rubbed her hands with antiseptic gels; she sprayed the kitchen table with a homemade concoction of vinegar and lavender oil, as if she could keep at bay what she began to call the subcontinental effect.

There were times when Penny thought India was colonizing her small French outpost. All three of them were besieging her by email and text messages. From his hotel lounge, equipped with free Wi-Fi ("one of the few things in this country that works"), Sandy offered detailed accounts of his indigestion. When he wasn't pondering his own entrails, he worried that Emily appeared completely besotted by this mysterious guru she'd never seen.

Over dinner one night, Emily had told Sandy that she would do anything that Rosheme asked of her. When Sandy asked would Emily jump off a bridge if Rosheme told her to, Emily replied that they would never ask her to do anything without a good reason. She had become very attached to one of Rosheme's followers, a young man called Samten who went to university in London.

Sandy also worried about Matthew's problem with "substances." Sandy had stopped drinking, in case she was wondering. Penny had been right to ask if it was a bit late for a gap year. But he was running late for so many things in his life that one more scarcely seemed to matter.

From an Internet café, Emily said everything was going as well as could be expected. "Dad is trying hard and sometimes he is very trying, but we're doing some fun things, getting out and seeing some of the amazing things around the town. We'll get there in the end. You're not to worry."

This immediately made Penny worry a lot, particularly as Emily had not been specific about what Penny wasn't to worry about. Matthew confined himself to cryptic texts.

"AAMOI why U marry him? AISI, nothing in common. Am seeing him 2moro. ADIP xxm."

Penny wanted to leave them alone, but they wouldn't let her. She replied dutifully to each email while thinking that, for a divorced family, they spent far too much time communicating with each other. It reminded her of their old life, how it didn't work. Remembering that dispelled the envy that somehow the three of them had managed a harmony that had eluded the four of them together.

Instead she began to feel guilty about spending money that could feed an Indian family for weeks, if not months. Annoyed with herself for feeling guilty, she walked down to the Wednesday market and bought more food for the dinner with Robert and Laura: a plump roasting chicken, freshly churned unsalted butter, and a perfectly ripe brie. On the way home, she dropped into Nigel's office and set up a standing order to Oxfam. It was something.

By five o'clock on Friday, the chicken was stuffed with onions and a great bunch of tarragon, ready for the oven. She washed potatoes, carrots, and spinach from the garden and baked an apple tart, looking up an old recipe of her mother's. She dusted off a good Bergerac red for the brie and chilled a white Montravel for the chicken. There was nothing else to do except wait for them to arrive.

The sun was already dipping behind the pines, but the courtyard flagstones were still warm. Fat bees hovered over the valerian and lavender, now in full flower. It was as she had hoped: a kind summer. She planned to take Robert and Laura along the goat path to the top of the hill and what she had imagined might once have been a cave. It was an ideal predinner walk, energetic but not strenuous, taking only an hour and a half. She was congratulating herself on keeping away from the mirror all day when she heard footsteps behind her. It was Robert. He was alone.

"Where's Laura?" she asked, wiping her hands on her trousers before going in for a quick peck on his cheek. This was not what she'd envisaged. She wanted a pleasant walk, a convivial dinner with three people. Now she had to wade through an evening freighted with possibility.

"That has to go down as one of the most downbeat welcomes I've ever had." He laughed. "But I guess I'll survive. Laura sends her apologies. She's got some kind of gastric bug and is lying low."

"I'm sorry," said Penny. "Sorry also for my very poor welcome. I need to brush up on my social skills."

In the kitchen, as he declined anything stronger than water, she watched him glancing around. She imagined her home through his eyes, probably too loving-hands-at-home for his New York taste; God knows what he would make of the latest doll's house project in the sitting room, its Palladian columns waiting for a roof, the three floors of rooms half-painted, bits and pieces all over the floor.

Head in the oven as she placed the chicken on a tray, she heard the clatter of his feet on the flagstones change to a thump as he reached the wooden hall floor, and then a muffled thud as he stepped through to the rugs in the sitting room. She stood up and waited, almost willing him to make fun of the doll's house, because then she would have a good reason not to like him and everything could revert to normal.

Silence. At the door of the sitting room, she saw Robert crouched down, peering behind the columns.

"This is amazing," he said.

"Ready to go?" she asked, thinking that he meant the opposite, as she did when she used that word.

"But I haven't finished admiring your work," he said. "It's quite something, so intricate."

Was he patronizing her? She couldn't decide. "There is a school of thought that says it's a stupid waste of time: I'm fiddling with matchwood while they in India are burning with inspiration."

Robert straightened, rubbing the base of his spine with his hand. The movement was endearing, a small indication of a physical frailty, that all was not whipcord muscle and perfectly balanced tendons.

"Why is what you're doing any less valid than what they're doing, or not doing? You know that old Hemingway dictum—don't confuse action with movement. Enlightenment or lack of it is not about geography."

"You're right. I shouldn't be so touchy about things." She smiled. "Let's go. We should catch the sunset from the top if we leave now."

# Chapter 40

FOR THE NEXT two days, Sandy tried to find a good time to apologize. He didn't know what he was going to say. He knew only that he had to say something. But Emily was too busy at the ashram for anything more than a five-minute coffee, and Matt said he had a stomach bug. Sandy was not to visit. It might be contagious. Sandy hung around his hotel sending emails, reading, and feeling sorry for himself. Finally Matt called and asked him to his hotel. "For tea," said Matthew. "Just a quick one." Sandy was out of the hotel and in a taxi in less than five minutes.

An almost-naked man, lean with a beard and matted hair, stood completely still on a corner, oblivious to the traffic and the crowded pavement. He was smiling, a beatific grin, as he lifted his head to the sky. Maybe, Sandy thought, he should become like this man, a sadhu. Just take off your clothes, put on a loincloth, and keep walking. Enlightenment and peace would surely follow. Or maybe not.

His reverie was interrupted by the driver swerving hard and braking outside the hotel. Sandy paid the fare, forgetting to bargain, and went inside. He was expecting it to be some kind of fetid doss-house, but it was surprisingly large and light behind the run-down exterior. Sandy peered beyond the foyer, where people lounged on a neat lawn in the afternoon sun.

It wasn't just a crowd of teenagers. There was a group of American women, all with gray hair, and the man sitting cross-legged on the grass was about his age. He hadn't minded about not staying with Emily, because she was living in the ashram. But to be hived off to some dump of a hotel, the name of which was an absolute lie, when he could have been here in comfort, near his son? Neither of them wanted him. It hurt.

He looked around for Matthew. Perhaps he was still in his room. But when Sandy asked the hotel clerk, the man stopped dusting his desk and beamed at him as if he was about to impart some wonderful news and produced a folded piece of paper from his pocket.

"From your son," the clerk said, giving it to Sandy. "Lovely boy, so kind."

Sandy quickly unfolded the piece of paper, worried that Matthew's stomach bug had suddenly got worse and that someone had taken him to hospital. Sandy saw the hurried handwriting, so like his own. Something had come up. Matthew couldn't make it after all. He would call Sandy later, or the next day.

> *I am gall, I am heartburn. God's most deep decree*
> *Bitter would have me taste: my taste was me.*

The lines swam into his consciousness unwanted and unbidden. Sometimes he wished old Gerard would take a running jump into someone else's psyche. He no longer yearned for success. He did not hunger for perfect note moments. None of that mattered anymore. All Sandy wanted was a chance with his children.

He decided to walk back to his hotel because each step would take him somewhere and physical movement would calm him, even though his sense of direction was erratic at best. The hotel was only about ten minutes' walk away, near a plump white dome of a temple. He'd seen it from his room. The dome would be a beacon.

He was confused in less than a minute. Somehow, his surroundings had shifted. The lane he found himself in was narrow and winding. There was another temple dome in front of him. Was it the same one?

Sandy wasn't sure, so he turned back to regain his bearings. In his head he kept hearing Emily's shouted accusations, and Hopkins's lines of self-loathing. He would never be able to make it up to his children. He was a fool to have thought it was possible. He had left it too late.

Everything was disjointed and disappearing into something else. He looked around him, certain the lane he'd walked down was lined with stalls selling rolls of linen and synthetic satins embroidered with fierce dragons. He remembered because the smell of chemicals on the fabric had made his eyes water. But the stalls had somehow disappeared and had been replaced by shops selling pieces of pipe and coils of wire.

"Mountain View Hotel? Please? Where?" he asked one of the shopkeepers. The man nodded and pointed towards a smaller lane. Sandy was doubtful, but the man insisted. "Yes, yes. Hotel." Sandy turned into a narrow row of food stalls selling spinach and carrots and piles of fresh ginger and turmeric. Further along a young girl flipped doughnuts in a vat of smoking oil. It was hot and airless. His stubbed toe ached. His ankles were chafed, probably blistered. Every step hurt.

A group of young men gathered around a bicycle laughed at him and shouted something. One of the men, shirtless, with his jeans slung low, raised his arms and pointed an imaginary gun. The others laughed and urged him on. Sandy was scared. If the men came at him, he could do nothing. There was no point of refuge, no shops or cafés with English signs where he could retreat to safety. Sandy turned his back on them and hobbled off in a different direction, down yet another lane. Snorts of laughter followed his progress.

Under the now-familiar aromas of cooking oil, chili, and cumin, there was a smell of something sweet and close. Before he could turn away, he saw a sad trickle of blood course through the dust, as a young boy behind a meat stall wiped his cleaver. On the table lay a small goat, still twitching, its pale eyes frozen in agonized surprise.

Sandy retched. Everything about the town was repugnant and alien. All he could think of was getting out of this hideous cruel place. But there were no taxis or cars anywhere, no Western tourists, only bicycles, carts, and far too many people crammed together, jostling for their own tiny piece of space. Everywhere he looked was another lane, another row of stalls or a dim alleyway, and there he was, just standing there, unable to move and not knowing what to do.

He needed to stay calm, to remember he was in a small town with a center and a periphery. It wasn't a maze, he told himself. He would walk with his shadow at his front and eventually find himself somewhere with a taxi or another white face. But the lanes grew even smaller, and it was so crowded that his shadow merged into all the others. When he looked up, there were no temple domes, just the haze that stung his eyes. He thought he would never escape.

Suddenly there was an eddy of air as the lane turned and widened. The press of people melted behind him and he was in an open square with buses, motorcycles, and perspiring white faces. All the time he had been lost in that other, parallel world, he'd been only minutes away from the comforting tourist landmarks of squares and cafés, now brightly lit by multicolored neon signs as the day fell away.

He passed tables of people drinking beer and salivated at the film of condensation on the bottle, the head of foam in the glass, remembering and craving the taste of it. He turned away and bought a Coke from a street vendor. He drank the bottle in one gulp, grateful for the distraction of the burn at the back of his throat as he waved for a taxi and told the driver the name of his hotel. All he wanted was a shower, even if it was only a tepid trickle, and a pharmaceutically induced sleep.

Later, in his room, just after he swallowed another pill, he sent a text to Emily and Matthew. He punched out the letters with painstaking care, cursing his clumsiness.

"Give me a chance please. I love you both so much."

Hi Mum,

A while ago, back in England, I went to this place called Jump. It was in Dorset, a kind of self-discovery thing. Emily talked me into it before she left. I guess she thought it might help. One of the things they asked us to do was to write a letter that you didn't have to send. I wrote one to Sandy. I only got through one page when I kept repeating again and again how much I hated him, how he was a fat arsey bastard who talked crap all his life.

It was a bit stupid. Anyhow this is another one I'm writing but not sending. The thing is, us being here, me, Sandy, and Em, it isn't working out. I had a bit of a blip, as we like to call it in what's left of our family, and got lost in more ways than one. Anyhow, Em and Sandy found me down some lane and dragged me out. Sandy had to half carry me until we found a taxi to take us back to the hotel. The first two taxis drove off because I'd been sick. Funny. I'd always thought of this place as being so filthy dirty. I'd never thought of anyone worrying about keeping anything clean. Let me tell you here and now, they're pretty obsessed by it, almost as much as we are, although in a different way. But I digress. After they found me, and on the way back to the hotel, Emily kept shouting at Sandy about what he'd done and that everything was his fault. I guess she meant me, or the mess of me and how I can't seem to make anything work for myself.

It made me remember when you used to nag him about doing things with me and not being around for me and everything. I suppose you thought I couldn't hear you. You used to whisper, but you still had the red voice thing going on. And you meant well, you were trying to look out for me, but it made me feel so shitty, because until I heard you say all that stuff, I hadn't realized that Sandy didn't want to spend time with me, or give me any thought, or that he was so obsessed by himself. I don't think I would have realized it either, not until I was a lot older, and then maybe it wouldn't have mattered. I reckon it would have been better if I hadn't known that.

So what I'm trying totell you is that I can't seem to get myself out of the past. Dad pisses me off, but I don't do anything about it. I don't want to be like him and yet I want him to like me. I want him to be proud of me. Em says, and she's right, that we had it absolutely fine. The thing is, I don't feel so fine. I used to imagine sometimes that you thumped us and that Dad had a crack habit or something. Or maybe you both left us, and we were on our own, just me and Em. That way, there would be something real to feel bad about. I'd have something to hang it on. How mad is that? Here where everyone is so poor, I feel guilty about having had so much and still moaning on, as you used to say.

I've started to go to this orphanage place, just to help out a bit. It's run by the Rosheme people, Em's fave. We make these enormous pots of vegetables and lentils, we boil up vats of rice, and that's what the kids eat. Every now and then there are eggs, but they cost so much money. There's this big sign up saying no one must kill any living thing, but they don't take much notice if they can afford meat every now and then.

There is this kid, Adjubal. He's about eight and he follows me around when I'm there. Maybe he thinks I'm his big brother or something. He had this big boil thing on his neck, so gross. I went to the Internet café to look up a cure. Some sites said tea tree oil was good, but I couldn't find any. The other thing they recommended was turmeric, so I made a kind of paste of it and put it on a bandage. I changed it every time I went there, and after about ten days, it was gone. Kind of exploded really, and there was this disgusting pus smell, but now it's better. I don't see him worrying about where his parents are or why they left him here. I wish I were more like him and not so caught up in myself. Okay, enough of that.

All the kids love football and think David Beckham is God, but they keep losing the balls because when they kick them over the wall, the people won't give them back. They say the children shouldn't be playing, they should be working. I'm trying to teach them basketball instead, because I found a hoop behind a shed. But we're not too sure of the rules.

This is about the longest thing I've ever written, longer than a school essay. The ones I managed to finish anyway. So I'll stop now and send you a text.

Love you Mum

# Chapter 41

"DO YOU THINK they ever repaint the ceiling here? Or it's just that color from everyone smoking so much in the old days?"

Tim peered inside the brasserie. "Does it matter?"

He drank his beer, wiping the foam from his mouth. Along with Arthur's, this restaurant always made Tim think of Sandy. Sandy in one of the corner banquettes, sometimes with Penny by his side, more often on his own, schmoozing producers and musicians, eyeing the girls with their carrier bags from Joseph across the road. Sandy drinking tea with that pop legend who ended up managing that tiny singer.

Tim watched the pigeons pecking under his table and waited a few seconds for the name to swim up to the surface of his brain. Adam Faith. And the singer was Leo Sayer. The three of them would chortle away for hours.

Peter shrugged. "All this DIY work at home has got to me. The ceiling isn't important."

Ever since Tim could remember, the ceiling had been the same nicotine color and the chairs the same burgundy leather. Even the perspiring waiters looked the same, simultaneously harassed and bored, dropping plates of steak and frites onto the tables with a clatter.

Unusually, Jeremy was late. They hadn't met since early summer. Jeremy had been away, then busy, and Tim had gone on a trauma management course in Cardiff while Peter had repainted Frieda's flat. Tim had pushed for a lunch, or at the very least a drink. For once, he had a story to tell in which he was the hero, the man with the money. A Dutch bank had approached him about working for them three days a week, a kind of one-man psychological health unit. Six lovely fat figures were mentioned. He couldn't wait to tell the others. How good it would be, to escape the usual role of passive listener, to be able to contribute something more than psychological maxims or anecdotes about the mad farmer down the road.

It was a day of confused seasons; the air carried late summer's heat and dust, yet the leaves had already begun to fall. Passersby flaunted what was left of their holiday suntans. A group of children dressed in red-and-white-checked uniforms waited at the pedestrian crossing. "Do you like your nanny?" Tim heard one freckled girl ask her friend. "I like the weekday one better than the weekend one," the friend replied, fiddling with her plaits. The traffic lights changed and their teacher marched them across the road. If Angie had been here, she would have said their parents didn't deserve to have children. She was so excited about the new job, suggesting a trip to Venice and making plans for the garden. A wave of affection for Angie swept through him. He scanned the menu, which appeared not to have changed in thirty years.

"Let's order," said Peter, looking at his watch. "Jeremy must be held up somewhere."

What was Peter's hurry? For someone who had scaled down their work commitments to the point of early retirement, Peter appeared unnecessarily agitated.

"Maybe another beer?" asked Tim. He wanted Peter to relax, so that when Jeremy arrived, Tim would have an attentive audience for his good news.

"Okay, but let's order at the same time," said Peter. They agreed on hamburgers. Together they flagged down a waiter, then sat in companionable silence until Tim felt, rather than saw, Peter stiffen as Jeremy got out of his taxi, and then, just as quickly, collect himself with a quick gulp of beer and a shifting in his seat.

The man approaching their table was stooped, with an old person's gait. The shoulders of his jacket hung limp and empty halfway down his arms and the collar of his shirt gaped around his neck. Only Jeremy's hair, balding and gray, was still the same. All the plumpness from his face had disappeared, and his eyes, staring out of hollowed sockets, were tinged yellow.

Tim forgot about his planned announcement and made an effort to assume his therapist's mode. He tried to look straight at Jeremy but somehow his eyes wandered above his friend's head. He wanted to say how scared Jeremy looked and how scared he was himself, but he couldn't.

"Jeremy, looking bloody trim!" Tim leaped up and clasped his elbow. He waved at a waiter, trying to think what to say, ashamed by his own lie.

"Good to see you, mate. Have a drink."

He should have known how to react when something was so palpably wrong. He should have been able to ask the question, listen to the answer, empathize, transfer, enable. He should be able to at least acknowledge the shocking change in Jeremy's appearance. But he didn't do anything.

Peter had taken refuge behind his glass, unable to stop staring at Jeremy.

"Beer? Or wine?" asked Tim.

"Maybe water," replied Jeremy, slumped in his chair. It was one of those uncomfortably small café chairs, and still it looked big for him. "Not sure if I'll stay on for lunch. Need to get back."

"All work and no play," said Tim. "You know what they say." No number of trauma management courses could help him escape his platitudes. He hated his own ineptness.

Beside him, Peter lurched towards Jeremy, almost elbowing Tim out of his chair. "Cut the crap, Tim. Jeremy, what is going on? What's wrong with you? You look bloody terrible."

"Ah," said Jeremy, leaning an elbow on the table. The back of his hand was covered with purple blotches, like a bruised and rotting plum. He must have seen Peter wince, because he removed it immediately. "You've noted something is amiss."

"Of course something is amiss," said Peter. "You look half dead."

"Actually," said Jeremy, his knee starting to judder against the table, "I am almost three-quarters dead. Pancreatic cancer. So efficient. From diagnosis to death in only three months. That's what my cancer team tells me. Don't you like that? Cancer team. So jolly."

He smiled. In his shrunken face, his teeth appeared enormous. White crusts of spittle had settled in the corners of his mouth.

"You don't have to make a joke about it," said Tim. "It's nothing to laugh about."

He wanted to reach over and hug Jeremy, to weep at this terrible thing that was happening. He wanted to do something to make it better. "There must be some treatment, somewhere," Tim said. "The Mayo Clinic, Sloan-Kettering, one of those places."

Peter interrupted with a sweep of his hand. "I reckon Jeremy would have that covered. What about Rosie?"

"We, ah, haven't spoken for a while." His voice faltered. In the afternoon sun, his face was beaded in perspiration. "I've decided not to have any treatment. Only palliative care, as the team calls it. I've decided, for the first and last time in my life, to let things just happen."

"You'll need support; you have us," said Tim, almost pleading. "Angie and me, Peter, we'll do anything, anything at all. Why didn't you call? Why didn't you tell us?" His questions dribbled into silence.

Jeremy shrugged. "There is nothing to be done."

Across the road two paparazzi on motorbikes were snapping at some girl leaving the hairdresser's. Her hair was pulled into a tight chignon. She posed at the traffic lights, hand on her hip, before darting into a waiting car.

"My mother used to wear her hair like that," said Jeremy, "though I don't suppose that girl would welcome the comparison."

"What about Sandy?" asked Tim. "Will you tell him? Do you want me to let him know?"

Jeremy sighed. "Matthew is my godson. I'm in contact with him. But no, since you ask, neither of them know and I'd rather you didn't tell them. Please. It's the one thing I am going to beg for." His hands were shaking and he tried for a smile. "God knows, you owe me that. I've paid for enough lunches in my time."

The waiter appeared behind Jeremy, brandishing their plates of hamburgers surrounded by heaped French fries and little jars of condiments. He banged the food on the table and strode off.

"He might have asked if I wanted anything," said Jeremy. "It's only polite." The smell of seared meat and toasted buns wafted about them. Just in time, Jeremy found his handkerchief and put it to his mouth, silently retching. Tim stood and rushed behind him, holding his jerking shoulders. It seemed there was no flesh left. It was hard to see clearly against the afternoon sun, but he felt sure Peter was weeping. Tim felt Jeremy sag against him, then recover himself.

"For heaven's sake, do sit down," rasped Jeremy. He wiped his mouth and put his handkerchief in his pocket, a small movement that caused him to wince. "Thank you, but I'm perfectly fine now. I'll just have some water and then I must go."

Jeremy's hand trembled as he reached for the glass. He tried to steady it as he sipped, but some of the water slopped onto his shirt and dripped down onto his trousers. "So clumsy of me, apologies."

He gave a small salute, heaved himself up, and almost limped to the edge of the pavement. But Tim was there before him. He embraced Jeremy, wiped away the cold beads of perspiration on Jeremy's forehead with his hand. He heard Jeremy's jagged breathing as Peter joined them. Tim felt Peter's arms lock around the two of them and then Jeremy trying to break clear.

A taxi stopped at the traffic lights. Jeremy hailed it and the door swung open. He got in, his hand shaking a final wave as he pulled the door closed. Tim took Peter's arm. He watched the taxi drive away, not noticing the girl on the scooter who nearly ran over their feet, not hearing the apologies of her mother. Tim didn't register anything at all until the waiter came over and asked had they finished eating. Tim nodded and, still holding Peter's arm, slowly walked back to the table, all the while thinking that he would never see Jeremy again, that money and power counted for nothing against something like cancer.

"What should we do?" he asked. Peter didn't reply. He slumped in his chair, his chin wobbling.

"What's happened to us?" asked Tim. "We used to be invincible, remember?"

Peter clenched his jaw and said nothing. They sat on, unable to talk and unable to leave each other. Half an hour passed and Peter got up. "I'm sorry, I have to go. I wish I could think of something to say or do, but I can't. It's too sad."

A quick embrace and Peter was gone. On his own, exhaustion crashed in on Tim. He thought of Jeremy, dying alone without the comfort of his daughter or Sandy and his other friends, almost as if Jeremy thought he didn't deserve anything more than a solitary death.

A shadow fell across the table. The waiter, standing impatiently, wanting him either to order something or leave. Tim paid and left. Suddenly, he couldn't wait to get home to Angie, to tell her what had happened.

# Chapter 42

THE THREE OF them turned towards the cave and walked in silence up to the gate. A hawker selling white scarves patrolled his pitch. Sandy waved him away, but Emily and Matthew bought one each. The hawker ushered them through to the path, which was steep with rough stone steps cut into it, each one as high as Sandy's knee. Ropes of faded triangular prayer flags festooned the stumpy pine trees growing on either side.

Emily looked around wide-eyed and bounded up the steps, with Matthew close behind her. Sandy fell behind, exhausted and disoriented. He was determined to keep climbing, although his thighs and calves had begun to shake. The path traversed back and forth up the mountain. He thought it would never end.

On a bend above him, Emily and Matthew paused, waiting for him as he stumbled and almost fell over the last few steps. He straightened and stood gasping for breath. His face ran with sweat. His knees buckled and he sat down with a grunt. Matthew lay sprawled on a rock. Emily gazed over the valley. She'd wrapped her hair in a scarlet-patterned scarf and wound it around her neck. Strands of blond hair escaped at her forehead and floated about her face as she stood there, her long arms and legs arranged like a Modigliani. They were both so at ease here. Every step he took jarred.

"Is this the sacred place?" Sandy asked, still breathing hard. He was expecting something physical: a sign, a statue, or even an etching in a rock. But there was nothing, only dead pine needles clumped in rough mounds. He kicked them apart as he left the path and walked over to the cliff face. Two small openings seeped black liquid.

Emily was behind him. "It's so holy . . . so sacred." Her voice was an awed whisper. "It's where Rosheme's ancestors came into being, the beginning of the line of deity which has continued until this day." Her words sounded formal, like a learned catechism.

"What is Rosheme like?" asked Sandy, although he wasn't interested in her answer. He wanted to delay going into the cave. He'd always hated being underground, felt claustrophobic on the tube. "Do you see him often?"

There was an audible intake of breath. "I haven't met him," said Emily. "Being in his presence is a privilege I'll have to earn, after huge amounts of study. Even Samten doesn't see him, even when Rosheme is not away. Samten only sees him in special audiences every now and then. You don't just walk up to Rosheme in the street. Half the time we don't even know where he is."

"Why not? Catholics know where the pope is," said Sandy. "And Anglicans know where the archbishop of Canterbury is. Why aren't you allowed to know where Rosheme is?"

"Maybe it doesn't matter where he is," Matthew said, skipping stones down the path. "What he says might be more important."

Emily rolled her eyes. "We sense his essence and study his texts. He's with me through them. Shall we go? I can take you inside, but not all the way."

They climbed into the caves, bending over to squeeze through the entrance. Inside it was dark, not fully black but an intense gray gloom. Sandy couldn't see anything. Gradually his eyes adjusted. They were in a small space with dripping walls and a slippery stone floor. It was barely high enough to stand up. Along one side was a rough ledge crowded with candle stubs and small offering bowls of moldy rice. At one end were two openings to smaller tunnels. It stank like a sewer, but Sandy didn't want to think about that.

The entire country stank as far as he could see. Everywhere he turned were piles of shit and rubbish. Children played in it, laughing as they threw cans to each other in air thick with smoke from smoldering bonfires. Adults fossicked through the rubble and dirt as though they were about to find a life-changing stash of rupees under a heap of cow dung.

His foot squelched on something soft. He could feel it, thick and cold, oozing above his sandals, through his toes. Emily stood still, hands clasped, eyes closed, and head lowered, nourished by some light only she could see. Matthew was beside her. He took her hand and they moved closer together.

Watching them, Sandy was besieged by a savage loneliness. He wanted to join his children but was paralyzed by indecision. He scraped some of the muck off his foot against a rock.

In the gloom, Emily turned to him. "Isn't it wonderful, Dad?" she breathed. "So beautiful. Can't you feel the peace and holiness here?"

"I might be able to if the place didn't stink and wasn't so filthy," he snapped. He knew he sounded like one of those demented keep-your-house-clean people on television, scurrying around in lurid rubber gloves, searching out life-threatening bacteria in the kitchen sink. But he couldn't stop.

"Why don't you and your friends come up here and get rid of all this rubbish everywhere?"

He kicked a sodden plastic bag. Emily was furious. "Can't you try, just for once, can't you try to see something apart from material things?"

"I am trying," he snarled. "But I can't see anything except what is in front of me and what I see is a great big pile of shit." He could hear his voice, harsh and bumping around the dim cave, furious that he'd wasted his life, that nothing he could do or had done was good enough or true enough, and that his children saw salvation and sacred peace in a place where he saw nothing.

# Chapter 43

THEY SQUEEZED THROUGH a hole in the hedge opposite the house and began climbing the narrow path. Robert went ahead, holding back branches for her, waiting on the bends, a perfect gentleman. Below them the town shimmered in the evening sun. She followed Robert in silence, winding up through the trees. The path was wider now and they walked abreast, Penny so aware of him beside her, the glint of the blond hairs on his arm, the smattering of freckles across his hands. So elegant, those hands with their long fingers, nails clipped clean and short with pale moons showing at their base.

She was sure the cave was to the left of the path, at the end of a narrow trail. Nigel had taken her once, soon after she had moved here. But she couldn't find the trail. "I know the cave is here somewhere," she said. "Perhaps I've taken the wrong turning. Maybe we should have crossed over to the next valley."

"I'm not too bothered," said Robert. He sat down on a broad boulder and motioned her to join him. She perched on a curved edge, feeling the sweat from the steep walk begin to dry against her skin. When they'd first met in the café, Robert's face was pale. Now it was deeply tanned and his hair had lightened from the sun and grown, curling against his shirt collar.

"One cave is really just like another. Dark, a bit smelly for my liking. And I've a confession to make." He smiled. "Don't look so alarmed. It's only that I don't like caves. I don't like being in the dark, feeling hemmed in."

"This wasn't a big dark cave with a dragon inside." Penny laughed. "It was more like a shelter with these incredibly intricate wave-shaped rocks. It's what you might imagine once was a cave. But just as well I can't find it. A lucky escape for you. So, let's go. Roast chicken awaits us."

Half an hour later, they were sitting in the courtyard with a glass of wine, their walking boots leaning together like old friends on the step and the chicken resting in the kitchen. The day's heat had disappeared. They would need a fire later on.

Robert was a good man to cook for, hearty and appreciative. "So good," he said, chewing on a chicken leg. Potatoes, carrots, spinach, and salad: he ate everything with equal enthusiasm and wiped his plate clean with bread.

"How is your work going?" she asked, relieved about the food, still anxious about the rest of the evening.

"Nearly done. Normally when I've finished something, I'm exhausted by the entire subject. But with Montaigne, I'm not. I think it's because he was so modest and yet so brilliant. He didn't propose any theories, he wasn't a great advocate of reason, and he didn't want to preach to anyone. So what's not to like?"

And then without pausing, he said, "I could say the same about you."

She was confused. "I'm no philosopher."

"I didn't mean that," he replied, looking up from his wineglass. "I meant, what's not to like?" He was the one who blushed this time, just a little.

They finished their cheese and walked through to the sitting room. The fire had gone into a sulk during supper. Penny fiddled at the grate until it was a cheering blaze again. They must have talked for a bit, but she never recalled about what. Did they discuss the comparative virtues of London and New York, his work, her life? Did they talk about visiting the big caves, the famous ones near Les Eyzies? Music? Novels? Cinema? They can't have not spoken at all, crossing and uncrossing their legs on that sofa that was just that bit too deep, looking at the fire. They must have said something.

All she remembered was both of them standing at the same time and moving closer together until she felt the warmth of his chest against her and his hands soothing her shoulders and back as they embraced. She remembered a small awkwardness before her body softened and bent towards him.

On the landing, they stopped for a first tentative kiss. She had forgotten how soft a man's mouth could be, how if you stood very still, you could feel the exact point where the delicate skin ended and the rougher bristly parts began. She had forgotten how pleasurable that was. They moved to the bedroom door and kissed again. His fingers traced the nape of her neck. Her mouth opened at the shock of it, all her nerves leaping at his touch as she tasted the warm secret skin of his inner lip.

He began to undress her. She tried to stop him, to scuttle off to the bathroom and emerge in some kind of enveloping gown, but he held her, all the while kissing her neck and mouth. She worried about her crepe-like skin, the bulge at her waist. His body felt so lean and muscled by comparison. The bedroom was dark but they could still see the hall light. As they kissed, she opened her eyes and saw him gazing at her. What did he see? A frowsy gray-haired woman, with the beginnings of a wattle neck and drooping breasts?

Now she was back in more familiar self-deprecating territory. He probably wouldn't look twice at her if they'd met in New York. Here in this French provincial backwater, pickings were slim. And yet she closed her eyes and felt his mouth move to her forehead, then his chin rest on her head. There was the smell of wine on his breath, fresh sweat, and above that, the musky rose of the potted geraniums on her dresser. Everything was still. She heard him breathing. She felt his heart beat.

"You know something?" he said quietly. "I'm nervous too."

The relief of his words. She forgot about herself and reached out to him. They kissed again. There was the gentle probe of his tongue and then the slow pull of his arms drawing her down onto the bed. They finished undressing each other, giggling at the clunk of his belt as his trousers fell onto the floor, the soft plop of her shirt on top of his boxer shorts. His hand brushed her breast. She felt herself quicken and she teased the hairs at his navel. They moved towards each other like familiar lovers.

# Chapter 44

EMILY AND MATTHEW pushed through the hotel door the next morning. Sandy jumped up and hugged them both so hard, they wriggled out of his arms. He couldn't help it.

"Sorry for my outburst," he said. "Let's just call it culture shock or something."

"Okay, Sandy, let's not get too excited," said Matthew. He looked like a child, fresh from the bath, his cheeks high with color and his hair slicked back.

"What's wrong with calling me Dad, the way you used to?" Sandy asked.

Matthew shrugged. "How about we get some breakfast, work out what to do with our day?"

They walked to the Nirvana Café. A rose-colored mist still covered the mountains. A group of girls in school uniforms giggled as they walked past, their tightly woven plaits bouncing against their satchels. A wizened woman bearing a giant straw pannier unloaded neatly chopped bunches of vegetables by a stall. Free of her load, she slowly straightened and rubbed her back. Her forehead was marked with an angry welt from the strap of the pannier. She smiled at them, teeth glinting with gold.

Emily foraged in her bag and gave the woman some coins.

"I thought you didn't give money," said Sandy.

"She's not a beggar, Dad. I buy my vegetables from her. Any extra goes towards her grandchildren's school fees."

"How do you know all that?" asked Sandy, puzzled. "Does she speak English?"

"No," replied Emily with one of her mysterious yet infuriating smiles, "but we manage to understand each other."

The café was already more than half-full. Sandy had been in the town less than a week, but already some faces were familiar: the loud spotty American girls who ordered pancakes every day and spent their time uploading pictures of themselves to their Facebook pages; the earnest German couple in walking boots and peculiar zip-apart trousers who consulted maps as they ate their porridge; and the beautiful pale woman with her shaved head and white robes, alone at her table drinking chai.

Emily ordered toast and tea for all of them, the most palatable option as the omelets were tasteless and rubberlike and the coffee bitter with a swamp of black grounds at the bottom of the cup. By the time they'd finished eating, Sandy had relaxed a little. He'd been all for making a major emotional statement of apology and explanation, but he remembered Carolyn's advice. Keep it light, she'd told him as she gathered her things before she left his flat. Don't drown them with your sentiment.

"I thought we'd go to the ashram and the temple this morning," offered Emily. "And you could meet Samten, my main teacher. He's great, isn't he, Matt?"

Matt nodded.

"Then," Emily continued, "we could have lunch and go for a walk. My friend Annie might join us. She said she was going up there today."

They left the café and headed towards the square in their little family crocodile led by Emily, then Matthew. Sandy brought up the rear, still bewildered by the noise and the people, the busyness of the place.

The town center was soon behind them. They walked through a series of lanes, Emily telling Sandy not to stare into the houses. But he couldn't help peering through openings where windows might once have been, or might be one day, to the women squatting on the bare earth, grinding spices and grains with oversized pestles as their children played around them. Dogs tied to posts snarled and leaped at them as they passed. There were no men anywhere.

The lanes became paths and suddenly they were in the country. Behind the small houses with their rusted, corrugated-iron roofs were terraced vegetable gardens and rice paddies. Along the length of the terraces, bent-over figures moved slowly up and down. Everything was neat and well-tended.

It was quiet now and the going much steeper. As they climbed the path, all Sandy could hear was the rasp of his own breath over the crush of pine needles under his feet, and the whisper of branches above. Daturas dotted the clearings, their elegant cream flowers swirling like Victorian tea dresses in the slight breeze.

Emily and Matthew strode ahead. Occasionally, he lost sight of them and paused to catch his breath in peace. Higher up he could see the dome of a temple floating above the tops of the trees.

"Wait for me," called Sandy into the silence. "I'm an infirm old man with a lifetime of bad habits behind me." He climbed on, his legs shaking with the strain, until he reached the top of the path, where Emily and Matthew lazed against a rock.

"You made it, well done," said Emily. Matt clapped him on the back and the three of them burst out laughing. Sandy wiped the sweat from his forehead and broke into a shuffling dance.

"Go, Dad, go." Emily laughed as Matthew gave a thumbs-up sign and punched the air. Sandy didn't deserve this moment, but he was going to relish it anyway. He was going to grab it and hold on tight.

The path had flattened out. It was wide enough for the three of them to walk abreast until the final curve, when Emily pulled ahead and they walked single file until they reached a vast terraced garden with a wide sweep of stone steps leading up to an intricately painted temple. On either side of the steps were terraced gardens planted with cascades of scarlet rhododendrons and azaleas. Here, in their own habitat, with the fluorescent colors he had always thought so garish in England, the shrubs appeared original and exotic, a reflection of the temple's beauty. Somewhere, someone began to play the bansuri.

"We have to stop and listen," he said. "One of the most beautiful noises in the world." The three of them stood listening to the languid and mellow music as it rose and dipped through the air. It might have been the altitude or a slight mist, but it seemed to Sandy that everything before him trembled. A perfect note moment, he thought, overwhelmed by his surroundings before remembering he was a nonbeliever.

"Can I see your room?" he asked.

Emily bit her lip. "Sure, why not."

He was sorry he'd asked. It was clear she didn't want to show him where she lived. But he was curious, so he didn't retract the question. The three of them walked behind the temple, through another garden into a kind of square. It was lined with small breeze-block cottages with a vegetable garden in the center with neat rows of spinach, and beans growing up bamboo wigwams. Someone had pegged orange robes on a drooping rope. In between hung pairs of boxer shorts and women's pants and bras. Straps from some of the bras had entwined themselves in the robes, like white ribbons.

Sandy immediately thought of Emily and sex and a lama, a thought so disturbing that he almost blushed. He pushed it away from his mind and followed Emily into one of the cottages. The light was dim and it took a while to see properly. The room was the same size as a single garage with a small, high window looking out to the square. Off to the left side was a cupboard-sized room with no door, a lavatory, and a cracked hand basin.

The walls were unfinished plaster. Someone, perhaps Emily, had painted the main room a sunny yellow, but they must have run out of paint or lost interest, because half of one wall was dull brown, with a few chaotic daubs across it. Her clothes hung on hooks. Neat piles of books lay on the cement floor and in one corner was a single mattress, made up into a bed with a quilt and pillow. Sandy looked down at the small box that served as a bedside table. On it was a hardback book in some language he didn't recognize and beside it a framed photograph of the four of them, taken long ago in Hyde Park. He reached for his handkerchief, pretended that dust had made him sneeze.

"Are you happy here?" he asked.

"Absolutely," said Emily. "Hey, Dad, if Samten is here, be nice to him. Please. For me. Don't be all cynical."

"Sure," said Sandy, collecting himself. "Anything." He turned to Matt. "How about you? What do you think of Samten?"

Matt waggled his head from side to side in that Indian way. "He's good. Better than most."

They walked through the garden and back to the front of the temple. Outside a pair of scarlet-painted doors stood a handsome young man in saffron robes.

"Lama Samten!" Emily called, and then called louder when he seemed not to hear her. "Samten, hello." A joyous smile spread across her face. "How wonderful to see you."

She bowed her head and joined her hands together. He clasped them and they stood still, hands joined together, heads bowed. Emily was so much taller than the lama that she had to almost crouch so their foreheads could touch. Sandy suppressed a smile at the two pairs of feet positioned so close to each other: Emily's dirty bare toes protruding from her Birkenstocks squared up to the monk's stout brown brogues.

She straightened and gazed adoringly down at him. "Samten," said Emily, "this is my father."

Sandy wiped his hand on his trousers and went to shake the lama's hand, but Samten ignored his outstretched arm and cupped both his elbows instead. Sandy tried to find some flaw in the perfect symmetry of his face, but there was nothing except a small dark mole on one high cheekbone that only accentuated his beauty. He was so close that Sandy could hear the static rustle of his robes and smell something sweet and intense, like rose petals. There was the same feeling he'd had with the doctor, Rupert, from the hospital. Again Sandy felt that if he laid his head on Samten's shoulder, somehow he would be made whole again. But again, that was a ridiculous idea and he pulled away. Samten smiled, showing small neat teeth.

"Hello, Mr. Ellison. So good to meet you at last. So, what are your plans?" he asked.

"I'm going to show Dad the temple and then we might meet Annie," said Emily.

"Will you be here tonight? To help prepare for the class?" asked Samten.

"Of course," she replied, bowing her head.

"Very good to meet you, Mr. Ellison," said Samten. "I hope you enjoy your time here." Samten joined his hands together in a farewell gesture and walked down the steps, his shoes clattering against the stones.

"It's so beautiful, isn't it, Dad?" breathed Emily, gazing at his departing figure. "Sometimes I think I'll stay here forever."

I'm jealous of Samten, thought Sandy, and I'm scared of losing her forever. She cares about him more than she cares about me. Even Matt had appeared starstruck, giving a little farewell bow.

Sandy wished he could see what they saw, but he didn't. That was the problem. He felt like old Gerard wrestling with his faith and his God and his loneliness. It was so much easier to be a rusty old cynic. And yet, if he really was a genuine cynic, a true nonbeliever, why did he cleave to a religious poet like Hopkins? The thing to do, Sandy concluded, was to stop thinking. It was clear his psyche was a stranger to him and always had been. No amount of exploration at this stage of his life would change things.

"What about lunch?" he said, sticking to the obvious. "Where shall we go?"

There was a café just outside the gardens, run by followers of the temple. The three of them perched on stools at a counter below a large window looking out over the valley, now shrouded in mist. On the horizon opposite, mountain peaks floated above the clouds. As they were deciding what to eat, Emily's mobile rang. It was Annie, saying she would meet them in about half an hour. They ordered vegetable curry and rice while they waited for her. Sandy was curious to meet Annie. Emily had told him she'd been at Oxford too, a bit after Sandy, but had left before finishing her degree.

Before their food arrived, he went outside to the toilet. He'd got used to positioning himself on the metal treads and was surprised to find a block of clean Western-style lavatories. At the other end of the row of urinals, he overheard two men talking.

"I can't work out why it took me so long," said one in a strong southern American accent.

"I know exactly what you mean," came the German-accented reply. "It's so simple and yet so true. I'm absolutely certain of the truth of it."

Well, thought Sandy. Good that someone was certain about something. He'd been so sure of everything when he was younger, at university. There were no blurred edges then.

Back at the table, a woman in her fifties was sitting with Emily and Matthew. Her face was thin and angled, dominated by wide-set hazel eyes. Her gray hair was pulled back in a ponytail, and her shapeless trousers and brown tunic almost, but not quite, obscured her lean frame. Like most of the Western women he saw here, she didn't wear makeup or jewelry.

Sandy introduced himself and sat down. The conversation meandered around teachings at the temple, mountain walks, and a retreat center further up the valley. Annie had lived in the town most of her adult life, working for a charity that built schools and provided basic medical care.

"You can do so much with so little here," she told Sandy. There was something familiar in the intonation of her voice, and its high, light tone, as if he'd met her before but couldn't remember where.

"At the first school we set up, most of the children had dysentery a lot of the time, and chronic eye infections. But with soap and water, just basic hygiene, we got rid of the infections pretty quickly," she continued. "It's often ordinary things that make a difference. And we're trying not to build empires. They've had enough of that. It's more self-determination we're looking at."

Annie might have lived away from England for decades, but she still stuck to old-fashioned conversational etiquette. They might have been in a London drawing room. She had spoken about herself. It was time now to talk about him.

"You must be so proud of Emily, what she's doing here, studying and learning. And Matt, for joining her." He hadn't thought of that. He'd always imagined Emily's time here as an escape from the real world, and Matt's decision to join her as an excuse to leave his druggy London life. He nodded, not knowing what to say.

"And you, Sandy," she continued in the same high, light voice, "Emily's told me about your songwriting. How wonderful to have a talent like that."

"I'm not sure I'd call it an actual talent." He was embarrassed, not having thought of himself as a songwriter for so many years. "But it was something I always wanted to do. And it worked for a while. I mean, I loved it. I loved music, the whole business. But I think my parents were right. Law or medicine would have been a steadier occupation."

Annie smiled. "Maybe then you wouldn't have been happy. Emily said you were at Oxford. Did you like it there?"

"It was a long time ago," he replied, "but yes, I did like it. I didn't realize then what a privilege all that was. I just took it all for granted."

A young boy, wearing jeans three sizes too big, deposited plates of steaming curry and rice in front of them. Sandy began to eat. He was hungry after the walk, and the food was delicious. Emily and Matthew were wolfing it down. Annie ate more decorously, looking out at the valley between mouthfuls, sipping her water. There was something about her profile, something he thought he recognized but couldn't recall.

"I was there too," said Annie. "But I didn't stay the course. I know everyone is meant to just adore university, but it wasn't like that for me. Too many fashions and cliques, everyone posturing and getting drunk, wandering around thinking they owned the world."

"What made you leave England and come here?" he asked.

She turned to face him. He hadn't noticed before, but her lower lip was unusually curved.

"I had a sister, a few years older than me. She was at Oxford too. She died." She smiled in the way people do in moments of pain, the false hearty smile designed to convince themselves, as well as the person to whom they are speaking, that the grief is over, dealt with.

Her voice, however, was flat and cold. She stopped eating and wiped her mouth with a handkerchief.

His hands, Sandy realized, were shaking. He felt this strange darkness, a closing-in from his past. He was absolutely certain that Annie was Polly's sister. All those minuscule pinpricks of recognition: it had to be her. She spoke like Polly, the same lyrical intonation. And her profile, the sharply angled cheekbones, the curve of her mouth. The smell of the curry, only seconds before so fragrant and tasty, was nauseating.

He would have to tell her, tell all of them. He would have to face Annie's anger, his children's revulsion at what he had done and how he had obscured it for so many years. Any minute now, he would have to speak, expose himself, and, yes, feel the scorn from his children for the crime he had committed.

"Everything okay, Dad?" asked Emily. "You look a bit done in."

"No, I'm good," he replied.

Sandy glanced at Annie. It was impossible to tell if she had been beautiful or plain as a young girl, what color her hair had been, the bloom of her complexion. Still, she had to be Polly's sister, even though he couldn't remember Polly ever mentioning she had a sister or a brother. The chances of anything else were too remote; the level of coincidence too high. Those degrees of separation, however many there were, had been whittled down to practically zero. He'd read about it on some website, during his online trawls back in Battersea. Everyone, somehow, had become connected to everyone else.

Annie trailed a long bony finger across the table. Her hand dropped to her lap. "I adored my sister," she said. "She was so kind, so beautiful and brilliant. There was just the two of us. When we were kids we were completely inseparable. Maybe it was because our parents were so much older, in a different world. So her death hit me hard."

He tried to arrange his face in what he hoped was an appropriate expression of empathy. He nodded and leaned back in his chair, thinking to offer some commiseration, act like a normal person. But the nerves in his cheeks and forehead began to twitch and jump. He couldn't regain his composure and he began to weep, gushes of tears running down his face.

"I'm sorry," said Sandy. "I'm so very sorry."

Emily and Matthew turned to him in alarm, but he couldn't stop crying or saying he was sorry. Everything turned in on itself. He was back by the side of the road, in the rain, Jeremy shouting and Sandy weeping as he stroked Polly's face, tried to keep her warm, willing her to live as her breath grew strangled and jerky and then, finally, ceased. Sandy wiped his cheeks, his face contorted and flushed.

"Could you ever forgive the person responsible?"

He put his hands over his eyes. There was a cool hand touching his, stroking it. The hand didn't feel like Emily's. It felt older, more paperlike, reminding him of his mother. The temptation to stay silent was overwhelming. But he couldn't stuff it all back inside himself again and pretend nothing had happened, exist like some blinkered zombie. He would have to face them—Annie, Emily, and Matthew—and be an honest human being for one of the very few times in his life. He would have to do it immediately.

Annie's voice cut across his thoughts. "It wasn't anyone's fault," she said. Her voice was calm but puzzled. "It was a terrible thing to happen to her and she suffered horribly at the end. But no one planned her death. No one knew it was going to happen. It was leukemia. My sister died of leukemia."

He heard the word, registered its four syllables and in his mind saw it spelled out. He remembered it came from the ancient Greek words meaning "white" and "blood" before he realized its meaning. He scrubbed at his eyes until they hurt and opened them, blinded for a minute by the light.

So everything had been coincidence and chance, despite the diminished degrees of separation. There had been no fate-laden synchronicity. Everything he thought was so familiar about Annie was based on nothing more than his own faulty and guilty imagination. He should have known. England was full of regions where people spoke with the same intonation, even the same timbre. It was a tiny, crammed island. In every crowded room, every airport or railway

station, complete strangers might claim kinship on the angle of a jawline, the flare of a nostril. Even then, thinking all this, contradicting everything he'd told himself only minutes before, it took some time to realize that Annie had begun to speak again.

"All cancer is so cruel, particularly at the end. I couldn't deal with it, and I ran away, had a kind of protracted breakdown. I couldn't stay in England. A couple of years later, my parents died and there seemed no point in going back. I prefer it here. People like Samten have taught me so much. Samten would say death is natural and we must accept it as inevitable. To face death in peace, we must learn to live in peace."

Tim would have said Sandy wanted the coincidences, so he would have an opportunity to confess, despite what his conscious mind told him. Tim would have said that Sandy needed to tell Annie and his children what had happened much more than they needed to hear it. Tim was no doubt right and Sandy had every intention of telling them. He'd told Carolyn, a stranger almost, and she had not turned against him. He had felt less alone afterwards.

He would say something to Emily and Matthew. But not just yet. Not here. Not now. He had to think it through, let the matter settle.

# Chapter 45

MATTHEW ANNOUNCED HE was going up to the retreat center to do a three-day meditation course.

"I think it would do me good, clear my head," he told them after breakfast one morning. "Want to come, Sandy?"

"Maybe next time," Sandy replied. The idea of sitting in silence for seventy-two hours was not appealing. He didn't know what to think, what to feel, after his outburst on the mountain. The others had explained away his tears and proclamations of apology by delayed jet lag and culture shock. Emily suggested it might be a possible religious awakening.

They could think what they liked. Apart from the black hole of himself, everything was beginning to work. The three of them were able to fall into contented silences as they walked through the town or wandered through the markets. He saw the easy love that existed between Emily and Matthew, how they accepted and supported each other. It pleased him but also made him feel lonely. He'd never had a sibling. There had only been a series of miscarriages followed by a bleak period when his mother stared out the kitchen window for hours on end. He missed what might have been.

He missed Penny too, the way she had believed in him and tried to make him a better person. It was one of the reasons he'd fallen in love with her. And, he realized now, one of the reasons he'd fallen out of love with her. She hadn't fixed him. He wasn't a better person. But why had he expected her to do what he couldn't be bothered to do himself? He bought some fruit from the stall favored by Emily, the one run by the old woman, and devoured a banana before starting on an apple.

"We've just finished breakfast," said Matthew.

"I know," said Sandy, "but I'm hungry all the time. It's like some-one flicked the craving switch from booze to food. I wake up hungry and I go to bed hungry. Talking of which, do you have to fast on the course?"

Matthew shook his head. "But there's no drinking or smoking, of course."

"Are you still smoking, Dad?" asked Emily.

Sandy smiled. "Not in front of you."

Emily wagged her finger at Sandy, then flung her arm around Matthew's shoulder. "You won't know yourself at the end of it, little bro. And best of all, it's just the beginning. Dad and I could get the bus up and meet you there. We could show him around, go for a bit of a hike?"

Sandy's calf muscles were already protesting, but he nodded his agreement. For the next two days, Emily spent most of her time at the ashram. Sandy was content to meander around the town and take long naps in the afternoon. The evening before they left to see Matthew, Sandy idled through the line of stalls near the temple, try-ing to find something to read until he met Emily for supper. But there was nothing except outdated tourist guides and a thriller he'd already read, so he walked over to join a small crowd of tourists waiting out-side the temple. He recognized the white-robed woman he'd seen in the café. There was a small sign, hard to read, advertising a lecture scheduled to start any minute. It was called "Rosheme's Guide to Heavenly Enlightenment."

I'll go in, he said to himself. It won't be Rosheme himself because he's off inhaling essence of spiritual enlightenment. But I'll go in and I'll listen to what they have to say. At least I can talk to Emily about it, even if it's only to disagree. After so many decades of doubt and ambivalence, he was uncomfortable around Emily's religiosity. Her beliefs made him feel shallow, and sometimes, although he was ashamed to admit it, Sandy was irritated by her certainty.

A skeletal boy with a shaved head pushed open the tall wooden doors, and the little group took off their shoes and placed them in

neat rows before shuffling inside. Sandy stowed his sandals in a corner, then sat on the floor on one side of the temple. Faded posters of a rotund beaming figure were taped onto the walls. Dead flies were stuck on the tape and the posters' corners were curling upwards. There was a smell of earth and sweat, of unwashed bodies.

The temple was half-full. Some seemed to be curious onlookers, like Sandy. Others sat with their eyes closed and their hands clasped in spiritual reverie as they waited for the teaching to begin.

From behind, there was a brushing noise, as if someone was sweeping the floor. Sandy turned to see a plump middle-aged Indian woman kneel down and prostrate herself on the floor, her hands stretched in front of her. Then she drew her knees under her body and sprang to her feet, flinging her arms above her head before kneeling again and lying prone on the floor. In this kind of demented jack-in-the-box fashion, she made her way to the front of the temple, where she crossed her legs in the lotus position, sat upright, and smoothed her hair. She looked only a bit younger than him and she wasn't even out of breath. Last time he'd tried to touch his toes, Sandy had been giddy from the effort and had to sit down.

Everyone waited patiently. A door banged loudly and the skinny boy who had opened the temple doors rushed in, set down a bottle of water, and rushed out. Minutes later, he ran in again, carrying a velvet cushion and an old-fashioned feather duster. He flicked the dais with it. Dust rose in a cloud and slowly settled. He ran out. Everyone waited.

Sandy began composing an anecdote in his head. He saw himself back in London, at lunch with Peter and Tim, making them laugh with his amusing description of the old woman and the young boy, and everyone sitting barefoot in the temple waiting for enlightenment that was running late.

His buttocks ached from sitting on the floor. There was no room to flex his stiff knees. His neck hurt. Just as he thought he couldn't tolerate any more discomfort, there was a rush of air behind him and a skinny, cross-looking lama strode up to the dais and sat down on the cushion. At first he was silent, content to stare through his black-

framed spectacles at his audience. Everyone gazed back in a reverent trance. The lama rearranged his robes and shut his eyes. He appeared to have gone to sleep. The young boy reappeared from the side and moved the bottle of water closer to the dais.

The lama jerked. His eyes opened and he looked startled, as if he hadn't seen any of them when he entered. He grinned, began to giggle, then laugh. He laughed so much that his knees shook. His head jerked backwards and forwards. He opened his mouth so wide that Sandy could see the glint of gold fillings, even from where he was sitting. The lama guffawed. He chortled. He giggled. He would not stop.

The audience joined in. A man slapped his thighs in glee. The Indian woman almost rolled on the ground in hilarity, tears of laughter streaming down her face. The man sitting next to Sandy honked loudly and dug him in the ribs as if to share the joke. Sandy glared at him. Mad, he thought. They're all mad.

Then there was a clap, abrupt as a gunshot. Everyone fell silent.

"Now we begin," said the lama. He spoke with a light accent. Every word was clearly enunciated.

"The only certain outcome of life is death," he said.

Everyone nodded eagerly, as if such a thing had never occurred to them before this moment.

"Anger has no eyes."

Sandy looked up to the ceiling. It was covered in water stains and in places the plaster had fallen away.

The lama fell silent for a few minutes, and drank some water before continuing with his collection of non sequiturs.

"He who is kind becomes rich.

"Sleep after a day's trading.

"If a man tells you he is a God, then he is lying."

There was a murmur of approval after every sentence. Some nodded. Others shut their eyes, their brows furrowed in concentration. Sandy committed their faces to memory, to add an authentic flavor to his planned anecdote. There would be a certain embellishment, of course. A good story inevitably contained an element of exaggeration.

"Rosheme says, 'Let us do whatever we can to bring light into darkness.'

"He tells us to be patient and kind to ourselves and others."

The lama shut his eyes again. His head lolled on his chest. His hands fell limp in his lap. The boy tugged at the hem of his robe and his head jerked. He stood up, grasping the boy's shoulder as he straightened, and clasped his hands together. The audience stood as well, before forming an orderly queue. One by one they approached the lama, solemn and expectant. Some, like the man next to Sandy, were shaking. Sandy recognized the look on their faces. It was the weak-at-the-knees, about-to-inhale-the-fairy-dust gaze that accompanied the appearance of every pop star he'd ever known. It was baloney.

As each person approached, the lama whispered something and patted their shoulder. Everyone returned to their place and sat down, their heads bowed in contemplation. Sandy was the only person not to present himself to the lama. It would have been too hypocritical.

The lama left, accompanied by the young boy. Everyone shuffled out of the temple and reclaimed their shoes. Sandy found his sandals and was about to give a small donation when there was a tap on his shoulder. It was Samten, grinning broadly and taking his arm, as if they were the best of friends.

"Aha, you do believe, maybe just a bit?" Samten laughed and waggled his finger as if he'd caught Sandy with his hand in the cookie jar.

"I'm trying to keep an open mind, for Emily's sake. And Matthew too," replied Sandy. "Although nothing your man said in the temple made much sense to me. Maybe I wasn't in the right mood."

Samten folded his arms. "Oh, Mr. Ellison. You are too hard on yourself. 'Not in the right mood. Doesn't make much sense.' You should be kind, let yourself out."

"What do you mean?" asked Sandy. "Let myself out?"

Samten folded his arms under his robes and giggled in that annoying way. "We are all in prison in some way, but the plan is to get out, not stay in. You put yourself in protective custody. Scared to be free. Hanging on to the past. No good will come of it." He stared at Sandy and repeated himself. "No good will come of it."

Christ, thought Sandy, he knows. Somehow he knows. No, surely not. It's not possible. But why else would he bring up this business of the past, if he didn't somehow know?

"I'll consider the ramifications of that." He could hear the clipped tone of the formal words. The defensive mode. "Self-imposed protective custody: well worth pondering. But now I must go because I'm late to meet Emily."

Samten smiled. "Protective custody. There is no need for that. Just be free. It's as easy as that. Be free. Think on it, Mr. Ellison."

# Chapter 46

"YOU OKAY?" IN the rear-vision mirror, the taxi driver rubbed his face anxiously.

"Perfectly fine," replied Jeremy. He thought he might faint. The effort of holding himself upright, walking the few steps across the pavement to the taxi had produced an exhaustion he had never before experienced. His hands were trembling. His legs were shaking and he was sweating profusely.

"Just take me to Cheyne Walk, please." If only he had water. His mouth was so dry.

The driver nodded, then shook his head, glancing in his mirror with every gear change. Jeremy couldn't stand it any longer. "Don't worry," he said, "I'm not about to collapse on you. And even if I do, the hospital is only a couple of minutes away."

He wouldn't leave the boat again, not until it was time to leave for the other place. The other place. He was referring to it mentally as another home, a country bolt-hole. He was tired of fooling himself. Someone at the London clinic, a male nurse from Glasgow, told Jeremy he would know when that time had come.

Now he regretted the lunch with Tim and Peter. Not that he ate anything or stayed longer than fifteen minutes. But it was long enough to see the shock and pity in their eyes. He knew they cared and wanted to help. But this thing was easier done alone. The effort of dealing with anyone else's emotions was too tiring.

Over the past month, he'd quietly shut down his business and arranged his affairs, telling as few people as possible that he had only months to live. It was one of the benefits of a busy corporate life, that he could absent himself without any alarms being raised or questions asked. Everyone, friends included, were used to his frequent short-term absences, his erratic silences and delays in responding to telephone messages and emails. They knew that his most significant and longest relationship was with the deal, any deal, that he would pursue it with a single-minded passion that excluded everything else.

Casual acquaintances were informed he was on a sabbatical in Southeast Asia. He'd written letters to Isobel and Sally and told his lawyer to send them at the appropriate time. He would have told Rosie, but Rosie no longer spoke to him. Another letter for the pile. There was one for Matthew. The letter that took longest to write was addressed to Sandy.

In the oddest way, Jeremy found the process of dying from cancer more peaceful than much of his life. The whole thing had been taken out of his hands by a group of rogue cells. When he was first told, Felix Summerscale wearing a forlorn expression, Jeremy went completely numb. When the numbness stopped, he didn't feel cheated or angry or any of the things people were meant to feel when told they had less than three months to live. What he felt was that someone, somewhere, had excused him from duty.

It came to him one night, as he surveyed his shrinking body in the bathroom mirror just before bed, that he imagined the spread of his cancer not as an invisible malignancy but as something else that was eating away the murderous secret sickness that had been part of him for too long.

He no longer had to worry about himself. He worried about the pain of dying but not death itself. When he was told that the pain could be controlled, first by morphine tablets and then by an intravenous feed, Jeremy was relieved. He spent most of his time on a lounger on the deck of the *Jezebel* in what was left of the summer sun. Maria cleaned and shopped, organized food deliveries, and cleared the refrigerator when it began to overfill. The doctors came and went. There was occasional discomfort but no pain. All he had to do now was lie in the weak sun and wait.

# Chapter 47

THEY LEANED AGAINST the wall, already warm from the morning sun, and waited for the bus. Women carrying buckets queued in front of a well with a squeaky ancient pump that was so heavy each woman had to lean on it with all her body weight to pull it down. The ground was littered with boxes of detergents labeled Fab and Wisk, labels Sandy recognized from his childhood.

There was a knee-deep pond on one side, where half a dozen men in worn underpants washed their hair and waddled around laughing with each other. On the other side were large stone slabs running with suds as tired-looking women scrubbed and pounded piles of clothes, then rinsed and wrung them by hand. A woman paused to straighten her back as she wiped the sweat from her forehead with her hand. Sandy smiled at her and she looked away.

"Don't the women mind?" asked Sandy. "The men seem to do nothing but loaf."

Emily squinted into the distance. "Annie says the entire country functions on the unpaid labor of women. But it'll change. It has to."

He rummaged in his pack for his flask of tea, poured a cup, and sat down on the ground to drink it. The earth was already warm and a thin breeze blew dust against the buildings. A pile of rubbish smoldered nearby. There were rusted cans and plastic bottles jumbled with threadbare rags, piles of paper, and what looked like human feces. A building was being constructed somewhere in the distance and there was the sound of jackhammers and tractors.

Even a week ago, Sandy would have been repulsed by the smell and general disorder. He would have felt the grit on his skin and longed for a night in a luxury hotel with fluffed towels and clean sheets, a place where you could drink Coke with ice in the evening and not worry about dysentery the next morning. How quickly he had become used to this town, this country. He no longer had the feeling he was in a Michael Palin documentary. Everything had begun to feel real. He thought of his flat in London, that small sad box, his very own martello tower, the last line of defense against himself.

There was a small pebble rubbing against his foot and he kicked off his sandals. Already there was a pale imprint on his skin from where the straps crossed over. He was thinking of tattoos and symbols, when he saw Emily laughing.

"What is it?" he asked, smiling but not getting the joke.

"Oh Dad, look, you're twice the size of everyone else."

"But I've been twice the size of everyone else since I arrived in this place," he said. "I've never felt so enormous, not in a superior way. I'm overgrown, overfertilized, or something. I'm too fat. I'm too tall. My feet are too big. I've got too much body hair, too many freckles. I can't help it."

Emily swung her pack on her back in one graceful movement. Despite her blond hair and blue eyes, she was at home here in the dust and the heat, while Sandy sweated and scratched at his welts and bites. A group of schoolgirls, neat in their uniforms and plaits, gathered in front of the well. He remembered Emily as a child, shivering in her school uniform, her knees mottled purple with cold.

"Come on, Dad, get a move on." Emily's voice roused him. "The bus is coming. I can hear it."

A small crowd had formed: women with babies, men carrying sacks of cement, with the schoolgirls giggling between them. Above the noise of the jackhammers, there was the wailing sound of a siren, and a white minibus, the type used by schools all over London, careered around the bend.

Sandy heaved his backpack on his shoulders, bumping the woman standing beside him. He still wasn't used to the extra space the pack occupied. Every time he turned, he crashed into something or someone. He apologized to the woman. She scowled and pointed to his walking boots, which were tied to the pack's straps. She wrinkled her nose in disgust and drew her scarf across her face.

"What have I done wrong now?" he asked.

Emily giggled. "Sorry, should have mentioned it. It's the shoes, Dad. Think where they've been."

He hurriedly unzipped his pack and stuffed them inside. A boy, no older than eight, collected rupees, and passengers rushed forward all at the same time. Sandy joined them to clamber on board, so clumsy with his big feet, stepping on bags and grabbing at the roof to keep his balance.

"Sorry, so sorry," he muttered like a mantra. Behind him, Emily was still giggling.

The bus had four rows of seats, not nearly enough for the people pushing to get a place. They crammed and squeezed and jostled and squirmed. Sandy perched between a woman carrying an enormous bag of flour and a man clutching a shovel. The woman leaned against him and he moved forwards, perched uncomfortably on the edge of the seat. A schoolgirl sat down next to the man. Four people in a seat designed for two. Not bad, he thought.

Emily had been carried in the wave of people to the back of the bus, where she sat squashed between women with children on their knees. Sandy managed a contorted turn and gave as much of a wave as his hunched shoulders allowed. She grinned and waved back. Her blond hair glinted above the dark heads and the dust motes in the air. He counted twenty-three people in a vehicle built for perhaps twelve. Before the driver pulled away, he gunned the engine and glared at Sandy. He muttered to the people around him and they nodded in agreement.

Sandy called out to Emily. "What now?"

"Dad, they're saying you're too big and you take up too much room. They say you've got too much stuff and they want to charge you for two seats."

Sandy tried to hunch into his seat and make more space, which made the man next to him drum his shovel on the floor in anger.

"I know I'm big," said Sandy. "But there's not a lot I can do about it now." The schoolgirl near him tittered and the bus drove off with a spray of gravel and a blast of its horn.

It was a morning of perfect pale sky and lace clouds. Above them the hills were patterned with emerald rice paddies. Women carrying huge panniers on their backs moved between the fields along narrow paths.

The bus rattled around corners, belching black exhaust fumes. The driver smoked a bidi while speaking on his mobile in one hand and steering with the other. Grit and dust flew in through the open windows. Sandy thought longingly of his bus trip from Delhi with one person to each seat, its regular stops at teahouses and temples. Every half mile or so, the bus braked and everyone lurched forwards while people got on or off. There were more passengers now, twenty-seven. They crouched on the floor and sat on each other's knees. A man hung out the door, a small girl crouched behind him, clinging to his legs.

Sandy wriggled and managed to twist himself halfway around to see Emily gazing out the window, a half smile on her lips. The woman next to him scowled and muttered again.

"Just how safe is this bus?" he called back to Emily. "Should we have got a taxi?"

"We're cool, Dad," she shouted back. "This is the way to go."

She smiled at him. Thoughts of seat belts and overcrowding sloughed away as the driver steered them around the sharp bends and up the mountain. The sun danced on the bus's ceiling.

"Hey, Em," he called back to her, as the woman beside him elbowed him in the ribs. "We're riding the magic bus." He drummed his hands on his knees and sang, "I'm on the magic bus at last."

"Dad, you and your pop songs. You don't even know the right words." She shook her head, but she said it with affection. As they neared the town, the rice paddies were replaced by clusters of houses linked by a trail of brown paths. The pines edging the road disappeared. In their place was the now-familiar sight of rusted axles, wheels, and fenders littering the roadside ditches. There was more traffic and the driver honked his horn as trucks whizzed past.

Sandy heard Emily shout they would arrive in about half an hour. He couldn't help himself. He punched the air in a gesture of triumph. The woman next to him sighed and drew her scarf across her face. He didn't care. Despite his discomfort and the heat, he tensed in excitement. Soon he would see his son. The three of them would be together. It would be a perfect note moment that had nothing to do with music.

A truck lumbered past them, a group of men clinging to the roof and waving like children. The bus accelerated around another corner. A familiar sound cut through the noise. "Eye of the Tiger" from one of those Rocky films. A ringtone. The driver picked up his mobile and took his hand off the wheel.

The bus slewed across the road. Clouds of dust and bits of gravel blew in through the windows. The woman beside him screamed and clutched her bag of flour. The bus skidded in the opposite direction. The dust lifted and on the side of the road Sandy saw the soft brown eyes of a cow slowly munching its cud as the driver tried to steer out of the skid.

Sandy was thrown against the woman. Her head smacked against the metal window frame. Blood trickled down her head and then her face. Sandy tried to wipe it away, but he was pinned to his seat by the man with the shovel. One of the schoolgirls wailed and Sandy shouted for her not to be scared, that everything would be all right. The bus veered back across the road. The man fell on the floor, still clutching his shovel. Sandy managed to turn around. Behind the cowering heads and terrified faces, he saw the back door of the bus swing open and the row of seats carrying Emily began to tilt. He couldn't see her face, only her hair. He tried to shove the people away, so he could crawl over the seats to grab her. He twisted and struggled to move but everywhere people were screaming and scrabbling for purchase.

The bus veered again and he banged his head on something sharp. For a brief second he was blinded. But still his hand pushed through the bodies and the arms and the legs. He thought he touched her fingers, thought he felt the small mole at the base of her wrist. He tried to hold on to her, but their hands slid apart. There was a rasping noise, of sheering metal buckling and giving way. Under the smell of engine oil was the metallic tang of human fear.

His vision cleared and he saw Emily gazing back at him. He saw the fine layer of dust on her face and her golden hair spread out behind her. She didn't look scared. She smiled. Such a beautiful smile, wide and full of trust and hope. Then she was gone, sliding out the door into the valley below.

The bus came to a halt on its side, its wheels stinking of burning rubber. Sandy clambered out and ran down to Emily, falling and scrambling among the rocks. He never remembered how he got there, but he must have got to her somehow. All he remembered was kneeling by her side, seeing the blood trickle from the edge of her mouth, watching her pupils dilate and grow dull before her eyes closed, hearing her breath grow shallow and weak. He stroked her head and saw his hand, wet with blood from some unseen wound.

People behind him were still screaming and weeping. Someone groaned in pain and someone else was shouting down a mobile for help. It began to rain and he took off his jacket to wrap around her, leaning over her frail form to protect her while cupping her face in his hands, begging her not to die.

"Em," he whispered. "It's going to be all right. You'll see, someone will come. You're going to be okay. Open your eyes, please, Emily, open your eyes."

Then there was a bellow, loud, elemental, obscene. It must have been him.

# Chapter 48

SANDY DIDN'T KNOW then, as he crouched beside Emily, that above them in the meditation center, someone had answered their mobile and heard about the accident. Someone else called for an ambulance. He didn't realize that Matthew knew the bus had crashed and had jumped on someone's motorbike and driven at breakneck speed down the winding, treacherous road until he arrived at the bend where the bus had overturned, a small trail of smoke still curling up into the mist and rain.

Sandy had no idea that Matthew would know what to do, that he'd thought to bring a blanket with him, so he could wrap it around his sister while he gave her mouth-to-mouth resuscitation; that he had the foresight not to let anyone move her until a truck arrived with stretchers and a doctor.

Other people must have been injured. Sandy remembered three stretchers being lifted onto the bed of the truck and Matthew telling him to get into the cabin with the driver and the doctor, then looking into the side mirror to see Matthew behind them, slaloming on the motorbike.

He never knew how long it took to get to the hospital. He only remembered that Matthew took his hand and held it while they watched Emily being lifted off the truck, moaning softly as the stretcher jolted on the ground and they wheeled her into a ward full of people injured in the accident.

It took two hours before a nurse appeared with an intravenous drip, another four hours before someone came with an X-ray machine, and then a doctor, sweating with fatigue, appeared to tell them that Emily's spleen had been ruptured, some of her ribs had been broken as well as an ankle, and that she needed an operation, but not here because they didn't have the equipment.

For all that time Matthew did not leave Sandy or Emily. There was an assurance about each of Matthew's movements that Sandy had never seen. Matthew found a clean towel to wipe Emily's face and mouth. Painstakingly, he fed her tiny sips of water as he soothed her forehead while talking to her in a low, calm voice.

Sandy could do nothing except shake as he held Emily's hand and brushed her hair away from her face. Sometime before dawn, Annie arrived with a thermos of tea and Matthew slipped away to telephone Penny. Annie sat on the floor by the bed and asked Sandy to pray with her.

"For Emily," she said. "So she knows we are here."

He nodded and closed his eyes. He tried to ignore the discomfort and the constant sting from the gash on his forehead. Nothing came to him, except for Samten's sermon on protective custody and the sound of the bansuri music shimmering in the air above the temple. He felt as he had when he'd first met Samten, and when the doctor had come to his flat: a sense that if he gave himself up, just leaned against the bed and held Emily's hand, everything would be all right. This time, he did not fight it. He felt his breath ebb and flow, the pulse in Emily's wrist beat weakly but steadily. Everything else dimmed before this rhythm. Sandy had no idea how long he sat there in this state. It might have been minutes or longer, even an hour, until through a haze, he felt Annie's hand on his shoulder and heard Matthew slipping in beside him.

"I rang Mum and told her what to do. She wanted to come right away," he whispered. "But I said she should wait. Until we know more about the operation and everything. She probably couldn't get a visa immediately anyway, even an emergency one."

The day passed like a dull dream. Emily opened her eyes, murmured, and closed them again. She drank more water. Sandy wept for the miracle of her survival. At some stage, Matthew must have called Jeremy, or Penny must have called him, because the next day an ambulance appeared to drive them back to Delhi, where Emily was admitted into the most modern and luxurious hospital any of them had ever seen. Matthew and Sandy were checked into the excessively comfortable hotel next door. When Sandy asked about tariffs and payment, the concierge said it was taken care of, sir. Your son has organized everything, sir, with the man in England.

They stayed in Delhi for a fortnight before flying back to London. Emily was still swathed in bandages. Matthew sat beside her, holding her hand throughout the flight. Every half hour or so, Matthew would turn to Sandy in the seat behind and tell him not to worry, that everything would be all right after all.

Penny was at Heathrow to meet them. As he pushed through the doors and saw her kind weathered face and her gray hair pulled back, Sandy wished that the four of them could be together, the way they never had been, the kind, comfortable way Penny used to crave and he used to despise. He wanted it with a ferocious hunger. He wanted them never to stop talking to each other. He wanted them to tell him everything. He wanted to tell them everything.

He wanted to tell Penny about Matthew, the person who his son had become in India. Matthew was no longer depressed and purposeless but someone new who taught children to play basketball, who cured a young boy's boil with an everyday spice, who leaped onto a motorcycle at the top of the mountain, competent and assured.

When Sandy was incapable of doing little more than slumping by the hospital bed, it was Matthew who supervised Emily's care, ensuring that she wasn't thirsty, that she was comfortable, that her pillow was at the right angle; Matthew had done all this with a quiet confidence, as if he had glimpsed an idea of who he was, of who he might become.

As Sandy fussed and worried to little effect, it was this new Matthew who consulted the doctors, who updated Penny and Jeremy each day and booked the flights back to England. Matthew did all this so easily that it was hard to imagine he'd never done anything like it before.

A sari-clad woman pushing a trolley of plastic-wrapped luggage taller than herself pushed past them, and for some seconds he lost sight of Penny's gray head. Panicking, he scanned the crowd until he found her again, looking at the cluster of drivers holding up their placards.

Beside him, Matthew patted Emily's shoulder as he pushed her. His hands slipped on the wheelchair handles and he wiped them, one at a time, on his trousers, leaving a cluster of fogged fingerprints on the chrome handles. Sandy reached out to touch him, but Matthew had moved ahead, swept forward by the wave of weary passengers leaning into their trolleys for the last stretch, buoyed by the anticipation of the embrace of home.

# Chapter 49

PENNY STOOD NEAR the information desk. She had been waiting there for nearly an hour, not wanting to move in case she missed them coming through the doors. Emily came first, pushed by Matthew. Her eyes were dark with fatigue and pain and she flinched as a child rushing past banged her bandaged ankle.

Matthew's hair was cropped so short Penny could see his scalp, even at that distance. Behind them was Sandy, pushing the trolley of luggage. He was brown and thinner than the last time she had seen him. She was reminded of Robert, also thin and brown: a disloyal thought, although she was not sure where the disloyalty lay. She maneuvered her way to the point where the barriers ended.

Penny crouched down to Emily and hugged her. She held her close, felt the bones in her shoulders and the roughness of the plaster cast as they both wept.

"We'd better get to one side," said Sandy. "Otherwise we'll get mown over."

She nodded and they moved to the main concourse. She turned to Matthew and clutched him to her. Over his shoulder, she saw a bored-looking chauffeur holding up a scrawled placard smile in their direction. She saw the four of them through his eyes, through the eyes of the people milling in the arrivals hall.

Just look, they would think. A regular English family. The middle-aged, sensible mother waiting for her middle-aged, sensible husband and their children, one of whom has had an accident but looks as if she will recover soon. Look at them embrace, watch them weep with happiness that they are together again. There should be more such families.

Penny wished that they were returning home to a reunion dinner, something like roast chicken, with a cake and candles to indicate this was more than an everyday meal. Then she was in Sandy's arms, tentative about physical contact with him after so long and also because she had recently rediscovered the responses of her own body. But the hug came naturally enough and she felt Sandy's cheek against her own, wet with tears.

A man in a turban behind them asked them to move because he was trying to film his son and new daughter-in-law and they were in the way. As she moved apart, she saw the chauffeur still smiling.

Penny suggested coffee and muffins, and the other three agreed, although no one seemed hungry or thirsty. Sandy found a table at the back of the café, where they sat shielded from the world by a semicircle of luggage.

"You're not too tired for this, darling girl?" Penny asked Emily. "Just say, and we'll leave right this second." She almost said that they would go home, but there wasn't one. Penny had arranged for her and Emily to stay with Frieda until Emily had fully recovered and then travel to France. Matthew and Sandy were going to his flat.

"I'm fine," said Emily, and burst into tears. "It's not true," she wept, clutching a paper napkin. "I feel sick, my stomach hurts. I don't know what to do, if I'll ever fit in here again. Where am I going to live? What am I going to do?"

Beside her, Matthew's chin wobbled. He rubbed her shoulder. Sandy took Emily's hand.

"Do you remember, Dad?" she said, still crying. "Do you remember what I said about the Michael Palin documentary? But this time it feels like England, my home, is unreal and India is the place where I feel comfortable. I don't know what to do."

"You don't have to do anything, darling girl," said Penny. "Just get better. Don't think about anything else."

Emily nodded, dutifully like a child, then told the story of the bus ride and the accident again. After Sandy and Matthew recounted their versions, they fell silent. They had run out of things to say to each other after the emotional charge of their reunion. Emily looked as if she was too tired to cry.

At the taxi rank, they hugged. "Can we meet before Mum and I leave for France?" Emily asked. Her question carefully addressed the spaces between them all. "Maybe for lunch or dinner?"

Penny felt a tinge of euphoria, an almost-forgotten pleasure from a previous time.

"What about Sammy's?" she said. "The place on Fulham Road, opposite the flower stand. It's a good halfway point between us all." She steered the wheelchair so that it faced the approaching taxis. "We used to have dinner there years ago," she said. "The four of us."

"I remember," said Sandy, as he opened the taxi door and helped Emily into the back seat. Together he and Matthew folded the wheelchair and stowed it in the boot. Now that they had left the terminal and there was no chauffeur smiling at them anymore, reflecting what Penny wanted to see, something had shifted. They were no longer a family greeting each other after a long separation but a group of four people about to leave each other.

# Chapter 50

SANDY AND MATTHEW took the tube back to Vauxhall, then the bus to Battersea. Sandy shrugged off his backpack and felt inside his pocket for the keys. He stepped over clumps of autumn leaves, noting a new spray-painted slogan on the wall of the bus shelter. "What part of illegal don't you understand?" It was the same scarlet color that he'd used to deface Jeremy's boat less than six months ago. Now it seemed an eon away.

In Delhi, he'd thought about making some kind of peace with Jeremy, if only to thank him for everything he'd done for Emily. It was easy for rich people to be kind because it cost them nothing, but Jeremy had done all that voluntarily. It had to count for something.

"Hey, Sandy?" Matthew's voice bisected his thoughts.

"What?" he asked, suddenly fretting that Matthew might want to leave and stay somewhere else.

"You've finally got it."

Sandy was perplexed. "Got what?"

"The art of carrying a backpack." Matthew smiled. "Congratulations. You haven't knocked anyone over all the way from the airport."

Sandy laughed. "So I learned something in India after all."

He fiddled with the lock and together they made their way up to his flat, pushing the door open against the pile of mail his neighbor had collected for him. The flat smelled damp and airless. A stray tea bag left on the kitchen table was covered in a bloom of mold. Matthew opened the windows, and they stood together in the sitting room, too tired to do anything but feel the gritty breeze circle the room.

Sandy told Matthew that the sofa was too uncomfortable, that he'd blow up the old air bed instead. The truth was that he couldn't bear to be apart from his son. He needed to hear him breathe through the night and see him wake in the morning.

They took turns to clean their teeth. Sandy gave Matthew an old T-shirt and made up the air bed. He collected the armful of mail and heaped it on the kitchen table.

From the bedroom, he heard the plastic mattress squeak and then settle under Matthew's slight weight. He heard Matthew sigh, then turn over. He would join him in a minute or two, after listening to his telephone messages. There could be one from the nursing home, about his mother. He sat down with a glass of water and pressed the play button. Of eleven messages, eight callers had breathed once, then hung up; one was from Carolyn asking him to get in touch when he returned; one was from Peter; and the last, left two days before, was from Tim. He played it three times, as if to make sure it was real. For some time, he sat absolutely still before finding himself reaching for the pile of letters.

Most were pamphlets or bills. Various people wanted to steam-clean his carpets or wash his windows. Others wanted money for one cause or another. The last in the pile was a leaflet advertising discounted bathroom fittings, and he was halfway to throwing it into the bin when another letter fell out from its pages and onto the floor.

Sandy recognized it instantly. He didn't have to pick it up to know the weight of the paper, feel the linen-like weave and the embossed letterhead. He stared at it for a while, then picked it up and placed it in the center of the table, very slowly, as if he was performing some sad private ceremony. He made himself a cup of rooibos and went into the bedroom. The sitting room lights shone on Matthew's fuzz of hair as he lay curled under an old duvet.

He flicked the switch and went back into the kitchen. He drank his tea. He put the mug in the sink. He gathered up the junk mail and put it in the bin. He moved the bills to one side of the table, then the other. When he could think of nothing else to do, Sandy opened the letter from Jeremy. It was only one page, brief and written in a strange, shaky hand.

"You were right about Forster," it said. "My mistake and one I have regretted for too long. For everything, my friend, I thank you. For everything else, I apologize."

He put the letter back in the envelope and wept silently, his head in his hands. He wept for Jeremy and for Polly. He wept for himself and Penny and his own mistakes, and when he was too exhausted to weep anymore, he turned out the light and went to his bed.

He sensed that Matthew was still awake but didn't dare to say anything. The night was so quiet. They turned in tandem. The bed springs creaked, the air bed squeaked. Sandy and Matthew lay in silence and listened to each other not sleeping.

Matthew cleared his throat. "Dad? It's good you came. To India, I mean."

A cab pulled up across the road. Its diesel engine rattled. The headlights swung on the ceiling as it turned around and drove away.

In the darkness, Sandy allowed himself a small smile. He was Dad again.

Outside, the lid of a garbage bin clattered. A fox screamed, high-pitched, like a scared woman. He waited until everything was silent again. "I'm pleased I came too, although I was scared of how you and Em might react. After all, I did invite myself and I wouldn't have blamed you if you didn't want to see me."

Sandy turned in the bed, so his body faced his son.

"Dad, it wasn't that bad." Matthew's voice wobbled.

Sandy reached down and rubbed his shoulder.

"You know all those songs you wrote?" asked Matthew. "The ones about love lasting, and everything? Did you mean them, or were they just something you did to make money?"

Sandy remembered the piano in the kitchen and Penny's encouraging smile. "I meant them, all of them. Most of them I wrote for your mum. It's just that I didn't know how things would turn out.

I was too careless about everything. I thought I could do anything I wanted, and I couldn't."

Matthew's breath came like a sigh of relief. Sandy heard the duvet rustle and Matthew's head turn on the pillow, then steady breathing. He lay on his back, timed his own breath to match Matthew's, and thought about what he would tell his family the next day.

# Acknowledgments

I am indebted to my agent, brilliant Kerry Glencorse, for her commitment to this book.

A huge thank-you to Susanna Lea and all at Susanna Lea Associates.

Sarah Branham at Atria / Simon & Schuster in New York and Alex Craig at Picador Australia have made me feel very welcome in a new world. Thanks to Deonie Fiford and Jo Lyons for their insightful editing. As well, thanks to Daniella Wexler.

Kylie Fitzpatrick encouraged me through early drafts and made invaluable suggestions, as did Elisabeth Gifford, Brett Hardman, Angela Lett, and Jennifer McVeigh.

Thanks also to Lyndall Crisp, Jacqueline Diedrich, Susan Haynes, and Corinna King.

My wonderful children have sustained me in ways I never dreamed possible. I owe so much to them. Visits to my daughter Laura, who lives in Nepal, provided invaluable background to the sections set in India. In England, my son Nicholas gave unstintingly of his quiet good humor and his intelligence. They encouraged me throughout and I could not have completed this book without them.

# About the Author

Suellen Dainty grew up in Sydney, where she worked as a journalist for the *Australian*, the *Sydney Morning Herald*, and the Australian Broadcasting Corporation. She moved to England more than twenty years ago and worked for many years as a producer for *Sky News*. She lives in Somerset.